NO PAIN

NO GAME

LUCIE ATAYA

NO PAIN
NO GAME

PROLOGUE

The little girl pulled the curtain aside and watched through the living-room window as police cars rushed down the street, stopping abruptly in front of their house. The cars' lights sent red and blue rays flashing all around them, bursting through the darkness, illuminating the sleeping street, reminding her of a firework display she had once seen with her father.

Men and women in uniform poured out of the vehicles, rushing into the front garden, marching in her direction.

The little girl glanced back over her shoulder. Her father was slouched against the doorframe between the entrance hall and the living room, his head in his hands, sobbing. She went to him, her stuffed rabbit hanging from her clenched fist. She knelt down next to him, placing her hand on his shaking shoulder. She did not quite know what to say, so she said nothing. When he looked up at her, his eyes were full of tears. She rubbed his arm gently, cocking her head to one side. He brought one hand to her face and cupped her cheek, with such love and tenderness that she felt maybe everything would be alright after all. He had always protected her. For so long it had been just the two of them against the world, surely this time again he would make it all ok. She gave him a smile, and he looked at her sadly. He kissed the top of her head. It was a gesture he had made so many times before, except this time it felt a bit different. She did not know why.

Outside, the pack of strangers was growing louder and more impatient by the second. They stormed up the short walkway to the house and pounded persistently on their front door. Someone was shouting something, though the little girl could not understand exactly what they were saying. She looked at the door, and turned to her father again, unsure what to do. But her daddy was looking only at her, watching her face in silence, tears rolling down his cheeks. That was when she felt scared too, because the look on her father's face was not the look of one who would make everything ok. He looked afraid, scared like she had never seen him before. She gripped his arm tightly, wishing for some reassurance. She did not understand what was going on. Everything felt different and strange.

Before either of them could make another move, the front door burst open with an ear-shattering sound and troops of people carrying guns stormed in, shouting and screaming and stomping their feet. The girl recoiled, curling herself up into a ball against her trembling father, her fingers squeezing his limp hand.

The police were all over the house now, zooming in and out of every room, up and down the stairs, gathering eventually in the little kitchen, from where the little girl could hear them talking animatedly. She buried her face in her father's stained, wet shirt, hoping that when she emerged back the strangers would have left and everything would have gone back to normal.

But that did not happen. Two strong arms grabbed hold of her and tried to pull her away from her father. She kicked and screamed and held on tight to her father's hand. He was squeezing her fingers in his palm now, but two men were on him, pinning him forcefully to the ground, pulling him away from her, forcing both his fists behind his back. The girl called out for him, terrified. Her father was shouting her name and all she wanted was to join him, to hide in his arms until all of this was over. The policemen surrounding her father were beating him with large black sticks, and the little girl screamed for them to stop, as loud as she could, louder than she had ever screamed in her life. A moment later her father stopped calling out her name. In fact, he had stopped moving altogether, and was lying still, facedown on the hardwood floor. The little girl struggled, craning her neck to get a glimpse of her father's face. His forehead and cheeks were bathed in red. He appeared to be asleep, just like her mummy was, on the kitchen floor. The little girl thought this an odd time for either of them to go to sleep, when so many people were in their home and she felt so alone and scared.

Two policemen dragged her father away, and she watched them disappear through the front door. She collapsed on the living room floor, her shaking hands clasped around her stuffed rabbit's ears. She felt suddenly very tired, exhausted by the effort of trying to understand all these strange things happening around her. The pain and terror were too much for her to comprehend and though she willed herself to stay awake, she could feel her eyelids growing heavier and heavier.

The last thing she was somewhat aware of was that she could see people hunched around her mother's body. She could almost glimpse the dark, velvety crimson liquid surrounding her mother's head like a halo on the white tiles of the kitchen floor.

And then, a moment later, she drifted into nothingness, and everything around her disappeared.

Fifteen Years Later

CHAPTER 1

SHAUNA MULLIGHAN

With just a few minutes to go before the live broadcast, the news studio was buzzing with activity. Shauna was sitting at her desk, at the ready. From her vantage point, she observed the incessant ballet of the members of the crew, rushing around as they attended last minute items ahead of the night's programme. In her two decades in the news industry, Shauna's favourite moment had always been the countdown to the live evening broadcast, whether she had been assisting in the background early in her career, or later as she had moved to the other side of the camera.

There was something intense about the chaos that preceded the well-organised and polished show the public eventually saw. Looking at the evening news, the glossy well-lit studio and the presenters' flawless appearance, one could not have guessed the frenzy that had been going on until the very last moment to build such a perfect facade. Being part of this well-oiled act of deception always made Shauna feel like she was privy to a secret very few could fathom. It gave her goosebumps every time.

She glanced at the giant digital clock on the wall in front of her, behind the cameras. The countdown to the start of the programme showed they had a little over three minutes to go. At the far end of the desk, the evening's two guests had already been settled down, their faces matte with the excess makeup they all had to wear. Neither of them was talking.

Shauna looked down at her notes and reviewed her headlines. Or, she thought, 'headline', in the singular. The one and only topic on which the country had focused for a long time now was their sole discussion point for the evening. She sighed audibly, shaking her head, like she always did when she pondered how exactly they had all got in this situation.

It had been the longest way coming, but eventually they had all paid the price for years of bad decision making. She wished she could pin it all on the government, but she knew too well that it was not true. A decade ago, mounting tension between the nation and its mainland allies had forced the government to offer the country its very own referendum. The people had rejoiced at the opportunity, so loudly and so openly that the noise of their contentment had covered the lobbying and brainwashing orchestrated by radical parties and organisations to influence their votes.

Shauna often said that one had to call it what it was. It had been a real shambles, and their great country had become a laughing matter for all of their neighbours, friends and foes alike. Politicians kept changing sides, contradicting each other, their own parties and, more often than not, themselves. Personalities from all walks of life had an opinion. It had become impossible for anyone to make out the truth from lies, the results of legitimate surveys from the unfounded threats of another world war.

A year after the referendum's announcement, the people expressed themselves and, by doing so, had proven many a sociologist's point by showing that not only could the masses be manipulated into believing anything, but that whoever caught the public's attention could influence the most crucial of national events.

The country had voted. And their choice was to sever their ties with the international coalition their country had been a leader in for well over half a century.

It had all gone downhill from there, in Shauna's opinion. It had taken years for the new political leaders to negotiate the nation's exit strategy. These had been dark times of division, uncertainty and failure, but it was nothing compared to what history still had in store for them.

'Live in one minute,' the producer announced in Shauna's earpiece.

She jumped and straightened on her seat, adjusting the papers in front of her and settling her face in what had come to be her live-television facial expression.

'Five... Four... Three...' The producer chanted, 'Two.... One... And we're live!'

'Good Evening, I'm Shauna Mullighan and you're watching the evening news on LiveTV2. The plan to which the Prime Minister gave his official consent a few weeks ago, designed to tackle the long-standing issue of the country's off-the-charts criminal rates and prison overcrowding, is finally due to launch tomorrow. The proposal was the brainchild of former Minister for Internal Affairs Valery Swan and entertainment tycoon and Channel55 CEO Sean Cravanaugh, and it has divided opinions ever since the idea was first put on the table. In tonight's edition we will review what little we know of the new plan and the reasons why it has caused so much controversy.'

Shauna turned to one side, and the cameras shifted, widening their angle to include an impeccably dressed young man sitting further down the long desk.

'Matthew Dalston, you're our Senior Economics and Social Affairs analyst here at LiveTV2. Before we go into further details about this new plan, can you remind our viewers of the chain of events which brought this about?

'Of course, Shauna,' Matthew smiled. 'One of the challenges our government faced after the breakup with its allies was the way in which the prison staff unions took advantage of the disruption to push for jobs and salary increases.'

The images on the screen behind them shifted to display silent footage recorded at the time.

'The government failed to peacefully resolve the situation,' Matthew Dalston continued, 'and within weeks, all prison staff across the country went on general strike. Prison inmates were left unattended for days on end until, one fine day, prisoners in the country's leading penitentiary establishment managed a mass escape. The first one of that scale in the history of our nation. Prisoners across the country followed suit and managed their own escape. By the time prison staff returned to their posts and police forces were deployed, the damage had already been done. Crime rates rocketed, setting the country on a path that was beyond repair.'

'Thank you, Matthew,' Shauna shifted back to face the main camera, 'and now let's look at the mysterious new plan aimed to solve the nation's troubles. Our correspondent James Carson is live from the capital. Over to you, James.'

Shauna kept looking straight at the camera. From the corner of her eye she saw Matthew Dalston quietly stand up and leave the studio. She waited for the image on the screen to split, allocating half of the space to her other colleague. James was standing rigidly on the spot, gripping a large and fluffy-headed microphone. A few seconds elapsed before he started speaking, as always with live connections. Shauna could never quite pinpoint why, but this handful of silent moments, where she had to stare fixedly at the camera, always made her want to giggle.

'Thank you, Shauna. I am standing here in front the Cradle Arena in the capital, which is where this new plan is due to be put into action tomorrow evening.'

The images on the screen shifted to show footage from their archives, illustrating James's commentary.

'Three years ago, the Prime Minister received the shocking results of a report by the NHRA, the National Human Rights Association, revealing that every single penitentiary establishment in the country was dangerously over-crowded. This meant the government had to release hundreds of convicts with minor offences into the streets each year for lack of space to keep them behind bars.'

The screen shifted to a colourful animated graph.

'We have also seen over the last few years a major rise in public discontentment,' James continued, 'causing the biggest exodus in the history of our country, with an immediate snowball effect on our economy.'

The graphs faded into footage of the Prime Minister, shown exiting his car and walking swiftly up the steps to the government's headquarters.

'Two years ago the Prime Minister put together a crisis cell and, of all suggestions on the table, the plan by Valery Swan and Sean Cravanaugh was designated to be put into action. Now,' James cleared his throat, 'this plan is controversial, to say the least, as it comes in the form of a competition, called 'No Pain, No Game', which is to be broadcasted live on television. Convicts serving a life sentence, or awaiting death penalty have been given the opportunity to sign up. The winner will see their sentence immediately waived and will be entitled to any cash made during the competition. The losers on the other hand, will be executed...'

The image refocused on James' somewhat incredulous expression.

'The exact rules of the game remain a mystery,' the camera spun around to reveal the crowd behind James. 'I'm standing here in front of the Cradle Arena where the opening ceremony will be aired live on Channel55 tomorrow evening. This is James Carson, live from the capital for LiveTV2. Back to you, Shauna.'

James' face disappeared as the camera zoned back in on Shauna, who had taken a seat with the night's guests.

'I am joined in the studio tonight by National Human Rights Association spokesperson Sarah Khan and Professor of Modern Economics Patrick Gregson. Sarah, you were involved in the original NHRA report commissioned by the Prime Minister, is that correct?'

Sarah Khan sat upright on her chair, trying her best to appear confident. To a trained eye like Shauna's, the young woman's nerves were obvious. She felt vaguely sympathetic towards her.

'That's right. I was the main project coordinator for the report,' Sarah Khan responded with defiance, betraying her apprehension at tackling the subject.

'Did you have any idea at the time that the report would lead to such a controversial solution?'

'Absolutely not,' Sarah said firmly, 'and I would by no means call this a *solution*,' she emphasised the last word derisively, her hands forming imaginary air quotes by the sides of her face. 'Suggestions in the report pointed towards the creation of more penitentiary establishments and increases in police forces on the streets. This lunatic idea of solving prison overcrowding through a televised game was most definitely *not* ours.'

'Of course, Sarah, and this is the position that the NHRA has been reaffirming ever since the proposal has been put forward. However, fresh controversy was sparked when Josh Carter, the Head of the NHRA, announced he will be a judge on the show.'

Shauna used the woman's first name deliberately, as if addressing a child, and she could see Sarah's face flicker with annoyance each time. The young woman sat a little straighter on her seat, a sure and probably unconscious sign, Shauna knew, that she was trying to make herself seem more assertive and in control than she actually felt.

'This is not an endorsement of the whole concept or premise of the plan. Mr Carter has been very clear since the announcement was made that he only agreed to be on the panel because he felt responsible for the ridiculous turn of events our report triggered.'

Shauna paused for a moment after Sarah finished talking, glancing knowingly at the camera, her eyebrows raised. This way of looking intently at the camera had become her trademark, as if she were exchanging some sort of in-joke with the audience. People loved that about her, or so their consumer polls said. She could not have made it plainer that she found Sarah's argument risible. Sarah's lips parted but Shauna knew better than to allow her to continue talking. She turned towards the second guest.

'Right,' she concluded with a tone that left no room for further discussion. 'Professor Gregson, you have been supportive of the 'No Pain, No Game' concept. I can't say that this has been a popular view amongst the people we have interviewed on our programme.'

Patrick Gregson was a well-kept man in his early forties, with an undeniable twinkle of charm in his manner that most likely fuelled the fantasies of more than one of his students.

'Certainly, Shauna,' he threw her a casual and irresistible smile. 'Something I often tell my students is that the measures taken to solve a problem have to be proportionate to the extent of the problem you are facing. With the degradation of the living conditions in our country and the major rise in criminal activity, we simply cannot get the nation back on track with flaky measures. Because the situation is so drastic, and none of the generic solutions worked, the government had to think out of the box. I agree with Miss Khan here, in that 'No Pain, No Game' is the most insane, loony idea our government has sponsored to tackle our horrendous criminal rates. Where I disagree, however, is that I believe only an insane solution can allow us to put an end to such an insane problem.'

'So you don't believe that the Prime Minister had a choice in the matter?' Shauna asked, ignoring Sarah's expression of incredulous outrage.

'Not anymore,' Patrick Gregson shook his head. 'Whether this new plan is the way forward, only time will tell, but at this stage it's worth a try.'

'Indeed. Looking at the panel of judges, alongside Josh Carter we'll have...' Shauna looked down at her notes, 'the founders of the plan, Valery Swan and Sean Cravanaugh, and pop star singer Camilla. Sarah, what do think of this panel?'

Sarah Khan appeared taken aback at being drawn back into the discussion and it took her a couple of seconds to regain her composure.

'Well,' she articulated slowly, 'I'm not sure how Camilla's nomination came about. This doesn't seem to be her natural area of expertise.'

'I can only agree', Patrick Gregson nodded. 'Camilla isn't someone people would have expected to take part in such a scheme. She's mostly known as a bubblegum pop star for teenage girls,' he chuckled, as though he thought it to be the most ludicrous profession in the world. 'I don't care one bit for her music, but my niece is one of her biggest fans! My guess, which is as good as any at this stage, is that Camilla is there to help bring a lighter touch to what could otherwise quickly become a very heavy and unglamorous subject matter.'

'Thank you both for joining us tonight,' Shauna turned back to stare directly at the camera. 'All will be revealed tomorrow. Stay tuned for more analysis on LiveTV2 as we will discuss the events in our evening edition. This was Shauna Mullighan, bringing you the latest news on LiveTV2. Goodnight.'

CHAPTER 2

SEAN CRAVANAUGH

Sean Cravanaugh was standing in the middle of the stage, which he had requested to be positioned right at the centre of the Cradle. He was looking up around him, turning slowly to take in the entirety of the arena, imagining what it would look like filled with thousands of his fellow citizens screaming and clapping their excitement.

When he and Valery Swan had first put their idea forward to the Prime Minister, a very, very long silence had followed their presentation. Derren Clarke, who was serving his second term as the country's leader, was looking exhausted and desperate. On that very day, he explained to both of them, he had received a final warning from the United Nations that there would be no more external help and that he was now to be left to his own devices to either salvage the situation or to finish burning the country down to the ground completely.

'Prime Minister, I understand you may be sceptical, but we are confident this will not only solve prison-crowding issues and lower crime rates, but also improve public morale and work wonders for your re-election campaign.'

Derren Clarke looked at Sean warily and rubbed his eyes with his thumb and index finger, as if to force the words he was hearing to fully sink in.

'This is quite a drastic approach, to say the least,' he finally said.

'Absolutely,' Valery intervened, 'and we are conscious of that. I must, however, beg you to consider it seriously.'

Derren Clarke stared at them from behind his desk. The dark circles under his eyes made him seem much older than he was. He sighed before sitting back down in his chair and leaning in towards them, his hands clasped on the wooden desk in front of him.

'Ok,' he finally conceded, 'run me through it one more time.'

Sean worked hard to suppress a smile. Nothing better than a desperate man to sign off on the most desperate of measures.

'We will select a hundred life sentence or death penalty convicts for the show. Convicts who aren't selected for the competition will be either executed, if they are awaiting death-row, or transferred to Cartford Hill in the North of the country, where they will be, shall we say, left to their own devices.'

'What does this mean exactly?' the Prime Minister asked.

'Off the record, sir, they will be left to die. At some stage, Cartford Hill may very well suffer from a disastrous incident. After all, gas leaks or fire breakouts are fairly common occurrences these days...'

There had been silence once again in the Prime Minister's office, as the implications of Sean's words sank in.

'What would we tell the public?' Derren Clarke voice was almost a whisper.

'The official answer, sir. That whatever happened was an accident,' Valery answered. 'All prison staff in Cartford Hill and anyone involved in the plan will be signing iron-clad confidentiality agreements before any of it is put into action.'

The Prime Minister sat back into his chair, his right hand resting on his cheek. Sean knew he was waiting for his conscience to kick in, for his well ingrained morals to take over and tell him he was insane for even considering what was being put in front of him.

'And this… what did you call it…' Derren Clarke glanced back at the folder marked 'confidential' open on his desk, 'this 'No Pain, No Game' competition. Do we have legal grounds for it?'

'We'll be taking convicts through to a pre-selection process, during which they will be made to sign a waiver,' Sean said. 'A revised version of a power of attorney consent form, which gives the government full control over any decision made for them, as far as life or death decisions, without them being able to appeal. The show,' Sean continued, 'will take place in the Cradle Arena, one of the capital's most symbolic locations. Contestants will go through a series of challenges, and the winner of the show will see their sentence written off. All of the others will be executed.'

'It seems a little drastic,' Derren Clarke's forehead wore a deep frown, 'it wouldn't make us any different to the Nazis!'

Sean felt Valery's stare on his shoulder but did not look across at her. The last thing they wanted was for the Prime Minister to feel cornered.

'The Nazis were on a mission to eradicate anyone who did not correspond to the criterion of perfection they had set for their nation. This is not what we are suggesting. Convicts are *criminals*, they made a deliberate decision to enter a life outside of the rule of the law,' Sean leant forward, his voice as cold as ice. 'It's high time the nation stopped sympathising with the very individuals who are sucking the life out of our economy. And, may I remind you that the proposal also provisions for the state to receive a generous share of the profits to rebuild the country from its ashes.'

The Prime Minister stood up and took a few steps to the window. Sean smiled internally, because that was the moment he knew victory was theirs.

Give anyone the choice between their own life and that of a stranger's and they will throw the stranger under the bus. Fear and pain, he had come to realise over the years, turned the most honest and decent citizen into a madman in a matter of seconds.

'I can't tell whether you're a genius or a lunatic,' the Prime Minister said, turning to look Sean straight in the eyes, 'all I know right now is I'm left with no other choice but to accept.'

~   ~   ~

Sean snapped out of the memory and readjusted the collar of his jacket. He could hear the murmurs of excited voices coming from outside the Cradle, where thousands had already gathered, setting up makeshift camping sites in a long and messy queue before the arena's entrance. Give them the entertainment and they will come, he always said. Whether you were presenting a singing contest, or a gladiator-style fight to the death, people would never fail to follow. Such was the desperate state of their nation, which had left its citizens craving distraction to the point of no return.

Sean had never been bothered by the so-called ethics, or lack thereof in this case, of the plan he had put together. Soon, he thought, soon the country would return to its former glory, rid of its vermin and welcoming its most valuable citizens back with open arms. Of course, he was a business man first and foremost, and he had ensured that whichever way this enterprise went, he would be a rich and happy man at the end of it.

Some called him cruel. Some called him insane. Some said he had no ethics. Most would neither care nor remember the names they had called him once the game started and they all became engrossed in its intricacies and the new purpose it gave their miserable lives.

All around him, members of staff were finalising the last details before the grand opening the following day. When the production team did a quick light check and the entire arena lit up in bright shades of white, red and blue, a deep and deafening wave of applause and cries resonated from outside the arena. Sean listened to the sweet sound of success with an appreciative smile.

'Ethics,' he whispered under his breath, rolling his eyes and shaking his head, 'my arse.'

CHAPTER 3

SEAN CRAVANAUGH

Sean stood behind the large wooden panels which delimited the backstage area, peering through a small gap, watching the proceedings on the stage. The arena was full and the audience had been waiting impatiently, their excitement growing palpably with every passing moment. When the lights dimmed, a sure sign that the start of the show was imminent, the thousands of men and women in the public exploded into a chaos of applause and delighted screams. Sean could not have hoped for a better omen.

They had opened the arena doors five hours earlier and it had soon become apparent that the fifty-thousand seats in the Cradle would not contain the immensity of the crowd that had gathered to attend the show. They had to setup last minute giant screens all around the arena for the thousands of people who had not made it into the Cradle. Similar screening areas had been improvised around the country, in parks, bars and restaurants. Cinemas across the nation were ready to broadcast the show live. Before it had even begun, 'No Pain, No Game' was snowballing into the most gripping and incredible adventure the country had embarked upon in a long, long time.

'Ladies and gentlemen,' the commentator's deep voice purred through the entire arena, 'Welcome to 'No Pain, No Game'! Please give a warm round of applause to your host, Tyler Benson!'

A roar erupted in the Cradle as the nation's favourite television show host jogged onto the main stage.

'Thank you! Thank you, everyone! How are you all today!' He said it more as an exclamation than an actual question, but the effect was immediate as the audience shouted their excitement even louder. 'Today, folks, we make history!'

The audience applauded loudly and reverberations of the crowd's cries outside of the arena gave anyone inside the Cradle the impression of being at the very centre of the universe.

'Please put your hands together to welcome on stage your 'No Pain, No Game' judges!'

The panel behind which Sean was standing with his fellow judges began lifting up. A cloud of smoke escaped around them, loud music blaring and bouncing off every single inch of the arena.

'Top of the charts superstar, Camilla!' Tyler exclaimed, as the audience exploded in hysterical screams.

Camilla waved at the crowd, a broad smile plastered on her beautiful face. Her blonde hair cascaded down her shoulders and her back, over a stunning red satin dress which floated down all the way to the floor.

'Former Minister for Internal Affairs, Mrs Valery Swan!' Tyler continued.

Applause continued as Valery nodded politely to the crowd, her hands raised in the air. With her modern navy-blue dress and her greying hair tied in a tight bun at the back of her head, she looked like someone's posh grandmother.

'Head of the National Human Rights Association, Mr Josh Carter!'

Josh Carter briefly waved at the crowd, but seemed reluctant to put up too much of a show.

'Last but not least... Ladies and gentlemen... Please give the biggest round of applause for your 'No Pain, No Gain' head judge, Sean Cravanaugh!'

The crowd rose to their feet in one single wave, as if under the same spell. Such was Sean's appeal. His brutal honesty and refusal to indulge in sugarcoating in times when all the public could hear were political lies had won him the citizens' support. They all loved the audacity with which he spoke his mind and always managed to get his way. He was admired, adored and feared.

Sean walked slowly down to the centre of the stage, the smile on his face as polished and impeccable as the dark designer suit he was wearing. He lifted his right hand to salute the crowd, and led the judges to their table, facing the stage, where they each took a seat.

'Tonight,' Tyler continued, 'we kick-off 'No Pain, No Game', during which one hundred convicted criminals will compete in a series of tasks. Starting tomorrow evening, over the next ten weeks we will see how they fare, because only one of them can win the ultimate prize... Before we introduce you to the contestants, let's have a look at their journey through the early rounds of the competition so far.'

Tyler turned around towards a giant screen behind him as the lights went down, plunging the arena in semi-darkness. The commentator's rumbling disembodied voice filled the Cradle.

'Over the last ten years,' the deep voice said in the background of a dramatic mixture of video footage and music, 'our country has fallen into chaos.'

The screen showed sections of news reports on street violence and crime scenes.

'We are outnumbered by criminals. Honest citizens are fleeing what once was the most prosperous land on earth.'

The audience boo-ed their support.

'Our government is struggling to keep all of these criminals behind bars, leaving horrible crimes unpunished.'

The audience was on their feet, their anger almost palpable.

'Tonight, we are bringing you justice!'

For a few seconds, the voiceover was drowned in the fury that had washed over the entire arena.

'From thousands, there are now one hundred convicted felons waiting to take part in the most challenging competition of their existence, in a fight for their freedom… and their *life*! From tonight, ladies and gentlemen, they will have to pay!'

The entire arena was in a mad frenzy of applause, screaming and foot stomping. The video ended and the lights slowly turned back on in the arena, illuminating the audience. Tyler walked towards the centre of the stage.

'Ladies and gentlemen, please welcome onstage your 'No Pain, No Game' contestants!'

A ray of light shot down towards the left corner of the stage where one of the side panels had lifted up, a cloud of fresh smoke filling the open space. A gigantic metallic cage was slowly advancing on the stage until it stopped right in its centre. The cage was divided into sections, with fifty men and fifty women standing, spread across four levels, facing the judges, their hands and feet tied with metal chains to the bars in front of them. They were wearing bright orange long-sleeved baggy overalls, over cheap grey trainers. Cameras and spotlights zoned in on them and they all appeared to recoil as one.

For a split second the entire arena seemed to freeze as the many observed and judged the few, with the hard cold stares of traders at a slave market evaluating the merchandise on offer. And for that one second the world stood still, on the verge of tipping over with the resounding crash of values and dreams shattering on the ground. Then the moment was gone, and the crowd was shouting profanities towards the hundred stunned souls on the stage.

'Let's get acquainted with our contestants,' Tyler announced.

The lights went down until one single ray of light remained, directed straight onto a woman standing at the left end of the cage's bottom row. She jumped with surprise at being singled out, her hands tensing around the chains securing her to the metal rail. One of the giant screens showed her dirty, tired face, whilst on another screen new video footage started. The commentator's deep voice was heard again as the images came and went.

'Contestant number one is Sarah Greensby. She was arrested eight years ago for the brutal murder of her brother, Daniel Greensby, over an inheritance dispute. She pleaded guilty to the crime and was sentenced to life imprisonment.'

As the commentator spoke, the images on the screen showed pictures of Sarah Greensby's smiling brother and images of his body after the killing had taken place. It all lasted a mere fifteen seconds, during which Sarah Greensby's face turned different shades of green and grey on the giant screen. Loud applause erupted as the video concluded.

The ray of light moved onto the contestant next to Sarah Greensby. The man looked positively terrified as his face appeared on the giant screens.

'Contestant number two is Greg Krane, also known as 'The Interceptor'. He was arrested four years ago for the robbery of the Herbert National Bank's main branch and then charged with the robberies of thirteen other banking establishments.'

The light moved on to the next person in line.

'Contestant number three is Alessio Martellini, infamous head of the Martellini cartel...'

CHAPTER 4

From where he was standing, Terrence Blake was not missing a second of the proceedings. The spotlight was now on convict number thirty-five, a man sentenced to the death penalty for multiple charges of rape and murder. Terrence glanced again at the number printed in bold black characters on the sleeve of his own orange overalls. Seventy-seven.

The audience had been on their feet, screaming and bumping their fists in the air towards the stage long before the commentator had introduced the first dozen convicts. Terrence had followed everyone's gaze, from the convicts' faces to the giant screen displaying bright images of the crimes they had committed, always accompanied by photos of their smiling victims, until the spotlight moved to the next man or woman in line. It seemed that the public was more vocal when it came to rapists and murderers than for convicts with a robbery or drug dealing history. Terrence was not surprised. When it came to illegal activities, not all criminals were equal. This was obvious even within prison walls, where child rapists or murderers were treated with a special brand of violence and disgust. It was only natural that it should be the same out here.

Terrence was a tall, forty-something man with broad shoulders. After fifteen years behind bars, he had lost track of his own age. He glanced down at his hands, chained to the bars of the cage in front of him. The black skin was rough and wrinkled. He looked back up towards the screen, and peered back in the direction of the spotlight to check where it was. Convict number fifty-nine was looking determinately in front of him, refusing to even glance at the giant screens. The commentator was listing the names of the victims he had brutally killed and the audience sounded like one angry beast ready to pounce on its prey and tear it apart.

What a concept, Terrence thought, with a shake of the head. He had not made the decision to sign up to the competition, of course. None of them had. When the plan was announced, he was given what was presented as an 'option' to register for the show. In state penitentiary terms, this was only a politically correct way of saying the wardens had made each and every convict sign the form placed in front of them, loosely administering a few strong blows with their batons to anyone who hesitated for too long. Some had signed right away, either not wanting to face a confrontation or naively believing they may have a chance of winning the stupid show and escaping their sentence. Some had kept on resisting, even after a violent beating by the guards. Those convicts had been taken away, bleeding profusely and half unconscious, and no one had seen them since.

Terrence had read the form from start to finish, all five pages of it. As a former primary school teacher, he was educated enough to understand he was being asked to sign his life away. Specific sections indicated that by adding his signature at the end of the form he was giving up any right to take action 'in case of trauma (physical or psychological), injury (fatal or benign)', or even, and this had made something inside him tighten with fear, 'death'.

Not having much choice, he had signed his name at the bottom of the fifth page and had handed it over back to the ward officer standing in front of him eyeing him like a hawk.

Terrence glanced down briefly at the cage to see who was standing in the spotlight. Convict number sixty-two's video footage was unravelling on the screen. Terrence shivered. The man standing in the ray of light stared right back at the crowd, a smile on his worn-out face. He looked like he was enjoying the crowd's anger, rejoicing in the disgust he was igniting in them. His eyes shone with that particular flame that kept a madman going.

His name was Spencer Martins, or Mad Spencer as he had come to be called. He had been sentenced to the death penalty for the rape and murder of six young girls. He had stalked each of them before drugging them and kidnapping them, keeping them locked up in the basement of his house. There, day after day, he had raped and tortured them until they died in agony. The fact that the man was still alive showed how desperate the penitentiary situation had become: lack of staff often meant a convict could be on death row for years before being executed. Terrence remembered that on Mad Spencer's first day in prison, once his story had travelled around every single corner of the building, a large group of convicts had joined forces to give him a beating he would never forget. Criminals had their own rule book on the hierarchy of crime, and Mad Spencer definitely ranked at the very bottom of the food chain, much below even prison wardens. The prison staff had been well aware of the plan to teach the newcomer a lesson but had neither said nor done anything to prevent it, giving the rest of the convicts their tacit agreement on what was about to play out. Mad Spencer had barely screamed or protested, as if he accepted that this simply was the way things were.

After that day, two unspoken rules had come into effect across the jail. The first one, that no one was to speak to Mad Spencer, and Mad Spencer was to speak to no one. The second, that even rival gangs could let go of their enmity if it meant teaming up to give Mad Spencer the beating he deserved for simply being the despicable piece of garbage that he was. The prison staff was by no means an exception to either rule.

When Mad Spencer's video ended, the audience was on their feet, protesting against the very existence of such a monster. Terrence could not blame them. The sight of Mad Spencer sent shivers down his spine, and he could never keep himself from imagining what the parents of those poor girls must have been going through. On some level, he could relate to them just a little too well...

As the spotlight moved to convict sixty-three, Terrence drifted back into his thoughts, trying not to acknowledge the dread building up in his chest, waiting for his turn to show up magnified on the giant screens. Several weeks before the show started, the convicts had been put through multiple rounds of tests, interviews and assessments and they could only watch silently as dozen of their peers did not make the cut, and disappeared one by one, never to be seen again. No one asked where they had gone, maybe because they were too scared they already knew the answer, and because asking questions might cause them to follow the same path.

When the commentator got to convict seventy-three, Terrence's chest tightened uncontrollably. He felt nauseous, unsure whether he would be able to take the spectacle he was about to be put through. A quick glance towards the remaining convicts game him the impression that he was not alone in his unease, but this did not make him feel any better, or alleviate any of his concerns. The light moved from convict seventy-three to convict seventy-four, who looked about to pass out.

Terrence glanced over at the panel of judges. Sean Cravanaugh's face was unreadable. The young woman sitting by his side, Camilla, did not look familiar. Her facial expression was difficult to read, halfway between anger and agony. On her left, sitting bold upright in her seat, Valery Swan was making no effort to conceal her disdain for each and every individual being introduced on the show. The last judge, Josh Carter, looked very white. Did he feel responsible for lighting the match that had enflamed the country, Terrence wondered, and had led to those hundred individuals standing like animals in a cage, on display for the world to target their hatred at?

The ray of light was now on convict seventy-six. Terrence started fidgeting on the spot. He saw rather than felt the trembling in his hands. His entire body was numb with fear. The moment the spotlight moved towards him, his first reflex was to close his eyes. When he opened them again, Terrence caught a glimpse of himself on the giant screen above the stage. He looked like a terrorised animal caught in the headlights of a massive truck on a country road in the dead of night. It took him the greatest of efforts to snap back into reality. He looked up at the second screen where the video footage of a time he had prayed long and hard to forget was displayed for all to judge. The moment the first images popped up on the screen, he wished he had kept his eyes shut. He willed himself to look away but remained staring at the screen, mesmerised, unable to even blink.

'Convict number seventy-seven, Terrence Blake, was arrested fifteen years ago and charged for the gruesome murder of his wife, Delilah Blake, in front of the eyes of their frightened five-year-old daughter Maddison. The police later also found him guilty of physical abuse on young Maddison. He has been condemned to life imprisonment.'

The video showed pictures of the crime scene, of Delilah's lifeless body soaking in a pool of blood, her face turned at an unnatural angle.

As the spotlight moved on to the next convict, Terrence found himself paralysed, his eyes wide open still staring up at the screen. He could barely hear the audience, or the commentator now narrating a different horror story. His hands were gripping the chains that kept him securely tied to the cold bars of the cage. He felt like a hole had been drilled into his chest, right where his heart used to be. Images he had wished to bury as far down as possible crawled their way back into his mind, dancing around in his head like a grotesque carousel. Delilah in her long white wedding dress... Maddison proudly holding up the spelling bee trophy she had won at the school fair... Delilah's blood-soaked hair swimming in a crimson pool on their kitchen floor... Maddison terrified, screaming her lungs out, begging him to make it all go away...

But he had not been able to make any of it go away. In the blink of an eye he had destroyed the only world she had ever known, depriving her of both of her parents in one single lack of judgment. But, as reckless as his behaviour had been at the time, he could live with his punishment. What he despised himself for was dragging his daughter down in his fall, and for single-handedly ruining the happiness of the best and brightest thing that had ever happened to him.

CHAPTER 5

TYLER BENSON

When contestant number one hundred's ordeal came to an end and the spotlights zoned back in on him, Tyler Benson knew he must look pale. He felt an awkward smile placate itself on his face, his jaw a little too tense. Tyler's fidgety eyes met Sean Cravanaugh's icy glare and he knew what his boss' silent command was.

When Sean Cravanaugh, *the* Sean Cravanaugh, had reached out to him personally to arrange a meeting, Tyler had not believed his luck. The entire industry knew that whatever the 'Great Cravanaugh' touched turned into gold, and whoever was lucky enough to be part of the journey had their career sorted for the rest of their lives. Tyler had spent the whole time leading up to the encounter unable to stand still for more than a few seconds. His wife, Constance, had actually estimated his record to be a little less than a minute. He had looked through his wardrobe over and over again, deciding on the right outfit and almost instantly changing his mind. He had made a list of the work experiences he had had so far, from his first runner boy internship on a mediocre television show, to his climb up the ladder, slowly and painfully until one day he had got his own big break. The co-anchor for one of the live shows where he was part of the production team had been found high off his face on cocaine in his dressing-room. After the initial few minutes of utter chaos, as the team realised they had only about four minutes to the start of the show, Tyler had grabbed his chance.

'I'll do it,' he had pleaded to the producer, 'put me in. I know the programme by heart, I'll do it!'

The producer had stared at this nobody, trying to gauge his options: running without an anchor and consequently having to explain what had happened, or letting one of the assistants on live television during primetime. He had opted for the latter and Tyler had been prepped for makeup and sat down on the second chair next to the co-anchor. She had looked at him quizzically, but had not commented.

Tyler could barely remember what the show was about that day, he only recalled how ecstatic he had been to be given a shot. It was a fair assessment to say that he had nailed it, demonstrating a level of confidence and wit on the screen he had not even known himself capable of. When the producer later announced that their audience rates for that night had almost doubled, after years of average performance, Tyler's fate was sealed. The country had fallen in love with this young fellow, appearing out of nowhere on their screens. He was a relatable, funny guy, average-looking enough to seem genuine, the producer had said matter-of-factly, and in such difficult times, people needed that.

From there on, everything fell into place until he got his own show, which had now been running for three years, consistently getting some of the highest audience ratings in the country. This was one of the reasons Sean Cravanaugh had picked him, he had told him when they finally met.

'The public loves you,' Cravanaugh had said, 'they love that you're just like them. A nice guy, married to a lovely girl, struggling for years on end to try and make it, and finally getting what you deserve. People need someone they feel isn't pretending or lying to them because some arsehole at the top gave them a script to recite.'

Tyler had simply nodded.

'I'm working on a new show,' Cravanaugh had told him, looking him right in the eye, 'and I want you on it.'

Tyler had stared blankly back at him, wondering if he heard correctly.

'You heard me,' Cravanaugh had added, as if reading his thoughts, 'I want you on the show. But it's not going to be easy, and unfortunately circumstances dictate that I can't tell you any more until you sign with us.'

Tyler had tried to process the situation as quickly as he could, but deep down he knew could not turn down the offer. He had signed the contract right there and then. Once Cravanaugh had talked him through the concept of the show and the stages of the competition, Tyler understood why he had needed to sign a legally binding document to become privy to the secret.

For someone who made a living out of talking constantly, and as naturally and wittily as possible, he had found himself unable to find the right words, or *any* words for that matter. Something inside of him was setting off an array of warnings to back out whilst he still could, but the memory of years of painful struggle trying to get to this very moment forbade him from raising any of his concerns.

'Tyler,' Cravanaugh had leaned in across the coffee table between them and had told him in a calm but firm voice. 'I cannot imagine anyone else hosting this show better than you ever could. There will be difficult times when it comes to standing on stage orchestrating all of this and you will need to remain strong. Whatever fear, concerns or morals are telling you now that something isn't quite right, I need you to silence them. Find that special place in you where none of this has a say because, for the sake of our country, we need you running the show like there's nothing wrong with it. And also...' Cravanaugh looked like he was trying to decide on the best way to phrase what he was about to say. 'Also, the contract you just signed binds you to the show from this very moment until the second it ends. There is no exit clause and any breach in this contract will see you owe Channel55 the financial value of your contribution to the success of the show. You're familiar enough with your own audience ratings, and you're a clever man...'

Tyler had felt all the colour drain out of his face. He flicked through the pages of the contract he had just signed until he had reached the 'Break Clause' section. His value had been grossly estimated and valued at hundreds of millions. He stared at the figure until he felt sick to his stomach. A note in italics indicated this amount was subject to change based on the success of the show and was to be re-calculated if and when the clause was to be put into motion. If Tyler thought he had been feeling uncomfortable until that point, he realised he had seen nothing yet. In the spur of the moment, he had surrendered his life to the most powerful man in the country.

~ ~ ~

Tyler tried to let go of the memory, and conjured up the most natural smile he could muster.

'Ladies and gentlemen, before we switch off for the night, let's see what our judges have to say. Camilla, let's start with you. What are your first impressions after learning more about each of the contestants?'

Camilla sat up in her chair, instantly releasing her grip on the plastic water bottle she seemed to have been torturing.

'Well, Tyler, I think we have some good contestants here, and I'm looking forward to seeing what they can do,' Camilla hesitated only for half a second, clearing her throat before she spoke again. 'I would lie if I said I haven't been horrified by some of the images I've seen tonight... But I hope I can be as impartial as possible in helping to bring justice to the people.'

As she said those words the entire arena was on its feet once again, clapping loudly, chanting her name repeatedly. Camilla stood up and turned around, taking in the propensity of their support and anger, one hand resting on her chest in a sign of appreciation.

'Mrs Swan, let's move onto you,' Tyler had to speak a little louder than normal, in an attempt to cover the crowd.

'Certainly,' Valery Swan answered instantly, her voice and manner were composed, and one could tell she knew the ropes of diplomatic answers. 'During my career, I have come to deal with a lot of situations where ensuring justice is brought to victims and their families is a challenge. I hope I can help anyone who has been a victim or who knows the victim of a crime to get the closure they need.'

'Thank you, Mrs Swan,' Tyler Benson said with a flourish. 'Mr Carter, what about you?'

He turned to Josh Carter, who readjusted his tie, as if trying to buy himself some time before he found the right words. When he finally spoke, his voice was a little coarse.

'If I'm entirely honest, Tyler, I was appalled, as we all were, by some of the footage we were shown today.'

His first comment was met with applause and cheers from the audience, showing their support.

'But in the spirit of *honesty*,' Josh Carter continued, 'I have to remind you that the reason I joined the show has been and still is to ensure that the contestants are being treated with the respect any human being deserves.'

He marked a short pause and for a couple of seconds it seemed no one really knew how to react to this comment, either because they were pondering the validity of his argument, or because no one so far had raised this line of questioning.

People in the audience seemed genuinely confused. They were looking at each other with frowning or blank faces, leaning in towards their neighbours and debating the matter in low whispers. Tyler waited for a few seconds to see which way the public would tip.

'What I mean is,' Josh Carter explained, a little uncertainly, 'no matter what crime a person has committed, Human Rights should be respected when they receive the sentence they deserve. This is what our justice system has set out to do and…'

'So, you think the justice system has succeeded in doing that?' Sean Cravanaugh interjected sternly.

'Well, to a certain extent…' Josh Carter started to answer, a little unsettled by the interruption.

'I'm not asking about *extents*, I'm asking you a very simple and direct question, which only warrants a simple and direct answer. Do you or do you not believe that the justice system has succeeded in giving criminals the punishment they deserve?'

'You could say that, in fact…' Josh Carter mumbled, only to be immediately interrupted again.

'*Do you*, or *do you not* believe that the justice system has succeeded?' Sean Cravanaugh's voice was as firm as ever, although he had not needed to raise his voice to quiet any other conversation in the arena.

Tyler had often wondered why Sean Cravanaugh had asked Josh Carter to be on the show and at times he had naively allowed himself to believe having such a respectable figure on the panel would help mitigate the public's opinion on the concept of the competition. At this very moment however, watching Josh Carter stuck in between tens of thousands of people and the most influential man in the television industry, Tyler knew what had been expected of the man all along. Cravanaugh had known

Josh Carter would speak for some of the citizens who might share his opinion. By doing just that on live television, Josh Carter had given Cravanaugh the perfect vessel to take his arguments and destroy them completely. Josh Carter swallowed with difficulty.

'I don't,' he admitted, 'but I firmly believe that this country needs to treat each and every one of his citizens with respect and…'

'Respect!' Cravanaugh barked, spitting out the words like they were poison, and banging on the table in front of him with his clenched fist. 'Were you dozing off when we were all watching the crimes each of these men and women standing on stage committed? Are you blind? Didn't you see what happened to their victims? Would you say *they* were treated with respect? And despite that, you'd still want to allow them a luxury they have so violently denied others!'

This seemed to have given the audience just the push they needed to make up their mind. They were shouting their support for Cravanaugh's words, their voices resonating like thunder in the arena.

'I mean, it's just…' Josh Carter struggled to find the words.

'Listen to them, Carter,' Cravanaugh said again, now standing, pointing straight at the people behind them, 'don't you think they deserve justice?'

He had now turned to face the audience, his clenched fist raised up high in the air.

'It's time we taught criminals that we will not sit and watch whilst they destroy what centuries of our ancestors' hard work has built! It's time for justice!'

The audience had risen as one, applauding and chanting 'Time for justice! Time for Justice!' Josh Carter slumped back into his seat, bitterly defeated. Tyler took over again, trying to make himself heard over the crowd.

'Thank you, judges, for sharing your thoughts! We will return tomorrow for the first challenge of the competition which will see some of our contestants face elimination. Before we switch off for the night, we'd like to say a huge thank you to our sponsors,' Tyler gestured behind him as fifteen different logos appeared on the large screen, 'for their support. Remember you can visit our website on www.nopainnogame.com for more information on the show and on each of the contestants. You can also download the 'No Pain, No Game' app to participate at each stage of the competition, or to share your impressions in our live feed. 'No Pain, No Game' episodes will be available for live streaming every week and on replay on our website for a small fee. Thank you for watching, and good night!'

Tyler waited for the little red light on the cameras in front of him to switch off, indicating that the live broadcast was over. Without thinking about it, he mopped his forehead with the back of his hand, only to realise the gesture had left a thick trace of foundation on the sleeve of the expensive jacket he was wearing. He swore under his breath. He suddenly had a burning desire to be home, slouched on the couch, on the other side of the television screen. He longed to watch the proceedings from afar, without being a part of it at all, because he knew better than anyone in the audience what was to come, and all he wanted was to run as far away from it as he possibly could.

CHAPTER 6

Terrence Blake

Terrence was lying awake on the paper-thin mattress he had been given for a bed. The production team had repurposed the Cradle's underground facilities to hold the convicts for the duration of the show. There were no rooms with bars, or secure heavy doors, so the convicts had been divided into groups of about twenty and tossed into tiny dressing rooms which had been emptied of all their contents. Even the carpets and wallpaper had been stripped off, so that all that was left was the hard stone floor and walls. Someone had wanted to avoid giving any of them any tools which could have been used for anything else than their intended purpose. The electric wiring in the room was gone as well, so that the small space was not only crammed, noisy, and smelly, it was also cold and completely dark.

Terrence's eyes were wide open, and for several minutes he tried to see if his vision would adapt to the pitch darkness of the room. This gave him something to do in between the waves of panic and fear which rolled over him. He was constantly seized by cold sweats and his heart was pounding in his chest as if trying to tear through his skin and escape. Once the wave had passed, he was left feeling empty and numb.

Flashes of the night's events were coming back to him, bit by bit, as if his mind was putting together a giant puzzle. When the memory of his wife and daughter popped back into his mind, he shut his eyes as tightly as he could, willing the images to disappear. How he wished he could have forgotten about it all.

He had never denied the crime he had committed. He, Terrence Blake, had killed his wife. But it had not been out of malice or cruelty. It had been an accident, although no one had ever cared enough to listen or wonder if they believed him. So, he had gone to prison without saying another word. After all, regardless of the reasons for Delilah's death, at the end of the day she was dead, and he was responsible for it. He tried not to think about Maddison, but the memory of her smiling face refused to go away. Here, in this dark room, crushed against the wall, Terrence could not keep hot tears of despair from rolling down his cheeks.

In the distance, he could hear people walking along the empty corridors, and see the shadows of moving feet dancing underneath the tiny space between the floor and the closed door. The smell of bodies huddled together seemed to hover over them like invisible fog. The floor was so uncomfortable Terrence could feel bruises starting to form under his back and shoulders. He was squeezed in such a tight space, the pressure on his ribs was becoming hard to ignore.

He eventually drifted off into a troubled sleep. In agitated dreams, he saw Delilah's face spin around him like a ghost, screaming at him to open his eyes and see what was going on. He saw Maddison's tiny hands grip his own, but the more he tried to hold onto her the more she slipped out of his grasp. He called out to her to be brave but she only looked at him sadly and shook her head. Suddenly he was thrown into a cage, the bars of which shrunk closer and closer by the second, until the metal dug into his legs and his ribs. He was trying desperately to push them away but there was no stopping them. He knew he must die and, just as the realisation hit him, he was dragged out of the realm of dreams back into the madness of his new reality.

'Get up, you lazy fuckers! Come on, get up!'

The guards were shouting, banging loudly on the doors of their makeshift cells. Terrence felt exhausted. Around him, the other convicts barely looked at each other, simply lining up in the room, ready to be taken outside. This part of the drill was vaguely familiar to them, since a similar routine was followed in prison. Up at six in the morning, for breakfast, and a quick and freezing cold shower, before being led back into their cells. In the afternoon, they were allowed thirty minutes in the prison yard to get some air. If the wardens were in a good mood this could sometimes last an hour, although this had become more and more of a rare occurrence over the last few years.

Terrence got in line behind the others. The door opened in front of them and they moved ahead, at a fast pace, in between the two lines of armed guards escorting them down the corridor. They were led into a room where several long tables and benches had been setup up. Small bowls of what looked oddly like pre-digested blobs of porridge were positioned at regular intervals, indicating where convicts were supposed to sit. They ate in silence, trying to ignore the pungent taste and smell of the lukewarm paste. Many of them had learnt to gulp it down without thinking about it too much, knowing full well that none of the other meals they would be given that day would be any better and that they simply needed to have some substance in their system to help them through the long stretches of boredom ahead.

The taste of it barely registered on Terrence's tongue. He was lost in reflection, wondering what the first challenge would be. The mere thought of it chilled him to the bones. Before they had gone on stage the previous day, he had tried to rationalise the whole concept, thinking that there was no way the public would back violence shown live on national television. He was not so sure anymore.

He had always been a firm believer in the human race, and in their ability to love and forgive, but his beliefs were being strongly challenged. He had misjudged how bad the situation had become. He wished that he could drop out of the show before it truly began. If he was to be paraded and humiliated live on stage, under the watchful eyes of millions of people who wanted him worse than dead, maybe the easy way out was preferable.

His thoughts were interrupted by the shouts of the guards, urging them to get up. They were escorted to a large basement room which had been repurposed as a giant bathroom. On one side of the room, dirty buckets were aligned against the wall. On the other side the walls and floors had been covered with white tiles. The room stank of human excrement, cheap soap and damp body hair.

As their group came in, they saw a group of female convicts exit the room at a fast pace, their hair soaking wet. The men were told they had ten minutes to use the buckets to relieve themselves. Of his entire time in prison, Terrence thought, he had never faced such poor and inhumane conditions.

After the allocated ten minutes, they were lined up against the tiled wall, facing five of the guards who were holding industrial size water hoses in their hands. The cold jets hit them before any of them could register what was happening. One of the guards screamed over the rumble of the water for them to turn around to face the wall. There was a short break during which they were able to use the small soap bars to shampoo their heads and wash their bodies. Within seconds the hoses were on them again.

Once it was over they stepped out of the wet area and got dressed again, ready to be led back into their tiny cells, for the first of many long and exhausting waits until the evening show.

CHAPTER 7

SEAN CRAVANAUGH

Across the Cradle, preparations for the first stage of the competition were underway. From his office in one of the large VIP rooms at the very top of the arena, Sean oversaw staff and construction workers running around to get everything ready for the first task.

On one side of the room, the window gave him an unparalleled view of the arena whilst the opposite wall had been replaced at his request by a giant glass window that allowed him to keep an eye on the growing queues of citizens waiting impatiently to get through the Cradle doors. Both windows were bullet-proof, and a small group of specialised security agents were arranged all the way from his office door along the corridor.

Sean walked over to the opposite window and looked out to count the number of stands that had been put up to sell the show's merchandise. After the previous day's show, he had requested twenty more to be set up and for their supplier to print out millions of tee-shirts reading 'Time for Justice' overnight. Both his head of Operations and their supplier had tried to explain to him why this was a difficult ask but he had not backed down.

He was not a man used to being denied anything. Either people got used to meeting his demands, no matter how challenging, or they would not last long in his circle, or any circle they might have previously been able to enter for that matter, since he was not someone to forgive and forget easily. Over the years, this had made him both respected and feared across the industry, and somewhat resented and lonely in his personal life. He did not mind either so much. It was the price he had had to pay to get this far, and if he had to do it all over again he would happily have paid it a hundred times over. He did not for one second miss having the burden of too many human relationships. He was admired by all, desired by so many, and had never needed to want for anything he was unable to obtain, or have someone fetch for him. In his books, one barely needed anything more.

Sean looked through the large window, towards the arena doors, along the queues of thousands of hopefuls excitedly waiting for the competition's first task. Whoever tried to tell him he should have proposed something more socially acceptable was simply misguided. He had rebuked anyone who had begged him to tame down his plan, and he had warned them that they would be the first to congratulate him on being so bold once the show started.

Sean snorted, and allowed his gaze to linger on the men and women lined up in front of the doors, all of them already madly engrossed in the show's vision. None of them cared for politically correct anymore, and Sean watched their little figures dancing before his eyes like so many piles of golden coins.

CHAPTER 8

TERRENCE BLAKE

It was only when he heard someone shout, waking him up with a jump, that Terrence realised he had fallen asleep. He stood up and got in line behind the other convicts. As they walked through the corridors, rows of heavily armed guards surrounding them, they heard a distant rumble. It grew louder and louder as they made their way up to ground level. By the time they reached their giant cage, the rumble had become so strong it almost made the metal bars vibrate before their eyes. Something about the intensity of the vibrations and the thunder-like sounds made Terrence shudder. It was an angry and frightening noise, resonating all the way to his bones.

Terrence looked around. Most of his fellow convicts looked apprehensive. Amongst the few who managed to keep their composure was Mad Spencer. He was standing straight, his expression calm, almost curious, like a pensioner about to be taken on a day trip. He must have felt Terrence's gaze on him because, without any notice, his head jerked back in his direction, his eyes suddenly shining. Terrence instantly looked away.

Their cage was rolled slowly along one side of the panels, until they arrived on the stage. The strength of the lights took Terrence by surprise after a day spent in semi-darkness. The rumbling noise hit him with full force, and it took him a few seconds to realise it was not thunder, but the roar of the audience impatiently waiting for their victims to be dragged before their eyes.

'Ladies and gentlemen, please welcome onstage your 'No Pain, No Game' contestants!'

Terrence squinted, trying to force his vision to adapt to the brightness of this alien environment. The show host, Tyler Benson, was standing in the middle of the stage, with his back to them.

'The very first challenge our contestants have to face tonight will be announced in a minute, but first let's take a moment to look at the rules. Each week, the contestants will have to face one challenge. Challenges will be revealed on the night, so there will be no time for them to prepare. Some challenges will be divided into two, with female contestants competing against each other, separately from the male contestants. Other challenges will see all of our contestants competing together. When the challenge ends, we will use our Wheel of Destiny…' he walked over to a giant, glitter-covered wheel which displayed numbers from one to forty in a random order, '…to decide how many of the contestants who came last will have to face a 'Punishment Card'. The punishment cards will be chosen by you, our audience, in the arena and at home. The losing contestants will then exit the competition and answer for their crimes by immediately facing the death penalty.'

Terrence's heart skipped a beat at the words. Had he heard this right?

'At each round, the contestants who come first in each challenge will earn points. The contestant who makes it to the end of the competition will see all their points converted into cash and will be allowed to take their winnings home. Most importantly, they will see their sentence entirely abolished. Now,' Tyler pulled an envelope from the inside pocket of his jacket and waved it in the air. 'I have in this envelope this week's challenge…'

He paused for dramatic effect, the envelope still high above his head, heavy with mystery. The sound of a drum roll resonated in the arena. Tens of thousands of eyes were fixed on him, and on the piece of paper he held brandished in the air.

'The challenge our contestants have to face today is...' Tyler Benson ripped the envelope open, 'the one thousand meter race!'

A jingle kicked off in the background, as two fire canons on each side of the cage breathed tall flames. The commentator's deep voice repeated the name of the challenge, which also appeared in bold letters on all screens around the stage. The audience applauded at the announcement.

'Whilst our contestants go and get ready for their first task, let's see what our judges have to say. Mrs Swan, let's start with you...'

CHAPTER 9

TERRENCE BLAKE

Terrence was so stunned he did not hear the wardens usher them all out of the cage, towards the backstage area. As they passed through the door one of the guards bent over to attach something cold and heavy to their right ankle. Terrence glanced down at his foot to see an electronic bracelet, with a small red light flashing faintly. The guards directed the women to an open-ceilinged cell surrounded by metal bars and the men to another cell a few meters away. The Head Warden stood in front of the cells, looking at them like he had never seen anything so despicable in his entire life.

'What's on your ankle is a state-of-the-art electronic bracelet. It is equipped with the most advanced GPS tracking technology in the world, but most importantly, it has this amazing feature which allows us to hit you, from a distance, with either an electric shock, or a tranquilliser to knock you out. *Or*, if you're really misbehaving, with a dose of a concentrated modified cyanide formula which will guarantee you the slowest, most painful of deaths.' He paused for a few seconds to let the words sink in, glaring at them. 'I'm personally excited to try that last feature, so I dare you to try anything other than what you're being told to do. Actually...'

He turned to the first officer standing behind him and nodded at him. The first officer instantly saluted and marched away purposefully.

'Why wait?' The Head Warden exclaimed, 'I've been dying to try this out! Pun intended, of course,' he chuckled at his own joke, and the other wardens smirked.

Screams and shouts erupted from somewhere backstage. The Head Warden barely glanced towards where the screams were coming from, his stare fixed on the convicts, obviously enjoying every second of the show he was putting on. Two guards dragged out a screaming woman, holding her tightly by the arms. She was fighting as strongly as she could, trying to slow their progress down. The guards threw her at the Head Warden's feet. She scrambled back up, her eyes mad with anger and fear. The Head Warden pulled out a small remote control from his pocket.

'Everyone, meet contestant one hundred and one. This woman was convicted for the brutal murder of her lover, his wife and their two children. She has been condemned to the death penalty, but has escaped it so far for lack of available resources to conduct the execution.'

A look of utter confusion spread across the woman's face.

'Now, let's see how well this works, shall we!' The Head Warden said cheerfully, pressing one of the buttons on the remote.

All eyes were on the woman as she immediately collapsed in front of them, screaming in pain. Her body shook violently, as if she was suffering from a seizure. Her voice became muffled by the electric shocks running through her from head to toes. Large drops of sweat poured were pouring from her forehead and down her face.

Terrence could not take his eyes off the woman. As much as he wanted to look away, he was transfixed. Something about the insanity of her torture and the detached attitude of the Head Warden paralysed him. After a few seconds, the Head Warden released the button he had kept pressed and looked around him with a satisfied smile.

'I'd say this is fairly efficient, isn't it?'

He waited for a few minutes until the woman had stopped shivering on the ground and nodded to a couple of guards. They immediately walked up to her and forced her up. She was so weak that she could not stand on her own. One of the guards slapped her back to consciousness. Her head jerked up suddenly. With another small nod of his chin, the Head Warden ordered the guards to let go of her. She wrapped her arms around herself, covering her stomach, wobbling on the spot.

'Any last words?' Grumbled the Head Warden.

She looked up at him, probably thinking she had not heard him correctly. Within a second, a flash of understanding crossed her trembling face and her expression distorted into a grimace of fear. Before she could even let out the scream that was forming on her lips, the Head Warden had pressed another button and she collapsed again right before their eyes. The pain seemed so intense that it prevented any sound from coming out of her open mouth. Her expression was one of absolute agony. Her arms were clutched around her body, her hands grasping at her skin like she was trying to pull all her organs out of her abdomen. She twitched on the ground silently, and Terrence thought of a slug covered in salt. Her suffering was mesmerising. No one uttered a single word. The woman shook violently, red foam gathering at the corners of her mouth, dribbling all over her chin and neck. Her skin was greying by the second, and her nails dug into her upper arms so hard that drops of blood started forming under her fingertips. The morbid spectacle seemed to last forever, until finally she stopped moving. She remained there, in utter stillness, her tongue and eyes popping out of her face in a grotesque fashion.

No one made a sound. Terrence could feel a hole carving its way into his chest, drilling through his vitals organs, suffocating his heart. Blood beat hard inside his ears, pounding against his temples. Somewhere in the distance he could vaguely hear the deep, resounding murmurs of the agitated crowd. When he glanced up, he saw the Head Warden looked satisfied with his little trick. He must have felt Terrence's stare on him because, ever so slowly, he turned his head towards him, his lips distorted into the most paralysing, blood-chilling of smiles.

CHAPTER 10

TYLER BENSON

'Call for an advert break, we need a few minutes to set up,' Tyler heard the producer call out in his ear piece.

He gave the slightest of nods towards the production room, a big glass room located on one side of the stage, high up above the rows of seats occupied by the audience, designed to give the crew a panoramic view of the arena.

Tyler heard himself announce a break and promise the audience they would be back shortly. He had thrown so many such announcements to so many such audiences he barely even realised when he was doing it anymore. Sometimes his wife teased him that she could tell when his mind was somewhere else, because he addressed her in the same manner, with his 'telly voice'.

Tyler forced the manufactured smile to remain on his lips, one he had come to perfect over the years, until he was certain he had gone far enough into the backstage maze that no one would notice the change in his demeanour. He walked quickly to his changing room and locked the door behind him.

He pulled a chair and sat facing the wide mirror on one wall. He patted down the side of his head, taming a few strands of hair which had come out of place. He adjusted his tie absent-mindedly, tightening its knot, straightening it down. He unbuttoned his jacket, and buttoned it again. He met his own gaze in the brightly-lit mirror and suddenly froze. The man staring back at him was a picture of perfection. Perfect hair, perfect skin, perfect suit and tie. Tyler could no longer be sure who the man so glossily reflected in front of him was.

He could not prevent a burst of traumatic images from popping into his mind, memories of the 'special training' he had undergone to prepare him for the job. On Sean Cravanaugh's instructions, he had been made to witness the 'pre-selection process'. Weeks and weeks of scouring through prisons and standing in the background as the Head Warden and his team worked tirelessly to find the best hundred men and women to make the show as entertaining as possible. If the contestants looked somewhat inoffensive on stage now, it was only because the brutality of the pre-selection had bent them into harmlessness. Tyler shuddered, because more than the pain of the convicts, what had shocked him most was the obvious enjoyment the Head Warden and his men seemed to get out of the experience. Tyler recalled how many of the convicts had refused to be enrolled in the show and sign the waiver, only to be beaten into submission. Tyler knew he would forever bear the scars of having had the front row seat to such violence. The images had been branded into his brain with red hot iron.

'Back live in one minute,' the producer's voice resonated in his earpiece.

Tyler remained frozen for a few seconds, almost unable to breathe, willing himself to snap back into action. As he stood up, slowly, shaking his head, he threw one last look at the man in the mirror. He could only hope that his beautifully manicured exterior would be enough to fool the world, and prevent anyone from catching a glimpse of the anguish he could feel building deep inside him.

CHAPTER 11

TERRENCE BLAKE

'And we are back on the stage of 'No Pain, No Game', live from the Cradle Arena!' Tyler Benson exclaimed to the crowd.

From where he was standing, Terrence caught glimpses of the presenter's back, as he stood facing the audience. Backstage, the contestants were arranged in two lines, with women and men on different sides. Around them, the guards' eyes were alert, batons hanging by their belts, machine guns across their chests. A short distance away, a young man with a headset and a clipboard was in deep conversation with the Head Warden, gesturing around as he spoke. The Head Warden said nothing for some time and when the young man finally stopped talking, he nodded briefly, immediately walking back towards the lines of contestants.

'Listen to me, you little shits!' He paused for a second to make sure he had their undivided attention. 'In exactly thirty seconds you will be brought on stage for your first challenge. The men will race first, then the women. The racers who come last will be faced with another challenge and will then leave the competition. Once you leave the competition,' the Head Warden continued, 'you will be executed. I won't keep up the suspense, *I* am the one in charge of that particular task... And I can't begin to tell you how much I'm looking forward to deciding in which way each and every one of you is going to die.'

Terrence's knees weakened at the thought. From the corner of his eyes, he saw a couple of guards wiping the blood and drool off the patch of ground where, a few minutes earlier, they had watched convict number one hundred and one perish.

The contestants were ushered at a brisk pace onto the stage.

'Ladies and gentlemen,' Tyler Benson exclaimed, 'you will notice our contestants are no longer in the protective shell you saw them in earlier…'

Protective shell, thought Terrence bitterly, that was quite a lot of effort to avoid calling it what it was. They had been parked in a *cage*, like animals.

'But don't be alarmed. You will see they are all now wearing an electronic bracelet, attached to their ankle,' he turned towards the large screens above their heads and pointed to the image which was now zoomed in on the convicts' feet. 'This is a high technology bracelet which allows us not only to track the contestants' location at all times, but also to immobilise them from a distance should there be any reason for us to do so.'

Immobilise. Terrence shook his head in disbelief. Here they were again with their politically correct nonsense. The distorted face of convict number one hundred and one flashed back, unbidden, into his mind.

'As you can see over here,' Tyler Benson walked across to the left edge of the stage, 'we have installed a race track. The tracks are two hundred and fifty meters long, so the contestants will need to complete four loops to finish the race. To keep it fair, the men will race first, followed by the women… Can we have the men on the race tracks, please!'

The guards ushered the fifty men forward, their guns pointed down, their eyes alert. The entire arena went quiet with anticipation. Terrence looked over at the judges' table. Valery Swan was observing the scene without the slightest hint of compassion. Josh Carter, on the other hand, seemed to have turned a weird shade of green. Terrence thought how much greener he would be if he was standing on the tracks, about to take part in a race which could very well cost him his life. The other two judges, Sean Cravanaugh and Camilla, were whispering to each other, their heads slightly bent sideways.

'Ladies and gentlemen, are you ready for our first challenge?' Tyler Benson turned to the audience, his arms lifting to the sky as he spoke.

The audience clapped and screamed back at him in excitement, their roar quickly turning into their new mantra:

'Time for justice! Time for justice!'

Thousands of clenched fists punched the air with each word. The chanting grew louder and more menacing by the second. Terrence swallowed hard as one desperate thought crossed his mind.

It did not matter how fast he ran, or how many challenges he faced, anyone still alive at the end of this charade would still be torn apart by an entire country's fury. He felt so hopeless his knees almost gave way. He forced himself to breathe. He willed himself to muster all his courage, and hoped that the years of disciplined jogging around the small prison yard would give him enough of an advantage that he could live through another day. The distorted face of convict one hundred and one flashed back into his mind and he gasped, as if someone had punched the air out of his lungs. He barely had time to regain his composure. His heart was beating madly against his ribs, in such a frenzy that he felt one of them might crack under the pressure. Around him, colours and sounds started to fade into a giant blur of noise and shapes. It seemed to him he was standing on a revolving stage, and the entire world around him was spinning endlessly. He tried to close his eyes, but was struck with such vertigo he immediately sparked them open again.

'On your marks...' Tyler Benson exclaimed, 'get set... GO!'

A loud gun shot resounded in the arena, instantly followed by absolute mayhem. The mass of convicts lurched into action in a chaos of bodies and tangled limbs. Some of the men sprang into motion at once, whilst others remained petrified on the spot. Terrence was caught in the crowd. He felt hands pushing him around, elbows jabbing into his ribs and legs kicking him. He looked around him, panicked, confused by the screams and shouts pouring down on him, the chaos around him drowning his senses.

It took Terrence several seconds to realise he, too, had started to run, madly, desperately, straight in front of him. He could not feel his body, nor the ground underneath him. He could only guess that he was doing what he was supposed to. Everything around him was a haze, one big abstract watercolour painting in which he felt he was the only sharp, distinct figure.

He ran. Not because he wanted to run, nor because he wanted so badly to win. He ran because some primal instinct made him run, emerging from deep within his guts, commanding him to move. He shoved men aside, ignoring the shouts around him, not turning back even once to see what happened to those he outran.

All of a sudden, a piercing pang of pain radiated from his ankle, and he fell, hard against the rough concrete of the tracks. He felt his skin scratch around his knees and palms, but it was nothing compared to the mind-blowing agony which reverberated through his leg. His vision blurred, and he could hear his heart-beat banging in every corner of his skull. A high-pitched buzzing sound bounced between his ears. When the pain subsided slightly he looked down to his foot, and saw the light on his ankle-bracelet was flashing bright red. Two guards were running towards him and he felt strong arms grab him from the elbows and force him up on his feet.

'…is quite unbelievable!' Tyler Benson's voice reached him from a distance, 'contestant seventy-seven didn't want to stop racing!'

Terrence looked up, his vision slowly adjusting to his surroundings. A giant burst of laughter came up from the audience, high above him. It sounded like the arena itself was mocking him. He frowned in confusion.

Down on the track, the race was still on and Terrence watched, powerless, as his fellow men ran for their lives. Some of them had not exercised in years and either slowed down, or collapsed in pain, hugging their stomachs and panting. None of them was allowed to forfeit their turn. If some of them took a little too long to get back onto their feet, the guards sent a few tactical electrical discharges through their ankle bracelets to spring them back into action.

One elderly convict, a small and wrinkled man with frail limbs and a tired face, whose overalls bore the number fifty-one, took such a long time to finish the four laps that the show host called for an advert break halfway through. Terrence watched the old man with growing unease, trying to fight the urge to run to him and carry him through the final meters. When convict fifty-one eventually finished the race, he fell to his knees just behind the finish line, his hands on his thighs, eyes closed, his face turned towards the sky. His lips were moving ever so slightly and Terrence wondered if he was praying for the strength to go through dozens of other such challenges, or for the mercy to have his life end right there and then. A couple of guards sprinted to the old man and dragged him off the tracks. The convict did not fight them, he let himself be carried away, in absolute surrender.

Terrence saw the show host striding over to him purposefully, a bright smile on his lips, a microphone in his hand. He was dazzled by the scene. He squinted, unable to focus. When he managed to step out of his state of confusion, he looked up to see Tyler Benson staring at him expectantly.

'It seems contestant seventy-seven is still high on adrenalin!' Tyler Benson chuckled.

It took Terrence some time to realise the he was being spoken to. Tyler Benson did not seem put off by his lack of a response.

'What's your name?'

Terrence hesitated slightly, for a second he was not too sure he could remember his own name.

'Terrence,' he said, 'Terrence Blake.'

'Oh yes,' Tyler exclaimed theatrically, 'the wife murderer and child abuser!'

The audience booed in unison.

'That was quite a performance you gave back there. How do you feel?'

The microphone had been pushed to Terrence's mouth.

'What?' He frowned.

Tyler Benson looked disappointed.

'Are you used to running? It seemed like you didn't want to stop racing.'

Terrence stared blankly back at him. Above them, the giant screens were showing a replay of the final moments of the race. He watched intently as the video showed him running madly, past the finish line, and then on for several meters before he collapsed onto the ground.

'Are you used to running?' Tyler Benson asked again.

'Yes.'

'Can you tell us what was going through your mind during the race?'

Terrence pondered the question for a moment, and realised he did not have an answer. He had not even really known he was running.

'Nothing,' Terrence answered, which was the truth.

'Really!' Tyler Benson exclaimed, 'because it looked like you were running for your life there!'

'I was,' Terrence was snapped back to attention by the ridiculous obviousness of the comment.

Tyler Benson seemed to judge it best to end the interview there.

'Well, let us all give a round of applause for contestant seventy-seven, Terrence Blake!'

A few faint claps emerged from the heights of the arena, but the sound died away fairly quickly. Terrence was taken away from the stage to join the other male convicts backstage. Before he was allowed back into the cage, however, the Head Warden came to face him. Terrence could feel the man's filthy warm breath against his cheeks.

'Someone isn't much of a showman, it would seem!' The Head Warden said coldly.

Terrence looked down. He did not think the comment warranted a response.

'Let me tell you one thing,' the Head Warden turned to look at the other convicts, 'don't delude yourself into thinking that your chances of surviving this process are any good. They're not,' he paused to let his words sink in. 'The only way you have of tilting the odds in your favour is to play along. Ultimately, the people who will be deciding your fate will be the audience and the judges. So, I strongly suggest you try as hard you can to get into the spirit of this competition. Who knows, maybe some of you despicable bastards can win the public's mercy…'

The Head Warden looked satisfied with his speech, and an air of sadistic delight had taken over his face.

For a split-second Terrence's mind wandered out of his body, and he was standing high above it all, dominating the arena, an invisible observant to the puppet show beneath his feet. He saw the public, their hands pointed straight in front of them, partial judges of the contestants' fates. With a flick of their fingers they could have them dead or alive. He watched the contestants, lined up like little chess pawns, waiting to be moved forward or back, one step closer or further away from the fire pit all around them. He could see it so clearly it made his chest tighten. A wave of nausea and desperation washed over him. He shook his head, forcing his attention back to the present.

The women were lead onto the stage and, though he could not see them, Terrence could picture them standing on the race tracks. He could imagine their confusion, and their fear at what they were being asked to do. He knew how terrifying the cheers of the crowd seemed, reaching them from high above, as though they were suffering the wrath of an angry God. Worst of all would be the knowledge that there was nothing they could do other than go along with it. That no one would come to their rescue and everyone around them was rooting for them to fail. What on earth could any of them do in the face of such a rigged game?

CHAPTER 12

SEAN CRAVANAUGH

From his privileged position at the judges' table, Sean had the best view in the house. He swivelled on his chair and breathed in the immensity of the crowds behind him. The sound of an excited audience was music to his ears, the audible proof of a successful venture. He closed his eyes briefly and took it all in. All around him, the excitement was like a giant ball of energy, bouncing off every corner of the Cradle. They loved it. Not only did they love it, but the safety of numbers, of others shouting and raging with anger around them, seemed to justify their hatred, and to allow them to let it out with mind-blowing intensity. He would have loved to hear anyone try and talk to him about whatever ethics they thought the scheme was lacking now, and see how they fared when faced with the thousands of enthused souls in the Cradle. Ethics, Sean thought again with a snort, remembering the arguments put forward by so many of his opponents just a few weeks before, *my bloody arse.*

He looked around and his eyes fell on Camilla's profile. She still looked deep in concentration, with her head slightly bent. Sean wondered what thoughts were going through her mind.

When he had first released the 'No Pain, No Game' proposal to the public, he had expected to get a lot of phone calls. He could have predicted most of them and, if he had been given a penny for each one he had got right, he would be even more insanely wealthy than he already was. One call he would never have guessed he would receive, however, was the one from superstar pop singer Camilla. When his secretary had popped into his office to ask whether he wanted her to put the call through to his direct line, he had asked her to repeat herself, certain he must have heard her wrong.

'Put her through,' he had said, incredulous.

He had sat down in the large chair behind his desk, his landline phone on speaker, and had waited for the call to be connected with growing curiosity.

'You're through to Sean Cravanaugh.' He had made sure to use his most businesslike manner.

'Hi, Mr. Cravanaugh. This is Camilla speaking.'

Her voice had been level, perhaps a little too much so, and he had wondered how many times she had rehearsed the conversation before going through with it.

'So I've heard,' he had responded, 'What can I do for you, Camilla?'

There had been a fragment of a pause on the other end of the line. Over the years, he had received a lot of calls from people begging for favours, and he had learned to recognise when he was about to be asked to grant someone a wish. He braced himself.

'I have heard about your proposal,' Camilla had answered, 'I want in.'

Sean had been stunned. Camilla was all glamour and glitter, the country's latest diva. He could not imagine why she would be interested in something as radical and, even he had to admit it, as sinister as 'No Pain, No Game'. He had felt like he was running one step behind her, completely blindsided, and that was a position he abhorred finding himself in. He had tried not to let any of his unease show, and forced himself to speak with the blandest of tones.

'Do you, now…'

'Yes,' her voice had been determined.

'And why would that be, may I ask?'

'I'm afraid this is not something I'm able to discuss over the phone. Let's meet,' she had answered.

She had seemed to expect his question. Sean had fallen silent, pondering his options. As much as he doubted that the singer had anything to bring to the table which could be of any value to him, he was too curious not to indulge her. He had sighed, loudly enough for her to understand he was doing her a favour.

'Fine. You've sparked my curiosity. I'll have my secretary arrange a time for you to come in.'

'Thank you.' She had sounded audibly relieved.

'Let me tell you, however,' he had warned her, his voice hard, 'that my time is extremely precious. Don't waste any of it, otherwise I can promise you will have to pay a hefty price for it.'

He had not meant for the words to come out sounding as harsh as they did. He had merely wanted to give her a chance to reconsider the obscure reason why she wanted to meet him, and to make sure it was indeed going to be worth his while, but somehow his suggestion had sounded like a downright threat. She had said nothing for a moment, taking in his words on the other side of the line.

'Of course,' she had eventually responded, 'I can assure you you will not regret meeting me.'

He had disconnected the call, and sat back in his chair, only realising at that moment that he had been hanging off the edge of his seat.

~ ~ ~

Sean looked up, dragged out of his reflection by Tyler's voice reverberating across the Cradle. He looked up at the screens, where images of the first round were playing, contestant seventy-seven's face stretched, magnified, over the giant screens. He was a tall man, with short greying hair. His face looked tired, resigned. Sean checked the thick volume of printed notes the producer had given him, and flicked through the pages until he found what he was looking for: 'Convict #77: Terrence Blake. Wife murderer. Child abuser. Sentence: life imprisonment'.

Tyler announced an ad break whilst they got the female contestants ready for their first challenge. The moment the red lights on the cameras switched off, the entire atmosphere in the arena relaxed. In the audience, small groups of people started standing up and walking around, making their way to the bathrooms or to the snack stands.

Tyler had disappeared backstage the moment the break began, and Sean guessed the pressure of holding up his cheerful attitude was getting to him. The host would probably be locked in his changing room, or in some hidden part of the arena, stretching out his facial muscles.

His attention fell again on Camilla, who sat next to him, eyes closed, fists clenched around the fabric of her dress gathering on her lap. He extended a hand and placed it on hers. At the touch, she sat bolt upright and her eyes flinched open. When she saw it was him, she relaxed instantly. He nodded towards her, silently asking her if she was ok. She nodded back briefly, but her face was tense and the look in her eyes betrayed her unease. How fragile she looked, how defenceless! No matter how much she tried to compose herself, and how determined she was to play her part, she seemed to struggle to keep a grip on her emotions. He had to admire her stubbornness to achieve her goal, whatever the cost.

He checked his watch. They had a few minutes before the end of the ad break. He tugged at Camilla's hand and motioned for her to follow him. She stood up without a word, and let him lead the way around the stage towards a small black door to another one of his private quarters. It was spacious and richly furnished, but above all it had no windows, and no other access point than the one they had taken to come in, giving it the undeniable advantage of being far away from any curious eyes and ears. He walked across the room over to the drinks cabinet. When he turned around, Camilla was standing in front of one of the plush sofas in the centre of the room, her face determined and fierce in the faint light. Her neck and arms were exposed, her soft, caramel-coloured skin almost glowing in the semi-darkness. She was a picture of perfection, at least in appearance. But he knew better than to stop at a cover to understand what a book was about.

'I need a drink,' she announced sternly.

Sean had guessed as much and was already pouring her a stiff scotch. He handed the tumbler over to her. She remained standing, sipping the brown liquid. She seemed lost in thought, and Sean knew not to interrupt her train of thoughts. He leaned back against the cabinet and studied her. Slowly, as she drank, the crease in her brow softened, and her fingers relaxed a little around the glass.

'You ok, kid?' He asked.

She simply nodded and gulped down the rest of her drink. She motioned towards the cabinet, holding up her empty glass. Sean followed her silent instructions and refilled her tumbler. She took a seat on the sofa, her arms stretched out wide by her sides, her legs crossed with her left ankle lying on top of her right knee.

After their first telephone conversation, he had met Camilla a handful of times, but he had known from their first meeting that they understood each other. On their third encounter, they had discussed the challenges of maintaining one's appearance in such a frivolous and scrutinising industry. She had told him that her attitude, clothes, everything up to her posture, was thoroughly designed by her manager and her team to build out the most perfect and consistent image. Over the years she had got used to sitting and standing straight, crossing her legs delicately one over the other, and checking her appearance before stepping outside her house. Sometimes, she had revealed to him, she would send all of her staff away, close all of the windows and curtains in her house, locking every possible access point. Then she would switch on very loud hard rock, pop open a bottle of vodka, strip off to her underwear and drink, and scream, and dance until she passed out on the marble floor. She did not particularly like hard rock music or the taste of vodka, but they were far enough away from her bubblegum persona to make her feel like she had not yet lost her real self completely. Looking at her at that moment, spread out on the couch, her legs crossed in quite a manly manner, Sean thought she could not have looked less like her pristine lady-like professional character.

He glanced at his watch.

'Time to get back out there. We'll be live soon.'

She looked at him with a wicked smile, and raised her glass towards him.

'Time for justice!' She declared with unhidden sarcasm before swallowing her drink in one go.

CHAPTER 13

TYLER BENSON

The women's race was almost over and Tyler was standing by the side of the stage, commentating on what was happening down on the tracks. Just like the men, a few racers collapsed long before the finish line. The guards then activated their ankle bracelets, giving them enough of a nudge to keep going. The show must go on, Tyler thought bitterly. He tried his best not to wince every time it happened.

'Smile!' The producer snorted in his ear-piece when it appeared that he was not making enough of an effort to control his facial expression, or at least not with enough success.

'Hello there!' He called out to the contestant he managed to reach first, his microphone held up straight in front of him. 'What's your name?'

The woman, whose overalls bore the number twenty-three, jumped a little. She hesitated for a moment, glancing around.

'Helen,' she growled.

'Oh, yes. Helen Stewart!' Tyler exclaimed, as information came through his earpiece, 'the passion crime!'

General echos of 'ohs' and 'ahs' came from the audience, followed by buzzing whispers of disapproval. Helen Stewart looked uncomfortable. Her fingers tugged at the front of her overalls. Her cheeks had turned bright red and, as she looked at him, Tyler could not help but take a small step back. He had a nasty feeling it was the exact same look of sheer anger and revenge the woman's victim must have seen just before he died.

'Erm…' He swallowed the hard ball of nerves which was building inside his throat, 'so, you did quite well in the race. How do you feel about that?'

By the end of his question, Tyler felt he had managed to restore his casual tone. Helen Stewart shook her head at him in disbelief.

'You want to know how I *feel?*' She repeated slowly, 'I've been serving a life sentence for the last ten years, the last time I exercised was so long ago I can't even remember that I ever did, and I've just run a thousand meter race on live television to entertain all of you fucking morons!' She barked at him. 'How the *fuck* do you think I feel!'

Tyler had not been expecting such animosity, and before he realised it, he had recoiled, crossing his arms instinctively in front of his chest. The audience laughed and he straightened up immediately, his face turning crimson with embarrassment. He tried to regain his composure, but his awkwardness and his inability to bounce back from the scene made the audience almost hysterical. He watched the guards lead the contestant backstage.

'Yes… Erm… Well…' He tried to speak again but his voice was flustered, and the more he tried to breathe the more he could feel his face burning with shame.

If ever there was a living nightmare equivalent for live television hosts of standing naked in front of a crowd in your underwear to recite a poem you did not know the words to, *that* had to be it.

'Are you alright, Tyler?'

Tyler looked up. At the judges' table, Sean Cravanaugh looked amused, although from that distance, and in his present state of distress, Tyler would not have sworn to it.

'Please, can we bring some water to our host?' Cravanaugh called out to the side of the stage, throwing the task out in the open for anyone to take ownership of it.

Someone from the production crew ran towards the edge of the stage. Tyler only caught the small bottle of water which was thrown at him a second before it was due to hit him in the stomach. He unscrewed the plastic top and took a few sips of water, his eyes closing briefly as he forced the fresh liquid to soothe the panic brewing inside him. By the time he flicked his eyelids open, the plastic bottle was empty, the audience had somewhat settled down, and his state of turmoil felt like a distant memory. He threw the bottle aside.

'Well,' he relaxed into a smile, 'that was interesting!'

The audience laughed, and he felt like he was finally back on track.

'And now, on to the moment you've all been waiting for. The results!'

More 'ohs' and 'ahs' resonated through the audience as the arena lights dimmed. In a loud ruffle of metallic clickety-clacks, the large cage was dragged onto the stage again.

'Tonight,' Tyler announced with a deep voice, 'we have seen our contestants face their first challenge. Some did well, some not so well, but *who* will make it through to the next stage?'

Two low notes punctuated the end of his sentence, resounding all around them, adding to the suspense of the situation.

'Now, I'd like to add here that the punishment cards our losing contestants will face are not random…'

Tyler stopped for a short moment to allow his words to sink in, and only spoke again when he was certain he had captured everyone's attention. The arena was dead silent.

'We have contacted the victims, and the family and friends of the victims of the crimes committed by our contestants…'

Another pause. The tension was spiking up by the second.

'We have asked them to create the punishments.' He gestured towards the cage, his gaze directed straight in front of him on the audience, '*Their* fate has been put in the hands of those they have wronged!'

He had spoken louder and louder, his voice mounting in a crescendo, until he was shouting in his microphone. The audience lifted, and their mantra once again bounced around the arena.

'Time for Justice! Time for Justice!'

CHAPTER 14

TERRENCE BLAKE

Terrence suppressed a shiver. He wondered if he would ever get used to this, to being a part of this, and whether he would ever truly get to grips with what 'this' was. He struggled to wrap his head around what was happening to him. The public's calls for justice banged like hammer blows inside his chest, as though coming from inside him.

'And now…' Tyler Benson announced, 'to the Wheel of Destiny!' The host walked to the side of the stage towards the giant wheel and dramatically pulled a large glittery handle. 'Here we go!'

The wheel spun round and round for several seconds, its pointed hand zooming madly past brightly coloured numbers, until it slowed down and finally stopped.

'Number two!' Tyler Benson exclaimed with a flourish. 'This means two of the contestants who took the longest to complete the race will face a Punishment card. Now, to make this exciting…' he added, and the audience went instantly silent with anticipation, 'we will reveal the *ten* contestants who came last in the race and it will be up to you, our audience, to vote for the two you want to see face the first punishments of the show!'

The audience's reaction left little doubt that they were pleased to be given a role to play. The images on the giant screens shifted to show head shots of ten convicts, five men and five women. The giant cage was plunged in semi-darkness, leaving ten individual beams of light, targeted at the ten unfortunate souls.

'You will have one minute to vote for the two contestants you want to see face a Punishment Card,' Tyler Benson announced, facing the audience. 'For the members of the public here in the Cradle, you may now pick up the electronic tablet located under your seats. For anyone watching at home, you can also participate using our app. The one-minute voting time starts... Now!'

A large countdown appeared on a second screen, and Terrence felt the tension immediately thicken around the arena. When the countdown reached the final ten seconds, Tyler Benson started shouting the numbers, quickly joined by the audience and the judges, until they reached the number zero.

'That's it! The voting line is now closed. I'm informed,' Tyler Benson widened his eyes, one hand pressed against his ear, 'that we have received five million votes. Oh, my!'

The audience roared and the judges stood up, clapping ostentatiously. The faint sound of drum rolls filled the silence.

'The two contestants who will face a Punishment Card, are... Contestant fifty-one and contestant twenty-five!'

Simultaneously, the rays of light covering the two convicts, a man and a woman, turned red and their pictures on the screen magnified.

'*You* have voted and *you* have picked the two contestants who will face the first Punishment Cards of the competition and exit the process!' Tyler Benson continued. 'And we will need *your* help once more, in the Cradle and at home, to pick the punishments they will face. These punishments are...'

Tyler Benson let the pause linger, the suspense wildly contagious. The tension was building up, like a thread had been extended between them and the host and stretched so much it was on the verge of snapping.

'To be revealed after the break!' He announced with a bright smile, whilst the public expressed their disappointment.

The tension dissolved instantly, and the whole arena relaxed, to the exception of the two convicts whose static emotionless faces stared out from the screens above them.

CHAPTER 15

SEAN CRAVANAUGH

Sean leant back in his chair. He closed his eyes for a brief moment, trying to focus all of his remaining senses on the arena, and the vibrations from the activity brewing inside it. The soft thumping of feet walking up and down in between rows of seats. The distant, buzzing murmurs of conversations, bouncing around the Cradle. Bits and pieces of technical conversations popping up around him, as members of the production crew walked by. Metallic sounds came up from the centre of the stage, where contestants fidgeted in their spots. The aromas emanating from his cup of freshly brewed coffee mixed with the smells of food and the crowd, as each and every individual carried their own collection of snacks and human odours along with them. To others, this might have been a repulsive mix but, to Sean, a fully packed arena carried the sweet smells and melodies of success.

At the sound of glass crashing on the ground, his eyes opened instantly, his head darting towards the noise. To his left, at the end of the judges' table, Josh Carter was faffing over the mess he had just made. Someone from the crew was kneeling, mopping the water and broken glass scattered on the floor. Josh Carter looked flustered, his cheeks pink, the corner of his mouth twitching uncontrollably.

'Hey, Carter,' Sean called out to him, leaning over the table.

Josh Carter looked up towards him. The collar of his expensive shirt was drenched with sweat.

'Breathe,' Sean reminded him.

Josh Carter only nodded. What an idiot, Sean thought, shaking his head.

He had never been a fan of the man, with his air of self-importance, his near fanatism for the rigid, well-oiled processes of hierarchy, and his posh mannerisms acquired during a wealthy upbringing and years fooling around the country's most expensive private schools. Josh Carter was everything Sean was not. He incarnated all the perverted, hypocritical and archaic values Sean abhorred. Josh Carter had coasted through life, the absolute opposite of the path Sean had to endure to carve his way into the world.

Sean knew that Josh Carter cared not one bit about his fellow men, that his role as the head of the National Human Rights Association was just a valuable addition to his curriculum vitae, a stepping stone to much bigger things. Sean saw that Carter did not give a damn about anyone other than himself. The Human Rights act was all for show, as had been the release of that fatal report, bringing the prison overcrowding issue to the forefront of public opinion polls. Without it, however, Sean's idea would never have even seen the light of day. In some strange way, he owed him, but this had not prevented him from using Carter as one of the many, many pawns in his big scheme. He had seen his value for what it was, like he did for every other human being he came into contact with. Having Carter at hand on the show gave him the undeniable advantage of being able to counter any possible piece of nonsense the man could come up with about human rights. Their very first confrontation on the first day of the show had been proof that Sean's strategy was working.

The ad break was coming to an end and, at the centre of the stage, Tyler was getting a foundation fix from one of the make-up artists. Whatever he had been up to during the short break seemed to have messed with his carefully arranged composure. They would need to do something about it, Sean thought. They had tried to prepare their host for what was to come by involving him in the pre-selection process, making him watch every minute of it until his face stopped turning quite so green with every blow delivered to the convicts. But it appeared now that it hadn't been enough.

'And we're back, ladies and gentlemen!' Tyler turned on his heels. 'Before we turn to the two contestants who came last on today's challenge, let's reward the two contestants who came first!'

A set of brightly coloured lights swept across the stage.

'Contestant seventy-seven and contestant eighty-nine completed the one thousand meter race in the shortest time and therefore receive a hundred points!' Tyler gave them his brightest smile.

Multiple rays of light converged to the spot in the metal cage where the two contestants were standing. A spark of movement in the giant cage caught Sean's eye as he saw convict number seventy-seven flinch. Terrence Blake was wearing a convincing poker-face. His expression was so blank it seemed as though he was not even fully there. He looked straight in front of him, past the judges, past the audience and the fully-packed arena. Sean looked at him more closely again, squinting in an attempt to block out the mess of lights and noise around him. The man's hands hung by his side, his fingers twitching slightly.

'Next to me are the two contestants who will be facing a Punishment Card', Tyler continued.

Contestant fifty-one seemed glued to his spot, a look of confusion spread across his face. He was the old man who had collapsed during the race and had taken the longest time to get past the finish line. Next to him was contestant twenty-five. Sean looked at the woman with curiosity. Her face was hard as stone, her lips pressed in a slim line. She seemed to be gathering all the strength she could to hold herself as straight as possible, her head raised high. Despite her effort to maintain her posture, all the colour in her cheeks had evaporated, leaving behind only a pale shade of egg-shell white. She leant heavily to one side, one of her legs looking oddly stiff. Sean shrugged, his arms crossed in front of his chest. Someone had to go at each stage after all, and just like in the larger game of life and evolution, the frail and broken ones would be the first to be eliminated.

Camilla shifted on her seat next to him. She threw him a side look, a knowing look, full of the secret understanding they had of each other's intentions. He nodded almost imperceptibly.

'It is up to you,' Tyler was moving on, 'our audience, to decide which punishment awaits our two contestants.'

Tyler turned back towards the giant screens, and the entire arena followed his gaze. On one screen was the headshot of contestant fifty-one, whilst contestant twenty-five's picture was displayed on another screen. A list of three options appeared underneath each contestant's picture. 'Wheels on the Bus', 'Take a Seat' and 'Spider Man' for contestant fifty-one, and 'Let's Dance', 'Mirror, Mirror on the Wall' and 'How's it Hangin'?' for contestant twenty-five.

A short baffled silence followed the appearance of the names, before the audience broke into a buzz of whispers. Sean smiled. They had designed the names to be purposely mysterious. The audience would soon realise that the lighter the name sounded, the darker the punishment would be in comparison. He could not wait to see everyone's reaction when they witnessed the contrast.

Tyler faced the crowd. Thousands of incredulous pairs of eyes stared back at him.

'The voting lines are now open!' He exclaimed. 'They will remain open for the next two minutes, so make sure you vote and have your say in our contestants' fate! We'll find out the results after the break!'

CHAPTER 16

TYLER BENSON

'Three, two, one. And we're off,' the producer called out in Tyler's earpiece. Tyler made sure that the red lights on the cameras were switched off before he dared to release the stiff smile he had forced himself to wear. He dismissed the make-up assistant distractedly with a wave of his hand, before setting off backstage, ignoring whoever was calling out to him to stay put. Whatever they planned to say to him, he knew for certain that he was not ready to hear it. He rushed into his changing room, past the jungle of crew members, guards, cables and props. He locked the door behind him and he sank into an armchair. The muscles of his neck slowly relaxed, reminding him of how tense he had been on stage. He closed his eyes. For a moment, however short it was, he did not have to pretend. He could let himself go, let his face bear whichever expression he wanted. He could allow himself to look as trapped and panicked as he felt.

His fingers started shaking uncontrollably at the thought of what awaited him after the ad break, but he did nothing to try and stop them. He knew that sooner rather than later he would have to maintain that constant pretence, and he wanted to make the most of the little time he had when he did not have to fool anyone. The audience might not know exactly what they were voting for, but he knew only too well the shock that awaited them. A loud knock on the door made him jump from his seat.

'Mr Benson,' a feminine voice called from outside the closed door, 'we're back live in a minute, and we need to do a make-up check.'

When he did not come out right away, the knocking intensified and a tumult of concerned voices grew behind the closed door. Tyler composed himself, unlocked the door and stepped out in the chaos. The looks on the production crew's faces told him they were concerned he was up to no good. He was ushered to the main backstage area, behind the large panels, where someone powdered his nose and cheeks, and lightly mopped the traces of sweat at the top of his forehead.

'Live in fifteen seconds!'

Tyler made his way reluctantly through the opening between the panels. He could tell the crew were suspicious of him, because two assistants remained flanked by his side, exchanging glances, until he had made it to the stage.

He plugged his earpiece back into place and stood facing the judges' table. Sean Cravanaugh stared straight at him, and Tyler was sure that his boss knew everything. He knew his distress. He knew why he now needed escorting to the stage. He *knew*. And, despite that, he was forcing him into submission, with that one single stare, reminding him of all he had to lose if he did not comply.

Three... Two... One...

The countdown resounded in Tyler's ears as if shouted out from heaven, even though he was certain the voice in his earpiece must have been nothing more than a murmur. He let his body, his years of stage experience take over, as if on auto-pilot. He tried to ignore the fact that his heartbeat was pounding against his skin like it was looking for the smallest gaps to escape.

'Ladies and gentlemen,' he heard himself exclaim, and he could only hope his face matched the cheerful tone he had managed to summon. 'The voting lines are now closed and we have received a whopping seven million votes! It's time to see what you have decided! Let us remind ourselves of the options you voted on...'

He swirled back towards the giant screens, and paused for a second, exaggerating a surprised look, raising his shoulders high against his ears, and popping his eyes wide open.

'Such mystery!' He joked.

Someone from the production crew walked up to him on the stage, carrying a golden tray. There was nothing on the tray but a large envelope with the word 'results' on it in dark red ink. Tyler picked up the envelope, dismissing its messenger with a nod. He held the envelope high above his head for a few seconds, showing it off the to the audience, soaking in their applause.

'Shall I open this?' He asked cheekily.

The crowds stomped their feet, clapping their hands, and he smiled at how easily their enthusiasm could be revived. It was like pouring gasoline on a dying fire. The moment his words reached them, they burst back to life, on the verge of explosion.

'Ok, ok,' he agreed, raising his hands apologetically. 'May I have a drum roll please?' He asked no one in particular, confident that someone would grant his wish.

He opened the envelope slowly, aware that millions of eyes were transfixed by every single movement he made. For those few moments he was on top of the world. Drum-rolls came out of the speakers above him.

Those might as well have been the beats of his heart. He could hardly tell the difference anymore.

He extracted a thick paper card from the envelope on which were written the results of the public vote. He looked up, and he knew the entire nation was hanging on to his every word. He wanted to make it last forever, to breathe in the power it gave him. Silence spread, like plumes of smoke covering them all.

'Contestant fifty-one...' He turned slowly towards the old man, 'the audience has voted. Your punishment today is...' His voice was low, his tone harder and colder than ice. 'Take a seat!'

The option popped in big bold letters on the screen below the man's picture, and the public's clamour rose like a storm.

'Contestant twenty-five... The audience has voted. Your punishment today is... Let's Dance!'

The woman frowned, because she would have no idea what it meant yet. *Yet*, Tyler thought with the smallest of shudders, and all he knew was that it would be something he would rather not witness.

'Now, whilst we get the stage prepared for this...' Tyler waved behind him, where tall black drapes had been erected, forming two large restricted square areas. 'Let's turn to our judges...' Tyler announced, 'and get their impressions so far. Camilla, shall we start with you?'

CHAPTER 17

SEAN CRAVANAUGH

S ean turned his attention to Camilla, studying her face closely as she answered Tyler's question with unrivalled control. He was proud of her mastery over her true emotions. He had known from the start this would not be an easy task for her. He had warned her enough times, and in no uncertain terms. She had assured him she could manage. Her goal, her ultimate objective, all of it took precedent over whichever weaknesses she may possess. It gave her the drive she needed to ignore everything else and stride ahead. Sean had had his doubts, but he was now learning to give her some credit. She was a woman with a purpose, and he understood that better than anyone.

The general attention shifted to the other two judges, and he listened distractedly to their answers. Valery Swan was a model of calm and sternness, and one could tell she had seen much worse over the years than what had been displayed before them so far. Sean actually knew for a fact she had also seen much worse than what was about to come. He liked that about her. The woman had a strength of character he could only ever compare with female cowboys in the the Far West. If she had lived in that era, she would have been carrying a gun and the hell of an attitude. He had crossed paths with Valery Swan several times back when she was in office, and they had got on instantly. She was an individual who would neither give nor take any nonsense, and they had soon found out they spoke the same language. When Sean had thought of the concept for the competition, she was the first person who had popped into his mind to help him fine tune the details. She had not hesitated for one second before accepting.

'What about you, Sean?'

Tyler's question forced him out of his train of thought.

'Well, Tyler, I'm really curious to see what stands behind those black curtains,' he nodded towards the stage, 'I'm sure I'm not the only one!' He exclaimed swirling his chair around to face the public.

The effect was instantaneous, and the whole arena agreed with him in a chaos of noise and clapping.

'Well, let's not make you wait any longer!' Tyler marked a small pause, and beaming, he threw to the sky his arm with a flourish. 'What time is it?'

'Time for justice!' The public screamed back, standing as one, their right hands stuck out above their heads in a fist, pounding the words.

'I can't hear you, what time is it?' Tyler repeated, his hand cupped in an exaggerated motion behind his ear.

'Time for justice! Time for justice!'

Sean settled back into his seat. He could feel the rhythm of the crowd dictating the pace of his heart. He sat there, savouring the warm satisfaction of money being made and people being as predictable as he always knew they were.

CHAPTER 18

TERRENCE BLAKE

Terrence froze on his spot in the giant cage. The handcuffs around his wrists were feeling too cold and too hot at the same time, sending both icy shivers and heat waves radiating from his fingertips to his shoulders. The crowd's chant was not dying down. If anything, it was gaining in intensity by the second, and he wondered whether he would ever get used to being the target of an entire country's anger and hatred. He doubted he ever could.

All of a sudden, the lights went out and the arena was plunged into darkness. With a loud crack, a single spotlight appeared, directed straight onto convict number fifty-one. The deep, booming disembodied voice of the commentator broke the silence, and Terrence felt like God himself was addressing the shivering man on the stage.

'Convict fifty-one, time has come for you to pay for your crimes…'

The man looked puzzled and frightened in equal amounts. The commentator kept speaking, the invisible judge of the man's fate.

'Eleven years ago, you killed your wife in cold blood,' the voice spat out the words like they were venom. 'You stabbed her repeatedly, until she bled to death in front of your eyes. For this unforgivable crime, the nation has picked your punishment… Take a seat!' The commentator exclaimed, as the black drapes around one of the restricted areas dropped down to the ground.

Another set of lights came on, bathing the stage in warm, yellowish rays. The audience immediately caught on the phrase and chanted it loudly.

'Take a seat! Take a seat!'

A large chair was positioned in the centre of a small pedestal. The chair itself was luxurious and resembled an old-fashioned throne, made of wood, painted gold. The seat was covered in a plush red velvet. It looked just a little too comfortable, and Terrence suspected that the nicer it looked, the more lethal it might turn out to be.

The guards grabbed the old convict by the elbows and led him towards the throne. He was made to sit down on the chair, and before he could react four leather straps were fastened around his ankles and wrists. A piece of fabric was roughly shoved into his mouth. He tried to spit it out but the gag remained stubbornly in its place. Terrence felt a ball of nerves the size of his fist build up in his chest.

'For his punishment, contestant fifty-one will remain on this chair for the next few minutes,' Tyler Benson's voice was grave as he spoke again, and Terrence was certain he could detect a slight tremor in his voice. 'The chair is linked to this electrical command box here,' he added, 'which will trigger three separate discharges, of increasing intensity. Each will last for a minute, and he will be allowed thirty seconds in between discharges to catch his breath. We will start with a thirty second countdown.'

The audience quietened down for a moment. The big angry lion had frozen, leaving the surrounding small prey animals to tiptoe their way into hiding, before the great beast sprung into motion again, hungry for a good chase.

The giant screens flashed to life, and the black background was replaced with a thirty second countdown, displayed in big, bold numbers. The numbers started to melt down from thirty at a sickening speed, and when it eventually reached the number ten, the audience started shouting the numbers in unison. Tyler Benson accompanied them, pounding the air with his closed fist with each passing second. The lion had made up its mind, it seemed, and had spotted its next meal. Terrence's eyes were glued to the convict strapped to the chair.

Ten... Nine... The old man was now wearing an expression of sheer panic, wriggling his wrists frantically. His eyes were shooting from the countdown on the screens, to the leather straps keeping him in place.

Five... Four... Terrence's stomach rose up and down with each passing second, and whilst he wanted to run to the man and free him from the chair, he found himself unable to move even the smallest part of his body.

Three... Two... One... With the final number, lights started flashing brightly from all directions, giving the arena the air of being in the eye of a thunder storm. One of the giant screens zoomed in on the seated man, whilst the other displayed a new countdown, underneath the first one, starting from one minute. For the first few seconds, the Cradle was quiet. The old man on the chair had stopped moving altogether, his body constricted in one broken line, his back arched upwards and his face distorted with pain. The veins underneath his skin were glowing, dark and blue, and looked as though they were about to burst against the thin pale envelop of his body. His teeth were gritted on the fabric gag. Terrence repressed the refluxes of vomit and bile gathering at the back of his throat, revulsion rising inside him, praying that the audience would sense this too, and put an end to the insanity of the situation.

For a moment, as silence lingered, he allowed his hope to grow, thinking that no one in their right mind could possibly endorse such a spectacle. Just as he allowed the thought to take root in his head, he heard a distant rumble. He looked up, able for the first time to detach his stare from the man suffering on stage. The rumble grew, like a shock-wave, making its way towards them.

Suddenly, as the sound grew louder and louder, he realised where it was coming from. It had originated from within the audience, a low murmur, which had slowly mutated into a deafening roar. After a few seconds of stunned silence, they had regained consciousness and their anger, parked to the side for a short instant, had built up speed again. It was a wave, an unstoppable tsunami of hatred and fury, fast-approaching the stage, threatening to destroy anything standing in its path. Terrence felt the rumbling drill its way into his heart, trembling against his chest and he swore he felt the moment of impact, that second where the wave engulfed the stage, and drowned them all in its muddy waters. The beast had awoken, and deciding upon not granting its prey any mercy, it had sprinted towards it at full speed, pouncing before allowing itself another moment of doubt.

The one-minute countdown ended, and the old convict's body dropped back into the chair, his limbs floppy, like a lifeless rubber doll. Another countdown started right away, for thirty seconds this time. The man's chest was moving feebly up and down, as though each breath required the greatest of efforts. His fingers were twitching intermittently, contracting and releasing in short bursts of motion. In the metal cage, many of the convicts were glancing around them, trying to catch each other's eye, breaking for the first time since the start of the competition one of the most important unsaid rules of prison life. There was disgust on their faces, but predominantly there was fear. Fear of the pain. Fear for their own lives. Fear that this was only the beginning, and that what they would have to go through would only be worse.

The new countdown was coming to an end, shouted out from the highest heights of the arena. Ten... Nine... Eight... This could not be happening, Terrence thought. This had to be a nightmare. It simply *had* to. If he forced his eyes shut for long enough, when he reopened them he was bound to wake up in his prison cell, about to face another random day of isolation from the world. He closed his eyes. He refused to believe that this was it, that the world he had fantasised so many times about rejoining, the world he had left behind so many years ago, had turned into this wild circus. He could not accept that this was the world his daughter had grown up in, so far from the hopes he had for her. Was she here, he wondered. Was she watching? Most importantly, was she also shouting, yelling out this sordid countdown? Was she a drop in the angry wave? His heart clenched and warm, salty tears rolled down his cheeks.

When the crowd's countdown ended, he could not help himself. He opened his eyes and instantly wished he had kept them shut. The strength of the discharge must have increased, because the old man was now convulsing on the chair, his body like a twig at the mercy of strong winds. He was tensing up and down, his back arching and releasing in quick pulsations. His fists were clenched, his wrists pushing against the leather straps. His head had dropped back, his face to the skies, his eyes popped open. This time the audience did not fall silent. They were screaming and shouting, pounding their feet against the metal grounds of the arena. The great beast had tasted blood, and it was going in for the kill for a second time.

The second one-minute countdown ended, and another one started from thirty seconds. The old man's body slumped back down into the chair, the angle of his head suggesting he had slipped into unconsciousness. Terrence noticed for the first time the guard standing behind the chair, controls in hands, as he stepped forward to poke the old convict's face. When he did not show any sign of acknowledgement, the guard slapped him, over and over again, until eventually the old man opened his eyes. He looked exhausted. He glanced around him slowly and tried to sit back up into the chair. He looked confused for a few seconds, and Terrence watched as recognition spread over the man's face, dread and panic quickly replacing the questioning expression. The countdown came to an end, and the final discharge kicked in. Terrence was now painfully aware of the guard standing behind the golden throne, and he wondered what it took to be the man pushing the button, knowing what would come of it. The guard's expression was blank, unreadable – almost bored, as if he had just pushed the button to call for the lift.

Terrence could tell the electrical charge was now reaching lethal limits. Seconds passed like minutes, with painful slowness. Time was on the executioner's side, mocking the victims, moving at its own sweet pace, defying the rules of logic. Each instant lingered, stretching to the point of breaking, before it reluctantly moved onto the next. The sixty seconds of torture felt like an hour. By the time it ended, the old convict had drifted back into unconsciousness, his head drooping lifelessly against one shoulder, his chest barely moving, rising up and down so imperceptibly one could have easily mistaken him for dead. Two guards unstrapped him from the chair, and lifted him up to his feet, revealing large dark strains on the red velvet fabric and on the convict's overalls. Perspiration, urine and excrement, Terrence thought, unable to control a gag.

'Well, well, well,' Tyler Benson's voice interrupted the Terrence's reverie. 'Let's see what our judges thought of our first punishment.'

Tyler Benson walked towards the judges' table, and addressed Josh Carter, who had turned very pale.

'Mr. Carter, what did you make of that?'

Josh Carter looked up, as if he was noticing Tyler Benson's presence for the first time. Sean Cravanaugh chimed in from the opposite side of the table.

'It looks like Josh Carter might be more faint-hearted than the rest of us!'

The crowd burst into laughter and Tyler Benson let out a chuckle.

'Mr. Carter, are you quite alright?' He asked with mock concern.

Josh Carter nodded vaguely, and grabbed the glass of water in front of him. He took a few sips of water, swallowing each one slowly.

'Tyler,' Josh Carter said eventually, 'if you want my honest opinion…'

'Of course we do, Carter!' Sean Cravanaugh interjected loudly, 'so come on, get it out, before we all start growing roots!'

Josh Carter seemed unsettled by the interruption, and even more so by the derision and laughter coming from the audience. He frowned slightly. Whatever he had been about to say, he now looked hesitant to share it.

'Actually…' he swallowed with apparent difficulty, turning back to face Tyler Benson, 'I thought this was a little too much…'

'A little too much!' exclaimed Sean Cravanaugh, jumping in again. 'I don't see anyone else looking nearly as dishevelled as you do, Carter. It does seem that you are much better at *commenting* on the country's issues, from the comfort of your office, than you are at overseeing how those issues are tackled… What do you have to say for yourself?'

Josh Carter's mouth dropped open.

'I am… I mean, I'm not! I just…'

He stopped talking abruptly when he saw Sean Cravanaugh silently mimicking him.

'Grow a pair, Carter, this is only the first round!' Sean Cravanaugh laughed.

'Stop it,' Josh Carter mumbled, stumbling on his own words. 'That's not what...'

'Yeah, yeah,' Sean Cravanaugh concluded. 'Whatever you say, Carter. Just let us know if you need us to call someone to hold your hand, ok?'

The crowd was hysterical. The one man who appeared to have taken the incidents of the day for what they really were was now being ridiculed for voicing the truth. Valery Swan was as much a picture of control and composure as Josh Carter had been one of misery. She commented on how impressed she was with the way the competition had been so thoroughly organised, and that she was pleased to see the public's support. When asked whether she agreed with Josh Carter, she simply snorted, leaving no doubt as to what she thought of her fellow judge's opinion.

'Tyler,' she said in a decisive tone, 'what we've seen today has been nothing more than what this man deserved for committing murder. Why should we be offended? His actions should come with consequences proportionate to the pain and agony he has inflicted on others.'

She paused, because the audience's reaction was so loud it drowned out her words. Sean Cravanaugh himself stood up and applauded her. Soon the entire arena was on their feet.

Terrence glanced over at the old convict, parked in between two guards on one side of the stage. There was to be no redemption for him. There was to be no future, only hatred, resentment and pain. The man must have known right then that he was going to die. Everyone knew in a way, of course. For those of them who were to die within the hard grey walls of their cells, it was simply a matter of when. Still, in their darkest moments, in the loneliest of hours, Terrence knew each and everyone of them still clung to the tiniest hope that they may outlive their ordeal. This was what got them through day after day, through the monotonous routine of prison life. An immense wave of sadness washed over him. It was not simply compassion for the man's distress, it was the realisation that he, too, was starting to know, to really *know*, his own end was near.

Terrence thought of Maddison, and he wanted to believe that she would be shaking her head at all this, that she would not approve. He could not know, of course, since he had neither seen nor spoken to his daughter since he had been arrested. She would be twenty years old now, and he wondered for the millionth time where she was and what kind of a woman she was turning into. His throat clenched as it hit him that if he had ever had even the slimmest chance of seeing her again before, now he was in this competition, he was sure to die without holding her in his arms one last time. He closed his eyes, willing the thoughts out of his head, and he silently prayed that he would be proven wrong.

When he opened his eyes again, he could have sworn he saw Sean Cravanaugh's intense stare fixed on him, but he was standing so far away, and his mind had been playing such tricks on him that he quickly convinced himself he had imagined it.

CHAPTER 19

SEAN CRAVANAUGH

Sean averted his gaze when he saw that Terrence Blake had seen him watching him. He had found himself looking at the man a lot. He felt oddly intrigued by him and he could not help wanting to know more.

Sean was not usually interested in people. He actually did not care much for other human beings. He tended to like people most when there were none around. The one part of social interaction he did care about was the way in which people could be useful to him. When it came to Terrence Blake, there was a sense of suspense surrounding the man that he could not quite explain. It was all a gut feeling and, if there was one thing Sean had full confidence in, it was his very own instincts.

Tyler was now announcing the start of the second punishment card. Contestant twenty-five was pushed forward to the centre of the stage, limping visibly, and the commentator's deep low voice took over. It looked exactly as though God himself was condoning her, leaving them all with the impression that the competition was not only supported by the law, but it was also approved by a much higher court of justice. Sean smiled to himself.

The silky fabric surrounding the second contraption dropped down, revealing a large transparent cube, placed on a black pedestal. Its walls were three meters tall, held together by metallic borders. The cube did not have a door, and a ladder leant against one side. The contestant was told to climb the ladder and to get into the cube. She hesitated for a second, then climbed slowly, carefully, one step at a time. When she got to the top she swung her legs across to the other side, and gripped the top of the wall, until she was hanging there, unable to let go. The guards ordered her to jump down, but as she looked towards the ground, she hesitated again. One of the guards raced up the ladder, and unhooked her hands, one at a time, sending her crashing down the bottom of the cube with a loud bang. When she tried to stand up, she winced in pain. Limping on one leg and hurt on the other... Sean rolled his eyes. This was going to make what was about to come even more interesting, although 'interesting' was probably not the word she would have used to describe her predicament.

'This cube is no ordinary cube,' Tyler explained. 'Its walls and floor are made of heat-conducting material. For this challenge, heat will be induced in three rounds of one minute each, with thirty seconds of respite between each round. The first round will start in thirty seconds,' he added, raising his arms towards the giant screens which were now displaying a thirty second countdown. 'Are you ready?' He announced towards the audience, 'Let's Dance!'

The first thirty-second countdown ended, instantly merging into another one, this time for one minute. The walls of the cube glowed a light shade of red, glinting menacingly, and the trapped contestant jumped with surprise as the ground got warmer and warmer underneath her feet. She forced herself to put as much of her weight into her stiff leg, as she attempted to relieve her twisted ankle, although it was obvious this was not coming naturally to her. She started shifting her weight from side to side, only able to leave it for a second onto her injured leg, before leaning back onto the other leg again. Sean glanced at the countdown. She still had half a minute to go. She was now hopping on her stiff leg, breathing heavily, her face a deep crimson. The exercise looked to have exhausted whatever little energy she had left in her, and without thinking, she leaned against one wall of the cube. She jumped back in pain as the heat burnt through the slim fabric of her overalls. By the time the one-minute countdown ended, light smoke had just started fuming from underneath her feet. The cube walls instantly lost their red tint, and the woman collapsed onto the ground, massaging her now swollen ankle.

A new thirty-second countdown started on the screens, and the audience screamed their impatience for it to end. Their chant 'Time for Justice!' erupted in one corner of the arena, and was quickly trickling down to every other part of the Cradle, contagious and gripping like an epidemic. When the countdown finally ended, a new one-minute round started and, as the cube walls turned red again, it became obvious to all that the heat level had considerably increased. The contestant could now barely stand for even a second on either leg. Heavy drops of sweat started rolling down her face, creating strings of hot steam as they crashed onto the bottom of the cube.

Halfway through the second round, the rubber soles of her trainers melted into a pool of gooey plastic, glueing her to the floor. With hasty, uncoordinated movements, she bent down, started undoing her laces and stood on top of her shoes. The public chanted the last ten seconds, and as they reached zero, the cube was powered off again. The heat was gone within a split second and the contestant once again collapsed onto the floor, puffing, rolling herself into a ball.

The thirty-second break came to an end, marking the beginning of the final round. The minute started. The contestant, still lying on the floor, let out a piercing shriek of pain. She stood, leaning on her stiff leg, her other ankle now not only swollen, but an abnormal shade of purple. She was back to standing on her melting trainers, but very soon even that was not enough. Slowly, painfully, she undressed. The sweat-drenched overalls dropped to the ground with a puff of steam. She gathered it in a ball on top of her trainers and stepped on it, wearing nothing but a dirty grey tee-shirt and soiled underwear. All over her body, her skin was bright red and a nasty smell of roasted flesh carried through the air. In the last fifteen seconds, the cube was so hot now that her skin was starting to bubble in places. She gritted her teeth but did not allow herself to make any noise. Maybe she had reached such high levels of agony that her body had just become numb, Sean guessed. He had once experienced the feeling first hand himself.

The moment the countdown ended, contestant twenty-five crumbled unconscious onto the ground. Several production assistants immediately ran up to the stage and dismantled the cube. Two guards trotted towards the contestant and lifted her effortlessly off the ground, dragging her backstage.

~ ~ ~

'Ladies and gentlemen! What. A. Night!' Tyler had taken to his microphone again.

Sean watched distractedly as Tyler closed off the evening, his final remarks prompting the entire arena into motion. The giant cage was rolled off backstage, and the audience got to their feet, making their way out of the Cradle. Noticing Tyler speedily marching off the stage, Sean grabbed one of the production assistants and whispered:

'Get Benson in my office. Now. Don't let him get away'.

He had known that he would have to keep Tyler in check throughout the competition, but he had not expected the first intervention to be needed so early on. As he stood up, he made a mental note to check with the security team he had assigned to monitor Josh Carter's every move whether he was also showing signs of causing him trouble. Camilla, who was still sitting in the chair next to him, glanced over at him, a questioning look on her face. He shook his head and rolled his eyes. Don't ask, he silently told her. She seemed to hear him and shrugged.

When Sean pushed the door to his office open, he saw that Tyler was already there, standing by one of the large windows, overlooking the arena. Tyler barely acknowledged his presence, and kept his back to him. Sean marched slowly to a small cabinet in the corner of the room and extracted a bottle of vintage scotch and two crystal tumblers from its shelves. He poured himself a generous drink and took a sip of the amber liquid.

'I believe you have something to tell me, Tyler,' Sean said simply, his tone even, walking towards the window.

He stood next to Tyler, swirling his scotch into the tumbler, enjoying the clicking melody of the ice cubes against the borders of the crystal glass. Tyler turned to face him. He looked exhausted, Sean thought, as he took in the dark purple circles around the man's eyes, peering through the heavy layer of make-up. For a few seconds Tyler looked as though he was going to say something, but he seemed to think better of it and turned back to face the window.

'Come on, Tyler,' Sean encouraged him, 'just spit it out.'

Tyler shook his head vigorously, his lips squeezed into a tight line, his gaze fixed on the window.

'Tyler,' Sean insisted, his voice more firm now. 'Say it.'

This time it wasn't a suggestion. Tyler shook his head from side to side, his eyes shut.

'Say it!' Sean shouted.

Tyler began shivering uncontrollably. He was so close Sean could see sweat forming at his temples, and small teardrops gathering at the corner of his eyes. Sean could tell he was not far from giving in.

'Come on, Tyler, say it!' He kept pushing. 'Say it, you little shit!'

Tyler exploded.

'I can't do it, ok! I can't do it! This is wrong!' He was gesturing frantically around him, and pointing towards the window behind them. 'All of this is wrong!'

If he had tried his best to remain silent so far, he now seemed unable to contain the flow of words pouring out of him.

'Don't you see!' He exclaimed, his eyes wide. 'We're *hurting* people! We're *torturing* them! And what's more, we're encouraging people to think it's right! It's not right. It's wrong! It's so wrong! I can't do it!'

He collapsed into one of the leather armchairs, his head buried in his hands, sobbing heavily, mumbling incessantly.

'I can't do it… I can't do it… It's wrong… I can't do it…'

Sean smiled, satisfied. Find a man's button, know how to press it, and you will have him at your mercy, he thought, triumphantly.

He downed the contents of his glass, walked over to the drinks cabinet and poured himself another scotch. This time he also filled the second crystal tumbler. He peered into the cabinet until he found what he was looking for. He picked up a small white plastic bottle. He popped it open and, holding his palm stretched out, he shook the little bottle until two small, round red pills fell into his open hand. He walked over to Tyler and handed him the second tumbler of scotch, followed by the two red pills. Tyler looked up quizzically, then, without another word, he took the glass and swallowed both pills with a generous gulp of scotch.

'Well, that wasn't so hard, now, was it?' Sean commented, sitting down in one of the Chesterfield sofas, his eyes never leaving Tyler's tired and desperate face. 'Tyler, can you tell me what the most important thing is?'

Tyler stared blankly back at him.

'Of all the things in the world,' Sean said again, as though addressing a particularly stupid child, 'what would you say is the most important?'

Tyler answered almost immediately, with wavering determination:

'Love.'

Sean burst out laughing. He had asked the same question to many people, and always got the same nonsensical responses about love, happiness, sex or money. Every time he found people's disillusion simply hilarious.

'You're wrong.'

Tyler's eyebrows shot up and he looked at if he was going to contest. Sean did not give him a chance to speak again.

'You're wrong,' he repeated firmly. 'The most important thing is *power.*' He paused there, enjoying Tyler's confused expression. 'Look at you, for example. You've lived your life as an honest man. You love your family. You love your wife. You love yourself, too, and all that you've ever done has been out of all this *love* you have in you.'

Sean was fully aware of the derision in his voice as he pronounced the word 'love', and he saw Tyler wincing each time he belittled the word.

'I, on the other hand, have *power*. For instance, I have the *power* to either make your career, or to end you forever, ruining you to such an extent you'll wish you'd never been born.'

All the colour slowly drained from Tyler's face.

'You see, you have all this *love*...' Sean continued, 'but right here, right now, where does that get you? Nowhere. At this very moment, your love is what is making you weak and vulnerable. You see, if you don't keep up your part of the bargain, then *I* have the *power* to end you. Not just you. Your entire family too…'

He took a sip of scotch, letting the words sink in, allowing them to fill up the entire room. Tyler looked fixedly at him, and so distraught and exhausted he seemed to have aged twenty years in the last twenty seconds.

'As you can see, *love* is nothing. It won't save you. If anything, most of the time it will be that one piece of rock tied to your neck making you drown when all you're trying to do is keep your head above the surface. *Power*, on the other hand, will be your saving grace.'

Tyler blinked, once, twice, and wiped the sweat which was now dripping down his face with the back of his sleeve.

'I don't… I don't know… How… I just…' He murmured.

Tyler was quiet for a little while. Sean smiled, his gaze strong and determined.

'How are you feeling now?' He asked.

Tyler was about to answer, when all of a sudden he stopped himself, a look a surprise on his face, and thought the question through, obviously reconsidering his response.

'I feel… Fine,' he said eventually, uncertainty permeating his words, like he could not believe himself, 'I feel *fine*,' he murmured again, a little more confidently this time.

Sean kept looking at him, and extracted the small white plastic bottle from his pocket. He opened it and dropped a few of the little red pills into Tyler's palm.

'Take two capsules, twice a day. Two thirty minutes before coming on stage, and another two before going home. These will help calm your nerves whilst the competition is on,' Sean explained.

Tyler stared at Sean, and then at the little red pills lying in his open hand. He hesitated, then he poured the pills back in the bottle, pressed the top firmly into place, and pocketed it without saying another word.

Sean watched Tyler stand up and leave, closing the door softly behind him. The man's shoulders looked slightly less hunched than before.

Sean thought that he had had to do a lot of things in his life that most honest citizens would not approve of. He had had to tell a lot of lies. He had had to cross the line many a time. He remembered the words of caution of the doctor who had prescribed the drug, when he had asked him if the pills could *hypothetically* help some under extreme stress and duress over a period of several weeks. The doctor, who had been developing the medicine as part of an ambitious ongoing medical trial, had insisted that it may not be ready for human consumption yet. All the tests to date had been performed on mice, with mixed results. Sean had refused to back down, because his research showed anything else currently available on the market was either too weak or too ineffective to achieve the results he wanted. The doctor had eventually conceded that although he supposed the stress relieving effects of the drug may remain over such a prolonged use, he could not vouch for the chances of recovery from some of the dramatic side effects.

'*Hypothetically*,' the doctor had warned, emphasising the words, staring intently at Sean over his glasses, 'if the patient were to survive the experience, it is likely that the rest of his days would be spent battling a severe addiction to the components of the drug.'

It had taken a generous amount of cash and an iron-clad non-disclosure agreement to secure a large stock of the medicine and to send the doctor into early retirement in a faraway land.

Sean had anticipated that Tyler would offer some form of resistance. After all, very few people would be able to stand so close to brutality and violence without flinching, and Sean had expected that none of those who could would gain the public's affection. If the show host was able to stand on stage and play his part until the final day of the competition, that was all Sean needed. Whatever happened afterwards was none of Sean's business, and he would be long gone before anyone realised what irreversible changes he had put into motion.

Sean downed the remainder of his glass in one go, thinking that, of all the lies and deceptions he had orchestrated throughout his life, this one had to be the most despicable, even by his own diabolical standards.

CHAPTER 20

SHAUNA MULLIGHAN

L iveTV2's news room was bathed in the bright glow of the powerful studio lights used to illuminate the presenter's desk. Shauna quickly made her way to her seat. She patted the top of her head and her temples to make sure no rebellious strands had escaped her neatly arranged hairdo. She checked her notes for what felt like the millionth time.

Shauna could not think of a time when anything had gripped the nation so quickly and with such force. The show had become everyone's favourite distraction from the bleakness of everyday life. She herself had tiptoed on the edge of scepticism when she first heard of the concept, but she had to admit that the way the whole thing had been presented was clever. It turned angry masses against a select guilty few.

The first episode had been tough to watch. She had been sitting in her local pub at the time, her hands clenched around a large glass of red wine, her jaw tense with apprehension. She had known she might not have the strength to watch it alone in her living-room. She had sat there, gulping down her wine, watching the small smelly pub fill with more and more people by the minute, until all the tables were occupied.

The pub staff had set up big screens, switched on to the correct channel long before the show was scheduled to start, as if to reassure people that they would be the first to know when it began.

Silent tension had settled in the air as the clock hands edged ever closer to the top of the hour. The sense of purpose had united them, strangers as they were, before it had even started.

Much later, when Shauna reflected on this time of her life, she realised that this very moment should have been her first clue. The earliest sign of the ominous journey they all were about to embark upon together and of the experience they would all share. But at the time, sitting alongside strangers at a wonky sticky table in her local pub, Shauna could only think how odd it was to feel so connected to so many people she had never spoken to.

The first video introductions set the tone, and spread an icy chill over the crammed pub. It was one thing to know that horrors took place around you, and it was quite another to hear of the deeds whilst watching their perpetrator's face, to see the pictures of the victims and crime scenes. It was enough to make your entire body constrict with revulsion.

It had taken one person yelling at the screen to start it off. Anger and disgust had washed over the little room like a wave, submerging them all. Discomfort had been replaced with outrage. They had all felt it. They had felt allied in it. On a couple of occasions, Shauna had even partaken in it too, finding release in the act of screaming at the screen. It had opened a window in her heart and allowed for all of her frustrations to be vented.

After a little while, Shauna had noticed her brain seemed to acclimatise. The warmth of the people around became a cocoon. She felt more connected than she had in longer than she could remember. She felt like she was part of something real, something much greater than herself, something which, for just an evening, gave her life a little more meaning.

And it had felt good. So good that when the time to watch the second episode came around, she had needed more.

'Live in one minute,' someone said in Shauna's earpiece, making her jump.

She arranged her notes again and gulped down the remainder of her coffee. The taste of the lukewarm liquid barely registered.

'Good Evening, this is Shauna Mullighan and you're watching the evening news on LiveTV2. Three days ago, we announced the much anticipated grand launch of 'No Pain, No Game' and today we gauge the public's reaction to the first two episodes. Our correspondent James Carson, who has witnessed the competition from inside the Cradle, reports live.'

The split screen revealed James Carson's upper body as he stood in front of the arena, clutching a microphone. The camera swivelled around to reveal the Cradle behind him, illuminated in bright colours and surrounded by a sea of people. Random onlookers glanced at the news team, some of them pulling faces as they got into view.

'James,' Shauna remained unfazed, 'everyone here in the studio has been watching the show, and many of us are shocked by what we've seen. Have the organisers commented on the reasons why none of the broadcast was censored?'

'Excellent question, Shauna, and yes, Sean Cravanaugh has been asked this question after the first two episodes. What he said was that the show is meant to give the public a chance to be a part of the justice-rendering process. For that reason, he feels it's important for everyone to be able to witness the punishments given to the contestants.'

'But, surely, they must have had complaints from people who were watching the show with children, or individuals with sensitive dispositions?' Shauna insisted.

'Based on the official reports, there have been a surprisingly low number of complaints. In LiveTV2's very own survey, we found out that over seventy-five percent of people didn't have a problem with the events being broadcast live on television for all to see. I'll be honest with you Shauna, I was sitting quite close to the stage, and at times I had to avert my gaze. But as the evening progressed, the atmosphere here in the Cradle and the absolute euphoria of the audience... I mean...'

James Carson paused, apparently lost for the right words. Shauna felt she knew what he meant.

'It was almost contagious. Whatever reservations anyone might have, they wouldn't keep them for long in that type of environment. Peer influence is definitely playing a part here on making all of this legitimate in the public's eyes.'

'Thanks, James, that's very interesting indeed. There was a lot of speculation before the show started about how the public would react, and I must admit I was amongst those who predicted it would flop.'

'A lot of us did,' James Carson agreed. 'But let us also remember who we're dealing with here. These people are *criminals* after all... And if you look around me here,' James Carson gestured excitedly around him at the crowd, 'you'll see people have already started camping out, hoping for a chance to get into the Cradle for the next show. I don't have the exact numbers with me here, but the crowd seems to have doubled from what it was ahead of the first show a few days ago. I don't think anyone could have expected such a resounding success from the very start.'

'Thank you, James, and we look forward to more details after the next episode, which is taking place this coming Saturday!' Shauna concluded, as the image of James Carson disappeared from the screen and was replaced with the weather forecast. 'And now, let's have a look at the temperatures for the week...' she continued brightly.

CHAPTER 21

TERRENCE BLAKE

I n the cemented guts of the Cradle, minutes turned into hours, hours into days and days into weeks. First came the rough nights and even rougher mornings, then the cold showers and the inedible lump of gooey porridge. And finally came the waiting in between each weekly task.

After the first round of the competition, a deep silence had settled between the convicts. The punishments inflicted at every stage of the competition haunted Terrence. They seemed to get worse with each passing stage of the competition. The terrified and agonised faces of the tortured men and women were forever engraved on the walls of his mind.

Week after week, challenges were put before them, and each time, a few of them were fed on a silver platter to the angry crowds. The audience appeared to be feasting on the contestants' pain, and on their desperation to survive. The more they fought back, the more the public's rage grew. Everyone around them already seemed to have forgotten they were still human beings, or maybe they simply no longer cared.

As far as he was concerned, Terrence had done reasonably well, given the circumstances, dragging himself through three more tasks since the racing round. They had faced a task on electrical repairs, a fitness task and even a cooking task. Of course, nothing ever was as straightforward as it sounded. Despite himself, Terrence had been in awe at how complex the methods of physical and psychological torture devised for the show were.

For the electrical repair task, they had needed to to fix a battery powered toy car. At random times, however, some of the pieces would emit an electrical charge, sending shock after shock through the convicts' fingers.

The fitness task had involved a neatly arranged circuit. Each of the ten stations they had to go through was placed in a large glass box filled with a collection of insects and reptiles fit for the vivarium of a national zoological park.

The cooking challenge had been the most deceptive. They had been taken to a large kitchen counter setup in the middle of the stage where they needed to assemble a simple plate of pasta bolognese. They had each stood in turn inside a large rectangular wooden box, their feet chained to the ground. As they cooked, the box slowly filled with oil. A plastic gauge, attached to one side, rose steadily with every drop of liquid. The moment the gauge reached a certain level, a long piece of string would unfold from the box, all the way to another contraption to the side which, once in contact with the string, burst into flames. The fire would then edge its way back along the string towards the oil. Convicts had to give the plate of food to the judges to taste, and only once they were done discussing the food amongst themselves would one of them press a button which released the shackles on the convict's ankles. At times, the judges took so long to finish their conversation that the convicts had to watch as the flames slithered towards them and spread like wildfire across the surface of the oil before they could escape.

Sometimes the results were defined by the time taken to complete the tasks, and other times the judges and the audience were left to decide who they felt had not performed as well as their peers. It was sheer madness.

Worst of all, in Terrence's opinion, was the unconditional support the audience gave to the show. The first week had seen just two convicts facing elimination and having to take on a Punishment Card, but the wretched Wheel of Destiny rarely fell on single digits. The second week six convicts were eliminated, then twenty-two on week three, and thirty-five on week four. As each punishment was revealed, so was the production team's latest twist. Soon enough, Punishment Cards began involving a member of the audience, who would take part in enforcing the punishment, for a chance to win a generous amount of tax-free cash.

Although he still felt unable to connect with the experiences he was being put through, Terrence had grown better at isolating his emotions from it all. How could he fight any of it, he thought, when the entire world was determined to see him suffer?

Terrence suppressed a shiver at the thought. Before the incident, long before he had gone to jail, he had been a firm believer in mankind, and in the power of men to make their own piece of heaven on earth. He had tried to impart his convictions to his daughter, but feared he had been extirpated from her life too soon for her to remember any of it. Once again, as he often did when his mind wandered off unchecked, he wondered whether Maddison was cheering at the screen or refusing to accept the monstrosity of the competition. As he hoped for the latter, he felt an immense sadness overcome him. He knew now he would never see her again, because that within the next few weeks he would be dead. If he was lucky enough, his end would be as quick and painless as possible, which was all he could hope for at this stage. He curled up in a ball on the cement floor of the makeshift cell and closed his eyes, wishing with all his might he would not wake up to face another day.

~ ~ ~

'Come on, you fucking slugs! Time to go!'

Terrence turned around with a start. The Head Warden's voice resonated around them, punctuated by loud bangs on the metal doors of the cell.

The convicts arranged themselves in a thin line. The size of their original group had been cut down by more than half, and whoever remained was now a shadow of the human being they had once been. The one man who astounded them all was Mad Spencer, who seemed to thrive on the process, as though he enjoyed every single moment of it. He revelled in the challenges and, astonishingly, in the disturbing spectacle of punishments.

The cell doors opened and all convicts were lead out in the long corridor, up the stairs to the metal cage. They took their places, leaving over half of the spots empty and trying not to remember too vividly what had happened to those who no longer stood beside them.

CHAPTER 22

TYLER BENSON

'Live in two minutes,' Tyler heard the producer say in his earpiece. He adjusted the collar of his shirt and absent-mindedly tapped his inside pocket for the reassuring little bottle of pills. He breathed a sigh of relief when his fingers felt the familiar contours of the plastic container.

The first weeks of the process, before the televised show had even started, had been hard but Tyler had managed to remain standing. After the first punishment rounds, however, he had felt like he was going to break.

As difficult as it had been at the time, however, he could now barely remember the distress he had felt. With each passing stage of the competition, his panic attacks started to fade into oblivion, as Tyler surrendered to the fabricated comfort of the little red pills. He had vaguely wondered what the medicine was, but he had quickly abandoned the line of questioning, telling himself that it was all for the best. Had he made a more persistent effort to be honest with himself, he would have been able to admit that he was simply afraid of the answer, which he knew with certainty would break the spell. The pills were his lifeline, helping him to get his conscience back on track. He felt in control. He felt strong and present. He was so aware of everything and everyone around him that he felt he might be able to fly if he tried. They were his own secret, one which gave him the courage to keep going. They created such a convincing illusion around him that at times he forgot none of the comfort they provided was real. The alternative was a much more frightening one, and he did all he could to hold on to the pills' cosy cocoon.

'Live in one minute,' the disembodied voice called out in his earpiece.

Tyler stood straight at the centre of the stage, readying himself to recite his opening lines. 'Good evening, ladies and gentlemen', he repeated silently, finding comfort in knowing that whatever he would have to do and say had been carefully scripted. All he had to do was to show up and have faith in the pills. Soon, he thought, he could put all of this behind him, once and for all.

As the producer's voice in his earpiece started counting down from ten, Tyler's blank expression turned into a broad smile. Anyone who saw him right at that moment might have thought he was the kind of person who was forever carefree and cheerful. For some fleeting moments he almost believed that was who he was, too.

'Good evening, ladies and gentlemen!' Tyler heard his own voice from afar, and he could only assume his body had taken over, leading him through the motions. 'How are you all tonight?' As he exclaimed the last sentence, he took a step forward, raising both his arms towards the crowd, prompting a loud and excited clamour from the audience. 'Welcome to week five of the competition. And, my, what a competition it has been so far!'

He could hear the roar of the audience extending beyond the high walls of the arena, across every grey narrow street of the capital, and to the furthest, most remote corners of the country. The nation was cheering him on.

'Please welcome onstage your 'No Pain, No Game' judges!'

Tyler sensed the large metallic panels behind him slide open, letting out puffs of grey smoke. He turned around just in time to see the four judges walk slowly onto the stage, bright smiles pasted on their faces, waving at the crowd.

'And the people without whom this competition would be nothing... Your 'No Pain, No Game' contestants!'

The crowd burst into applause as one of the side panels slid open, and the contestants' cage was rolled onstage. Tyler had been amazed at the interest the contestants had sparked throughout the country. It had started with tabloids and gossip websites until the demand had been such that even respectable publications and television channels had followed suit. Sociologists studied the public's response to the competition, analysts investigated the impact on the country's economy and profilers gave their twopence worth of opinion on each contestant. It was an exciting time to be alive, and the nation took it all in its stride, pulling itself back onto its feet with a fresh wave of enthusiasm. Tyler, on the other hand, had stopped ingesting any form of news a long time ago. He was already getting enough of 'No Pain, No Game' as it was.

'It is now time to reveal tonight's challenge, and let me tell you this is one that greatly excites me!' Tyler exclaimed. 'The challenge our contestants will have to face today... is.... The singing round!'

The response from the public was as instant as it was deafening. They welcomed the announcement like they had just been told they were all about to become millionaires.

'Each contestant will be coming on stage, one by one, in a random order, and they will be singing a song of their choice. You will rate each contestant at the end of their performance, and we will spin the Wheel of Destiny to see how many contestants will face a punishment card.

Whilst our contestants go and get ready, let's turn to our judges and see what they think of today's task…'

CHAPTER 23

SEAN CRAVANAUGH

To say that Sean felt pleased with himself was quite an understatement. The success of the show had turned into the biggest achievement of his entire career. Whatever he had had to do to get here was worth it. No matter the consequences.

Sean sat back in his chair, and watched as two guards escorted the first contestant to face the singing challenge to the centre of the stage. The woman, whose overalls bore the number thirteen, looked distraught, the way anyone would if they were pulled onstage, in front of a large audience, on live national television, and expected to sing without having rehearsed for it. Sean knew their struggle would make for better entertainment.

'To make this interesting, and to provide just enough encouragement for our contestants to participate fully in this challenge, we have added another element to this task,' Tyler added with a knowing smile.

He walked to a small round platform which had been arranged next to them. A microphone on a stand stood on it, ready for the challenge to kick off. Sean could feel the entire arena holding onto his every word, their mouths watering with the expectation of a great twist.

'This may look like a very inconspicuous platform. However…' Tyler paused. 'This platform is designed to conduct heat. Our contestants will need to perform a song of their choosing for a full two minutes. If the contestant sings, then the platform will remain switched off. If they *don't* sing, or if they stop before the end of the allocated time, the platform will heat up, reminding them of the task at hand!'

Sean smiled. Surveys on audience preferences so far had shown that the public had particularly enjoyed one of the very first punishments they had setup on the show. The audience's response to Tyler's announcement confirmed Sean's conviction that they had done the right thing in giving them more of what they wanted.

The contestant gasped, and horror rippled through the ranks of convicts within the giant metal cage. Sean's eyes fell on convict seventy-seven. Terrence Blake's expression was resigned and hard. Sean wondered what song he would sing. What type of music would he have liked, back when he was a free man? Would he be a good singer? Would he even know the lyrics to any one song? A shiver trickled down Sean's spine, making him wriggle on his chair with anticipation.

Meanwhile contestant number nineteen had been pushed onto the small platform, her nose pressed towards the microphone. The arena plunged into semi-darkness, a lone ray of bright yellow light directed straight at the shivering woman. The public fell silent. For the first time in a long time, there was no sound in the Cradle. The platform started glowing from the lightest shade of orange, increasing in intensity with each passing moment, until it turned bright red. The contestant did not seem to notice it at first, tangled as she was in her state of fright, but very soon, the heat under her feet seemed to drag her back into reality. She backed away, but two powerful pairs of arms popped out of the darkness and maintained her firmly in her place. Sean watched carefully, as suddenly, something seemed to click in her mind. Whatever was holding her back so far had just been overwritten by her instinct for survival and a few shaky notes came out of her mouth. Immediately, the red tint of the platform started fading away.

Sean did not recognise the song, but it did not matter. The public was clapping, the live band was improvising a background track, and the contestant kept singing. It was a success, he thought, yet another one. When she uttered her final note, the audience jumped to their feet, exhilarated by this new turn of events, this new challenge they were embracing.

Whilst the woman was escorted back to the metal cage, and the guards signalled to the next contestant to take her place behind the microphone on the small platform, Tyler asked the judges what they thought of the performance. For the first time in weeks, Josh Carter actually seemed genuinely relieved. How marvellously the brain works, thought Sean, and how beautifully one sees only what they want to see. Valery Swan made a brief comment on how she probably was the only ancient creature in the arena who would have recognised the song, old fashioned as it was. Camilla's contribution was more in depth, drawing from her experience as a professional singer. Sean added jokingly that if none of their contestants had a better sense of tune, this could very well be the longest night of his life. His comment prompted a burst of laughter across the audience. In the giant metal cage, there was not even the shadow of a smile.

As the evening progressed, it took contestants less and less time to kick off their songs, as undoubtedly those in the cage had a chance to think of a song, any song, to which they knew even half of the lyrics, before their turn came.

Halfway through the line of contestants, Sean felt Camilla's entire body tense beside his. He darted a quick look towards her and saw her eyes were fixed right in front of her. He followed her gaze, and knew immediately the reason for her reaction. The next contestant to come on-stage was Spencer Martins. Before he could stop himself, he touched Camilla's thigh under the table. She was trembling uncontrollably. He pressed his hand down on her knee until she eventually stilled. She did not look at him, but he felt her relax in her chair. Finally, she nodded once, her eyes still directed towards the stage, and he removed his hand.

Spencer Martins walked up to the platform. Of all the contestants who had taken this challenge, he definitely looked the most at ease. He walked in an almost nonchalant manner, as though he had just popped out to buy some milk. He stood on the platform for several seconds, and he did not flinch in the slightest when its colour gradually changed to yellow, orange and almost crimson. He closed his eyes, his face tilted upwards, and Sean had the disturbing feeling that the man was enjoying himself. It looked as though he was feeding off the pain and, far from trying to make it stop, he was deliberately letting it linger. Eventually, with a loud sigh, like he did not really want the moment to end, Spencer Martins bent towards the microphone and started singing. He did not hesitate for even a second. He seemed to have known all along the song he was going to perform, and from the broad, blood-chilling smile creeping up on his face, he was delighted to be given a chance to share it with the world:

'*Shhh, be quiet. No one will hear anyway.*

Why the kicks, why the tears, on such a beautiful day?

Don't you worry, don't you cry,

the pain will soon go away.

Don't you worry, don't you cry,

soon it will be time to die.'

Spencer Martins finished the verse and paused to breathe in the deadly silence around him. His song, his terror-inducing melody cast an instant spell on the Cradle, as if he had pressed a giant pause and mute button.

Before anyone could react, he started the verse again, and he went on singing it on a loop, his voice growing louder and shrieker each time, his hands motioning wildly around him, as if in absolute ecstasy. His body rose and fell with each word, each syllable. He had an air of madness about him, of utter delirium, so much so that at times he appeared to be barely human. He was no longer a man, he was a creature of insanity and indecency. He was every shadow children feared underneath their beds, every unknown movement at the corner of dark little streets, and that fresh breeze of panic one shuddered from when standing too close to the edge of a cliff. As he stood there, before them all, blasting out a song all now knew to be his own, with little doubt as to when and where it might have been used, Spencer Martins was the living embodiment of all that ever went wrong with a world they had all once known to be pleasant. He was evil. Pure, unadulterated evil. Far from looking to be affected by the heavy judgement all around him, Spencer Martins seemed to feast on it. He soaked in their anger and their shock.

By the time he reached the fourth repetition, the audience finally woke up. A shower of loud, angry shouts rained from all corners of the arena, shortly followed by shoes, plastic bottles – anything anyone could put their hands on. Several of them fell short and ended up amongst the audience, and around the judges' table, until one particularly heavy, metal-soled boot reached the stage and caught Spencer Martins straight in the face.

The entire arena cheered, uniting as one, and their clapping spread far beyond the walls of the Cradle, to the crowds amassed outside in front of the giant screens, all the way across the capital. In their metal cage, the convicts lunged forward as one, brandishing clenched fists and shouting obscenities at Spencer Martins. The nation stood up in unison, bound as they were by their revulsion.

Spencer Martins dropped to his knees. The metal sole of the lone boot, propelled from the depths of the arena, had hit him across his left cheek, leaving a deep, bloody cut along his face. He looked up, picked up the shoe and studied it for a few seconds. He turned it around, inspecting all of its borders and edges, eyes wide, as though he had never seen anything like it before. Then unexpectedly, he threw it back into the audience, bursting into laughter, like he had just cracked the best joke in the world. His laughter was as icy and petrifying as his song had been, and it just seemed to infuriate the audience even more. Four guards rushed at him, and grabbed him tightly, dragging him off the stage. He kept on laughing frantically. He did not try to resist. The audience was wild with fury, and Sean wondered for a moment if they were about to charge the stage to carry out justice on this man themselves. With a wave towards the production room, he caught the producer's attention to immediately call for an advert break.

When he turned to look at Camilla, Sean saw that she was frozen in her seat. Her face had lost all of its colour. She had been biting the corner of her lip so hard she had pierced through her skin, and plump drops of crimson blood were rolling down her chin, dripping slowly onto her neck and her dress. Sean quickly turned around, and grabbed a member of the crew who was rushing by. He whispered a few words to the young female, motioning towards Camilla.

As Camilla was made to stand up to be carried away back to the make-up room, Sean caught her eye. She looked as thought she had just seen a ghost.

'Come on, kid,' he murmured as she walked past him, 'you can do this.'

CHAPTER 24

TERRENCE BLAKE

Terrence felt like the advert break went on forever, but he admitted it might just have felt longer because of the turmoil Mad Spencer's performance created. The backstage area where their cage had been rolled to was buzzing with chaos, but it was nothing compared to the uproar emanating from the crowd.

'Get Benson back onstage,' Terrence heard someone shout.

It took a good couple of minutes for the production team to locate the show host. He appeared backstage, disheveled and pale-faced, dragged along by two sturdy-looking young men. Terrence thought he looked like the last thing he wanted to do was to get back out there, but failed to feel sorry for the man. The make-up girl hovered around him, powdering his cheeks, whilst the man who had previously ordered Tyler Benson to be fetched was talking at him animatedly. Judging by the look on his face, Terrence wondered whether the show host registered anything that was being said to him. He had an air of absence about him, spread over his eyes and his smile, the air of someone too used to have his body express one thing whilst his mind thinks quite another.

From where he was standing, Terrence could not quite make out what the man was saying to Tyler Benson, but his face was stretched out with so much tension he could have been trying to talk him into murdering a man.

Ironically, Terrence thought, if that been the case he could have found more than one person willing to oblige him. Suddenly, they both brought a hand to their ears and listened intently. A few seconds later, the man brushed the make-up girl aside, nodded at Tyler Benson and patted him on the shoulder as he walked past him, disappearing into the backstage maze. Tyler Benson stood on the spot for several seconds, his hands hanging limply by his sides, his shoulders slouched. His gaze was fixed somewhere in the distance. Then all of a sudden, his absentmindedness was gone. The shift happened so fast Terrence wondered if he had imagined it. Gone was the uncertainty, gone was the daze. He was a different man altogether. He straightened up, rearranged the collar of his shirt and the lapels of his jacket. He seemed to have grown several centimetres taller in a fraction of a second. He conjured a brilliant, dazzling smile on his face, and strolled onto the stage with a spring in his step. One of the panels slid aside and the giant metal cage followed onto the stage.

'Wow,' Tyler Benson said dramatically, 'that was quite something wasn't it?'

Tyler Benson was about to speak again when he stopped in his tracks. Sean Cravanaugh stood up from his chair, slowly, deliberately. The audience fell quiet. Sean Cravanaugh turned to face the crowd. He leaned nonchalantly against the judges' desk.

'Listen,' he said, his tone grave, 'I don't think any of us here can pretend that what we all just witnessed didn't happen.'

Murmurs travelled across the audience.

'I don't know about you,' he continued, 'but this was the most sickening, disgusting thing I have ever seen… And I have seen my fair share of crazy stuff!'

The crowd let out a small, uncertain laugh.

'This…' Sean paused, as if searching for the right words, '*this* is why we created this show. Because there are too many people like this piece of shit who are still living and breathing, when so many others have suffered. Some people might think prison is enough to teach people like him a lesson. I say it isn't enough. I say we need more!'

His tone had gone up gradually, so that before anyone could realise it he was shouting.

'We need these outlaws to pay for what they've done. To pay for the lives they've taken and the happiness they've destroyed. This show exists to give the people of our great nation something they deserve and have been denied for too long. Revenge. A chance to make these fuckers pay!' He bellowed, pointing at the cage behind him, his gaze still on the crowd, 'this is *our* time! Our time to take control, to make our own justice!'

The crowd was incensed once more.

'Time for justice!' Shouted Sean Cravanaugh, his tight fist in the air.

'Time for justice! Time for justice!' Chanted the audience.

Terrence saw a few of the convicts exchange incredulous glances. He looked at Sean Cravanaugh. He wanted to catch the look on his face, to read his expression, but he was too far to see properly. He had to give it to the man for being such a skilled orator. Terrence might despise him, yet he could not help but feel a little awe for his technique.

When Sean Cravanaugh sat back down, Tyler Benson announced the next contestant, and went on having each and every man and woman dragged out of the cage and onto the platform. He watched them struggle, some more than others, commentating on each person's desperate attempts to escape the heat beneath their feet.

'Quite a performance from this contestant,' Tyler Benson exclaimed, watching a male convict being half led, half carried off the perilous platform. The man had attempted to sing what was probably the only song that had come to his mind, and incidentally the one song that would be bound to infuriate the audience almost as much as Mad Spencer's tune: the national anthem. The convict had barely been able to get past the first verse when a deluge of shoes, metal can bottles and, to Terrence's astonishment, even rocks, had poured at him from every corner of the arena. Unable to utter another word, he had crouched down, his arms over his head, in an attempt to protect himself from the projectiles. The platform however, or rather *whoever* was operating it, had no sympathy for the man's predicament, and before long, the ground under his feet was bright red. As objects kept raining over him, he fell to the ground. His hands were fuming, his skin burnt raw. It had taken quite a while for the guards to show mercy. They trotted towards him, and carried him off back into the cage. The man collapsed onto the spot, a few feet away from where Terrence was standing. He had been so subdued by this gruesome spectacle that he had not heard Tyler Benson's commentary start again.

'It looks like convict seventy-seven is getting a little cosy in there! Let's give him a bit of a nudge to join us, shall we?'

The words had barely registered in Terrence's mind, when the familiar sharp pain shot through his ankle, spreading fast, until it was radiating through his entire body. He thought he heard himself cry out in pain, but his mind was so taken on what was happening within him that he could not have been sure what was going on on the outside. The pain stopped as instantly as it had started, and he found himself on all fours, large beads of sweat trickling down his face and neck. He looked up to see what felt like a million pairs of eyes fixed on him.

He made his way slowly out of the cage towards the platform. He looked at the judges' table, and he thought Sean Cravanaugh was holding his gaze, as if daring him to try anything funny.

It was only when he stepped onto the platform that he remembered what was expected of him. It baffled him that while he had stood watching his peers going through their own ordeal, he had not for one second thought of what he would do once he was in their place. He needed a song. He had barely spoken ten words together since he had been incarcerated, let alone sung anything. He wracked his brain for any song he could remember, but anything he could think of only came back to him in fragmented memories which did not quite seem to belong to him.

He closed his eyes, trying to stop the fresh wave of panic from rising in the pit of his stomach. A song. Any song. Anything. All he could see swirling through his head were blurry images, patches of colours and indescribable shapes. As he fought his way through the maze, the one and only sharp image was that of Maddison's smile. Her eyes turned towards him, her hands clasped in delight.

'Again!' He heard her voice emerge from a distant memory, 'again!'

In his mind's eye, she was laughing, clapping her hands along in excitement, her beautiful soft dark curls bouncing around her face like a halo. The words to a long forgotten song slowly made their way into his mind, a tune from a past he was not entirely sure was his own anymore. He thought he heard his voice float out of his parted lips, but all he could focus on was Maddison's happy, giggling face.

'Baby girl, You waltzed into my life one day;
All those feelings came rushing my way.
Couldn't stop them if I tried...
Baby girl, your fingers wrapped around my heart;
Can you believe it was beating so fast.
Couldn't calm it if I tried...

You're fast asleep there in my arms,

The world just seems to melt away.

Your angel face, and such tiny palms…

You guide me through day after day'

He felt like he had opened gates he could no longer close. The words poured out of his mouth like a waterfall, lyrics he had not uttered in years nor allowed himself to even remember, vestige of a life he had destroyed.

'*You called me dad, and I rejoiced.*

As priceless as diamonds and pearls,

This bond of ours, the dreams we created,

Forever will be true, darling little girl'

The last words gripped his chest with such force they had barely come out as a murmur. His heart was pounding, resonating in every single cell of his body, creating a skull-breaking tumult between his ears. His cheeks and chin felt just a little too wet, and it took him some time to realise it was no longer from sweat, but from tears flowing behind his closed eyelids. His hands instinctively raised towards his cheeks, brushing the moisture away. All around him he could sense the all too familiar feeling of the crowd looking down on him. He could almost sense their breaths on his skin. He allowed himself to drift away, to stay lost inwards for a second longer. Now he had stepped back into the memories, back into the warm glow of his daughter's smile, he never wanted to turn back. His insides tightened at the thought of the sight awaiting him when he finally faced the world again, and it took all of his might to keep his eyes tightly shut.

CHAPTER 25

SEAN CRAVANAUGH

Another sort of silence enveloped the arena and Sean wondered how something so similar in theory could feel so different. Silent horror had followed Spencer Martins' performance. A veil of quiet confusion now replaced it. It was like the audience was struggling to reconcile the idea their contestants could appear so human. Sean was certain that for a fleeting moment they had all forgotten who the man was and why he was standing before them.

Sean had been watching Terrence Blake week after week, and instinct told him that something was amiss about the man. Because he prided himself on being a remarkable judge of character, it bothered Sean that he had not yet been able to pinpoint what it was that nagged him about this particular individual.

He looked at Terrence Blake more closely. He was standing still, his arms by his sides, his hands clenched into fists, his eyes still closed. His cheeks glistened with tears and exhaustion. He looked like the saddest man Sean had ever seen. It was not a superficial sort of sadness, the kind of melancholy one could experience upon hearing unfortunate, but not life-altering news. It was a form of sorrow, of heart-breaking nostalgia which seemed to envelop him entirely.

Sean wondered what the man was thinking. He wondered where the song came from and whether Terrence Blake had written it, because he could not for the life of him place it. But most of all, he wondered how a man accused of killing his wife and abusing his child could breathe so much emotion and tenderness into words. Sean caught himself frowning.

And, suddenly, he knew. And it was so blatantly obvious, he wanted to laugh. The answer had been dangling in front of his nose the entire time, and now that he could see, now that he *knew* he could not believe he had missed it until that moment. He felt like jumping on the table in front of him and shouting out his victory for all to hear.

He had not planned for this situation. If he was honest with himself, as he often was, it had not even crossed his mind. For all he knew, all of the so-called 'contestants' were destined to die one way or another, whether it happened on live television or beyond the Cradle, as each of them exited the competition. What he had not anticipated was that one of them would get out of this experience alive. They had planted such hatred in people's hearts that no one would even care if all contestants met with an untimely demise. If anything, they would be glad to see every single contestant painfully perish before their eyes. They would demand it, even. Such had been Sean's theory, and so far, he had only been proven right.

But things were different now. Everything had changed. For the better, of course. Anything that bonded the audience together was an added bonus, and this would bring them the one thing missing from their lives: hope. They would be united, even more than they already were, and Sean knew that this would justify everything and anything that happened to any other on the show, no matter how horrid. Sean's mind was buzzing with action points, with marketing slogans, with all that needed to be done to put his new plan into action.

How he wanted to laugh. How he wanted to rejoice in his own luck. How he loved the predictability of all of the good people around him, because he knew exactly how to lead them where he wanted them to be. Their gullibility would make his fortune. Nothing could get in his way now. He had found a rare needle in the haystack of hundreds of thousands of guilty, incarcerated bastards. Prisons had been full to breaking point with men and women whose filthy hands were covered in blood. How fortunate was *he* to have found Terrence Blake, the country's one and only wrongly-accused, genuine, innocent man.

~ ~ ~

The rest of the singing task passed in a daze, Sean could barely focus on what was happening around him. He was certain he was right, his instincts had rarely led him astray in the past. Still, he was eager for a chance to confirm his theory, and this could only be done once the day's show was over.

He willed time to go faster. More convicts were put through to a punishment round, but even their yelps of pain and terror could not drag him away from the excitement of what he wanted to set in motion. He was oblivious to reactions around him, to the indignation rising and falling in the audience. Their anger flowed past him. He was no longer present. His mind was so focused on his latest realisation, it had taken a will of its own, racing ahead. Like a chess master, he was carefully calculating his next ten moves.

As a child, his mother had often complained that he would suddenly switch off like this. They would be having a conversation and without warning, his brain would latch onto something. Sometimes it was something she said, or a thought that popped in his head. Sometimes the episodes were sparked by only one random word in an entire conversation. It snowballed into a giant path of causality, threading along the sinuous strings of his own unfathomable sense of logic, and there was nothing anyone, including himself, could do to stop it. Without any warning, he would appear absent, his eyes fixed on a point ahead that he was not really seeing. His whole body would gently rock forward and back, his arms tightly wrapped around himself. He knew this because his mother would later describe his own behaviour to him.

One day, she had filmed him, and she had made him sit and watch the entire thing, from start to finish. Sean had thought she was trying to make a point, although he had failed to see which one. He had watched on, fascinated, an outside observer, as if it had not really been him on the small screen. His mother used to say she could almost see the cogs in motion in his brain, and on the rare occasions she was in a pleasant mood, she would tease him and say she could see smoke coming out of his ears from the effort of so much thinking. When he was really young, he had not understood the joke and had found himself rushing to a mirror to check his ears. His mother had laughed so hard. He had stared at her in disbelief. Then resentment and shame settled in, and he taught himself to reel in his most childlike impulses.

His mother would refer to the episodes as his 'quiet moments'.

'He's just having a quiet moment,' she would say apologetically to anyone who had the misfortune of being around when such an episode was triggered.

At times she had found it endearing and she marvelled at his intelligence when he shared with her the outcome of his silent reflections. With the passing of years however, it transpired that she had expected her son would outgrow his 'quiet moments'. She had longed for him to turn out 'like other boys', although he had never quite figured out what that meant.

Sean had loosely wondered if this was when his mother's drinking had started, or if it had been there all along and he had simply failed to notice it. They never spoke of her habit openly. On particularly bad days, her favourite topic was how strange her son was and how unlucky she was to have brought such an unusual character into the world. She would wail at what she knew the neighbours must be saying and at how he did not behave like a normal boy. He would never get a job, she would say, and he would never be able to take care of her like she had cared for him. He would be homeless and they would both be miserable and die a slow, painful death.

Luckily, her prophecy had not proved right, at least not for him. He had made a life for himself. He had found success beyond that which she could ever have imagined. On one thing she had been right though: he had not taken care of her. He had cut all ties with her and had left her to drown in the pitiful state she had got herself into. Far from trying to stop his 'quiet moments', he had learnt to harness their power. Growing up in such impoverished circumstances and with little to his name, he had soon come to realise his brain was his most valuable asset. He had sharpened his instincts, allowing them to take the driving seat in his life. He had rarely been disappointed by the result. If his mother, or for that matter everyone around him, did not see that, it was their loss. He had sworn to himself he would prove them wrong, and that one day they would all despair in their stupidity, in having casted him aside, in shaming him for who he was. He would show them, he had professed silently, and their regret would be a small price to pay for making his early years hell. His mother was no exception.

When the show ended, Sean waited for the red lights on the cameras to switch off, indicating the live transmission was over, before waving a production assistant over towards him. He whispered his instructions, pausing to ensure he had been fully understood. The production assistant looked puzzled, but nodded and jogged off.

Sean turned over to his right and glanced over at Camilla. She still looked pale, although she seemed to have recovered some of her composure. Her gaze was lost, somewhere far beyond the edge of the stage. He nudged her with his elbow and she glanced over at him.

'You alright?' He asked quietly.

She nodded once, and the motion was sharp and stiff, as though this was as much as she could manage.

'Need anything?'

He must have looked more concerned than he felt, because she forced her face to release into a smile and she shook her head. He placed his hand on hers and squeezed it once, reaffirming the unique and silent understanding they shared. There was much more to go through before it was over and they both knew she needed to be strong.

Sean made his way back to his office, his pace quick and his mind focused. A lot was resting on the outcome of his next move. The crew stood aside to let him pass, groups of people splitting before him and merging back in waves behind him. For a moment he reckoned he knew what Moses might have felt when he parted the sea. Not that he believed for a second he had existed, or that anyone anywhere was watching down on humanity, helping the righteous and punishing evil. Nonsense, he thought, shaking his head. His own life had convinced him there could be no higher power as long as such unfairness transpired in every second of every day across billions of lives. With so much suffering, with so much pain, he wondered how anyone could ever claim any of it had been purposefully designed. Had there been a force out there to keep the balance steady and the world in check, there would have been no need for this show. There would have been no problem to solve and the topics on live television might have been rather more vanilla than what they had come to be.

He closed his office door behind him, strode straight to the far end of the room and circled his desk to sit in the comfortable leather armchair. He remained there, tuning in, gathering every single ounce of concentration he had in preparation for his next encounter. He closed his eyes and brought his awareness to his breathing. He tuned in entirely, his body completely still, his mind alert.

A knock on the door dragged him out of his meditation.

'Come in,' he called out.

The door handle lowered and the producer walked in, closely followed by contestant seventy-seven, who stood tightly squeezed between two guards.

'Thank you,' Sean jerked his head towards the staff, 'you may leave now.'

The producer looked dumbfounded.

'Sir…' He started hesitantly.

'I *said* you may leave now,' he interrupted him, more firmly this time, not giving him a chance to voice his concerns.

The producer and the two guards exchanged a disbelieving look.

'Get out!' Sean barked, losing his patience, 'now!'

The startled members of staff needed no further telling and finally left the room. Sean turned his attention to Terrence Blake, who had not moved an inch. The contestant looked mildly disconcerted. If he was afraid, he was hiding it well. For a moment, their eyes locked and they took the measure of each other. No animosity passed between them, simply interest. For Terrence Blake, it might have been curiosity as to why he, of all people, had been summoned. For Sean, it was the opportunity to watch the man more closely and to make a final call on how to broach the topic on his mind.

'Take a seat,' Sean said in an even voice, gesturing to the Chesterfields.

Terrence Blake did not move. He frowned, looking from the sofa, then to Sean, and back at the sofa.

'It hasn't been tampered with,' Sean added, taking a seat himself. 'Sit down.'

Terrence Blake stepped slowly forward and sat down. Sean could tell the man's guard was up. He could see it in the tension in his jaw and the sparks of movement in his hands. It was like he was expecting someone to jump out from behind him and stab him in the back. Who could blame him, Sean thought, after the last few weeks.

'Anything to drink?' Asked Sean, suddenly remembering social conventions.

He stood up and walked to the drinks cabinet, pouring himself a glass of scotch. As he had received no response from his guest, he peered back. Terrence Blake was staring at him intently.

'No,' Terrence Blake said simply, not taking his gaze off him.

Their eyes met again. An electric current shot up Sean's body, an instinctive reaction he could not control, making the hair on the back of his neck stand up straight. He walked back to his seat, glass in hand.

'That was quite a performance you gave us tonight.'

Terrence Blake did not respond and Sean started to think their conversation was at risk of becoming dangerously one-sided.

'Do you know why you're here, Mr Blake?' He asked, changing tactics.

'No.'

'Take a wild guess,' Sean's tone left no doubt that this was not just a suggestion.

Terrence Blake looked away, surveying the room around them with disinterest. Eventually he sighed and turned back to face his host.

'How can I possibly guess what you have in mind?' He said sternly, 'you came up with all of this,' he gestured around vaguely, 'and I will forever struggle to comprehend how anything of the sort ever saw the light of day. Don't ask me to guess your motives, Mr Cravanaugh, your brain obviously works in ways that defy all reason. I'm afraid I'm not gifted with such powers of imagination.'

Sean stared at Terrence Blake. A heavy silence settled between them, thick with tension.

'Human-made reason, perhaps,' Sean shrugged, 'but not *all* reason.'

Terrence Blake said nothing.

'Humans…' Sean continued, 'humans make rules that make no sense. They trap themselves in idealistic systems that are doomed, bound to fail, because none of them is clear-headed enough to see the very flaws that limit human beings. We'd like to think ourselves the masters of the universe, but in reality all we manage to do is lock ourselves up in a game limited by our own understanding of the world around us, and within us. Humanity is its own worst enemy, it's destined to pain and misery. Why should that be encouraged? To do nothing is to be compliant. To take part in the charade is to be as guilty as the people who made the stupid rules in the first place.'

Terrence Blake's expression was hard as steel. Sean's words seemed to trigger something inside him, something that made the corner of his eye twitch.

'You're mad,' Terrence Blake's voice was ice cold.

'Mad for wanting to take our race to the next level? For taking action to see it flourish?'

'Mad to think you can make a difference,' Terrence Blake countered, 'and deluded for believing you're doing any of this for anyone other than yourself.'

Sean studied his opponent more closely. He was at the same time surprised and pleased at hearing his answer. It was rare for him to come across anyone who not only dared to challenge him, but was also able to cut to the chase and see things just as they were, rather than how they wanted them to be.

'Look around, Mr Blake,' he motioned around the room, and towards the big glass windows overlooking the arena, 'haven't I already made a difference?'

Once again, Terrence Blake said nothing, his eyes wide with anger and disbelief. Sean took a sip of his scotch before speaking again.

'What do you think is the most important thing?' He asked.

'The most important thing?' Terrence Blake looked surprised at the randomness of his question, 'in what?'

'In everything.'

Terrence Blake considered the question for a moment, shaking his head, as though he could not believe what he was hearing.

'Does it matter?'

'Doesn't it?' questioned Sean.

Of all the times he had asked the question, that was an answer he had never received.

'No.'

The two men stared at each other.

'Enlighten me, then,' Sean sat back in his chair. 'Why would it not matter?'

He had just realised that he had been leaning forward from the edge of his seat, invigorated by the turn the conversation was taking. He studied Terrence Blake's face, still unsure what his judgement of the man was. One thing he could tell with absolute conviction was that the contestant was no sociopath. It takes one to know one, Sean thought, and of the two of us, I'm definitely the one with that affliction.

CHAPTER 26

TERRENCE BLAKE

'Enlighten me, then. Why would it not matter?'

Terrence let out a dark chuckle, heavy with derision. Sean Cravanaugh was looking at him intently, and Terrence held his gaze. Terrence shook his head, still unable to believe they were even engaging in such a conversation.

It had been some time since he had had a discussion with anyone that did not revolve around the simple logistics of staying alive. In a former life, one that seemed a million years away, Terrence had been a teacher. He had been engrossed in the joy of seeing young minds flourish, learning to observe and question the world around them. One of his favourite debates had happened when a seven-year old boy had asked where the evil in people came from. Were some people born with it, he had asked innocently, or did it come later? Were some people good and others not, just like some seeds grew as beautiful flowers and others as weed? Terrence had looked at his pupil in awe, a sense of amazement and pride overtaking him, as he watched the boy's little brow furrowing, and listened to him ponder the strange concepts of nature versus nurture.

Right there and then, sitting on a sofa opposite one of the most powerful men in the nation, Terrence could not for the life of him remember what he had told the little boy. He hoped that he had given him a sensible explanation. If the boy had walked in through the door at that very moment, Terrence knew what his answer to the same question would have been. No one is born evil, he would have said. No baby comes to life with a demon lodged in their heart. But all of us have to interact with the world around us. Sometimes good things happen to people, and sometimes bad things happen. With time, we make of each event in our life what we will, and whilst we cannot control our environment, what we *can* control is how we respond to it. Children will replicate the thoughts and behaviours they have been taught, or the ones they have seen enacted around them. In desperate times, some will turn to desperate measures, simply because no one might have showed them that there ever was another way. Terrence wondered what had led the man facing him to turn into the despicable being he was today. He exhaled sharply.

'One who has nothing can have no desires. One who has no worldly possessions can have nothing he values most. Importance loses all meaning. Whatever once made a difference, or sparked joy, becomes irrelevant.'

Sean Cravanaugh looked at him intently and Terrence could tell he had the man's attention.

'I have been in jail for many years,' he continued, 'people might think freedom would be the most important thing to me. But I don't have any freedom, nor will I ever be free again, so should I allow myself to even consider it as important? Wouldn't I go mad if I did? When you have nothing, it doesn't matter what's important or what isn't, it all becomes irrelevant. It all loses its value from being so out of reach. Pointlessness. That is the price to pay for such an existence,' Terrence shook his head. 'It doesn't matter,' he said again, 'none of it does.'

Sean Cravanaugh did not respond right away, and silence stretched between them.

'What happened the night your wife died?' Sean Cravanaugh asked abruptly.

Terrence was taken aback by the sudden change of topic. Shock and rage bubbled inside him, but he said nothing.

'I know you didn't murder your wife,' Sean Cravanaugh insisted, 'I know you're innocent.'

Terrence sat very still, because for as long as he remained silent, maybe he could make himself believe his ears had tricked him. He glared at Sean Cravanaugh, silent fury fizzing deep inside his guts, a wave of indignation threatening to break loose. What did this stranger know! What arrogance he had to stand before him passing judgement! Who did he think he was?

'Come on, Mr Blake, let us speak openly. I can help you. All you have to do is tell me the truth.'

'You. Know. Nothing,' Terrence seethed, enunciating each word as clearly as he could, the trembling in his voice barely under control.

'I know enough to be certain that whatever happened that night is not what we've been led to believe,' Sean Cravanaugh asserted, 'and I can help you.'

'Help me!' Terrence erupted, jumping to his feet. '*Help* me! The only person you're ever looking to help, Mr Cravanaugh, is *yourself!* Who do you think you are? You may be playing god around here, but it gives you no right to…'

'It gives me every right!' Interrupted Sean Cravanaugh in a firm voice, his tone raised. 'In this part of town, Mr Blake, *I* decide who lives or dies. I'm not *playing* god, I *am* god. I snap my fingers and tomorrow you're a dead man,' he reeled, snapping his fingers for dramatic effect. 'But you've made it amply clear that your own life isn't what matters to you… Maybe you feel differently about your daughter's life.'

Terrence was stunned. For a second he thought he had heard incorrectly. He opened his mouth, and closed it again, unable to utter a single word.

'I thought so,' Sean Cravanaugh said with a cold, triumphant smile, 'why don't you sit down, Mr Blake, and hear me out.'

Terrence paused for a moment before taking a seat again.

'On one thing you're absolutely right. I don't *want* to help you. Frankly I don't care if you live or die. What I do care about is what your living or dying does to my show and to its audience levels. Now, whilst the nation has rallied behind the competition and united in hatred of the lot of you…' He motioned to nowhere in particular, his eyes fixed on Terrence, 'I do believe there is something even stronger than hatred. Something that has the potential to make the value of this entire enterprise shoot through the roof. Can you see what that might be? No? Let *me* enlighten you then.'

Sean Cravanaugh barely paused, hinging forward on his seat, a glimmer of excitement painted over his entire face.

'Hope,' he murmured in false confidence, 'hope unites people so much better than hatred! Hope gives people a purpose, a motive, renewed energy. Can't you see!' He exclaimed. 'Can't you see how brilliant this all is!'

Another long silence settled between them. Terrence could not believe his ears. Sean Cravanaugh's words had rendered him nearly speechless.

'You're mad,' Terrence repeated, because no other words came to his mind.

'Yes, yes. You've said that already,' Sean Cravanaugh said dismissively, 'let's just agree to disagree, shall we?' He added, his face serious. 'We will tell the country the true story of what happened that night and gather some momentum. We can fine tune some of the details to make them stick in people's minds better. Now is the perfect time, after your singing performance. We will make sure you win, Mr Blake. You *will* go free. All you need to do is cooperate. After all, even I would rather an innocent man walked free at the end of all this than one of these other thugs.'

'I'm not innocent,' Terrence insisted.

Sean Cravanaugh looked straight at him, visibly annoyed.

'Did you listen to a word I have said? I *know* you did not murder your wife, don't you think now is a good time to cut the crap and come clean?'

'I have *told* you…' Terrence raised his voice.

'That's bullshit!' Sean Cravanaugh exclaimed angrily, throwing his empty glass against the wall.

The crystal tumbler crashed against the hard concrete with brute force, and exploded into what looked like a million pieces.

'*You* know it, *I* know it, and soon the entire nation will know it,' his tone was menacing now, 'and if you refuse to help, we will fish out the one other eye witness for that night. Maybe young Maddison can give us her account of what happened the night her mother died.'

Before he knew what he was doing, Terrence had bounced to his feet and launched himself onto Sean Cravanaugh. His outstretched fist collided with the man's face and he felt the murky crack of breaking bone under his knuckles. The two guards erupted into the room and grabbed Terrence by the arms, pinning him to the floor. He felt someone's elbow crash into his back. The familiar burning sensation burst in his ankle, as one of his assailants activated the stun function on his security bracelet.

'Mr Blake,' Sean Cravanaugh said, holding his bleeding face, a tinge of disbelief in his voice, 'I'm disappointed that you have chosen to react this way. This *will* all go ahead as I have stated, whether you like it or not. All that you can do is comply, unless you want your daughter to be dragged into this. Maybe sleeping on it will encourage a change of heart. Take him,' he commanded to the two guards.

The guards dragged Terrence, half stunned, out of the room.

'I'm not innocent...' Terrence pleaded feebly.

Sean Cravanaugh looked at him hard, his face contorted with pain, warm, thick blood now trickling down his neck. Wide gloomy scarlet stains were forming on the collar of his white shirt.

'I'm not innocent...' Terrence heard himself mutter again, before everything plunged into darkness.

CHAPTER 27

TERRENCE BLAKE

When he awoke, Terrence was lying on cold hard floor. His eyes flickered open, but it took some time for his vision to adjust to his surroundings. He did not recognise the room he found himself in. It was a very small cell, similar to the one he had spent most of his time in over the past weeks, except he was alone. The walls were so close together he could just about lie or sit properly and, for a moment, he was thankful that he had never suffered from claustrophobia. The tiny dimensions of the room were actually strangely comforting, because he could easily keep an eye on every single corner of it. Sitting up, with his back against the rough cement wall, he gave the pounding in his chest a moment to quiet down.

Flashes of his meeting with Sean Cravanaugh a few hours before were coming back to him now and he found himself struggling to put them together in a logical order. Pangs of pain erupted from his ribs and ankle, and his entire body felt sore.

Had he imagined the whole encounter? As his mind reconstructed the conversation piece by piece, he felt anger rising in the pit of his stomach. Who did this man think he was to be making such assumptions? What did he know of the hell he had gone through? What did he know of the pain and guilt that never left him? Terrence took a deep breath but failed to calm himself down.

The more he willed himself to breathe the thicker the air around him felt. Before he knew it, he was panting and covered in sweat. His face felt puffy, like he had been crying for hours. Time extended and stretched to breaking point. He had no idea of how long he had been locked up in this new cell, though, in a way, he appreciated the solitude. He pressed a cheek against the cold wall and let out a small sigh of relief as the soreness in his skin gently subsided.

His conversation with Sean Cravanaugh came back clear as day in his mind now, and he knew he had no choice in the matter. Terrence doubted the man had ever been refused anything. It pained him to think that Maddison might be pulled into this. The ache in his heart was so intense he had to grasp at his chest with both hands to contain it. He had loved his wife, but it was the absence of his daughter that caused him the most pain. Every single day without her, without even knowing where she was or if she was happy, was like a dagger through his skin.

Deep down, during his disturbed patches of sleep, a thought emerged at the back of his mind, and he hated himself immediately for allowing it to form. For just a moment, he longed to see her so much he hoped Sean Cravanaugh *would* find her. Instantly he thought of what this would do to her, how shameful an experience it would be, and disgust hit him like a punch to the stomach. He had no right to wish for her company. He had lost that right the moment he had ruined her happiness forever.

Closing his eyes, he saw Delilah's face. How he had loved her. For many years they had lived happily and he had done everything in his power to keep her content. As a school teacher, he was not making as much as he had wished to give her, but they had shared joy all the same. She worked part-time in a flower shop, and filled their tiny house with fragrant bouquets every day. They had been happy.

He could pinpoint the exact moment when everything had changed. The very second something dark took root within his beautiful wife. It was all over the day she announced that she was pregnant. He had physically leapt off his seat with excitement. He loved children and he had been longing for one of their own. In his exhilarated state, he had failed to notice that Delilah, quite far from joining in his excitement, had turned very quiet. He had missed the very first sign that something was not quite right.

The pregnancy itself had gone smoothly, despite Delilah's alarming state of silence. Terrence had thought she was tired. She was nurturing their child after all, that was bound to take a toll on her. That was the excuse he had created for her. Surely her lack of interest for the baby, for his or her name, for the things they had to buy and prepare, was due to the exhaustion of growing a human being inside her own body.

As her mood deteriorated and she stopped speaking to him altogether, he had kept defending her. How could he know what it was like to be pregnant? He had to allow her to handle it however she wanted. All he could do was support her as best he could. She stopped working, long before her pregnancy forced her to. Not that she had consulted him on the decision, or even informed him of it. Suddenly she was not getting ready in the morning and he had to go to the flower shop to be told she had quit. He started tutoring after school for extra money to buy the things they needed. He would come home to find Delilah lying motionless on the couch, the television turned on to some random mind-numbing programme. When he cooked for her she refused to eat. He would leave a plate on the coffee table by her side, only to find it cold and untouched when she had gone to bed. One evening she locked herself into their bedroom, and despite his best efforts he could not persuade her to open the door to let him in. That was the first night he spent on the couch. The first of many nights.

But Terrence had kept his good spirits. If Delilah was struggling through the pregnancy, he had to be strong for the both of them. He took care of every single logistical element of their lives. When the baby arrived, he knew, everything would be well. His wife would come back to him, they would be a family. He knew it was just a matter of time until Delilah's state improved. How could it not, when she held their child in her arms for the first time.

Several months before the birth, she refused to visit their midwife. No amount of begging had changed her mind, and Terrence found himself in the consultation room, on his own, making yet another excuse for her. She was exhausted, he had heard himself say. The midwife had frowned but had not commented further. Visit after visit, the midwife stopped asking when Delilah would be attending, or warning him about the lack of medical supervision during the pregnancy. Without ever getting into details, Terrence and the midwife had come to a tacit understanding that this was the way things were.

The day Delilah went into labour, he had to carry her, kicking and screaming into the ambulance he had called. She fought so hard the paramedics had needed to administer an injection to calm her down. At the hospital, Terrence had watched, powerless, as his beloved wife was carried onto a bed and taken to surgery for a caesarian. The midwife had failed to convince Delilah to cooperate in pushing their baby out into the world.

When Delilah was still asleep, recovering from the anaesthetic, a nurse walked up to Terrence, a little bundle of pink cloths snuggled into her arms. She had handed him his daughter without a word, a broad smile stretched over her face. Terrence remembered exactly what it felt like to hold his baby girl for the very first time. It had been as if the last nine months had only been a bad dream. All of it ended with the human being fast asleep in his arms. How tiny she was, he had thought. How very frail! In that moment, nothing else existed but the two of them and together they could have taken on the world. He was a father, and that was the best, most wonderful feeling he had ever had in his life.

Delilah expressed no interest in the child. Terrence brought their daughter to his wife and she refused to hold her. She barely took one look at her, and it was a glare so full of hatred and disgust that Terrence had not been able to make light of it. He had not been able to make an excuse for her again. He had not been able to brush it off like he had every single other sign so far, because now it was no longer about either of them. It was much bigger and far more important than him or Delilah. He had a responsibility to keep their daughter safe, and the murderous look in his wife's eyes filled him with dread. Whatever darkness he had endured and allowed to creep up between the two of them, he could not allow it to reach their daughter.

He had reported his concerns immediately to their midwife who looked unsurprised at the news. She had suspected it all along. Severe antenatal and postnatal depression, she called it. The doctors recommended that Delilah stay at the hospital, while Terrence went home with the child. Delilah would be safe there and would benefit from daily sessions with a psychiatrist.

And so Terrence left his wife in what he told himself were capable hands, and he went home with their baby. Delilah had refused to name her, and since he was increasingly pressed by the ward staff to register her, Terrence had made the decision on his own. He named their daughter Maddison.

Delilah was moved to the psychiatric ward. When Terrence tried to visit with Maddison, he was told Delilah was unavailable. When he persisted, day after day, a tired-looking psychiatrist took him aside and advised that Delilah should be left alone for some time. He promised they would let him know when she was ready to come home.

'Give her some time,' the man had said.

Terrence had believed him. When he thought of it later, on one of the many sleepless nights he had spent in prison retracing his steps to the moments that should have caught his attention and alerted him that something was wrong, he knew that he had not really believed the doctor. He had *wanted* to believe him more than anything else, because the alternative was too terrifying to consider.

Terrence's only consolation was that despite everything, Maddison was growing up to be a wonderful, cheerful child. She had inherited his ability to see the best in everyone and everything around her. She marvelled at the smallest aspects of everyday life. A colourful sunrise, a pretty flower, a delicious meal. She took it all in with a smile on her face.

Four years passed before Terrence got the long-expected call. Delilah was ready to come home, an unknown disembodied voice told him over the phone. He knew he should have been happy, that he should have been relieved. He knew he should have been looking forward to the moment their family would be reunited. But Terrence could not help but be apprehensive. Somewhere deep inside he had a daunting feeling that the comfortable life Maddison and him had built for themselves, although far from perfect, was about to end. He brushed the feeling aside, and attempted to convince himself that all would be well. Maddison needed her mother. At times he could even convince himself that he needed his wife back.

They went to the hospital to pick up Delilah. It had been a beautiful, sunny day. Maddison was strapped in the back seat of the car, humming a tune Terrence did not recognise. She was hugging her stuffed rabbit, Leon, in her arms. As they approached the hospital, he heard her speak to Leon. In hushed, reassuring tones, she was telling him not to worry, that it would all be fine. Of course, she said in a tender voice, he did not know 'mummy', he had not met her, but daddy said that she was very loving and kind. Surely, she had added, stroking the stuffed animal's soft head, she will like him and they would play all his favourite games. He should not be scared, she said, hugging him tighter, everything would be fine.

Terrence had observed her in the rear view mirror, a heavy knot forming at the back of his throat. Maddison was a very precocious child. She had learnt everything very early on. Walking, talking, drawing. It had all come to her so naturally that Terrence kept forgetting how young she actually was. The pride and joy he felt for her was beyond words. Looking at her, he felt his heart might have burst open with love. She had become his entire world, and he hoped rather than believed that welcoming Delilah back into their lives would leave their happiness intact.

Boy, had he been wrong.

CHAPTER 28

SEAN CRAVANAUGH

Alone in his office, Sean mulled over his encounter with Terrence Blake the previous day. He had not expected the convict to embrace his plan right away, but he had thought the promise of justice and freedom would bring him round to the idea in the end. He had definitely not expected to get punched in the process. He knew for an absolute fact Terrence Blake was not a murderer, and that changed everything.

He was so sure of it he would have bet his entire fortune on it, and that was saying something. The man *was* innocent, and yet he denied it fervently. Howsoever Delilah Blake had died, her husband must have felt responsible for it for some yet unknown reason, so much so that he had spent fifteen years in jail for it. The righteousness of the idea baffled him.

Sean had never been an honourable man, nor had he ever tried to become one. The lessons he had learnt early in life were that honour was overrated, at least where he grew up. Had he followed such admirable principles, he would never have made such a successful career, or such a fortune for himself. He had never quite understood what could make a man give up property and gain for the sake of values and principles. He had tried to make sense of it, he truly had, if only because it gave him the tools to better use the people who lived by those odd self-imposed rules.

Sean had been bullied as a child. He had always known he was different from other children, and he had quickly learnt that this was reason enough for his peers to pick on him. He had suffered so many public displays of embarrassment he had long stopped counting them, or feeling saddened by them. Instead, he had grown angry, and his mother's failure to take his side had done little to appease his rage. Worse, when she had suggested that she agreed with the rest of the world, and sided against him, he had retreated almost entirely into himself.

He had started playing tricks back on the children who chose him as a target for their jeering and nasty remarks. Someone's notebooks mysteriously ended up in a gutter, another's lunch in the toilet. But what had started as fairly harmless pranks soon grew into more dangerous acts of revenge. One girl who had once poured his milkshake over his head because she did not like the sight of him was found one day in the girls' bathroom, unconscious, her head entirely shaven. A boy who had made an unwarranted joke about his run-down clothes had been caught with stolen jewellery in his bag and was expelled, though he had always claimed his innocence. With time and practice, Sean had become more agile at covering his tracks. To this day, he had never been caught. He had developed a mastermind expertise in plotting and fooling others. He remembered every single one of those acts, because he had forever wanted to recall the look on his targets' faces as it dawned on them that there was no way out of the mess they were in. *That* was his favourite part.

Sean still remembered the moment his spirit of revenge had cemented into a more definite outlook on life, and the ugly event which had led to it. When he was ten years old, he had discovered that the local antiques shop was selling a first edition of Machiavelli's *The Prince*. His favourite book. He already owned a much more recent copy of the book which he had read more times than he could count, but the idea of owning the ancient version soon became an obsession. He had entered the shop to enquire about the price, only to be told that the item was worth more than he could probably earn in years. But young Sean was already not the kind of person to take no for an answer. After much bargaining, the owner had agreed that he would not sell the book to anyone else, and that the boy would come and assist in the shop after school, until he had worked enough hours to afford it. Sean had calculated that if he worked at the shop two hours on weekdays and ten hours on weekends, he would be able to take the collector's item home within eight months. The job had involved a lot of mind-dulling, menial tasks, but Sean's mind was made up. For months he had gone to the shop, day after day, toiling away. Every time he left the shop to go home, he would walk up to the glass box the book was kept in, and mentally count the days left until it was in his possession.

Eventually, that day arrived, and Sean's heart was pounding so hard he thought he might self-combust with excitement. The shop owner had grown rather fond of his little helper, and he had made a ceremonial show of closing the shop early and gesturing the boy over to his study. There, he had put the glass box down with immense care on his desk, and had fished out a small metal key from his jacket pocket. When he had opened the box and had lifted the book, Sean had felt himself hold his breath. Feeling the book in his hands for the first time was a moment forever engraved in his memory.

Sean had walked out of the shop, his most valuable possession carefully wrapped inside his backpack. It was a winter evening, and despite the relatively early hour, darkness had already fallen and engulfed the streets. He had quickened his pace, eager to get home and lock himself into his bedroom to examine the book in more detail.

As he turned the corner of a dimly lit lane, he had seen them. A group of three older boys who attended his school. He had instantly turned around and tried to retrace his steps but it was too late. They had seen him too. They were mean, arrogant boys from the wealthier part of town, star athletes from the school's cricket team. From the moment they had set eyes on him, Sean had become their favourite piece of entertainment. One of them called after him.

'Hey! Freak! Where are you going?'

To this day, Sean could still hear the jeer in his head as clearly as though he were there. He remembered how he had started running as fast as his short legs would allow.

But the boys had been fitter and faster than him, and before he knew it they had circled around him. One of them had pushed him in the back, sending him tumbling forward towards the second boy, who had pushed him in the shoulder, making him trip to the side. They had pushed him around for a while, throwing insults at him. Eventually one of the pushes was too strong, and Sean had fallen to the ground, his hands scratching against the dirty pavement. He had tried to stand, and one of the boys had stepped a foot onto his back to keep him down, whilst another had grabbed his bag from him and zipped it open.

'No!' Sean had exclaimed, realising his mistake the moment the sound escaped his mouth.

The boy who was holding the bag had looked up, a triumphant smile on his face as he realised he was about to come across something of value. He had turned the backpack around, spilling its contents on the filthy pavement. The carefully wrapped book had shone like gold amongst Sean's other gloomy possessions. The boy had bent over to pick it up and Sean had turned very still, knowing that any sudden movements may cause irreversible damage to Machiavelli's masterpiece. He had watched as the older boy unwrapped the parcel and extracted the book. Disappointment spread across the boy's face like wild fire across a dry field. He turned the book around, like he was missing a trick. He flicked through the pages, turned the book upside down and, holding it by each side of the cover, shook it vigorously. Sean knew he had expected it would conceal money. When nothing happened, the boy looked at his two acolytes, baffled, then turned the book again to check the cover.

'The Prince…' He had read out loud.

Slowly, malevolently, a wicked grin had stretched over his face as he raised his eyes to look at Sean.

'Check this out, guys, the little freak likes fairy tales!'

'What a loser!' One of the other two kicked Sean in the ribs.

'What are you, a little girl?' Added the third, kicking him in the thigh.

Sean had been powerless. He had known there was nothing to be done other than to let them have their fun and hope with all his might that they would leave the book alone. But the first boy had seemed displeased at their victim's lack of participation in the scene.

'Where's your cash?'

Sean shook his head.

'Hey! Freak!' He called out, still holding the book, 'we're talking to you. That's a bit rude of you not to respond.'

When his tease was met with more silence, the boy suddenly jumped forward and kicked Sean hard in the stomach. Sean doubled over in pain, certain he could feel his lungs shrink as air was expelled out of him.

'Once upon a time,' the first boy started reciting in a high pitched voice, 'there was a little freak, who liked fairy tales…'

Sean gasped for air. The boy fished for something inside his pocket.

'He knew that there was a price to pay to be a little freak. But he had left his wallet home…'

When Sean finally opened his eyes and looked up, what he saw made his blood freeze. The boy had taken out a lighter. The feeble flame was shining in the night, sending shadows dancing across the boy's face.

'Where's your cash?' He asked again, menacingly, edging the flame dangerously close to the book.

'I don't have any!' Sean protested, trying to get to his feet.

The other boys kept him pinned dow to the ground with their feet. The boy holding the lighter held the flame a little closer to the corner of the book.

'Are you sure?'

'I don't have any! Please! Don't!' Sean heard himself protest, panic now rising from his guts.

But it had been in vain. If the boy had missed the financial value of the book, he had understood how much its owner was attached to it, and that was good enough. He had nodded to his accomplices who pressed Sean more firmly down onto the pavement, and brought the flame to the book. Sean kicked and punched the air, trying to free himself from the grasp of his captors. But they were too strong, and he could only watch in despair as *The Prince* was consumed by the flames. It happened slowly at first, and then the fire caught so suddenly the boy had to drop it to the ground. They all watched as it was reduced to ashes. Sean could still remember the mean sneers on the boys' faces. He could still smell the warm scent of burning paper and dust. He could still feel the unbearable feeling of despair vividly, as the tragedy he could not prevent plunged him into maddening sadness.

After a few minutes, the book was no more than a little pile of blackened powder. The boys kicked Sean some more for good measure, but he barely felt the blows. His entire body and mind had gone numb. He stayed lying on the cold hard pavement long after they had gone, his eyes fixed on what little remained of what had been, for a few minutes only, his most valuable possession. Months of focused discipline, of irrecuperable hard work, burnt to ashes.

Something very deep inside him had broken that day, shattered under the weight of the unfairness of it all. He could not say how long he stayed there, motionless. He lost track of time. When he eventually stumbled back his feet, his resolve was of iron. If this was the way the world worked, then he had no interest in playing by everyone else's rules. He would rise above them, create rules of his own and build a world in which he was king, one where no one could ever cross him and live to tell the tale.

CHAPTER 29

SEAN CRAVANAUGH

Although surprised at first by Terrence Blake's reaction, Sean had come to see that the convict simply was one of these self-righteous individuals who felt they had to pay full price for mistakes they might have only partially been responsible for. He knew there was more to the man's supposed crime than met the eye but since he had refused to cooperate, Sean saw no other option than to find out the truth in another way.

The day after his meeting with the contestant, he sent an anonymous tip to a well-known blogger in the capital. Medina Salim was the founder of the 'What Really Happened' blog, and specialised in bringing to light the hidden and often ugly truth behind well-publicised affairs.

The girl, who was in her early twenties, prided herself on being the voice of the people, giving them the truth, and nothing but the truth. In such difficult times, when people needed a role model, she was a breath of fresh air for her fellow citizens. She presented herself as a fighter for what was right, for those whose voices were too repressed to be heard.

Sean had used her several times to advance his own agenda. Because she always investigated the tips she received, she was Sean's surest way of leaking out information no one would have ever taken as genuine had it come from him. Medina Salim was, after all, one of the people. One of 'them'.

The tip Sean sent in this time was simple. It was a plain brown envelope containing a printed note: 'Terrence Blake is innocent.' He knew Medina Salim would bite. The blogger had been rather vocal in her criticism of the show, calling it inhumane and evil, and he knew she would never pass on a chance to build a case against it.

As much as he disliked most people, Sean did find their predictability somewhat reassuring. No matter what happened, he could always rely on people's ability to behave exactly as he expected them to. At the root of every human action was a primal inner desire to dominate others, be it with excess wealth, resources or outstanding sexual prowess. Anyone pretending otherwise was fooling themselves. Knowing this was like holding the key to the human brain. It made everyone so much easier to read. Find out what people want, Sean had discovered, what they truly, deeply long for, and you can make them do your bidding. Either by dangling that very thing in front of their eyes, or by threatening to take it all away forever. Greed and fear were his most powerful allies, and over the years they had never let him down.

What young Medina Salim really wanted, Sean was convinced, was a chance to prove herself. As much as she might want to deny it, her entire blogging enterprise was entirely ego-led. Whatever had happened in her life to create that need, she wanted the whole world to see her worth. And that very craving was what made her such a perfect target for Sean to convey to the nation whatever news he wanted.

Terrence Blake was a trickier one to read, but Sean appreciated the challenge. When everyone around him seemed to be built only on one layer, Terrence Blake's mind and perspective on the world had been on point, quite unexpectedly so. Rather than decay with imprisonment, his reasoning sounded like it had sharpened with time, as though confinement had given him a chance to look at the world and humankind from afar. Sean had expected Terrence Blake to want his freedom back, to agree to anything. After all, was it not what all convicts wished for? But Terrence Blake had held his ground. He had refused to admit what Sean knew to be the truth. He had proclaimed his guilt. He had refused freedom when it was handed out to him on a silver platter. Sean had been momentarily stunned to see his endeavour countered so unexpectedly.

Later on, when he sat at his desk pondering the situation, replaying their conversation in his head, the answer came to him as clear as day. Whatever part Terrence Blake had played in the whole affair, he felt responsible for it to such an extent that he had sacrificed everything. To Sean, this had been a surprise, as he had rarely met a truly righteous individual, one of those who abided by the rules of a fair universe, regardless of the fact that they were the only ones doing so. His own self-preservation instincts prevented him from ever seeing the value of doing something that would get himself in trouble, whether or not it was the right thing to do. He looked at a situation and saw only the way out.

He recalled once sitting in a front row seat at a sought-after, sold-out show in one of the capital's oldest theatres. As the audience came to take their seats and the theatre filled with the buzzing chatter of people settling in, he remembered looking up at the richly decorated high ceiling and thinking that if anyone were to plan an attack on this place, that moment would have been the ideal time to do it. One could go up to the highest levels of the theatre, lock the main doors and gas the whole audience. If one were wearing a gas mask then one could easily watch the debacle and panic happening below, before exiting through the staff doors on the higher grounds. Then, from that vantage point one would also be best placed for a mass shooting, targeting the people sitting below. Sean had caught himself playing both scenarios in his head and making a note of his exit strategy in the unlikely event in which either, or both, took place. He had been pulled out of his reverie by his companion for that evening, a young model he had been casually sleeping with. He enjoyed the fact that his fame made him irresistible to gorgeous women. He did not care much for their company, or for the favours they tried, and failed, to extract out of him in exchange for their affection, but he liked indulging himself from time to time, just because he could.

'What are you thinking?' She had asked him.

'Nothing,' Sean had lied, finishing his train of thought with the mental note that if the shooting scenario occurred, his date would make a most effective human shield.

CHAPTER 30

SEAN CRAVANAUGH

Sean's handiwork was such that, within a couple of days, the nation's eyes were on the mysterious convict who had sung such a beautiful song for his beloved daughter. Terrence Blake became a sign that something good may possibly come out of an unfortunate situation. With the country in disarray, its citizens needed someone to renew their long-lost faith in the future. Speculation kicked off, fuelled by Medina Salim's blog investigations.

Terrence Blake was kept in solitary confinement, away from the other convicts and from anyone he may want to claim his guilt to. Sean needed the masses onboard before the next live show. Once people were convinced the man was who they thought he was, it actually did not matter whether he was an angel or pure scum. Nothing could beat a good marketing campaign.

The nation was obsessed. Who was this man? Who was this heart-broken father? Medina Salim's hashtag #whatreallyhappened was soon joined by a myriad of other catch phrases. Social media was buzzing with #breakthelie, #freeterrence and #timeforjustice. By that point, very little information had been released on Terrence Blake. The man's past was a dust-covered mystery, and no one seemed to be able to shed light on the night's events. Doubt, however, was enough to make people see the situation in a different way.

On Wednesday morning, just four days after the singing task, Sean was reviewing the latest audience reports from the production team, when his assistant knocked on his office door.

'I have Medina Salim on line two asking to speak to you. Should I put her through?'

Sean nodded, a triumphant smile spreading over his face. He had wondered when the young blogger would contact him asking for an interview with Terrence Blake. He needed her to make the request.

'This is Sean Cravanaugh.'

He heard the young woman inhale sharply at the other end of the line.

'Mr Cravanaugh, this is Medina Salim, from 'What really happened'. I'd like to ask you a few questions, I...'

'Miss Salim,' Sean interrupted abruptly, 'I'm a very busy man, I don't have time for another one of your far-fetched conspiracy theories.'

He did not want to give in easily. Being accommodating was not in his character, nor was it in line with his reputation, and it would only have made her suspicious.

'This is not a conspiracy theory!' She exclaimed, offended, 'I want to talk about Terrence Blake, one of your so-called *contestants*,' she spat out the word with audible disgust.

'What about him?' Sean snapped.

'Don't you read the news?' Her voice was full of disdain, 'he's innocent!'

Sean snorted loudly.

'Miss Salim. Convict number seventy-seven is *not* an innocent man. He's been incarcerated for fifteen years. Surely even you can see that if he had not murdered his wife in cold blood, he would have been set free a long time ago.'

He knew his referring to the man as a number would infuriate her.

'How blind do you have to be to say something like this! Our justice system has been flawed for decades now, and you're ready to torture an innocent man without even looking into what happened?'

Bingo. Now onto another little trap, Sean thought.

'Oh, don't you worry, Miss Salim, I spoke to the criminal myself, and he eventually confessed his guilt,' his voice was cajoling.

There was a short pause on the line. Sean said nothing, wondering if she would take the bait.

'*Eventually...*' She repeated in a hushed voice, 'what means did you use to get him to *eventually* confess?'

'I'm sure you understand I'm not at leisure to discuss this with you, Miss Salim.'

She was quiet for a moment. He gave her a few seconds to let her imagination kick in.

'Ok,' he said, finally breaking the silence, 'if we're done here...'

'No!' She called out, and he could hear a tinge of desperation in her voice, 'wait.'

He waited.

'Let me speak to him,' she pleaded.

Sean said nothing.

'If you are right and this man is guilty, then my investigation will only confirm that,' she argued, 'but if he is innocent then he deserves to have his voice heard.'

'And if he *is* innocent,' Sean retorted, 'which I highly doubt, this will discredit the entire competition! Not to mention our judicial procedures.'

'Don't you care about human lives? Would you rather condemn an innocent man rather than find out the truth and save his life!'

She sounded outraged now and Sean knew he had her by the proverbial balls.

'Fine,' he conceded finally, 'you may come to talk to the man but I can assure you he is guilty as charged. When he confesses this to you, as he did to us, I expect a full apology live on your website for the unfounded insinuations you made today. Do we have a deal?'

'We do, and I look forward to proving you wrong.'

'I feel sorry for you, Miss Salim, I really do. You're still young, there is so much you need to learn about the world. I hope you don't get too hurt when you realise it's a much darker place than you thought it was.'

He knew his condescending remark would hit a chord and he smiled when he heard her hang up abruptly. Now all he had to do was sit back and watch the situation unfold.

CHAPTER 31

MEDINA SALIM

Medina slammed the phone down. She had needed to interact with the media magnate before, on other cases she had investigated, and every time it awoke in her violent instincts she never suspected she had. That man was simply too self-important for his own good. There was a sense of entitlement about him. He always made sly comments about her, as if he knew some deep secret about her even she was not privy to. It infuriated her, probably because she felt on some level she did not truly know herself. She wondered if he had sensed that about her somehow and if he made a game of angering her about it. Maybe it was payback for her sticking her nose where he thought she did not belong.

During one of their encounters, Sean Cravanaugh had asked her if she had ever wondered why she even cared so much for what she called 'truth', adding that no one leading a happy, healthy life would ever care so much about random strangers. She was investigating a political scandal at the time, and though she never doubted the validity of the work she was doing, his comment did bring to the surface a line of questioning she had worked hard to bury deep inside her.

The search for truth was something she had felt an instant attraction to from a very young age. She had early memories of being read a bedtime story by Miranda, something about an ugly duckling and a bunch of arrogant bullying ducks. She was unsure whether she actually remembered the dialogue that followed with Miranda, or whether it had been retold to her so many times that she had built the recollection in her mind. Who is the ugly duckling? She had asked. Where does he come from? Why do people call him ugly? Is it just because he is different? Where is his family? Medina had read the book again, searching for clues, even visiting the school library the next day to loan all the versions of that story she could find. She had compared them carefully, making notes on variations between them. She had been amazed at the details certain versions focused on, which others completely omitted. When she had filled a notebook with her findings, Clive had jumped in and bought her a whiteboard, which she had soon covered with scribbles, questions and book cuttings. Eventually, after weeks of research, Medina had painted a rough story for the ugly duckling. She had given him a past. More than anything, she felt she had given him justice, and a brighter future. A place where he was no longer judged for being different or called ugly. A place where his origins were defined and gave him the strength to carry on with his life. Deep down she felt she had helped him.

She was only nine years old at the time.

The reality of the matter, Medina knew, was that her very first investigation had merely been a catalyst for pursuing questions that had haunted her for as long as she could remember. Miranda and Clive, as kind and well-intentioned as they were, where not her biological parents. They were a a couple in their late forties, who had struggled to have a child of their own. And so they had adopted Medina, when her own parents had abandoned her. Despite the love and care her new family had given her, Medina had always known something was missing. Her history, her origins, her mystery start in life had carved a sizeable whole in her identity. Miranda and Clive had received no information about her parents when they took her in and, maybe for fear of having their adoptive daughter look for a connection with her former family, they had not insisted on the matter with the social services representative. Medina knew they hoped that providing for her and loving her would be enough. She could not blame their wishful thinking. Year after year, however, she had failed to get past her insecurities. She herself remembered nothing of her past life. It had not been for lack of trying to search the darkest corners of her memories. She had been too young for any of it to truly register.

On some level, she felt that her story had created a bond between her and every other broken individual on the planet. She had the sensation of being connected to anyone whose truth had been stolen from them and she had given herself the task of helping others where she could. Had she looked deep enough, she would have seen that none of it had anything to do with anyone other than herself. Had she faced her very own demons, she would have understood why Sean Cravanaugh's remarks touched her soul as much as they did. He knew nothing about her, and yet he seemed to understand her better than she understood herself.

Just a few days' worth of research on Terrence Blake's story had convinced her that he had been wrongly accused, and she threw herself into her investigation with more fervour than ever before. She was a little surprised to be granted an interview the following day, as she expected the show's production team would want to keep him under locks, rather than risk leaking the news of his innocence to a wider audience. Maybe Sean Cravanaugh had known she would not stop until she had spoken to the man and wanted to save himself the trouble of fending off her calls? She could not be sure. What she knew however was that she would have her chance, and she must prepare for it.

She grabbed her wallet from a messy pile of papers and newspaper cuttings and walked out of her little studio, locking the door securely behind her. When she emerged on the pavement, she buried her hands in her jacket pockets and set off at a brisk pace. It was unwise to linger. The world she lived in was one of danger and fear. It was a place where children were taught defensive measures and curfews at school. An atmosphere where criminality pervaded the air that surrounded all of them. Her adoptive parents often spoke of the old times. A faraway life, over a decade ago, when streets were still safe and the country had not reached the point of no return it currently faced. Miranda had owned a little handmade jewellery shop and Clive had been working a high-level job in a global corporation.

And then everything had changed. It had crept up on all of them, slowly and silently like a deadly beast. By the time it was upon them, it had been too late for anyone to do anything about it and those who could not afford to flee had accustomed themselves to the new paradigm and attempted to get on with what life threw at them, until fear and suspicion was so deeply ingrained in their minds it became second nature. She could understand why anyone who had a choice had left country. No one in their right mind could possibly want to sacrifice their progeny's carefree innocence in this way.

Miranda's shop eventually went out of business. Clive held on to his corporate job for as long as he could, but within a year or two the company had shut down their activities across the nation and relocated. Unable to get the right paperwork to follow them abroad, Clive and Miranda had accepted their bitter fate. Clive found a job with the national transportation agency, working as a clerk selling train tickets in a station across the city. Miranda accepted a part-time job restocking shelves in a local supermarket. It had been a difficult transition, but they had ploughed on, placing all of their hopes and dreams on the child they were so desperately trying for. When that did not happen, they opted for adoption. They had to wait several years before being selected to give a little girl a home. The child, they were told, had been left, shivering and confused, on the doorstep of the agency building. The adoption agency had little details on her provenance, or even her exact age, and they had warned the couple that although the girl seemed to have no recollection of her former life, she may develop unexpected signs of trauma at a later stage.

For Miranda and Clive, Medina had been a benediction. She became their saving grace, the reason for going on living a life that had been stripped of so many of its former joys. Medina's existence had turned around, and the more time she spent in her new normal, the further away from her previous, mysterious life she shifted. She knew she was not the only one in that situation, that many children were adopted every day. She hated that it made her case so common. She wanted to feel unique. She wanted to have something about herself that was special. She wanted for whoever had abandoned her to know how unlike everyone else she was and how wrong they had been in rejecting her. But, most of all, she hated herself for even caring.

Miranda and Clive had been generous with her, and they did their best to support her. They had found a local support group for adoptive parents and adopted children, and had granted Medina a safe platform to have any dialogue she needed. She knew they meant well. Little did they realise that finding herself amongst this crowd of unwanted progeny was the harshest of tortures. It acted as a reminder that she had been rejected. It did not matter how good a child she could have been, how all she ever desired more than everything else was to love and be loved. If she had not been good enough for those who had brought her into this world, those who should have inherently, unconditionally loved her, how worthless must her existence be?

At times she tried to convince herself that it was not so, that her biological parents must have had some valid reason for casting her aside. She imagined an adventurous life for them, one in which they had needed to give her up to protect her, until it was safe for them to come back for her. And, sometimes, on rare occasions, she could almost believe it herself.

But meeting with these other adopted children, all as broken and incomplete as she was, all victims of life's unfortunate circumstances, reinforced her deepest, darkest fears that nothing in her story was as special as she wished it to be.

Medina strode up a narrow alley, rapidly turning a corner onto the busy high street. She walked fast, her entire body tense with heightened awareness. The pavement was littered with rubbish and a murky layer of dust. Dirt seemed to cover everything. Almost everyone she passed walked with their heads low. Those who looked confident of their own safety were exactly the ones to avoid. As she often did when she found herself outdoors, she wondered what it might have felt like to stroll down this same street, free from the fear that dangers lurked behind ever step. She could not even imagine it.

When her destination came in sight, she quickened her step. *Francisco's* was a small Mediterranean takeaway where she ate lunch almost everyday. The namesake owner, Francisco, was her god-father. He had been a close friend of Miranda and Clive's for many years and had seen her grow up. The small shop was one of the only places where she felt remotely out of harm's way.

The door bell jingled as she stepped in. It was close to lunchtime, and Pedro, Francisco's son, was serving a long line of customers at the counter. He winked at her and she nodded back, before taking a seat at one of the old formica tables in the far end of the room. It was only when she stopped, when she took a moment to pause, that she realised how short her breathing was. Her entire body was tense. It always took her several minutes to release some of the tension, knowing full well that complete relaxation was way beyond her reach, so second nature had this state of apprehension become.

She watched the customers queuing up by the counter, glancing at the sandwiches, hot plates and salads on offer, scratching their heads. She loved observing people. She loved seeing their unconscious gestures. She always tasked herself with decoding their body language, second-guessing who they were and where they came from. Having her mind occupied in such a way prevented her thoughts from wandering too much. It gave her a point of focus to gather her attention on, and helped her clear her head.

Before she knew it, Pedro was making his way towards her, carrying an appetising plate of hot lasagne. She felt her stomach grumble with pleasure in anticipation.

'Freshly made,' Pedro announced, 'and entirely Medina-friendly,' he added with a smile before she could comment.

She thanked him. She knew the trouble he and his father went through to cater for her long-standing vegetarian diet. Pedro stepped away as another wave of customers entered the shop, and Medina tucked into her food.

She ate quickly, as she always did. Being on the cusp of unravelling a mystery meant never having time for anything else than her research. Since she had started her blog, a few years previously, she had made space in her life for little else. Potential friends and romantic interests had come and gone. Most people never had the patience to break through the walls she had built around herself.

She had always wanted to study journalism, but as hard as they had tried, Miranda and Clive's savings had never been sufficient to allow it. Medina had been unfazed at the realisation that higher education was not on the cards for her. With time she had got better at parking her emotions. She had made her own way, driven by a deep, inner call to action to fight the odds. She had started working at the age of sixteen, against her parents' wishes, taking on any small job she could get. Seeing her determination, they had let her be.

Now, at just twenty years old, she had gone through an almost constant stream of menial jobs, working in cafes and shops, post offices and delivery companies, even once landing an evening cleaning job at a television news channel. She had watched as the set was prepared and the presenter covered in layer after layer of foundation. The thrill of it, even from a distance, was palpable. That was the night the blog was born. Maybe she could not take a conventional path, but she *was* going to build her own future, one way or another.

She gathered her empty plate and her cutlery and brought it around the counter into the tiny, brightly lit kitchen, placing it mechanically into the dishwasher, as she had done hundreds of times before.

'Off again?' Pedro called from the shop floor, which had cleared from customers.

'Yep,' she answered distractedly, her fingers scavenging inside her jacket pockets for some change.

When she finally gathered enough for her food and went to hand it to Pedro, he took a step back, his hands high up in the air.

'No, no, no,' he protested. '*Ni lo intentes.*'

Don't even try.

'You know the drill. My dad would kill me if he knew I'd let you pay.'

'Come on!' She insisted, taking a couple of steps towards him, 'you never let me pay! I don't want to be the one sinking your business. I won't tell Francisco, I swear!'

'Ha!' He exclaimed, and with a cheeky grin he added, 'if anything is going to sink the family business, it sure as hell won't be your one plate of rabbit food a day!'

She edged closer to him, smiling innocently. Pedro eyed her suspiciously. When she hopped forward, reaching for his right hand, she knew he had seen her coming. As she reached for his hand, he moved aside, chuckling. She grabbed his arm and tried unsuccessfully to open his clenched fist to give him her change. It was a game they had played many times, and which she always lost. Before she knew it, Pedro was around her, laughing out loud now, holding her arms behind her back. She knew the only way out was to surrender.

'Okay, okay,' she admitted, catching her breath, 'you win. Again.'

He did not move.

'*Segura?*' He whispered in her ear.

Are you sure?

His face was so close to hers she could feel the warmth of his breath against her cheek, and the sensation made her skin prickle.

'Yes!' She exclaimed, 'I swear! Let me go!'

She tried to wriggle herself out again, but his hold on her was too strong.

'Because, you see, this is exactly what you said last time, and the moment I released you, you stabbed me in the back.'

'I put the money in your pocket and ran,' she rolled her eyes, 'I would hardly call that stabbing you in the back.'

'Did you just roll your eyes at me, *señorita?*' He purred in her ear.

She felt herself stiffen unconsciously.

'No...' She breathed slowly, but she knew her voice betrayed the truth.

'Ah, then I guess you know the punishment, young lady!' He burst out with a grin, tickling her frantically as she squirmed in his arms, breaking into a nervous giggle.

'Time out!' She screamed between barely controlled outbursts of hysteria. 'Time out! You win!'

He released her. They each took a step away, panting, the same broad smile painted on both of their faces. She shook her head slowly.

'I can't believe that after all these years you're still holding that against me!' She exclaimed in mock indignation. 'Tickling is cheating!'

'*En el amor y en la guerra, todo se vale,*' Pedro chuckled unapologetically.

All is fair in love and war.

She stuck her tongue out at him, and popped the money back into her pocket.

She and Pedro had grown up together and there was little they did not know about each other. When Miranda and Clive had brought Medina home for the first time, she had been completely disorientated and had retreated into herself. Her mind had shut out where she was coming from and she did not know where she had arrived. Nothing around her or inside her felt even remotely familiar. It was like she had been catapulted all of a sudden into existence. Miranda and Clive, despite their good intentions, struggled to get through to her. Francisco and his young son, Pedro, visited often. Maybe Miranda and Clive had felt Medina could do with the company of other children. Pedro was a few years older than her, and from the moment they met, he seemed to take it upon himself to protect her. He had always been blessed with a bright, lively nature, but it was his quiet patience which had broken down young Medina's defences.

Every time he and Francisco visited, which had been almost every day, Pedro would bring something for her, a small token of friendship. Medina would be sitting in a corner somewhere, her little arms hugging her body. Pedro would come and sit next to her in silence. He would place his little gift on the floor between them, sometimes a pretty stone, or a book, or one of these little wooden figurines he collected and hand-painted, and they simply sat with each other. At first she had not even reached for the items, she had looked at them from a distance, too scared to make a move. For a long time they never exchanged as much as a glance. When he left, she would take the gift and store it with the others in a box under her bed.

And then, day after day, she had found herself looking forward to his visits. She became more relaxed around him until she realised she liked this strange boy who came to see her and sat with her for hours on end without ever uttering a word. She had wanted to know more about him, to talk to him. And so he was the one who, one fine day, had heard her speak for the very first time. For a second he looked ecstatic at hearing the sound of her voice, but he immediately controlled his enthusiasm and responded to her as if they had been conversing regularly. She had felt grateful to him for not making a big deal out of it.

He had got through to her, as one tames a terrified wild animal. When everyone around her was doing their best to talk to her, to organise activities for her, to engage with her, Pedro had known what she needed most. Without knowing a thing about her, he had *known*.

They had been inseparable ever since.

Over time, and as Pedro stepped into adolescence a few years before she did, she had suspected that their friendship had taken a turn in his mind which she had not quite been ready for. She could see the unique kindness with which he smiled at her and that twinkle of expectation in his eye. Deep down, buried under a mountain of her own denial, she knew he loved her more than he would a friend, in a way she was not ready to reciprocate. She felt that he had been waiting for her to catch up with him ever since.

As he grew into a handsome young man, he started attracting generous amounts of female attention. He always feigned ignoring it, or at least he did so when Medina was around. He pretended that he could not see how attractive he was becoming or how the delicate accent that tainted his every word affected the opposite sex. He behaved as if he did not know that the fitness regime he enjoyed so much was changing his body, making it deliciously toned and firm. He acted like none of it was even worth noticing, because all that mattered was the two of them. Their friendship. Their bond. And his everlasting desire to please her in any way he could.

Being the way that he was, he never pushed her, but his quiet understanding made her feel oddly more pressured. That one day or the other, she would *have* to be ready. What if she never was? What if she could never mend herself in the way she needed to be mended in order to be there for him? She knew she could not make him wait forever, and the idea of losing him completely because she took too long to heal her broken soul, or because she could never make herself whole again, made her sick to her stomach.

'*Qué paso?*'

What happened?

Pedro's voice resonated in the distance, and drew her back to the present moment. Medina extracted herself from her thoughts to find his worried face straight in front of hers, his hands resting on her shoulders.

'Medina, are you alright?' He asked, concern pouring out of his every word.

She nodded slowly, blinking hard as she felt the tears starting to swell behind her eyes.

'I'm fine,' she looked down, walking away. 'I've got to go.'

'Medina, *cariño*...'

'Thanks for the lasagna,' she interrupted, running towards the door. 'Say hi to Francisco for me.'

She barely had time to finish her sentence before the door shut behind her. She broke into a sprint, heavy tears now rolling down her face.

CHAPTER 32

MEDINA SALIM

By the time she reached her apartment, Medina was completely out of breath. She hurriedly locked the door behind her and collapsed on the floor, half sobbing and half gasping for air.

It took her several minutes to calm herself down. She rose to her feet, undressed and dropped all of her clothes onto a nearby chair, which was already heavily littered with discarded items of clothing. She marched into the shower and spent considerable time under the piping hot jet of water, waiting for it to work its magic, washing away her panic. For some reason, water had always been a sort of refuge for her, it had a purifying effect which little else did. It was her hiding place. In fact, the only exercise she had ever taken to was swimming. The feeling of being underwater, that sensation of the outside world fading away entirely, of diving into a universe where sound and motion slowed down healed her busy mind. Sometimes, when the shower just would not do, she would go to the nearest swimming pool and immerse herself entirely, staying under the surface for as long as her lungs would allow, over and over again. She would look at the limbs of other swimmers pedalling up and down the lanes without a sound and the calmness of it all would permeate her anxious heart. She had even made a habit of taking her swimming kit, a sporty black one-piece suit, swimming cap and goggles, everywhere with her in her backpack. She had realised very quickly that she could never predict when she might need some time out, and carrying her gear around gave her the option to retreat at any time.

The moment the hot water ran out was her cue to step out of the shower cubicle. Dried and dressed, she walked up to her desk and sat in her chair, skimming through her notes on her laptop. Turning towards the wall, she reviewed the large brown cork board which was now full to the brim with newspaper cuttings, handwritten notes and pictures. Pieces of different coloured string linked certain items to each other, making the entire thing look like a multicoloured spider web. Bit by bit, she had built the picture of Terrence Blake, though his past had turned out to be much blurrier than she had anticipated. She knew little of him, beyond the sordid image that had been painted of his story on that horrible show.

As she surveyed the board, her gaze travelled over the rest of the studio. It was a small room, with a single bed in one corner and a tiny kitchenette stuck between the entrance and the door to an even tinier bathroom. Her desk and research area, as she called it, occupied the majority of the space. An entire wall was devoted to whichever case she was working on at that time. What predominated more than anything, however, was the indescribable mess that reigned over the entire space. Piles of clothes were everywhere, books were stacked on shelves in no particular order. Paper in every form was king and laid scattered in every nook and cranny of the studio. The bin was full of empty take-away boxes. The chaos of it all was like a refuge to her, drowning the even bigger chaos of her own identity.

Miranda and Clive had been strongly opposed to her getting her own place at first, just as they were reluctant to consider any of her most daring suggestions. The day she turned eighteen, she had packed her bags and moved to the first studio she could find within her means, and located within minutes of *Francisco's*, where Pedro and his father lived above the shop. Miranda and Clive had come home from work to find her room empty and a note inviting them over to dinner at her new place the following day. It had been a period of great tension between them, not least because they both feared for her safety. These were not times for young women to be on their own. Medina's saving grace had been Pedro, coming to her rescue once again, vouching for her and promising to keep a watchful eye over her. He dropped in on her almost every day after closing down the shop, on the way back from his run around the neighbourhood.

Medina reviewed her notes on the Blake case. She had managed to find some of the press archives with what had come out in the newspapers at the time, but the more she looked, the more she realised how badly the affair had been documented. The man had appeared so obviously guilty that no one had wasted much ink writing about his story. In one of the press cuttings she had found a mention of the street where the Blake family had lived. Serenade Row. The article also included a quote by 'an anonymous source' that although Delilah Blake's death had come as little surprise, Terrence Blake's part in it had been a shock. The journalist had failed to look into the insinuations behind the source's words. To Medina, it seemed blatant that something had been going on, and she cursed under her breath at such a bad investigating job.

The article did not mention the source's name, but Medina was determined to get to the bottom of it regardless. A visit to Serenade Row was in order, and she made a plan to go there straight from her interview with Terrence Blake the following morning. With less than three days to go before the next sordid episode of the competition, she had no time to waste.

She started on her list of questions, pondering the value of each one as the list expanded, so that she could make the most of her short sixty minutes with the man. When she finished her list, she glanced at her watch and realised with surprise how late it was, only noticing then that the studio was plunged in semi-darkness, the setting sun forming distorted shadows on the walls. She was just wondering what she should do about dinner, or whether she should skip it altogether, when the doorbell rang, resonating across the still air of the room.

'*Soy yo,*' Pedro's voice cracked through the intercom.

It's me.

She could not help a grin, because she was ready to bet he had come bearing a delicious-smelling dinner bag. She buzzed him in, unlocked her front door and waited for him on the doorstep. She closed her eyes. She could have recognised the light but determined sound of his foot steps as he came up the carpeted stairs amongst a million.

'Hey,' he smiled at her as he reached the final steps.

Her eyes opened and fell on Pedro. He was wearing his running gear. Baggy shorts and a short sleeve tee-shirt that accentuated his toned shoulders. He was carrying a brown takeaway paper bag which looked very much like her favourite brand of Japanese takeaway.

'Hey,' she grinned back, and the tenderness in her own voice surprised her.

Pedro must have also noticed the sudden softness of her tone, because he paused for a second, uncertain, one foot floating mid-air over the very last step. He cocked his head to one side, inquisitively.

'You're in a better mood,' he lifted an eyebrow, as she moved aside to let him in and locked the door behind them.

She frowned a little, because by then she had forgotten about their encounter earlier in the day. She recalled how they had parted, or, to be correct, how she had flipped out and run out on him. She felt her cheeks heat up with shame.

'Oh… Yeah, I'm fine,' she said, eager to dismiss the topic. 'What's for dinner?'

His eyes lingered on her face for a moment, clearly deciding whether or not to push the subject. He handed the brown paper back to her and sat on the edge of her bed.

'You know *exactly* what is for dinner,' he answered, laughing at her excitement as she unpacked the takeaway onto the small coffee table.

She was skipping on the spot as box after box of food came out of the bag, and her delight brought a sparkle of joy to Pedro's eyes. When she looked up from the feast laid on the table she met his gaze and the intensity of his affection sent a shudder through her entire body. She diverted her eyes quickly, making her way towards the kitchen area to take out plates and cutlery. When she turned back towards him he was standing in front of her spider web wall, observing the connections she had made.

'You're investigating this Blake guy, right?' He asked, his back to her, his head moving as he went from one piece of the puzzle to another.

She mumbled something indistinct, busy as she was already, sat cross legged on the floor by the coffee table, gulping down mouthful after mouthful of takeaway delight. Pedro sat opposite her.

'Have you made any progress?' He asked, grabbing a fork.

She nodded vigorously. 'I'm interviewing him tomorrow.'

Pedro's head jerked up and he froze, staring at her in disbelief.

'You're... *interviewing* him?' He enunciated slowly.

'Yep,' she kept her voice casual.

She knew full well where the conversation was heading. They had variations of this same discussion every time she took on a new case. Pedro opened his mouth, ready to add something, but she lifted a hand at him to stop him.

'Listen, Pedro. I know you're worried, but I can take care of myself. I'll be fine.'

He glared at her.

'I need this,' she added, in a more supplicating tone than she had intended, 'this is the key to the whole story!'

When her eyes met his, it was her turn to freeze. Pedro's look was one of such anger and agony that she did not know what to do with it. She could not bring herself to look away.

'Medina…' He said, his voice shaking a little.

'Listen…' She started, but he interrupted her before she could say another word.

'*Escúchame*,' he rose his palm at her to stop her, 'you know I have always supported you, and I know how much your blog means to you, but this is insane! Don't you see what they do to people in the name of their competition? Do you think they would hesitate one second in hurting you if they wanted to? Don't you realise how dangerous this is?'

'Pedro…' Medina started, but he was far from finished.

'No!' He exclaimed, banging his clenched fist on the coffee table, so hard that some of the takeaway fell over and spilt onto the floor. 'No, Medina! This is too much, I won't let you put yourself at risk like that! That's it, I won't allow it!'

They stared at each other and his words hung in the air between them.

'You won't *allow* it?' Medina said slowly, her eyes narrowed.

Understanding seemed to dawn on Pedro, and the emotion on his face changed as he realised his mistake.

'I didn't…' He struggled to find the words, 'you know what I mean.'

Medina looked at him intently, as though seeing him for the very first time. Her face was closed, her lips pressed in a thin line.

'I don't need your permission, Pedro,' she retorted. 'I don't need anyone's permission.'

'You know that's not what I meant.' He extended a hand towards her.

She brushed him away with a flick of her arm.

'Medina…' Pedro's voice was pleading now, but the desperation in his tone angered her even more.

'I think you should leave,' she said coldly.

'Come on, Medina, I'm sorry...'

'Leave!' She repeated, much louder this time.

She stood, her gaze on the floor, ignoring his attempts to meet her eyes. Pedro remained glued to the spot. None of their altercations to date there had ever resulted in her kicking him out of her sight. He stayed very still, as one would refrain from sudden movements when faced with a wild animal. The silence between them stretched and, for a moment, they were frozen in time, sizing each other up, one radiating with fury and the other with concern.

All of a sudden Medina grabbed one of the takeaway boxes and threw it at Pedro. The gesture was so aggressive and unexpected that he did not have time to react. The container crashed on his chest, its stir-fried contents spilling all over him. He stared at Medina, baffled. The noddles and vegetables dribbled from his tee-shirt and onto the floor in almost comical slow-motion, but he did nothing to clean up the mess.

After what felt like an eternity, Pedro slowly stood up and left the room without another word or glance in Medina's direction. When she heard the door slam behind him, Medina collapsed onto the floor and burst into tears.

CHAPTER 33

SHAUNA MULLIGHAN

'Hey, Shauna! Are you there?' The voice in Shauna's earpiece made her jump out of her reverie. She glanced around, realising she had been paying no attention to what the expert criminologist was saying.

'...fact that very little is known of Blake's past is fuelling a lot of speculation,' the criminologist, one of the two guests for the evening, explained.

Shauna nodded and smiled, wondering what to say next. She was saved by the second guest, a renowned psychologist, who jumped in the conversation.

'Mystery is generally great for collective imagination,' the woman said.

'In fact,' Shauna chimed in, glancing down at her notes in an effort to compose herself, 'many people have tried to dig up elements of Terrence Blake's story and failed.'

The two guests nodded in approval.

'The affair was so poorly investigated back in the day,' Shauna added, 'and the organisers of the show have denied anyone access to Terrence Blake.'

'Indeed,' the criminologist leant forward, 'and since keeping him quiet is helping to spark public interest, you can't blame them for wanting to keep their star contestant well hidden!'

Shauna flicked through her notes again, looking for a particular piece of information her own research had brought up.

'We've just heard fresh rumours today that the 'No Pain, No Game' production team have granted a single interview with Terrence Blake...' Shauna scoured over the pages quickly until she found what she was looking for. 'Medina Salim, the founder of an investigation blog called 'What Really Happened'...'

Shauna could not keep the bitterness out of her voice. She herself had tried her hardest to secure an interview with him and all of her requests had been rebuked unceremoniously. This did not sit well with her.

'Of course, LiveTV2 will bring you all the details of the interview, after it has taken place, so stay tuned for more information! Thank you both for joining us tonight and sharing your expertise,' Shauna nodded at her guests and straightened up on her chair, ready for the transition to her next segment. She turned to face a different camera. 'Coming up next on our programme today, Clearing High, a penitentiary establishment in the South of the country, closed its doors today, after over two decades in operation. Our special correspondent, James Carson, reports live. Over to you, James...'

CHAPTER 34

MEDINA SALIM

It took a long time for the tears to dry. Medina sat in the darkened studio, her knees hugged tightly into her chest. She could not chase the hurt look on Pedro's face from her mind. His handsome features, stricken with surprise and pain, had carved themselves into her head. She hated herself for lashing out at him. The worst part was that she did not even know what had caused her fury. She knew exactly what he had meant, and despite his poor choice of words, he only had her best interests at heart. She had seen him overcome his concern at many of her choices so that he could support her as best he could.

Slowly, she propped herself onto the bed. She slipped under the covers, not bothering to undress, and drifted into a deep heavy slumber. It felt like barely a handful of minutes had passed when she opened her eyes again, but a glance at her watch proved her wrong. Morning had come, creeping its way slowly into the room. Medina's head was as heavy as lead, her senses numb with fatigue. The memory of the fight with Pedro hit her with full force, as clearly as if she had been facing him right there and then. She swallowed hard. Looking at the time again, she decided that she could afford another ten minutes in bed. She pulled the covers over her head and curled up into a ball. She wished she could stay under the warm protective barrier of the duvet forever.

Thirty minutes later, when she could no longer postpone facing the world, she dragged herself sluggishly away from the comforts of her bed. She stayed under the shower until the hot water ran out, allowing the initial jets of cold water to slap her awake. Today was a big day. She forced her mind to focus on the task at hand, refusing to dwell any more on the painful reflux of the previous evening's argument with Pedro.

She got dressed quickly, gathered her things, grabbed her backpack and stepped towards the front door. She could not afford to waste any time if she wanted to make it to the Cradle for her allotted slot. Her indulgent snooze in bed had cost her the leeway she had allocated for delays of any sort, and she no longer had the luxury of being still for even another second. She set off at a brisk pace, surveying the streets around her as she walked. She reached the bus stop in the nick of time.

Medina stepped off the bus a couple of streets away from her destination and walked the remainder of her journey at a fast pace. The excitement of where she was headed made her almost run the final meters. When the entrance to the Cradle finally came in sight, she found herself holding her breath. It was not the main entrance of course, she had been told to come through one of the side doors, which was guarded by two bulky and blank-faced security agents.

Medina looked around, taking in her surroundings. The street was quiet. A little too quiet perhaps. In the distance, she could just about make out the sounds of everyday city life. A few cars were parked along the street, and with a sudden knot in her stomach, she thought for a moment that she had seen someone behind the wheel in one of them. She turned around to face the vehicle, but the driver's seat was empty. She frowned. She could swear she had seen a silhouette there. She shook her head, as much to try and chase the image away as to convince herself she had imagined it.

She walked up to the Cradle door, forcing herself to look much more confident than she felt. She was intimidated by the whole situation, and the closer she got, the taller and the more aggressive the guards looked. One of them nodded at her silently and she handed out her phone displaying the confirmation email she had been sent by Cravanaugh's assistant. One of the guards mumbled something into a walkie-talkie and a crackling confirmation immediately came back. Medina was led in through the door, flanked by a third man, this time wearing military green tracks and a heavy-looking machine gun. The man's face looked a little too neutral, like he was at the same time not watching her but still registering her every move. Medina thought that this was the type of person who could kill someone without flinching or ever thinking about it again after it had happened. The thought made her insides swirl with fear and, all of a sudden, the concrete windowless corridor he was guiding her through seemed to shrink around her.

It was at that moment that it dawned on her what she had walked into. It was not that she had not known before, but the entire concept of what had been created within these walls had only just fully sunk in. This was no game at all. Regardless of the amounts of glitter they spread across the stage, it remained as serious a situation as ever there could be. With a silent pang of pain, she thought that maybe Pedro's reaction had been justified after all, and she quivered with shame as she recalled how she had treated him.

The armed soldier led her through corridor after corridor, up a flight of stairs, down another, so that before she knew it it would have been impossible for her to find her way out. He stopped in front of an open door and stepped aside to let her in. Medina walked in uncertainly. The room was small, with no windows and no other escape than the door she had just walked through. Guards were standing in each of the four corners of the room, weapons in hand. A small table and two chairs had been set up in the centre of the room. A young woman in a tight-fitted dress and high heels sat half perched on the table, deeply absorbed in something on her smartphone. She looked up when she heard Medina walk in.

'Miss Salim?' She held out a perfect manicured hand towards her. 'Hi, I'm Nancy, Mr Cravanaugh's assistant. We exchanged a few emails.'

Medina shook the woman's hand.

'So,' Nancy continued, her manner quick and efficient, 'why don't you take a seat here, the contestant will be here in a minute. We'll have security throughout and I do have to remind you that the entire conversation will be recorded,' she added, pointing at a camera set on a tripod in one corner of the room, 'for *security* purposes.'

Nancy emphasised the word 'security' ominously and ushered her to a chair, instantly going back to her smartphone. Medina shifted in her seat, her gaze roaming around the small room, and she wished she had been allowed to take pictures. A photo could speak a thousand words, and she would have wanted the world to see what it felt like to be on the other side of the show's pristine exterior. She placed her phone on the table, along with her notebook and pen. She was very much aware of the four soldiers' presence around her and her chest tightened a little.

'There we go,' Nancy announced, looking up from her screen as the door flung open.

Two more guards stepped in, dragging a third man in with them. Medina stood up unconsciously as she took in Terrence Blake's emaciated appearance. She held her hand out to him, only to realise he was handcuffed, and his wrists were tied to the ankle shackles on his feet by a long metal chain, restricting the movements of his limbs. Medina dropped her hand and looked down, embarrassed. She had wanted to make a good first impression but she was starting to think the whole endeavour might prove trickier than she had thought. When she looked up again, she could not help but take a step back when she noticed Terrence Blake's expression as he stared at her. It was a look of utter disgust.

He *hates* me, was her first thought, though she was unsure how anyone could develop such an instant dislike to someone else. A second thought bubbled up in her head, popping at the surface of her mind with a burst of fear. What have they done to him?

'Well,' Medina heard Nancy's business-like voice, blurry and distant like she was talking to them from the top of a mountain, 'we'll leave you two to it.'

Medina looked at her slowly and nodded. She walked unsteadily back to her chair and sat down. Terrence Blake did not move, his face still constricted with such violent emotions that Medina felt truly threatened. She thought of Pedro, and suddenly she missed him so much she found herself praying she could be anywhere but in that dark and suffocating room with armed soldiers and a man who looked ready to strangle her on the spot.

CHAPTER 35

TERRENCE BLAKE

I t's a trick, Terrence thought as he stood facing the young woman sitting at the little table in front of him, it's just another trick.

He thought of all the games these people had been playing, of how easily they had toyed with human lives. He recalled his conversation with Sean Cravanaugh and anger rose inside him. The idea that his existence had become a trivial matter infuriated him. His memories, his previous life, his long-lost happy moments were the only things he had left and they were now trying to take these away from him too. He would not let that happen.

The girl at the table was looking at him, her gaze uncertain, a little scared almost. Good, Terrence thought bitterly, you can't just get away with being a part of this.

And just as the thought had appeared in his mind, another followed which brought pain to his heart. Whilst he knew they were trying to manipulate him, he had to concede they had struck a chord. The girl was the spitting image of his wife. He could almost make out Delilah's traits in her face, the softness of her jaw, the intensity of her eyes. Her hair was different, long and wavy whilst Delilah's had been short and curly but that was pretty much the only detail they had missed.

Terrence's heart sank, because though he knew the resemblance was a ploy, it did not make it any easier to swallow. And in that moment he hated everything. He hated the world and everyone in it. He hated that physical and psychological torture was considered acceptable. He hated that he was being punished for refusing to play dirty. He hated the people who were doing this to him. But most of all, he hated himself for caring and for falling into their trap. He had been called a murderer for a long time now and he had always denied that the word fit him in any way. Right there and then however, in this prison of lies, after enduring weeks of inexplicable ordeal, facing a girl who had been planted there just to hurt him, he was in so much pain he swore he could have killed someone with his bare hands.

The girl cleared her throat, and the noise made him jump.

'Mr Blake?' She asked, the shyness in her voice making her sound much younger than she probably was.

Terrence said nothing, refusing to engage.

'Mr Blake, my name is Medina Salim, I run a blog called 'What Really Happened' where I investigate the truth behind the cover-ups of our country's elite and the failures of our justice system.'

She had spoken the words quickly, like she had rehearsed them before, and wanted to get them right before she forgot what she was meant to say. She took a short breath in and paused for a second, looking at him expectantly. When he did not respond, she started speaking again, her voice uncertain. Inside Terrence's mind, a little voice was pleased that his attitude unsettled her. Whatever was to become of him he did not know, but he would not bend before them without putting up some resistance.

'I'm here because I've been looking into your case and I have a sense that what was portrayed on the show isn't the whole story.'

Terrence felt suddenly exhausted. He could not stand having to second guess everyone and everything, and he loathed having to figure out people's hidden and cruel agendas. He missed the relative simplicity of his life behind bars, where rules were straightforward and unspoken. People knew what to do and what not to do, what to say and what topics never to broach. In the early days of his incarceration he had often missed the outside world, missed the mundane tasks of day-to-day existence. Now that he could see what the outside world had become, he wished more than anything to run back to the safety of his cell. *That* was one thought he never guessed would ever cross his mind.

'Mr Blake...'

The girl's tentative plea reached him from afar. He sat down at the table, facing her.

'Is there anything you can tell me about what happened that night? I found this article...' She rummaged in the folder she carried with her, 'it says that someone who knew you didn't believe what the police said. I couldn't find that person's name anywhere but, look...'

She slid a printed newspaper article in front of him. Although he had not wanted to play along, he could not help the reflex which made him glance down. The title of the article hit him like a punch to the throat: 'school teacher convicted for murder and child abuse'. The margins were covered in handwritten notes and scribbles. The girl's finger rested on the side of a paragraph covered in yellow highlighter. The passage was a quote from a 'close friend of the family who asked to remain anonymous'. He read the lines. The words were tainted with shock, incredulity and denial. The tone used to speak of him, of his character, of his family, were kind. He knew exactly who the person was who must have uttered these words.

Mrs Allen, once upon a time their next door neighbour. She was an old lady, a caring and thoughtful person who had been Terrence's closest...

What? He thought. What had she been really? A friend? A mother to him and grandmother to Maddison? She had been there for him when he had no clue what he was doing. She would show up on a school night, a baked pasta dish in hand for him and freshly mashed purée for his daughter, rescuing him from an evening of failing to juggle all that life was throwing at him. He always wondered how she had known when he was most out of his depth and needed rescuing. He had never explained their situation, or how he had become a temporary single parent, and she had never asked.

After Delilah's return, Mrs Allen's visits had become sparse, until she was never around anymore. Terrence had come home from work one day to find his wife in a wretched state of anger, and whilst he could never get out of her what happened, he got the feeling that Delilah was not as welcoming of Mrs Allen's kind attentions as he had been. He had gone to apologise to his neighbour on Delilah's behalf and the old lady had simply nodded, her face a little sad. She had patted his arm and looked at him with concern.

'Take care of yourself, Terrence.'

Her words had carried so much emotion and so much meaning that Terrence felt a dreadful shiver run over him every time he thought about it. It was in that moment that he realised she had probably known everything all along, that somehow she had guessed. After his arrest, her parting words had haunted him, filling him with remorse at the thought that, had he seen things as clearly as she had, his life could have taken a different turn.

'Do you know who this might be?' Medina Salim was asking. 'Or can you tell me what really happened that evening?'

Terrence looked at her blankly, his mind still lingering on the memory.

'You can tell me,' Medina Salim insisted, 'I'm here to help you. I'm on *your* side.'

At her words Terrence snapped back to attention. *What* had she just said? *Help*? *His* side? The anger came pouring out of him.

'Help! Help?! I don't need your help! I didn't ask for your help! I didn't ask for any of this! I have nothing to say to you, so spare me your little tricks!' He was screaming now, unable to control his temper. 'If you want to go harass my neighbours to know who said what, suit yourself, but leave me out of it,' he banged his fist on the table, 'just leave me alone!'

The guards around the room had taken a step forward but something, or maybe someone watching the scene from afar and calling the shots, made them refrain from taking any action. The girl had jerked back into her chair. She clutched the edges of her seat, her mouth hanging open, her eyes wide with fear.

'I just…' She mumbled, 'I just wanted…' After a second or two her expression changed as her mind caught up with something he had said. 'Wait…' She frowned, leaning forward, grabbing her notebook and a pen, 'so you think the person who might have given that quote was one of your old neighbours? Do you know who it could be? Maybe they know something which could help us prove that…'

'Prove what?' He barked at her, unsure whether he was more annoyed at her for listening too closely to his words or at himself for letting something slip, 'there is nothing to prove, you hear me?'

As she started scribbling a note on a blank page he jumped to his feet and slammed both his hands on the table. He stared into her eyes, summoning the darkest and scariest expression he could muster.

'I killed my wife,' he growled. 'I. Killed. My. Wife.' He waited a moment for his words to register on her face. 'I killed her. It was all *my* fault. Do you understand?' His voice was icy now, a threatening rumble that made the girl tremble. 'Do. You. Understand?' He repeated, insisting on each word.

She nodded, her body cowering away from him. Terrence stared at her, and once again he marvelled at the resemblance. He suspected whoever had planned this knew it would unsettle him, get him to lose his countenance and blurt something he should not have. In that regard, he thought bitterly, they had succeeded. He sat back down in his chair, elbows perched on the table, his head resting in his hands, his body slumped and tired, hoping beyond hope that someone would come and take him away.

'But...' Medina Salim's timid voice broke the silence and, peaking at her through his fingers, he willed her to stop talking. 'What do you mean it was 'your fault'?'

Terrence's jaw tightened against his palms.

'Was it...' she murmured, 'was it an *accident*?'

Terrence was glued to his chair for what seemed like an eternity. They were good, he thought, he had to give them that. But whatever game they had woven him into, he was not interested in playing. He had had enough. He did not want to be there anymore, in this tiny, stuffy room.

He was not sure where the inspiration came from but before he had a chance to think about it properly, his body had sprung into action. He jumped to his feet again and screamed. He screamed all of the air and all of the frustration he had in him. He screamed the pain and sorrow he had kept bottled up for too long, and which was threatening to engulf him. He screamed with delirium until the scream consumed him entirely. He screamed and he banged his fists on the table and sent his chair flying to one corner of the room and he made to throw himself at the girl. He gave the best performance of madness he could muster, and it felt so freeing, so real, that for a split second he wondered how much of it he was really faking, and whether he had not just gone truly mad.

The familiar sting erupted from his ankle, paralysing his body and sending him crashing down, face first onto the floor. Something warm and sticky trickled over his nose and lips and he knew he was bleeding. One guard ushered the girl through the door. She looked so scared that for the shortest of moments he felt a little guilty. He did not get any time to indulge in his own inner turmoil however. The other three guards were on him within seconds, grabbing him by the arms and dragging him back toward his cell.

CHAPTER 36

SEAN CRAVANAUGH

Sitting in the warmth of his office, Sean pressed a button on the remote control and the large screen in front of him went dark. He had been watching the live interaction between Medina Salim and Terrence Blake with great interest and he praised himself for leading them both right where he wanted them. Sean thought of Terrence Blake's outburst. He had to admire such a remarkable performance.

He walked to the drinks cabinet and poured himself a glass of scotch. He swirled the liquid around in its tumbler absentmindedly, making his way to the large window overseeing the arena.

He wondered if Medina Salim had got it right, and the wife's death truly had been an accident. If that were the case then it would be a profitable twist. He thought about Terrence Blake's reaction and he knew that whether or not the blogger had figured out the truth, she had definitely hit a nerve.

Well played, he thought, raising his glass in a silent toast. Well played indeed.

CHAPTER 37

MEDINA SALIM

The walk back out of the Cradle was such a blur that Medina had no idea how she found herself on the pavement in front of the arena's back door. She vaguely remembered one of the guards shoving her bag into her arms and escorting her at a fast pace back down the stream of corridors through a heavy metal door.

Medina could not recall much more beyond that. It occurred to her she might be in shock. She stood there motionless, stunned by the turn of events. She had assumed Terrence Blake would be glad to receive her help, that he would be grateful to have someone fighting his corner. She had built up a picture of the man in her head from her research that turned out to be in direct contrast with the person he actually was. She had pictured the school teacher, the loving father, the educated man, and she had convinced herself someone like that could never hurt a fly, let alone a human being.

And now… She wondered if she had been mistaken all along. Surely anyone who could lose their temper so suddenly and so completely was capable of unimaginable things. Medina shivered. How wrong she had been. How naive. How… she made herself think the word she hated so much. *Childish.* She thought about Pedro and how she had rebuked him. His caring face flashed into her mind's eye, bringing her to the edge of tears.

It took her a moment to get her bearings and identify the shortest route to the next bus stop. As she made her way decisively to her destination, a low rumbling noise made her pause. She listened intently, trying to work out where the sound was coming from. Her heartbeat quickened as her body responded to the immediate sense of danger. Medina took a few steps forward, realising the noise was coming from around the other side of the arena. The closer she got, the louder it became, eventually growing into a constant, persisting buzzing.

When she turned the corner and she suddenly came face to face with the source of the noise, she froze. A sea of people was amassed in front of the Cradle's main entrance gates. The numbers had to be in the thousands, she thought as she took in the scene in front of her. People of all ages sat on the floor, huddled around little camping tents, or stood in small groups, chatting excitedly. There were human beings everywhere she looked, their mass stretching so far ahead she could not see the end of it. Medina stood, transfixed. For all of the show's insanity and horror, it had such powers of attraction that countless hopefuls had settled by the Cradle, bowing at its giant feet, hoping for a chance to be a live witness to the next gory episode.

Medina glanced over the bobbing heads to the next street, where her bus stop was. She had never been keen on crowds, she did her best to avoid them wherever she could, but right now the only way forward was through the sea of people. She thought of turning back and finding another way, but the weight of the last couple of days was starting to bring her down, and all she wanted was to be home. She wanted to see Pedro, to snuggle into his arms and forget that the world around them even existed. She craved his presence with such force it knocked the air out of her lungs.

She made her way carefully through the edges of the crowd until, before she knew it, she was completely engulfed. Everywhere she turned there were bodies breathing and talking. She was no longer sure whether she was going in the right direction. No one paid her any attention. Despite so many pairs of eyes around her, she felt invisible. She became very aware of the constant humming of conversations, of the excitement she neither understood nor shared. All of these people united in the same inexplicable cause, bonding over their hatred and the years of suffering they would never get back. The further along she walked the thicker the crowd became. The air stiffened. There was so much going on, so many people crawling in every corner, it was becoming too much. Medina's heart rate accelerated. She spun round, desperately searching for a way out. Suddenly, she could no longer breathe. She stumbled, gasping for air, her hands clasping at her throat, her heart threatening to go into overdrive inside her chest.

'Hey! Watch out!'

Inadvertently, she had stepped onto someone's limb, hand or foot she could not tell. The reprimand made her jump and kicked her into action. She started running, slaloming between people, knocking elbows along her way, ignoring the complaints of those she ruffled. She kept running and running, the people around her like branches of so many tangled trees, blocking her way and making her exit all the more difficult. When she finally saw a beam of light on the other end, she knew she had reached the other edge of the crowd. She broke into a mad sprint towards the light, until she found herself on the pavement, a few steps away from the mass of human beings she had almost drowned in.

She bent over, hands on her knees, her head heavy and her breathing hard. It took her a long time to get her bearings again, but she realised with a sigh of relief that she was standing just a few steps away from the bus stop. She jogged to the worn-out sheltered bench, paying little attention to the graffitied plastic walls and broken, flickering light. After what she had just experienced, even this degraded, sorry excuse for a bus stop felt like an oasis of safety.

CHAPTER 38

MEDINA SALIM

Medina went straight to *Francisco's*. Her longing to see Pedro had turned into an obsession, a pain that had become almost physical with every excruciating stop the bus made along the way. In the end she hopped off a couple of stops before the one she needed, and ran along the final streets to her destination. When the faded shop-front came into view, she slowed down, smoothed her hair and her clothes, and readjusted her bag on her shoulders.

She walked through the door and was greeted by a chirpy Francisco. Though Medina was always happy to see her godfather, she frowned inwardly. At this time of day, Pedro was generally the one manning the store. She knew the only reason he insisted on taking that shift was that he wanted to see her when she came in at lunchtime. Not today, though.

'Medina! *Pequeñita*! *Qué tal estàs?*' Francisco made his way around the counter and gave her a bear hug.

Medina, darling. How are you?

Medina coughed under the strength of his embrace. He released her and looked at her, his hands on her shoulders, the biggest of grins plastered across his face. Medina smiled back at him. Of all the people in her life, Francisco had always been a pillar of strength and positivity. Despite everything, and even though the very same afflictions affected his family as much as anyone else's, he had taught her to always keep on going. She could see where Pedro got his quietly optimistic attitude, his resilience, and most of all his caring nature.

'*Pedro està aquí?*' She asked.

Is Pedro here?

Francisco shook his head excitedly, letting go of her shoulders. The words almost burst out of him.

'He's on a date!' He beamed, bouncing with joy.

Medina's eyes widened. She could not find the words to respond, but thankfully Francisco was so pleased at the news that he took care of the conversation singlehandedly.

'You know my friend who owns the convenience store in the west end? He has a daughter, you know.'

Medina nodded. Of course, she knew. Francisco's great ambition in life was to see his son married. Well, not *just* married. Francisco wanted Pedro to settle down with a nice girl, who shared their culture, and of whose lineage he approved. Ever since Pedro had reached adolescence, Francisco had been mentioning this friend's daughter, and that friend's daughter, from all these respectable Spanish families around town. Pedro had always deflected his father's attempts at arranging his matrimonial happiness. He had repeated patiently that when the time came he would take care of his own nuptials. Francisco's problem was that he knew *exactly* what that meant. Pedro was waiting for Medina.

Medina knew that whilst Francisco cared for her, it hurt him to see his son seemingly wasting his youthful years on what he considered childhood infatuation, pining for a girl who was nothing like the ideal daughter-in-law he desperately hoped for. The worst thing was, Medina could not blame him. Who would want a broken in-law like her?

As unfair as it was, she knew she *had* expected Pedro to wait forever. She knew she was being selfish, but it did not make the news that Pedro felt finally ready to give up on her, on *them*, any easier to digest. She just nodded, no longer hearing Francisco's contented commentary.

Back at her place, Medina stood by the front door, keys in hand, unable to bring herself to go inside. She could not face the enclosed space just yet. She could not stand to look at the leftovers of the previous night's argument. She was not ready. She turned back and walked for a while absentmindedly, her heart heavy. She needed a swim. Desperately so.

The swimming pool at her local leisure centre was busy with lunchtime swimmers, but it did not matter. Medina slipped into the water, her body shivering at its coolness. She started swimming and the remnants of the morning slowly started to fade away, as her mind found a new point of focus. One arm, the other, legs beating, to the end of the pool and back. The repetitiveness of the activity soothed her.

By the time she got back to her apartment a couple of hours later, she was feeling marginally better. She hung her swimming gear to dry in the bathroom and dumped her bag on her desk. She could deal with the case later. She set about making some food for herself, only then realising that she had not eaten anything all day. She managed to find just enough ingredients to make a sandwich, if dry bread, pickles and cucumber qualified as a sandwich. She had discovered some unusual combinations whilst scavenging for scraps in her kitchen, at times too busy and others too uninterested to go out for something decent. If it was not for the hearty meals she got at *Francisco's* or the takeaways Pedro brought her, she probably would never eat any proper food.

Pushing the thought of Pedro away, she busied herself with reviewing her notes, rearranging pins and pictures on her wall display, all the while munching absently on her makeshift sandwich. Slowly but surely, ideas started to emerge in her head. She lined up the pictures she found of the Blakes' house, and though she did not have the full address, knowing the street name was a definite start. She felt convinced that there were answers to be found there, and that her next step should be to pay the neighbourhood a visit. She glanced out the window, only to find the outside world plunged in darkness. It would have to wait till the next day.

The ring of the intercom took her by surprise. She pressed the microphone button and Pedro's unmistakable voice came crackling through.

'Medina, it's me. Let me in.'

His tone was pressing. She hesitated for a second, her fingers hovering over the buzzer that released the door.

'Medina, *dejàme entrar!*' Pedro insisted, frustration audible in his tone.

Let me in.

The unusual briskness in his voice made her press the button immediately and soon she could hear his footsteps galloping up the stairs. She started to panic. What did he have to say that was so urgent? Was he here to tell her about his date? Her throat constricted. She could not see him. She could not hear what he had to say. She refused to face this Pedro, this man who, not too long ago, was hers alone, but who was now looking for a wife. Without thinking about it, she bolted the door lock and reattached the safety chain. The handle moved as Pedro tried to get in. He tried a couple of times, in vain. He banged on the door and the sound resonated in her small studio. She did not budge, frozen as she was on the spot.

'Medina. Please. *Abre la puerta*,' Pedro called out.

Open the door.

She stayed still, listening to his presence on the other side of the wooden door.

'Medina, I know you're there! Open the door, *joder*!'

Medina shuddered. Pedro was not usually one for swear words. Silence settled between them and a minute passed without the smallest of sounds.

'*Cariño…*' Pedro's voice was pleading now.

She could not bring herself to let him in. She thought she heard him rest his forehead on the door and sigh. She leaned against her side of the door. She was not entirely sure why she was acting the way she was. Bitter disappointment filled her heart, and tears swelled up in her eyes. She did nothing to stop them. Mainly, she realised, she was angry. Angry at Sean Cravanaugh for being such a tyrannical bastard. Angry at Terrence Blake for treating her offer to help with such disdain. Angry at Francisco for forcing his son into this stupid date and angry at Pedro for agreeing to go on it.

But most of all, she knew, she was angry at herself. She was angry that had she said the word, it could have been her on that date. Angry that all these years Pedro was waiting for her she had done nothing to show him how much she wanted to be ready for him. How much she loved him. What an idiot she had been to think he would be there forever. How selfish and arrogant of her to think she was worth his wait. She missed the time when they were children and there were no expectations on either of them. All she wanted was for them to sit together in silence, like they had countless times before, understanding each other beyond words, not needing to put any label on what they had.

A long time passed and Pedro was still quiet. Not hearing any noise outside the door, she peered through the peephole. The corridor was empty. Her heart sank in her chest. He must have left and, lost, in her thoughts, she had not heard him walk down the stairs. He had given up on her, for the second time that day. She dragged herself to her bed and, burying her head in her pillow, she burst into tears.

CHAPTER 39

TYLER BENSON

By the time Tyler walked through his mansion's front door on Thursday evening, night had fallen on the capital. He closed the thick door behind him, locking it carefully. He took one step forward and felt himself wavering a little. He caught himself just in time, leaning against the wall, and breathed in deeply. It had been a long day. Sean Cravanaugh had called an emergency strategy meeting with the marketing team, something about new developments in the competition which they all needed to prepare for.

Tyler was actually not entirely sure what the meeting had been about and, as he stood in the darkened hallway, straining his memory to recall any valuable piece of information from Sean Cravanaugh's long presentation, it occurred to him that he had no clue what had been said. Not a single word of the four-hour meeting had registered in his mind. Tyler shuddered. This competition had taken a strange toll on him, and he found himself sliding through most days with little awareness of what happened around him. He had been tired and overworked before, but never quite to this extent.

Habit, more than anything, made him pull his phone out of his pocket. It was one thirty in the morning, and he had eleven text messages and twice that amount of missed calls, all from his wife. He frowned as he struggled to remember whether he had told her that he would be late. He could not be sure he had. The thought certainly had crossed his mind when the meeting was announced, but the deluge of missed calls and unread texts on his phone suggested he definitely had not acted on it.

'Fuck,' he whispered under his breath, suddenly more exhausted than ever.

He knew Constance would have waited up for him and he did not have any energy left for an argument. He walked cautiously to the bottom of the stairs and glanced up, trying to gauge whether the master bedroom light was on. He wondered whether he was safer crashing in the guest bedroom for the night, but knew he would have to face his wife sooner or later.

Dragging his feet, partly because he dreaded the confrontation, and partly because of the sudden wave of tiredness that had washed over him, he climbed the stairs to their bedroom. Sure enough, Constance was sitting in bed, propped up against some pillows, flicking moodily through a fashion magazine. He paused at the door, watching her in silence. How beautiful she was, and how very out of his reach.

Years of strenuous demands from his career had created a wedge between them, until all they truly shared was their two children, a living space and a stack of bills. The romance they had enjoyed when they had nothing but a small roof over their heads was gone. His work had taken him through never-ending travel, late nights and stressful episodes. He had missed more recitals, birthdays and anniversaries than he cared to admit. The thought of quitting had crossed his mind many a time. He missed his wife. Not just the person whose name was on the brass plaque alongside his on the front door, but the lover and friend who had held his hand through their early life together. He missed the simpler existence they had before fame and fortune polluted their happiness. By the time he had realised what had happened, it was too late. Gradually, he had come to accept the way things were, because they had quickly got used to the standard of living his generous pay cheques afforded.

He let out an exhausted sigh. Constance looked up and her eyes fell on him. Tyler saw in her gaze how furious she was. Oh God, he thought, what have I missed this time?

He walked into the room and sat on the edge of the bed, unlacing his shoes and unbuttoning his shirt, waiting for the storm to kick off. Constance was observing him, frowning.

'You look terrible,' was all she said.

He did not respond. He was well aware of how beaten he looked and there was little point in denying or confirming her comment.

'I tried calling you,' she continued.

Here we go… Tyler thought.

'Why didn't you tell me you were going to be so late?' She probed.

'They called a last minute meeting at work, I just…' Tyler started, but she cut him off.

'What? You just *what*, Tyler? Decided you wouldn't even bother letting me know?' Constance's tone was glacial, her jaw tense with anger. 'Ellie was so disappointed…' She added, 'you promised her you would be there this time.'

Ellie, their youngest. It was Tyler's turn to frown. He could not remember what he had promised, or what meaningful event he had missed. His silence confirmed what Constance already knew. He had forgotten.

'For fuck's sake, Tyler,' she hissed, 'why do you even make our children promises you know you won't keep? Do me a favour, will you, why don't you just stop talking to them altogether.'

She threw her magazine to the floor, turned her back on him, pulled the covers over herself and switched off the lights. This was how most of their arguments ended these days. Constance did not even bother giving him lengthy lectures about how appalling his parenting or marital skills were anymore. She barely said anything in fact, and seeing how she had resigned herself to the idea that their marriage and family life was no longer worth saving spoke louder than if she had said a hundred angry words to him. Tyler sat on the edge of the bed, his hands clasped in his lap, his head dropped, his heart aching.

'I'm sorry,' he whispered, but Constance did not react and he never knew whether she had heard him, or whether she even cared for yet another feeble apology.

He made his way to the ensuite bathroom and grabbed his toothbrush, wondering if he even had the strength for a task as small and mundane as brushing his teeth. As he lifted the toothbrush to his lips, he looked up and froze. He barely recognised the man staring back at him in the mirror. He was pale and tired, and looked like he had aged ten years in the last few weeks. But what made Tyler stare at his reflection in such horror was not so much how unhealthy and old he looked. No. What gave him a chill of terror was the trickle of blood slowly dripping from his left nostril.

He glanced back towards the bedroom, towards Constance's motionless figure under the plush duvet. He almost called out for her, but something held him back. The time when he could count on his wife's unconditional support was gone. After all, was it not his own fault if his ungodly working schedule started to affect his health?

With trembling hands, he wiped the crimson streak off his face, brushed his teeth and got into bed, as though nothing had happened.

CHAPTER 40

MEDINA SALIM

When she woke up the next day, Medina could not remember falling asleep. She lay on her bed, fully dressed, feeling numb inside. Where the night before there had been pain and anger and disappointment, now there was nothing but emptiness. She went through her morning routine on auto-pilot.

What next? She asked herself, as she stood in the middle of her living room, showered and dressed. Her eyes fell on her wall, and the new rows of article cuttings she had pinned the day before. She had to find Terrence Blake's house. Even the thought of a new lead in her case did nothing to awaken a reaction within her, which was unusual. She gathered her things, packed her bag and readied herself to leave.

She unlocked the front door and, as she opened it, something heavy collapsed at her feet. She let out a scream, and jumped backwards. When her vision refocused, she could not believe what she saw. A sleepy-looking Pedro was finding his wobbly way back onto his feet.

'Did you sleep here?' She asked, incredulous.

Pedro nodded, stretching himself and massaging the back of his neck. He walked into the flat with heavy steps, slamming the door shut behind him.

'Do me a favour,' he groaned, his voice coarse, 'next time, at least throw me a pillow or something.'

He fished out a glass from a cupboard and poured himself some water from the tap. He drank it all in one go, his back to her.

'I thought you'd left,' she said quietly, watching him from a distance.

Pedro froze with his hand in mid-air and simply turned to stare at her. There was so much in his eyes. Tiredness, annoyance, but also relief and concern. He shook his head at her, almost in slow motion, and before she knew it he had marched over to her and encased her in a tight hug. She nestled her head against his chest and breathed into him. Her arms locked around his waist. She felt the tears rise again and roll down her face. He held her close, his cheek brushing against hers, his nose in her hair. She could feel his breath against her neck.

'*Pero, qué tonterías dices...*' He whispered in her ear.

What nonsense are you saying.

'Do you really not realise how much I love you?'

At his words, she looked up at him, her face streaked with salty tears. The pain from the last couple of days vanished with the way he looked at her in that very moment. She brought a hand to his face, and caressed his cheek with her thumb.

She did not know what made her do it, all she knew was that if she were to remain true to herself, she could not do anything else. She pulled his face gently towards hers, and pressed her lips against his. Time slowed down. Pedro seemed unsure at first, letting her lead. When she slid her other arm around his neck, locking him in, his confidence grew, and he tightened his grip on her too. He was returning her kiss now, slowly, gently, tasting her. Medina felt herself melt. It was as if her entire body had burst into flames. Every single particle of her had ignited, awoken by his touch, and she wondered how she had never noticed that she was not truly alive before. Their kiss intensified. Pedro had one hand at the nape of her back, and one cupping her face. Her arms were around his neck. Before she could stop herself she jumped up and wrapped her legs around his waist. He caught her seamlessly. He moved forward, leaning her back against the wall, and the hardness of the concrete behind her spine sent delicious shivers through her body. Pedro's breathing grew faster. Medina could feel his arousal hard against her inner thigh. She was overwhelmed by his desire for her. She lost track of time, finding that it did not matter anymore. She wanted him, with a force and longing she had never experienced before. Her mouth still locked with his, she moved her hands to his waist and slid her fingers under the fabric of his tee-shirt. The warmth of his skin fuelled her craving. Before her hands had travelled much further however, he put her down, and grabbed her hands firmly in his, breaking their kiss. He rested his forehead on hers, eyes closed, breathing in deeply. He opened his eyes, and she gave him a grumpy look which instantly brought a broad grin to his face. He kissed her nose, and took a step back.

'Trust me,' he murmured, 'I want this even more than you do…'

Medina moved forward to bring her body against his again.

'But,' Pedro said, his face serious, 'when it comes to us… It's not something I want to rush.'

Medina pouted and the expression on her face made Pedro chuckle.

'Come on,' he grinned, 'I'll take a quick shower and we can go and grab some breakfast.'

When he spoke the words, Medina remembered her earlier plans. Pedro knew her too well to miss the guilty look she knew had flashed across her face. He took in her outdoors jacket and the backpack she had dropped when she had opened the door. He raised an eyebrow.

'Were you going somewhere?' He asked.

She nodded sheepishly, diverting her gaze. She wanted more than anything to avoid a repeat of their argument. Pedro crossed his arms and leaned against the chest of drawers, his eyes on her.

'Whereabouts?' He asked again, and there was no mistaking the shaking in his tone, though he was visibly trying his best to pretend her answer was inconsequential.

When Medina explained her plan, Pedro's eyes widened. She watched his face turn white with disbelief, then concern, then anger. Pedro inhaled deeply. When he spoke again, his voice was measured.

'I'm coming with you,' he said firmly.

The memories of her most recent solo excursion were still fresh in her mind, and she felt a wave of relief knowing she would have Pedro as back-up on her next one. She simply nodded.

'Give me ten minutes, and then we'll go.'

She watched him disappear into the bathroom and listened as the shower came on. Her mind drifted off, lingering on the thought of him, naked under the hot water. Her hand lifted absently to her mouth, and her fingers rested on her lips. Her kiss with Pedro had been her first. Not just her first with him, but her first *ever*, and it had felt more natural and more exhilarating than she had ever thought possible.

Realising she had inadvertently walked all the way to the bathroom door, standing with her hand hovering over the handle, she rushed back to the kitchenette, where she busied herself, pottering around to make two cups of coffee. She was stirring the milk in when Pedro came out of the bathroom, fully dressed, his dark hair still wet.

'Coffee?' She asked, looking at him over her shoulder. 'We can grab something to eat on the way.'

As a response, he walked up behind her and wrapped his arms around her, resting his chin on her shoulder, his cheek brushing hers.

'Yes, please,' he breathed against her neck, and the feel of him sent a fuzzy shiver through her stomach.

Medina closed her eyes and leaned her head against his. At that very moment, nothing else mattered beyond the two of them. She found herself thinking that there was nothing life could throw at them which would shake her anymore. And, in that short instant, snuggled in Pedro's strong and reassuring embrace, she almost believed it.

CHAPTER 41

MEDINA SALIM

Medina felt much safer with Pedro by her side. She had filled him in on her latest findings, glossing over the incident at Cradle so swiftly that she knew he suspected she was not being entirely truthful. He had not probed however, just as she had not lingered on the topic of his date. A tacit agreement had been made between them to leave both topics aside and move forward.

They drove Pedro's rusty old car down Serenade Row slowly, carefully examining the door fronts, comparing them to the pictures from Medina's newspaper cuttings. It took quite some imagination to match the now decrepit and doorless building to the lovely and colourful home it had once been. The house in front of them had clearly been abandoned for many years, probably since the Blakes left so suddenly.

The windows had been blocked with large slates of dirty, splintering wood and the door had been kicked in, giving the whole building the vague air of a haunted house. Some of its features remained however. A row of terracotta pots was neatly aligned along the front wall, though most of them had been smashed to pieces, and none of them contained the flowery array of begonias and petunias the pictures showed anymore. The paint on the walls had faded and crumbled, and many aspiring artists had used large patches of blank facade to test their graffiti skills.

They climbed the steps and peered through the vacant doorway. The entrance was dark and dusty, despite the bright sunny day. With a glance at each other, they stepped in, switching on the flashlights on their phones to see where they were going. To say that the house had seen some uncaring visitors over the years was putting it very mildly. The walls were stained and most of the furniture trashed. The floor was littered with rubbish and, to their dismay, what looked and smelled horribly like excrements. Broken glass bottles and suspicious instruments suggested more than one squatter had come around to indulge in drink and drugs. They walked through a door on their left, which led into the living room. The walls of the room had been graffitied, too.

'What are we looking for, exactly?' Pedro asked, looking around.

'Anything useful,' she shrugged, knowing full well how unhelpful an answer this was.

They went through the whole house with slow, careful steps, until they reached a small bedroom on the first floor. Pedro pointed his flashlight inside over Medina's head, shedding a ghostly glow across the room. Medina stopped abruptly on the door step. They had reached what must have been the little girl's bedroom. The walls were painted a faded yellow, which she imagined must have been bright and cheery at the time. A single bed was pushed against a corner, and a couple of shelves carried toys and books. A wooden toy crate sat in one corner. Leaving Pedro on the threshold, Medina approached the wooden crate and, kneeling down, opened it. The metal hinges croaked and a cloud of freshly unsettled dust flew out of the box, making her cough a little. A selection of old-fashioned wooden toys and stuffed animals were piled inside the box.

Quite surprisingly, whilst the rest of the house had been ransacked, the contents of the crate looked like they had been left entirely untouched. It was as if all of the intruders who had invaded the premises over the years had agreed to leave that one little parcel from the past intact. Medina picked up one of the stuffed animals from the box and brushed the dust off it with her sleeve. She turned it over in her hands to examine it. It looked handmade. It might have been an elephant, or at least this is what she supposed since the misshapen worn-out toy had what appeared to be a trunk poking out from the middle of its face. The fabric was a patchwork of colourful pieces, a rainbow of different shades, patterns and textures, sown together in thick and rough wool lining. Whoever had made this toy might have had the best of intentions at heart, but the result was very amateurish.

They did a second round of the house, this time opening drawers and cupboards, flicking through old papers and post they found lying around. Their search, as thorough as it was, was fruitless.

Medina sat on the dusty bed in the master bedroom, and directed her flashlight across the room. She checked the drawer of the closest nightstand, which was stuck. As she wrestled with the wooden handle, she dropped her phone. The device plummeted to the ground, sliding over the carpet under the bed with a soft swishing noise. Medina knelt down to peer under the bed. It was quite low, and her phone had slid so far under the bed she needed to flatten herself against the dirty floor and extend her arm to reach it. As she patted around for the device, her fingers scraped the wood covering the bottom of the bed. She froze. Amongst the wooden panels, her fingers had sensed a different material altogether. There was something else there, though she was not quite sure what. She motioned to Pedro.

Pedro propped his phone in his mouth, aiming the beam of light in front of them. They both gripped the side of the bed and lifted it, revealing Medina's phone underneath it, and sending spiders zooming away in all directions. Medina bent down to grab her phone and gasped as she saw the large brown paper envelope tapped to the bottom of the bed. She wrenched it away from its hiding place. They dropped the bed back into place and sat down on it, exchanging an ominous glance. Whoever had placed the envelope there had been intent on keeping it out of harm's way. Medina peered inside the envelop and tipped the whole contents of it onto the dusty duvet.

There were papers and drawings in there. Medina carefully lifted each to her face, looking at them closely. The drawings had clearly been made by a child. Here was a crayon drawing of a little girl wearing a bright yellow dress, next to a tall manly figure wearing a white shirt and black trousers. Behind them was a colourful house with little round pots lined in front of it. Next was another drawing, with the two figures, alongside a third one. The third character appeared to be a woman, with grey hair, holding sticks and circles. There were father's day cards and 'I Love you' cards, all written in the same uncertain child's handwriting. Medina was mesmerised. She could not take her eyes off the drawings.

She looked up at Pedro, and was about to share her observations when she noticed the look on his face. Pedro seemed uneasy and his traits were tense.

'What's wrong?' She asked him.

Pedro shifted uncomfortably on the bed.

'I don't like this place,' he pulled a face, 'it gives me the creeps.'

Medina felt there was something he was holding back, but at that moment, a cracking sound resonated on the ground floor and they both jumped to their feet. They froze. Pedro motioned at her to be quiet and walked slowly to the door, switching off his flashlight. Sounds were coming from the bottom of the stairs, like someone rummaging though pots and pans in the kitchen. Medina quickly shove the papers in her backpack. They stood motionless for some time, listening intently to the sounds coming from the floor below. After several minutes, the house became quiet again and Pedro guided Medina down the creaking staircase. Halfway through, he gestured to her to stay where she was, whilst he went down the final steps. Medina watched him disappear into the kitchen and emerge back almost immediately, a wide grin on his handsome face.

'Come and see who the culprit is…' He chuckled, beckoning at her to join him.

Walking into the kitchen, Medina gasped. Two tiny black kittens were roaming around the table and counter, scavenging for food, ruffling through rubbish and broken utensils. Her eyes met Pedro's and they exchanged a smile.

They left the kittens to scavenge to their hearts' content and made their way out of the house. On the front lawn, Medina looked around for inspiration on where to head to next. The next task was to be aired live the following day, and there were still much of the puzzle to assemble. As she looked at the house next door, her eyes caught sight of a woman, standing on the front porch, staring at them. When Medina took a step in her direction, the woman quickly walked back into the house and closed the door behind her. Medina followed, almost jogging to the house next door, and knocked. It took several attempts to coax the woman into opening the door.

'Yes?' she said, her face suspicious, one hand on the back of the door.

'Hi,' Medina tried her best to keep her tone as friendly as possible, 'we're wondering if you knew the people who used to live next door?' She pointed at the worn-out house they had just searched. 'The Blakes?'

The woman looked at them uncertainly.

'We're not here to cause any trouble,' Pedro explained calmly, 'My friend here…' He jerked his head at Medina, 'is looking to prove Terrence Blake's innocence.'

The woman glanced back over her shoulder, listening to something behind her. The woman was silent for a moment and, finally, looking resigned, she opened the door to let them both in. She led them down a corridor, through to a small conservatory bathed with warm morning light. There, on a creaky rocking-chair sat an old woman wrapped in colourful woollen blankets, a skinny black cat curled up on her lap. She looked up at them, her gaze resting on Medina's face for some time.

'Would you like anything else, Aunt Audrey?' The woman asked the old lady.

Audrey shook her head, then motioned at her visitors to take a seat on the small couch opposite her. Medina and Pedro sat down. Audrey had a kind gentle face and a knowing look which made Medina feel she could guess all of her secrets at once. Medina looked away, unable to hold her gaze.

'So,' Audrey spoke in a tired, croaky voice, 'you want to prove Terrence Blake is innocent?'

'Yes,' Medina nodded animatedly. 'Did you know him? Did you know the family?'

'Yes, I knew them. A long time ago,' Audrey said with a sad smile.

'Is there anything you can tell us about them? About what happened that night? I've been looking into their story,' Medina added, 'and some of it really doesn't add up...'

Medina went on to reveal what she had found, telling Audrey about her blog and her mission. The old woman listened quietly, her hands absentmindedly stroking the cat on her lap, her feet gently rocking the chair back and forth in a soothing motion. Pedro sat very still, his hands knotting and unknotting on his thighs. When Medina stopped talking, Audrey remained silent for a moment. When she spoke again, her question took Medina by surprise.

'Why?' She asked simply, her eyes searching Medina's face.

'I... I'm sorry?' Medina frowned.

'Why are you doing this?' Audrey asked again.

'I...' Medina started, unable to finish her sentence.

The many reasons and justifications she had created for herself over the years to justify her obsession for truth and justice suddenly escaped her. Why *was* she doing this? The look on Audrey's face was so intense, so genuine, so wise that Medina could not possibly give her any of her half-baked ready-made answers.

'I don't know,' she whispered.

'Mmmm,' Audrey muttered.

The two little kittens they had found rummaging in the Blakes' kitchen trotted in through the open door and settled at the old lady's feet.

'Terrence Blake was a good man,' Audrey commented, 'I don't know exactly what happened the night he was arrested. I have my suspicions, of course...' Audrey's voice trailed off.

'What do you mean?' She asked when the old lady's sentence was left unfinished, her voice more pressing than she had intended.

But Audrey simply shook her head.

'Every story, young lady, is there to be uncovered only by those who are meant to unravel it. It is not my place to try and guess what happened in that house on that day. All I know is that the man I knew was a kind and loving father, and a good husband. Everything else is conjecture. If you are meant to find out what the past held, some day you will.'

Medina opened her mouth to protest, but thought better of it. She felt she was within reaching distance of the truth, yet just a little too far to even graze the surface of it. They stood to bid Audrey goodbye.

Audrey's niece guided them back through the corridor, and Medina thought she looked relieved to see them go. As they walked past the living room, something caught Medina's eye. On the coffee table, nestled in a small wicker basket, sat a few rolls of brightly coloured wool and a pair of long knitting needles. They climbed into Pedro's car and Medina allowed herself to think. She felt Audrey knew more than she had shared with them. She was convinced the old lady had played a bigger part in the Blakes' lives than she had let on. Grey hair and a colourful knitting kit. She had identified the third character on the little girl's drawings.

CHAPTER 42

PEDRO MORENO GARCÍA

Pedro settled behind the wheel of his car. Medina nestled herself in the passenger seat and they drove all the way back to her apartment in silence. He kept glancing sideways at Medina, who was lost in her own thoughts. He stopped the car in front of her building, and watched her get out. She walked around the car and came to a halt by his open window.

'Are you coming up?' She asked, tilting her head.

There was hope and expectation in her words, and he wished he were able to fulfil the silent request in her eyes. Soon, he thought, wishing she could hear him, but not now. Now, he knew, he had things to take care of.

He shook his head apologetically and made a vague excuse about having to go and help his father in the shop. Medina looked disappointed, her beautiful face falling a little, but she conjured up an unconvincing smile. She took a couple of steps towards her front door, then stopped abruptly and walked straight back towards him. She leaned through the open window, brought a hand to his face and kissed him. Pedro's heart melted instantly. His hands found her neck and face, as he kissed her back. His heart pounded in his chest, pumping excitement madly through every single part of his body, his skin tingling. He could feel himself harden under her touch. All he wanted was to grab her hand, run up to her studio and lock both of them up in there forever. He wanted to forget everything and everyone else. Forget the world and her wild goose chase after a truth that did not matter. Forget the suspicions that their morning escapade had awoken in him...

As the thought crossed his mind again, he gently pulled back, keeping her face in his hands and smiled at her. How he loved her! How he longed for her! How complete she made him feel! She was everything he had ever wanted since the very first time he had laid eyes on her, though he had been but a child at the time. It had not mattered whether she was his, or whether she would ever return his affection. All that ever mattered was that she was safe and happy. He loved her no matter what, regardless of where she was and what she did. He did not love her because he thought she would one day love him back. He loved her utterly and completely, without conditions. Seeing joy on her face was all he wanted, whether or not he was the source of it.

She gave him one of her spoilt-child pouts and he smiled even wider. He had got her used to having her every wish granted and it amused him to see her reaction when he did not oblige her.

'I'll see you later,' he promised, watching as she turned around and walked in through the door.

When he was certain that she had gone, he slid a hand into the back pocket of his jeans and extracted a small pile of photographs, held together with a piece of red ribbon. He had caught a glimpse of the photograph on the top when Medina had tipped over the contents of the envelope on the bed in the Blakes' house. The moment his eyes had fallen on the first picture he knew he had to take them all away. He had not been entirely sure why. Medina had been so absorbed in the child's drawings at the time she had not even noticed him grabbing the small stack of photos and sliding them into his pocket.

He untied the ribbon and flicked through the photographs, looking at them one by one. He shook his head, bringing the photos up to his face, as if a closer inspection would prove him wrong. It did not. If anything, it made him even more certain that his instincts were right.

With a deep sigh, he popped the pile of photos into the glove compartment, turned the key into the ignition and started driving. He knew exactly what he needed to do.

CHAPTER 43

SEAN CRAVANAUGH

Sitting in his office at the top of the Cradle, Sean was satisfied. He had just finished going over the marketing figures he had requested during the emergency meeting with his team, and the numbers looked very good indeed.

He read through the schedule for the following day's episode, and reviewed the graphs showing contestant elimination figures so far. They had planned to increase the amount of men and women leaving the competition every week, building up to mass punishments and eliminations. For the past three episodes, they had struck contestants down in large groups, and the public had embraced the carnage, as they had everything else so far. On the eve of the sixth task, they were already left with only ten contestants, which Sean considered a good amount to make the next few rounds as exciting as possible.

Sean pulled another folder from the pile on his desk, and read through its contents with attention. The report, which was hand-delivered to him every morning, detailed Josh Carter's comings and goings. Sean had requested that the head of his security team keep him informed at all times of what Carter was up to, an added precaution he had decided was necessary, especially since the fourth judge was getting more vocal about his disapproval of the proceedings during the live shows. Sean could not risk him trying to sabotage the competition when everything was going so well.

Sean looked up as his cell phone rang. He picked up the device and checked the screen. He knew exactly who hid behind the blocked number, and answered immediately.

'Tell me,' he said abruptly.

After all, he did not pay the person on the other end of the phone to waste time in pointless chit chat.

'She went to the Blakes' old house. There was a guy with her, too. Didn't look like they found much, but they ended up going into the neighbours' house. I followed them back to her place, she's been there ever since.'

'Anything else?' Sean grunted, unable to keep the disappointment out of his voice.

'I saw her pulling some stuff out of her bag when she got home, so she might have picked up some things either from the Blakes' or the neighbours'. I've tapped her phone and hacked her emails, so I'll keep you posted if I find out more.'

'*When* you find out more,' corrected Sean, 'or you can kiss the second half of your fee goodbye.'

Sean hung up moodily without giving his caller a chance to respond. He hated it when the people he contracted failed him. He picked up the phone receiver on his desk and pressed a button. His secretary's voice resonated on the other end instantly.

'Get me the producer on the line,' his tone was sharp.

'Yes, Mr Cravanaugh,' came the immediate response, followed by a brief beep as the call was transferred.

'Mr Cravanaugh,' the man greeted him curtly, 'what can I do for you?'

Sean explained what he wanted done, and how incredibly important it was that it should be finished in time and in the most absolute discretion.

'It's a bit short notice, sir, maybe we could...' The producer responded, after hearing Sean out.

But Sean was not a man used to being bargained with. It had been a long time since he had needed to take orders from anyone, and he was not about to take any steps back now.

'You will do as I instructed, and you will do it discreetly. Use a skeleton team. Let it be a surprise for everyone else,' Sean interrupted.

If the nation was standing behind Terrence Blake, then Sean had to give them something to truly fight for. It was a standard marketing exercise really, and he loved how easily people's allegiances could be swayed with cleverly worded material. The world's best marketers were its ultimate puppeteers, carefully pulling on everyone else's strings. Sean could almost picture the audience's reaction when they saw what he had in store for them the following day. The country had wanted a distraction, a cause to rally behind, and all he had to do was to oblige them and give them a good show.

CHAPTER 44

MEDINA SALIM

Medina had laid out all of the drawings from the Blakes' house on her carpet, and was pinning them up one by one on her wall. When she was done, she took a step back to admire her handiwork. And now what? The next episode was going ahead that very evening, but she felt no closer to the truth. She stood there for some time, feeling like she was missing something obvious. There was this one thing, she knew, which was staring at her in the face but which she simply could not see.

She made her way to the kitchenette to make herself a cup of tea. Maybe stepping away from the problem would clear her mind and allow her to come back to it with a fresh perspective. She was waiting for the kettle to boil when her phone rang. She checked the caller's name and picked up.

'Hi, Mum,' she responded mechanically, placing her tea bag in the cup, the phone nestled between her ear and shoulder.

'Hi, love! How are you?' Miranda asked cheerfully.

'I'm good,' Medina fiddled with the string of her tea bag as she spoke. 'How's everything your end? How's Dad?'

Listening to Miranda's response, Medina's mind quickly wandered from the conversation. It occurred to her that Miranda and Clive had never asked her to call them Mum and Dad. But Medina had felt a little left out at school, because all the other children referred to their parents that way, so one day she too had done the same. It had stuck ever since.

'...you know how he is, love,' Miranda continued, unaware of Medina's lack of attention, 'Dad's just like that. Today it's backgammon, tomorrow it'll be something else.'

Medina had no clue what the first part of the monologue had been, so she just made a sort of non-committal sound.

'Mmmm...' she mumbled, picking up the kettle and pouring boiling water into her cup.

'So, what's new with you, love?' Miranda asked, 'how's your latest project going?'

Medina grinned. She knew Miranda and Clive worried about her investigations, but neither of them ever failed to take an interest. She was grateful for it.

'It's going well,' Medina said, unsure how much to reveal. 'I'm making progress.'

'Oh, that's good, love!' Miranda exclaimed, 'when will you come around and tell us all about it?'

Medina chuckled. All her conversations with Miranda included a not-so-subtle suggestion that she should visit them more. She knew she was not being the most exemplary of daughters, especially after all that Miranda and Clive had done for her, but she got so engrossed in her investigations that she often forgot they were even there. What a terrible thing to even think, she reproached herself silently.

'I'll come over soon, I promise,' Medina heard herself say, though she had no idea when she would be fulfilling her promise.

She removed the tea bag from her cup and threw it in the sink. Picking up her cup, she turned around, her eyes falling on her wall. The canvas of photos and strings and notes was staring back at her, as incomplete a puzzle as it had ever been. She walked slowly towards it, pausing to stand in front of the freshly pinned drawings.

'You know we're here, dear, if you need anything,' Miranda's voice was gentle.

'I know, Mum,' Medina answered, 'I just have a lot on at the moment, but I'll come over soon.'

'I'm here for you, love,' Miranda insisted, a tinge of concern now colouring her words. 'You know that, right?'

'Yes, Mum,' Medina answered, rolling her eyes, 'I know you're there, and I know where to find you if…'

Medina's words trailed off. She stared at the drawings on the wall. How could she have missed it before? How could she have not seen it?

'Mum, I'll call you back,' she blurted into her phone, before hanging up.

She stared at the wall, taking in every single drawing. The little girl. The father. The old lady next door. Here again. The child with her father. The child, the father, the neighbour. Medina knelt down on the floor, her eyes wide. Of all of these pictures the little girl had drawn, none of them included her mother. Where on earth was the mother?

If what the papers said about Terrence Blake was true, and he had been a violent man, who, one fine day had gone too far and killed his wife, then why did his child make all of these loving drawings showing the two of them having the adventures of their life together? Why was the only female figure the old lady next door? Where had the mother been all this while? If accusations against Terrence Blake were true, then why did his daughter seem more attached to him and the next-door neighbour than to her own mother?

Medina stood up again, inspecting the drawings closely, her fingers hovering over each character depicted in each of them.

'Where's your Mum, little girl?' she whispered.

Suddenly, Medina realised there was one other pressing question she simply had not seen before. It was so obvious and so blatant that she could not understand how she had missed it before.

Where was the child now?

CHAPTER 45

TERRENCE BLAKE

Deep in the Cradle, Terrence woke up in a cold sweat in his cell. He sat bolt upright on his makeshift bed, trying to catch his breath, willing the images from the nightmare he had just had to disappear.

Maddison's bruised little arms, Delilah's body resting in a pool of blood. Over and over again, the visions taunted him. He cried out in frustration, a long, intense wail which brought the guards banging on his door yelling at him to shut up. Terrence collapsed on the stone floor, his head back in his hands. He had had enough. He had lived enough, if what he had endured in the last fifteen years could really be qualified as living. All he wanted now was to die. An easy way out of this nonsensical farce. He was tired of the games, tired of the tricks, tired of having to drag himself from one day to the next, with no prospect of it ever ending. He lay down and curled into a ball, closing his eyes, hoping that he would never wake up.

But wake up he did, to his dismay. His cell door opened again and he was shepherded to a spot in the giant metal cage. He looked around and saw that many of the other convicts were staring at him suspiciously, probably thinking he was getting some sort of favour treatment. There were so few of them now, just a handful of men and women, looking more worn-out and emaciated than ever.

Backstage, the usual hustle and bustle which preceded the live shows was at full steam. From behind the large panels, Terrence could hear the crowd getting restless. The jingle boomed through the arena and the audience clapped and shouted their delight. He saw Tyler Benson disappear through a gap in the panels and heard the audience cheer as he came into sight.

'Welcome everyone' Tyler Benson exclaimed, 'to a new episode of 'No Pain, No Game'!'

The crowd roared as he called in the judges, and the cage was rolled onstage. Terrence took a deep breath in, his knuckles white from clenching the metal rail in front of him. Somewhere behind him Terrence heard Mad Spencer laugh. It was a low, sickening laugh which gripped Terrence's throat in an instant.

'From one hundred contestants we are now down to ten! Tonight, our contestants will face a new challenge…' Tyler Benson paused for dramatic effect. 'The wrestling round! The losing contestant from each wrestling pair will leave the competition.' Tyler Benson paused again. 'And now,' he said in a low, serious voice, 'let's see who each of our contestants will be facing!'

Tyler Benson turned to face the large screens over the stage. The first pair popped on the screen, showing the picture and number of each convict, separated by a large 'VS.'. Pair after pair was announced, each of them creating more and more applause from the audience. When his own portrait appeared on the screen, Terrence gasped. A chill descended over him. Next to his headshot on the other side of the letters 'VS.' was Mad Spencer's photograph. He sensed rather than heard Mad Spencer's delight from somewhere behind him, but he did not dare look around.

Was that how he was going to die? Tortured and beaten to death by a madman? Terrence could think of no worse way to leave this world. The screens flashed the final wrestling pair and the production team installed a brightly coloured wrestling ring, branded with the show's logo, onto the stage.

'Let's welcome to the ring our first pair,' Tyler Benson exclaimed.

A woman and a man were escorted to the ring. Terrence was pretty sure he could tell the outcome of the fight before it had started, because the woman was only skin and bones. The man, on the other hand, was a stack of fat and muscles and was wearing an angry look on his face.

The guards positioned each contestant at opposite ends of the ring and Tyler Benson spoke again.

'The fight will happen in three rounds. To win a round, one of the contestants needs to hold the other wrestler face down onto the ring for ten seconds. Best of three rounds wins the task.'

Three loud beeps resonated around them, followed by the sound of a bell, indicating the first round had started. The man launched himself at the woman, who jumped aside, her light frame making her much more agile than her opponent. The man turned around and charged again but, this time, the woman was expecting him. Jumping to one side again at the last moment, she quickly spun around on her feet and pushed the fat man onto the floor. The man fell face down and as his body hit the ground the layers of fat around his stomach jiggled. The woman reacted quickly, jumping onto his back. He wriggled around, like a tortoise struggling to get back on its feet, but before he could rid himself of her, he had lost the first round.

The audience cheered the skinny woman on, making the other contestant shiver with rage. The three beeps came, then the ring of the bell, and the fight was on again. The man seemed to anticipate the woman's moves. As he charged towards her again, he whirled around at the last moment, slamming into her as she jumped aside to avoid him. He crashed into her with full force, grabbed her by the arm as she tumbled, and turned her on her front just before she hit the ground. His fat arms pinned her to the floor, ten seconds passed, and the score was evened out.

The third bell rang. They chased each other for some time, both avoiding predictable moves. After a moment, the man slowed down a little, and doubled over, his hands resting on his thighs, apparently struggling to catch his breath. The woman stopped a little distance away from him, unsure what to do next. That was her mistake. The man jumped at her, throwing a heavy hook punch which landed on her temple, knocking her out cold. He walked slowly to where she had collapsed and, sith a push of his heel, he turned her around on her front, resting his foot onto her back to keep her in place. Ten seconds went by, and the match was won. Two guards came to drag the unconscious woman off the ring. No one checked whether she was still breathing.

That's it, Terrence thought, I'm a dead man.

By the time the next two pairs had faced each other, Terrence felt his turn had come too soon. He was not ready. He was led unceremoniously into one corner of the ring, and Mad Spencer was brought to the opposite corner, glaring at him with perverse amusement. Terrence shivered.

He heard a beep. Then another. Then a third. And finally the dreaded bell went off, signalling the start of the first round. Mad Spencer did not move. He stood in his corner, smiling a mad man's smile, his head tilted to one side. He let out a little amused laugh, as though this was the most fun he had had in a long time and there was nothing else he would rather be doing. Mad Spencer was pacing around the ring in small, bouncy steps, muttering something high pitched and unintelligible to himself. Every now and then he jumped out at Terrence, like a child jumping out behind a friend to give them a little scare.

Terrence was petrified. For a split second he got a sense of what Mad Spencer's victims must have felt. He was playing with his head, displaying the most incongruous behaviour, taunting him. The scariest thing about a mad man, Terrence thought, was his unpredictability. One could not anticipate the other's moves because, by definition, they defied reason. And then it happened. Mad Spencer pounced on him, with much more force and agility than he had seemed capable of. He launched himself at Terrence, punching him in the chest, then jumped off to one side, resuming his awkward and terrifying dance. Terrence fell to the floor, clutching his ribs, gasping for air. He was very much aware of Mad Spencer roaming around him, closing in on him, and he knew he had to get back on his feet soon.

But Mad Spencer did not attack again. Instead he waited patiently for Terrence to stand up, gave him a wicked smile, and lurched at him a second time. Terrence's arms shot in front of his face instinctively, awaiting the blow. But it never came. Mad Spencer brushed past him and collapsed on the floor, clutching his ankle. Terrence looked at him, confused.

Then, before he could think about it twice he leant over and turned Mad Spencer on his stomach, pressing down on him as hard a he could until the ten second countdown had finished. The moment the first round victory was declared to be his, he jumped back panting into his corner. Mad Spencer stood up slowly. He was still smiling, but the smile was no longer amused. It was a calculating, hateful, nasty smile which told Terrence that they both understood this was to be an unfair battle. Glancing down at his opponent's ankle bracelet, Terrence thought that today might not be the day he died after all.

The countdown to the next round resounded around them but this time Mad Spencer remained very still. Only his eyes were moving, darting from side to side, catching every single sliver of movement around him. Terrence wondered what to do. No matter how much he tried to push himself to lurch forward, he could not move a single muscle. They stood facing each other for an agonisingly long time. He wondered what Mad Spencer was waiting for. His own legs started to tremble, tired as he was trying to keep his entire body engaged and ready for the fight.

Slowly, Mad Spencer lifted a bony hand up to his face, and looked at it in mock amazement, as if he was seeing it for the very first time. He turned it and swayed it in front of his eyes, his face lit up with wonder. Then he lifted his other hand and examined it with the same interest. He raised his arms, moved them around, observing them with curiosity. The whole thing was the oddest, most tantalising of ballets. Terrence frowned, his attention focused on Mad Spencer's dark, eerie dance.

It all happened in an instant. A pang of pain flashed over Mad Spencer's face, snapping Terrence straight out of his reverie. He suddenly realised how close Mad Spencer had got to him. He had been so entranced by his arms and face, he had failed to see he was edging his way forward, slithering in his direction like a poisonous snake. He glanced down, to see his adversary's ankle bracelet was flashing red. Someone somewhere was determined to keep the game interesting by giving him a slim chance of winning. Mad Spencer interrupted his dance, but this time he did not retreat. The ankle bracelet flashed again and again, a sign that shock after shock was being administered. Mad Spencer's face twitched with every single jolt, but he seemed to use the pain to fuel his determination. He took small steps, giggling all the way, as though the sharp unbearable pain Terrence knew he was enduring were mere tickles. Terrence sprung back to attention and shifted to one side. Mad Spencer adjusted his trajectory, moving with slow painful steps towards him. Suddenly he jumped at Terrence, his hand outstretched, his face contorted in a look of perverse amusement. His fist caught Terrence in the throat, sending him face down onto the ground.

It was pain like Terrence had never experienced before. Like drowning and burning and suffocating all at the same time. His hands wrapped around his throat as if to free it from its invisible shackles. He curled up on the floor, unable to breathe, willing his lungs to draw in some air.

A voice in the distance announced his opponent the winner of the second round, and Terrence felt a painful sense of dread at the idea of having to face another fight. He lay motionless, his breathing ragged, his body limp, hoping that if he stayed still for long enough people might forget he was even there.

What was the point of fighting? He wondered. What was the point of any of it when, even if he *did* win the battle at hand, he may only be buying himself another few days of purposeless existence. Right there and then, curled up on the floor, he was amazed that he had gone on living all these years. Yet he *had* crawled from one day to the next, from dawn to dusk, cruising through his own mind and body like neither were truly his own. What was it, he thought, that had kept him going?

And then, he knew. Of course, he knew. He had always known. The one and only thing he craved.

Maddison.

Her name flashed in his mind like lightening, echoing through his chest and heart. Maddison. Deep down he had kept on hoping. Hoping against all hope that she was at the end of whatever twisted road he was on. If he could see her one last time, it would make every single agonising second of his life in jail and on this joke of a 'show' worth it. As much as he had tried to bury that wild hope, it had been waiting, just below the surface, to manifest into reality.

He could not give up, not now. Not after everything he had endured. Not without seeing his daughter again. The thought of her blew fresh air into his lungs and pumped blood into his feeble heart. He struggled to his feet, slowly, painfully. He looked up towards the other corner of the ring and his eyes met Mad Spencer's wild gaze.

Then, in the background, Terrence heard something strange. Like the sound of millions of people whispering at the same time. He turned around, looking at the audience, remembering for the first time since he had stepped on the ring that they were even there. The sound of their clamour hit him right through the stomach, as if someone had ramped up the volume all of a sudden. They were not whispering, they were yelling and clapping and stomping their feet. All four judges were on their feet, clapping their hands and punching the air with their fists. He gazed at the arena, dumbfounded, realising with a knot in his throat that they were cheering for him. They were *supporting* him.

Terrence caught Sean Cravanaugh's eyes and a primitive sense of fury overtook him. It was anger he had rarely felt before, all-consuming and deadly, sparked by the look of smug satisfaction on Cravanaugh's face; the look of a man used to getting his own way, regardless of how anyone involved felt about it.

Somewhere in the distance the fight bells rang, and without thinking about it for even a second, Terrence spun on his heels and threw himself at Mad Spencer, taking him by surprise. Terrence plummeted into him at waist height, sending his adversary flying against the ring cords. He could no longer stop himself, his body and his brain were no longer connected. He got hold of a handful of Mad Spencer's dirty hair and pulled him forward again. He let go of him, violently pushing him to the ground and started kicking and punching, kicking and punching, kicking and punching until he no longer knew what he was doing or why. His limbs were doing their own thing, lashing out with all the strength that he had left, against the injustice of it all. He was kicking and punching for all that was unfair, for people like Sean Cravanaugh having so much power over everyone, for scum like Mad Spencer still being alive despite the unspeakable things they had done, for how out of control his own life had spun, despite his best intentions.

The bell indicating the end of the fight rang loudly, snapping him awake, back to reality, bringing before his eyes the horrible mess he had made. Mad Spencer's limp figure lay on the ground, face down, bloody and bruised. Terrence's heart skipped a beat. Had *he* done this? What was happening to him?

He raised his hands, only to see they were trembling uncontrollably and covered in blood. He took a few steps back, dread pouring over him. He felt strong hands take hold of his upper arms and walk him back to his spot in the metal cage, under roaring applause from the audience. Terrence's disconcerted face searched the crowd, looking for some ounce of sense in this madness. He found none. He glanced back over his shoulder to see two guards dragging Mad Spencer away, his head bobbing at an awkward angle, all signs of life gone from his face. Terrence shuddered. All around him, the audience was chanting 'Time for justice! Time for justice!' over and over again.

Was *this* justice? Terrence wondered. Was making one man compromise his soul to shatter another, no matter how despicable his opponent may be, any sort of justice? If any of it was at all fair, then what kind of world was this?

CHAPTER 46

TYLER BENSON

Pitching the country's favourite underdog against their most despised contestant had been genius. And, as with all twisted genius ideas on this show, it had been Sean Cravanaugh's. Tyler watched uneasily as the last contestant fell to the ground and the very last bell rang. He patted his jacket pocket absentmindedly, checking for the small container. Knowing the pills were there gave him some comfort. He tried his best to ignore the prickling pain in his chest and conjured up his brightest, shiniest smile.

'What a show!' He exclaimed, in that impeccable tone he had learnt to master. 'Wasn't that something! Of our ten contestants we now have five winners, which also means we have five losers…' He paused for suspense. 'Whilst our five winners will go through to the next round, our five losers are now all at risk of leaving the competition. But…' The audience held its breath as one. 'We have a surprise for you tonight! One of our losing contestants will be given the opportunity to remain and proceed further in the competition…Who will remain and who will leave the competition… Find out after the break!' He exclaimed, and the red light on the camera in front of him went off.

Tyler kept his smile on, and walked off the stage, finding refuge backstage. He found a quiet corner, somewhat hidden from view and leaned against the wall, resting his head back, closing his eyes. He took a deep breath, giving his heart a moment to catch up. The prickling sensation came and went these days, a clear sign that he was allowing the stress of his current assignment to get to him more than he should. He fished out the bottle of little red pills from his jacket pocket and twisted the lid open with shaking fingers. He swallowed a couple of the pills and closed his eyes again, waiting for them to take effect. The relief they gave him generally came swiftly, though in the past week or so he had noticed that their action seemed more and more delayed. He wondered whether he needed to increase his dosage, but since he was already taking more than he had been prescribed, he had not dared. A little voice at the back of his head told him to enquire, to ask exactly what he had been given, and to look into whether it could trigger any side effects. But the voice was very low, almost inaudible in fact, and the more pills he took, the more of a murmur it became.

Whatever the pills contained, they made everything alright, albeit for a short while. It made the failure of his marriage and the trap of his work contract a distant memory. For a while, he could just about pretend that his regrets and bitterness did not exist. Whilst the mystery substance from the pills coursed through his veins, he was young again, at the peak of his success, back when he and Constance still had a life together. For a few precious moments he still had hope that things were unchanged, that his money and fame did not affect them, that his marriage would go on forever.

No, he knew, with such sadness it was almost unbearable, the little voice questioning the pills really stood no chance.

A faraway voice announced in his earpiece that they would be live again in one minute. He gulped heavily, trying his best to swallow the lump that had formed in his throat and threatened to suffocate him. Before he had time to think of anything else for too long, he was back on stage, facing the main cameras, intently listening to the countdown in his earpiece, ready to go again.

'And we are back again, live from the Cradle!' He exclaimed jovially, and the audience roared, as they always did. 'Behind me are the losers of the last round, who all face elimination. However, one of them has been randomly chosen during the break for a chance to remain in the competition. The contestant who has been drawn will face an additional challenge after which they will go through to the next round.'

A flicker of excitement rippled through the crowd.

'And without further ado,' Tyler said conspiratorially, 'I can reveal that the contestant who will take the extra challenge and remain in the competition... is... contestant... sixty-two!'

Contestant sixty-two. Spencer Martins. As Tyler uttered these last words the audience rose in uproar as they realised who was being handed a lifeline. Of course, Tyler knew, this was no random picking at all. He caught sight of Cravanaugh. His boss was wearing what he knew was a false expression of shock, like he was as surprised as everyone else to discover this turn of events. Tyler watched as he stood up, a microphone tightly clenched in his fist. The audience magically fell quiet the moment the large screens reflected the image of the head judge.

'What the hell just happened?' Sean Cravanaugh looked outraged, instantly receiving loud approval from the audience. 'This...' he denounced, pointing a finger behind him, 'this is *exactly* why we made this show. So that anyone who tries to get away with the horrible things they've done can be properly put to trial. And I'm not talking about courtrooms here, because we've all seen how well *that* turned out...' He rolled his eyes and made a derisive gesture with his hand. 'I'm talking about the trial that we, as a country, all get to be the judges of. Today, *you* get to be the judge, jury and executioner, so that a piece of scum like that man right there no longer gets to get away with raping and murdering little girls! Are you with me?!'

His words were like oil on a blazing fire, it spread through the crowd at record speed, fuelling their hatred. Cravanaugh raised his fist above his head.

'Time for justice! Time for justice!' The audience chanted in unison.

Tyler knew he had to make the transition as smooth as possible, though he felt a knot tightening at the pit of his stomach.

'The challenge the contestant will face, which was drawn at random, is 'A Game of Darts'.'

A murmur of anticipation flew through the crowd. Tyler felt his chest constrict and he struggled to keep his smile on. He forced himself to stay calm and to breathe. His hand was clenched around his microphone and it was as much as he could manage to keep it from shaking. He could feel beads of sweat form along his temples.

It lasted a second, and within a flicker of a moment it was over.

'May we have the contestant to the centre of the stage?' Tyler asked loudly, dismissing the moment with a shake of the head.

Two guards brought Spencer Martins to the middle of the stage. The contestant was tied, spread eagle, to a wide rectangular wooden panel by his wrists and ankles. A thick leather strap secured his waist.

'For this challenge,' Tyler commented in as chirpy a tone as he could muster, 'we have invited two of the world's best darts players to join us. They will play three games of darts together, right here on this stage… but…' He paused for a fraction of a second, '*but*, the board they will be playing with is no ordinary board!'

The production staff were setting up a large opaque fabric panel, with a magnified darts board printed in its centre, in front of the wooden panel the contestant was tied on.

'Our two darts champions will be playing on this very special board. Each area has a different colour and each colour wins the player a certain amount of points. Each player will get five throws each per round. The player who comes up with the highest score at the end of three rounds will win a monumental one hundred and fifty grand cash prize.'

The audience gasped audibly and Tyler smiled.

'Let's welcome our players onstage. Please give them a big round of applause!'

Two rowdy-looking men walked onto the stage towards the darts board. Behind the fabric panel, a guard stuffed a large gag into Spencer Martins' mouth.

'Let the game begin!' Tyler announced with a flourish.

The first player carefully picked a dart and inspected it. Its metal spike was longer than normal darts. The man aimed for several seconds and threw. The dart zoomed ahead, piercing the fabric panel with a soft sound, ending its course in Spencer Martins' arm, lodging itself deeply into his flesh. The moment the metal point came in contact with his body, the contestant made as if to scream but, gagged as he was, no sound came out. His eyes closed and his face constricted, a ripple of pain travelling across his entire body. His hands contracted into tight fists. Pearls of blood peaked through the fabric of his overalls, forming a dark red circle around the dart's tip. The second player aimed and threw, his dart aimed straight at Spencer Martin's stomach.

On and on it went for twenty-eight more throws. In between each round, the board was changed, becoming each time more precise and more intricate, aligning the high value targets with Spencer Martins' more vulnerable body parts.

Tyler watched, nestled in one corner of the stage, his stomach lurching with every throw. The previous weeks had brought some insane challenges, each more gruesome than the one before. But the more he saw, the harder Tyler found it to bear. It was not only the blood and pain he struggled with, although this was definitely taking its toll on him. What had made the experience so soul-shattering for Tyler had been how easily the country had rallied behind such a massacre. Never in his wildest dreams would he have imagined that people – hard-working, honest, law-abiding citizens – could fall down to such a level. Tyler could not fathom how anyone could bear to witness the slaughter of another human being in such atrocious ways, let alone encourage it and enjoy the experience. Was he the only one to think this way? Could no one else *see* what was going on? Or was there something wrong with *him* for questioning it all?

The challenge eventually came to an end, points were added up, a winner was declared and the two darts players walked off the stage, waving at the crowd, one of them carrying an oversized cardboard check under his arm. An advert break was called whilst the panels were discarded and the darts extracted from Spencer Martins' bleeding body. Tyler fought the gag reflex which spurted something bitter and acidic against the back of his throat and tongue. He wondered whether he had time to sprint to his changing room and relieve his unsettled stomach, but someone was already announcing they would be live in a minute. Tyler swallowed hard, wishing he could find a hole to hide in for the rest of his days. He adjusted his tie and smoothed out the lapels of his jacket, popped a couple of the red pills into his mouth, and walked back onstage.

'Before the break, contestant number sixty-two went through an additional challenge, a lifeline allowing him to go onto to the next stage of the competition,' he said, in a voice which did not quite feel like his own anymore. 'And what a challenge it was! Let's see what our judges thought of that.'

He strode to the judges' table and stood in front of them. Josh Carter seemed pale, his face an odd shade of light green. He looked uneasy and swaying, as if he was about to pass out, or vomit, or both.

Camilla, like Josh Carter, looked a little whiter than usual although, contrary to her fellow judge, the expression on her face was hard and cold. It was a strange expression on such a pretty face. Next to her, Sean Cravanaugh appeared at ease. He had one arm resting on the back of Camilla's seat, and the other nonchalantly laid on the desk in front of him. Tyler saw him glance furtively sideways at Camilla, a look of concern in his eyes.

'Mrs Swan,' Tyler turned his attention back to the task at hand, 'what did you think of our contestant's performance on this last challenge?'

Valery Swan leaned forward and clasped her hands together on the desk in front of her.

'It was definitely entertaining,' she said.

The audience laughed a little, and Tyler tried to keep up his smile as the word 'entertaining' kept bouncing and spiralling around in his head.

'But my colleague over here clearly has a different opinion on the matter,' Valery Swan turned to Josh Carter, who had his head hidden in his hands.

The audience started booing. Josh Carter looked around him, looking dizzier and more frightened than ever. It was clearly one thing watching the audience shout their disgust at the contestants, and quite another to be at the receiving end of it. Something seemed terribly off with Josh Carter. Tyler did not know what to do, or even whether he should be intervening at all. As he took a step towards Josh Carter, the man stood up, vacillating awkwardly on his feet, and ran off in the direction of the backstage entrance, one hand tightly held over his mouth. The audience's jeers followed him every single step of the way until, before their very eyes, Josh Carter could not contain himself any longer and vomited loudly, just a few steps before the safety of the backstage area. The audience burst into laughter and the sound of it felt cruel and harsh. Josh Carter stood there, white as a sheet, bent over halfway, with his hands on his knees and his eyes closed, apparently unable to take another step. With a click of his fingers, Sean Cravanaugh sent two production staff to Josh Carter's rescue and they all watched him be half-escorted, half-dragged off behind the wooden panels.

'I don't think our little friend Mr Carter is up to the task after all,' smirked Sean Cravanaugh, and his comment sent more ripples of harsh laughter through the crowd. 'Shall we continue without him?'

Of course, the audience roared in agreement. They were on their feet and their clamour rose up through the arena's open roof, higher and higher until it felt like the night sky was full of their determination to see this through to the end. They would stand, Tyler was certain, until the very last contestant had taken their very last breath. Never in a million years would they let any of them escape now. It's over, Tyler thought, and there was nothing any of them could do to change the course of history. It's over, Tyler thought again, though he was not sure he even begun to grasp the enormity of the words.

CHAPTER 47

MEDINA SALIM

Medina sat in the little waiting room on the ground floor of the 'Stronger Together' office, a charity which provided free legal advice and social services to low income households. One of their services included support in rehoming children from broken families, providing precious and much needed assistance to the over-flooded government-funded service.

Since her latest realisation, Medina had been working tirelessly to find out the various organisations which could have handled young Maddison's case at the time. She had drawn a list of all possibilities, based on the services they provided and whether they covered the specific neighbourhood the Blakes had lived in. She had methodically called every single option on her list, at times choosing honesty to justify her request, and other times lying through her teeth to get any scrap of information she could. She met rejection after rejection, but her persistence had coaxed shreds of information from some of the people she spoke to.

By Thursday morning, her research left Medina with four organisations which could have rehomed the little girl, and she set off to visit them all. She quickly managed to cross the first two off her list, having convinced the people behind the reception desks in both places to confirm the information she needed.

When she tried her little speech on the receptionist at 'Stronger Together', she realised that finding out what she wanted here would prove much harder than it had been in the other places. The lady at the reception desk gave her a cold, disgusted look, and barked at her to go away. Medina did not answer back, instead she went to sit down in the waiting room, wondering what to do next. She could see the receptionist glaring at her from her desk, watching her closely. Medina pretended not to notice. Her eyes glossed over the posters around the waiting room. In the corner of the room, a faded poster gave information about the social and rehoming service the charity offered. Medina stood up to look at it more closely. The background was an old, faded shade of green and large white text told of the care and attention with which the charity's staff handled every single rehoming case. It had a picture of a child with his back turned, holding a stuffed bear in one tiny fist and clinging to a woman's hand with the other. Medina looked at the poster, unable to draw her eyes from it, wondering where she might have seen it before, because it looked vaguely familiar.

Movement around the reception desk caught her eye, and she glanced over her shoulder to see the receptionist giving her seat to a young man. The woman noticed Medina watching them and she leaned, whispering, towards her colleague, pointing at Medina unashamedly. The young man nodded, and the woman left, with one last nasty look at Medina.

Medina looked back at the poster, knowing that the change in employee was a chance for her to try her luck once more. She approached the reception desk once more.

'Listen,' the sound man rose a hand to silence her before she could say a word, 'I can't tell you anything. We're legally not allowed to provide any information to any third parties about the cases we handle.'

Medina opened her mouth to speak, but the receptionist was on a roll, and he did not give her a chance to comment.

'Now, if you were one of the clients we rehomed, a parent, or a legal guardian that would be a different story but...'

'I am!' Medina spurted out before she even had a second to think it through.

The young man looked at her in shock, his eyes wide open and his mouth hanging open almost comically.

'I am one of your former clients,' Medina repeated, her hands shaking, her brain working as fast as she could to weave a convincing lie.

The young man looked at her suspiciously, unconvinced.

'I came here fifteen years ago,' she said quickly, taking out one of the article cuttings she carried around with her everywhere, and showing it to the young man. 'I must have arrived around this date,' she pointed at a highlighted section in the article which stated the date of Terrence Blake's arrest.

The young man leaned over to read the article and looked up at her again, a glint of awe in his eyes.

'You're...' He mumbled. 'This...' He struggled to find his words. '*The* Terrence Blake? The one on telly?'

Medina nodded gravely, almost holding her breath. The young man took the article from her and looked from the page to Medina.

'Look,' Medina whispered, her voice shaking a little, the weight of the lie threatening to tie her tongue, 'I don't need much information, I just want to know whether this really is my story. My adoptive parents didn't tell me anything, but I've been piecing it up together and think this is where I came from,' she pointed again at the article. 'Can you just tell me if I'm wrong or not? Then I promise I'll leave and I won't bother you again.'

The young man looked at her closely, and Medina could see the cogs turning and clicking in his head whilst he decided whether or not to believe her.

'I have a right to know,' she pleaded, pulling together her best impression of a damsel in distress.

'Do you even have any proof?' The young man asked, 'any paperwork from your adoptive parents?'

Medina shook her head, suddenly worried her opportunity might slip between her fingers. She had to think, and think fast.

'When I asked them,' she said, her voice breaking a little as she tried to conjure a tear or two from the corners of her eyes, 'they said they burnt everything. They didn't want me to find out...'

She did a little backflip in her head when she realised that she had managed a few tears. She felt guilty at making up lie after lie to this rather innocent-looking young man's face. The receptionist stared at her for a few moments, his mouth twitching slightly.

'If I give you any information, I could lose my job,' he shook his head apologetically, and Medina's heart sank a little. 'I'm sorry I can't help you...' He winced.

Medina went back to sit in the empty waiting room, unsure what to do next, the feeling that she was close to a breakthrough building inside her gut. She closed her eyes and forced herself to breathe. She could not tell how long she sat there, refusing to give up.

Eventually, some noise in the room made her open her eyes and jerk her head to the side. Over at the reception desk, the young man was talking to a small group of smartly dressed people. Medina watched as the receptionist led the new arrivals around the corner and down a corridor, until they disappeared from sight.

She did not give herself time to think. She got to her feet and strode to the desk. She listened carefully for a sign that someone might be coming, but the place was completely silent. She looked down the corridor, checking that no one was around, before hurrying down the end of the corridor, checking the sign on every door, until she came one that read 'filing room'.

She placed her hand on the handle, her heart beating fast, and looked around, half expecting an army of security guards to lunge at her any moment. But the corridor was empty and she could hear no sign that an alarm had been raised. With one last glance around, she stepped into the room, closing the door again behind her.

The room she found herself in was not as big as she had expected. It was full of tall shelves, lined one after the other from one edge of the room to the other. Every single shelf was stacked with cardboard boxes and files. The crammed space smelled of dust, mould and ageing paper.

Medina walked around the room, trying to understand the filing system, but after a minute or two she had to concede that whatever logic was in place escaped her. She roamed between the shelves slowly, looking at the labels on the boxes at random, wondering what to do. Where should she start? Was there even any point, given the little time she had and the mammoth task at hand?

She took a few steps and froze, as her ears caught the distant noise of a conversation. The voices were getting louder. She looked around frantically. Did she have time to run to the door and leave? By the sound of it, the people were coming directly towards her. She switched off the light and strode all the way to the furthest corner of the room, crouching between the side of a shelf and a tall pile of boxes. She cowered in her makeshift hideout, listening intently as the voices approached and, as she had feared, the door handle turned. The door opened, sending a beam of light through the darkness of the room.

'... And I tell her, why don't *you* go and do it yourself! Isn't that what you're paid for?' A male voice said, causing the other person, another man, to snort in agreement, 'she's a real piece of work, I tell you!'

'Yeah, I wouldn't be sorry to see the back of her!' The second man agreed, 'anyway, where should I put this?'

'Just chuck it anywhere you find space. No one follows the system anymore,' the first man responded, confirming Medina's earlier suspicion.

There was a ruffling noise, as if someone was shifting some boxes and paper around, and sliding cardboard around on the shelves. Medina listened intently as they finished stacking their boxes and left, plunging the room into darkness again. She stood up, picking up her phone to light up the way ahead. She had no time to search, and her new priority was to get out of there.

She stood behind the door quietly, listening for any sounds on the other side. She could not hear anything at all, and decided to risk it. She opened the door slowly and ran up the corridor. When she zoomed past the reception desk, the young man called out to her, but she did not turn back and kept walking straight out the main door. Once on the pavement, she ran. She sprinted down the street and around a couple of corners, zigzagging from street to street, without really knowing where she was going, thinking only of putting as much distance as possible between her and the building she had just exited.

Eventually she slowed down, glancing around her to check she had not been followed, though she already knew no one had set off after her. She took out her phone to check her live map application and see where she was. She noticed as the screen lit up that she had several missed calls from Clive and Miranda. She frowned. The last time she had spoken to Miranda, the previous Saturday, nothing had sounded particularly out of the ordinary. But again, she remembered, she had not been truly listening to the conversation at the time.

First, get home, she thought. Then, once she reached the safety of her studio she would call Miranda and Clive and find out what they wanted.

CHAPTER 48

MEDINA SALIM

When Medina reached her apartment, she was surprised to see Miranda and Clive waiting for her by the stairs to her building's front door. They both looked pale and tired.

'What's wrong?' Medina asked as she reached them, suddenly worried.

Clive and Miranda exchanged a weary look.

'Why don't we go upstairs, where we can talk,' Clive said, in his usual gentle soft-spoken manner.

They climbed the stairs to her apartment in silence. Medina felt her anxiety rise with every single step she took. Once inside, Miranda headed straight for the kitchenette and busied herself with making them all a cup of tea. Medina frowned. Tea was Miranda's answer to pretty much every single problem in life, something that Medina had always thought oddly patriotic.

'What's going on?' Medina asked, unable to take any more of the silence which had stretched between them.

Miranda kept her attention straight on the boiling kettle, dropping tea-bags into three mismatched cups. Clive, who was studying her wall of investigations, came to sit on the edge of her bed and beckoned her over.

'Sweetheart,' he started calmly, 'there's something we need to talk about, and it may come as a shock.'

Medina swallowed hard, but said nothing. Miranda came to join them, carrying three cups of tea and a small jug of milk, which she placed on the coffee table in front of them. Clive breathed in deeply. When he spoke again, his voice was uncertain.

'We need to talk about your biological family.'

The words hung in the air around them. This was never a subject they had broached in great detail, as they had both always insisted they knew nothing of what her life had been before she came to live with them. Medina had eventually stopped asking, finding no reason to believe they would conceal anything from her. She waited for Clive to continue.

'When we got you,' Clive added, 'we were given the option of hearing where you came from. At the time, your mother and I discussed it and we thought it best if we knew nothing of your previous circumstances. It gave us all a chance to start afresh.'

Miranda sniffed loudly. Big tears were rolling over her cheeks. Clive glanced at his wife and Medina saw the pain in his eyes.

'Maybe it was a selfish decision on our part,' he sighed, 'maybe it was not so much to give you a new start in life, but rather a way for us to ensure you would never want to leave us to go back to your family.'

Medina felt a ball grow and tighten inside her throat.

'Either way,' Clive continued, 'this is the decision we made at the time. I hope one day you can forgive us if you think it was the wrong one...'

His voice broke a little. Medina waited, hanging off the edge of her bed, wanting to shake Clive, to scream at him to hurry, to keep speaking. But all she could do was sit there, with her hands knotted on her lap, her knuckles white with tension.

'The agency who handled your case at the time must have seen this happen a hundred times, because they repeatedly told us we could come and retrieve your file at any time. They said that one day we might want to know or that...' He paused to take a breath, 'that *you* were likely to ask about your family. The child therapist who saw you when you arrived at the agency said you suffered from traumatic amnesia, and that your brain had blocked out your previous life as a protective mechanism. She wasn't sure whether any of it would ever come back to you...'

Clive looked up at Miranda and nodded at her. Miranda hesitated, then reached for her handbag, pulling out a large brown envelope and placing it on the table in front of them.

'We paid a visit to the agency yesterday and asked for a copy of your file,' Clive studied her face. 'We haven't opened it. We've never felt the need to know. To us, you are and you will always be *our* daughter, regardless of what happened before.'

He paused again, and looked at Miranda, who was still crying silent tears. Medina said nothing. She was mesmerised by the brown envelope. There it was. Within reach. The answer to her life's biggest question, to years and years of doubt and self-loathing. And yet she could not bring herself to move a single muscle. Never in her life had she been so close to the truth, to uncovering the most important clue of them all, to solving her own case. Despite that, she did not feel excited. She did not feel anything she thought she would when she finally got to this very moment. She felt scared. Terrified, in fact. Because it was one thing to be angry that she did not know, angry at her previous family for abandoning her, angry at the world for letting her lead a life where such a huge part of her was missing, but it was quite another to be so near to knowing whether those years of anger had been justified.

'Why now?' Medina asked, her voice just a whisper.

Clive and Miranda exchanged another look.

'We thought we might have an idea who your family was,' Clive said.

Medina stared at him in disbelief.

'Do you mean you figured it out? Out of nowhere?'

'Not *quite* out of nowhere,' Clive conceded. 'A couple of days ago, Pedro came to see us...'

'What does Pedro have to do with any of it?' Medina blurted out.

'He came to us after you two went on your little... erm... excursion,' Clive chose his words carefully, 'he said you had gone to visit Terrence Blake's house for an investigation on your blog.'

Medina nodded.

'He gave us something he found there,' Clive reached into the inner pocket of his jacket, and extracted a handful of photographs, which he handed over to Medina.

Medina took the pictures with shaking fingers and flicked through them. They were aged black and white shots, depicting the Blake family. Most of them showed Terrence Blake with his daughter, or the child on her own. One of them showed the entire Blake family. The child was in her father's arms, her little arms wrapped around his neck. By their side stood a slim woman, whom Medina figured was the mother. It suddenly struck her as odd that despite her thorough research she had not come across any photos of the woman who was so close to the centre of the story.

She studied that last shot, glancing at the faces on the picture. The girl and her father were looking at each other, smiling. The mother however was standing rigidly by their side, her expression strained. Medina could not take her eyes off her. The picture was a little faded and damaged by the years, but something about the woman's face seemed strangely familiar. She kept looking at it, unable to identify where the feeling was coming from.

She looked up to find both Miranda and Clive staring at her with sadness.

When she looked down at the photograph again, she knew.

She understood why the woman's face looked so familiar.

She knew why she felt she had seen it before. She saw it every single time she looked in a mirror. The face of the woman in the photograph was so obviously like her own that she could not understand why it had not struck her right away. The woman was like an older version of herself. Only their hair was a little different. Medina froze as the realisation dawned on her.

She put the photographs down on the table and took the brown envelope from the table, already knowing what she would find in it. She flicked through every page of the file. It felt like an eternity passed before she dared to look up again, before she met Clive and Miranda's eyes. Miranda reached into her handbag again and deposited something on Medina's lap.

'You had this with you when we picked you up…' Miranda's voice was a barely audible murmur.

Medina looked down at the object and gasped. It was a worn out, colourful stuffed rabbit. Its ears were different lengths, and one of them seemed to have been sown back on many a time. It was made of the exact same amateur patchwork as the other toys she had come across in the Blakes' house.

She brought the rabbit to her nose and inhaled deeply. A familiar, long-forgotten fragrance travelled up her nostrils and soothed the back of her throat. She closed her eyes. Fragments of memories came rushing back in a disorderly flow. Images and colours and sensations she had sometimes dreamt of without realising they carried any significance. A wide blurry typhoon of broken events swirled round and round in her mind. Her brain was overwhelmed with the realisation. Her heart was aching, though she was not sure whether it was because she was glad to finally remember, or sad that she had once forgotten.

She held the stuffed rabbit to her face and wept silently, the years of ignorance hitting her with full force now. She felt her sobs drench the soft fabric of the stuffed toy but she did not care. She brought it to her lips and kissed it softly.

'Leon…' She whispered.

CHAPTER 49

SHAUNA MULLIGHAN

The atmosphere in the studio was so intense that Shauna had to force herself to sit still on her chair and stop herself from fidgeting. She had been rearranging her notes, fiddling with her mug, stirring her sugar in the now stone-cold coffee, and constantly getting up to chat to the production staff to check on various items before the live news broadcast started. It was Friday evening, one day before the next 'No Pain, No Game' episode, and there was a sense of great expectation in the air. The news item on their agenda was not just news, it was *breaking* news, and no one else in the country had the story yet.

Shauna caught herself nibbling on her nails and slapped her hands back into the desk. Never in her entire career had she felt so much anticipation. So far, the competition had been an isolated news item. It had followed its course without affecting anything or anyone else. Or so they had all thought. In reality, a multitude of smaller pieces had been carefully and discreetly moved around the giant chess board they now all started to see more clearly. There had been single incidents here and there. Penitentiary establishments closing across the country for 'lack of qualified personnel' and inmates being shuffled around in small groups, causing barely a ripple on the news. The voices surrounding the televised game had been so loud that no one had paid attention to anything else, especially since

Terrence Blake's singing performance and the speculations around his alleged innocence.

Shauna was amazed at people's capacity to create their own truth. How wonderful it was that shreds of suggestive messaging could create such an assertive collective narrative, as long as it was packaged in the right way. Shauna knew the country had been desperate for change, for something, *anything*, to happen, but she would not have thought it possible for people to unite behind something which was barely better than what dictatorships perpetrated all over the globe. Now, it seemed, the degraded life they all had to endure justified the horror. Shauna shivered at the thought.

She looked down at her notes again, pleased with her angle. She wanted to make people see the situation for what it really was. She wanted to throw a curveball into the mix, something to challenge the strange equilibrium the show had brought to people's day-to-day. Her version had been a hard sell to her superiors, because it was bound to create controversy and many argued that it would be best not to challenge the status quo. Had it been a different topic, Shauna might have given up, but not this time. This was too big and too important to be hushed down.

Today, finally, she would spring to the next level in her career. In a time where most people followed the trends, she was about to set herself apart as someone with the guts to go countercurrent. Someone mature enough and confident enough in her own skin to dare to defy mass opinions. She would be surprised if she did not get a few calls from larger channels on her way out of the studio later with lucrative job offers. This was her moment, the one she had been waiting for her whole life. She just could not wait to grab it with both hands and run with it.

As the clock displaying the countdown to the live broadcast showed that they had two minutes to go, Shauna saw a small group of people approach her desk. The man leading the way was her superior, Mr Richards, closely followed by the director of the channel, Mr Brand. Close behind them was a young man she thought might be some sort of assistant on the team, and a couple of men in black suits. She straightened up immediately. Her boss gestured to the others to wait behind and he walked up to her on his own, sitting on the edge of her desk, his hands crossed on his lap.

'Is something the matter?' She asked, unable to hide her apprehension.

Mr Richards sighed and leaned in towards her.

'Shauna,' the tone he used was like the one he might use to reason with a grumpy child, 'we have to change our angle on tonight's story. We're going with the accident.'

Shauna's eyes widened and her mouth felt open. She was not sure whether she was more shocked at the news themselves or the patronising way in which they were being delivered.

'What?' She breathed. 'But we've been over this just this afternoon, we...'

'I know, I know,' Mr Richards cut her off dismissively. 'Listen, this is not coming from me,' he jerked his head back to the group of men waiting on standby behind them, 'this is coming from way above you and I.'

Shauna opened her mouth, ready to defend her case, but her superior did not seem open to a collaborative discussion.

'The decision has been made, Shauna. Now, you can either go with the revised script, or we can find someone else to present tonight's programme.'

Shauna snorted loudly. Who would they find at such short notice to replace her? And even if they did find someone at the last minute, this was *her* show. People expected *her* to come on the screen, as she had for years now.

'It's up to you, Shauna. Are you happy to go with the new angle?'

Shauna was unable to gather her wits and find an appropriately sharp response. Behind Mr Richards' head, she could see the countdown clock edging closer and closer to the one minute mark.

'Shauna, it is yes or no? We have someone ready to jump in for you if you're uncomfortable with changing your story.'

'What?' She snapped, 'you can't just *replace* me! This is *my* broadcast! Our audience is expecting *me!*' She hissed, and even to her own ears she sounded childish and desperate.

Mr Richards sighed and shook his head.

'No one cares,' he smirked, 'no one gives a shit about you or your stupid broadcast. All they care about is the *news*, they won't look twice at who's delivering them.'

Shauna rose to her feet, but before she knew it the two men in the black suits she had seen waiting were upon her. Security, she realised too late. They grabbed her by the arms and pulled her away from the desk, towards the door. Glancing over her shoulder she saw with a sharp pang of disappointment Mr Richards and Mr Brand settle the young man into her seat.

CHAPTER 50

SEAN CRAVANAUGH

Sean sat in his office, sipping a scotch, the television switched onto LiveTV2. He wondered if the channel's executives had managed to convince Shauna Mullighan to change her story. He had, of course, been one of the first people alerted the moment the events had occurred, and both he and the Prime Minister had campaigned hard to contain the news. They were too close to their goal to let anyone mess with their plans. They had given the story to LiveTV2, with the condition that they would follow a precise script. The executive team at LiveTV2 had not taken long to agree. Whatever the angle used, they had seen the value in being the first national channel to break the news.

The news programme's jingle came on and an unknown young man appeared sitting behind the presenter's desk.

'Good evening, I'm Cedric Stock and you are live on LiveTV2 as we bring you the day's breaking news. Earlier today, a fire erupted in Cartford Hill penitentiary, one of the country's few remaining establishments, located in the north of the country. The fire is thought to have started in one of the kitchens, and quickly got out of hand. The flames destroyed several of the building's failsafe systems, including the automatic launch of the emergency water supply through the ceiling valves. The rising heat jammed the electric system controlling the opening of the emergency exits.

By the time the prison staff was able to open the doors to rescue the inmates, it was too late. There was no casualty amongst the staff, but the fire brigade who arrived on the site earlier this evening reported that there were no survivors amongst all five thousand and thirty-five inmates. Our special correspondent James Carson reports live from the scene. Over to you, James.'

Sean sat back into the plush sofa, a satisfied smile spread across his lips. The images on the screen changed to show the burnt mass of the prison buildings, darkened and ghostly, whilst a horde of firemen, prison wardens and emergency services staff roamed around in the background. The correspondent commented on the scene behind him, emphasising how hard the rescue team had worked to try and help the inmates, showing the very marks on the doors where they had tried to take them down with axes.

Sean flicked through the channels, noticing how several others tried to catch up with the news, though all they could do was piggy-back the same information LiveTV2 had shared. The news was spreading like wildfire. People talked of the bravery of the prison staff for risking their own lives to try and save those of unworthy mécréants. They spoke of the fast response time and hard work from the fire department. There were talks of how unfortunate it was that so many security systems should fail at the same time and speculation that inmates themselves had started the fire. There were figures coming out about how the country's criminal rates had improved over the past few months.

What no one wondered was why there were so many inmates on the site, when Cartford Hill had been designed to hold just a thousand convicts at a time. No one questioned the deficiency of the fire alarms or water valves. No one lingered on why all the exit doors had jammed at the same time. No one raised the point that at the very moment the fire started, not a single member of staff could be found amongst the inmates. No one wondered why the emergency axes, purpose-built to take down the very doors locking the convicts in the furnace had been inefficient in serving their purpose. No one asked at what time the fire brigade was called.

If anyone had asked any of these questions, Sean knew, they would have found that over the past few months, the country's criminal population had been shifted around like so many pawns. Some were moved from one penitentiary to another, some simply disappeared without a trace. A large portion of the surviving convicts had been transferred to Cartford Hill, slowly but surely, until the prison walls could barely hold them.

If anyone had questioned the events, they would have noticed that the prison staff had all left their posts discreetly, mere minutes before the fire was discovered in the kitchen. By the time the convicts noticed, all doors had been locked and security alarms disabled from the main control room. If any of the security cameras had survived the fire, which of course they had not, anyone watching the tape would have seen the wardens barricading the doors from the outside, and getting to the safety of the control tower, watching the events unravelling on the security cameras, until not a single soul survived within the brasier. At that time, the fire brigade was called, a few feeble attempts at breaking the doors down were made. By then, it was already too late.

No one asked, Sean knew full well, because no one cared. Amongst the discussions and debate, there was an unmistakable underlying sense of relief. Of course, it was unfortunate that there should have been so many casualties, but, really, was it not for the best? Did these people not deserve to die? With each passing hour the line of discussion morphed into something Sean had predicted, back when the events had been carefully planned. People were *glad*. Whatever had happened at Cartford Hill felt like the first step to recovery, and it no longer mattered that thousands of people had been burnt alive.

Sean had the sudden urge to laugh, because everyone who had ever tried to convince him of the good in people and their empathic abilities had been wrong. So. Bloody. Wrong. He, on the other hand, had always known his kind to be mind-numbingly gullible. A mass which could be manipulated with fancy ideas and clever words, for whom the security of numbers justified everything and anything, as long as enough of them were on the same side. He felt like he alone held the world in the palm of his hand. He could do *anything*. Better even, he could get anyone *to do* anything. He did not believe in God, but if he had, he would have guessed that where he was at that moment was pretty damn close to being almighty.

CHAPTER 51

SEAN CRAVANAUGH

The noise about the Cartford Hill fire was soon drowned by the much louder voices anticipating the semi-final of the 'No Pain, No Game' competition. After that night's episode, six would become three, until eventually, three would become just one.

Sean checked his reflection in the full-length mirror in his walk-in wardrobe. He checked his watch, satisfied to see he was on time. When he stepped out the front door, he was surprised to come face to face with a man in a clean black suit. Behind the man, a luxury black car was parked along the curb. The back seat window slowly came down and Camilla's impeccably made-up face poked through.

'Come on,' she called out to him, 'we can ride together.'

Sean slid next to Camilla on the back seat. He gave her an appraising look. She looked stunning, as always, clad in a tight turquoise dress which accentuated her figure to perfection, her hair tied back into an elaborate bun.

'This is a surprise,' he watched her closely, 'one might think you're having a change of heart...'

She looked him straight in the eyes, her beautiful face strained with anger.

'No,' she breathed sharply. 'If anything, I wanted to check that you are still ready to hold up your end of the bargain.'

'Why wouldn't I?' He asked, a hint of curiosity in his words.

Camilla shrugged and looked away. Sean sighed.

'Rest assured that nothing has changed, everything will go ahead as planned,' his voice was low, and though she did not turn to look at him again he saw her shoulders relax a little.

'Good,' she said finally, her eyes still fixed on the window.

They drove in silence for the rest of the journey to the Cradle. Sean knew they were getting closer to their destination because he could hear the now familiar rumble of the crowd waiting by the arena. By the time the driver had stopped the car at one of the main entrances, cordoned off to make a way for them to the door, the noise was so overpowering it seemed to press against the car like a waterfall.

The driver stepped out to open their doors and Sean shifted, ready to face the crowd. Camilla turned to look at him intently. There was pain, concern and fear in her eyes. She placed her hand on his and looked as thought she was about to say something, but no words came out. Her palm closed around his knuckles. She tilted her head to one side and gave him a weak smile. Sean understood, and he gave her fingers a squeeze.

'I know,' he said softly. 'It's ok.'

They stared at each other for a fragment of a second, then Camilla gave her window a little knock, letting go of Sean's hand. The door opened and she got gracefully to her feet, making her way up the red carpet, waving at the crowd, smiling at the unknown faces, stopping here and there for a picture or an autograph. Sean watched her for a moment, a strange sense of pride washing over him, until his own door opened and he followed her up to the Cradle door. He, too, waved and smiled and posed for badly-angled selfies.

When he reached the door, he offered Camilla his arm, and she slid her hand through, letting him escort her inside the building with a last wave at the people screaming their names behind them. It was not long before their smiles were gone, once they knew for certain they were out of sight. In their line of work they all had to develop a second face to wear on such occasions.

There was little room for genuine behaviour in the public sphere, and those who survived the longest were the ones who built the most convincing personas. After a while, it became second nature. Only when they reached the safety of their own company could they let the monster out. It always lay low somewhere, cowering in a corner, growing bigger and stronger with time, and the only way forward was to keep that monster under control, tightly chained in a recluse part of themselves. The world of fame and fortune was a solitary one, and not everyone was cut out for it.

Sean took Camilla to her dressing room and paused in front of the door.

'You alright?' He asked.

Camilla nodded.

'See you on the other side, then,' Sean whispered, and she gave him a small, unconvincing smile in return.

He watched as she stepped into her dressing room and closed the door. He heard the lock turn with a distinct 'click'.

~   ~   ~

Forty-five minutes later, Sean made his way to the backstage area, where he found Camilla and Valery Swan already waiting. Camilla was staring in the distance, fiddling with the thin gold bracelet dangling around her wrist. Valery was plunged deep in concentration on something on her phone. They both nodded at him when he approached. Tyler stood by the opposite end of the wooden panel, looking rather ill, next to the door he was scheduled to walk through. Josh Carter, however, was nowhere to be seen. Sean called up the head of the security team he had assigned to Josh Carter.

'Where's Carter?' He snapped.

'I'm afraid we've lost him, sir,' the head of the security team responded sheepishly. 'He left for the Cradle a couple of hours ago. We followed his car but lost him in traffic on the way…'

'What!' Sean exploded. 'Are you fucking *kidding* me? Why the *fuck* am I only hearing about this now?!'

'We have men searching the arena now, sir,' the man's voice was uncertain, 'we thought he might already have arrived, since the show's about to start. I apologise, sir, this is clearly our mista…'

Sean hung up the phone, cursing under his breath. After Josh Carter's reaction on the last episode, he had reinforced his security detail and had instructed them to keep an even closer eye on the judge than usual. What was the point of his careful planning if others only ever let him down? How he *hated* it when people failed him. He summoned a group of passing production staff and ordered them to search the premises for the fourth judge. They were due to go live in less than ten minutes and they were running out of time to get all of their ducks in a row, quite literally. The staff dispersed, spreading the word as they went to others around them, until very quickly the entire backstage area resonated with murmurs about the missing man.

It took most of their allotted time to find Josh Carter. With just over four minutes until the go-live time, a couple of staff members came dragging him backstage. Josh Carter was gesticulating and protesting, trying to free himself from his guardians. One thing was amply clear: Josh Carter was completely drunk. His gaze was unfocused and he swayed dangerously on his feet. He looked utterly confused, like he was trying hard to remember where he was and why he was there. The moment he saw Sean standing in front of him, he advanced menacingly.

'You!' Josh Carter yelled at Sean, a shaky finger pointed straight at him, 'you fucking… Insane… *You*!'

He was struggling for words, wobbling from side to side as he looked for the rest of his sentence in the muddled pathways of his drunken mind.

'You fucking lunatic!' He finally screamed.

Sean could smell Josh Carter's breath on his face and splatters of tequila-flavoured saliva landed on his cheeks, but he remained very still.

'What the *fuck* is wrong with you!' Josh Carter continued, 'who in their *fucking* right mind would do something like this?' He added gesturing around him wildly. 'I agreed to come here to defend… to defend…' Josh Carter paused, swaying dangerously on the spot, looking for a moment like he had already forgotten what he had meant to say. 'To defend fucking human rights!' He added angrily, the words coming out flowing out of his mouth now in a furious, tangled speech. 'But you don't fucking care about that, do you! You don't fucking care about anything! You fucking used me! You bastard! You used me! For your little circus! Sean Cravanaugh, the fucking puppet master,' he sneered, 'but you can't control *me*. No, no, no. No, sir! You can't keep using me! I won't be a part of this…' He hiccuped loudly. '…any… more! You hear me, you son of a bitch! I quit! I quit! You can do whatever you fucking want to but I won't be a part of this anymore! You hear me? You freak! You fucking *freak*!'

Josh Carter paused for a moment. Sean looked at him hard for a second and, without any warning, punched the drunken man in the face.

The jab sent Josh Carter flying backwards, stumbling dangerously, until he hit the ground. He groaned and struggled to his feet, grasping desperately for any leverage around him to help himself back up. His cheek was cut and his nose was bleeding. He brought a hand to his face and the sight of the red streaks on his fingers seemed to send renewed anger flooding to his pale face. He made as if to take a step forward but Sean was faster and, more importantly, sober and much more in control of his abilities than his opponent. Sean grabbed Josh Carter by the collar of his shirt and pushed him against the nearest wall, barring the man's throat with his forearm.

'Listen to me, you little shit,' Sean hissed.

His voice was low, but the backstage area had fallen so instantly quiet that his words seem to reverberate much louder than they actually were.

'You're right, I don't give a rat's arse. The only thing I *do* care about is the contract you signed when coming on the show. I'll accept your resignation, but only because the legal battle you're about to embark upon with my solicitors will strip you from everything you own and everyone you ever cared about.'

Josh Carter gripped Sean's forearm, trying to free his throat, desperately gasping for air.

'Now, you have thirty seconds to get out of my face or I swear to you, someone will need to carry you out of here in pieces,' Sean spat the words at Josh Carter's face, and pushed him aside.

A sudden look of recognition dawned on Josh Carter's face and he looked, terrified, at Sean, who was still towering over him. Josh Carter made as though to speak, but Sean grabbed him by the collar and threw him towards the nearest door. Everyone watched in absolute silence as the fourth judge scrambled to his feet and left. Two security guards hurried off swiftly after him. From his spot in the metal cage in the corner of the backstage area, Spencer Martins laughed and clapped, and his laughter resonated around them, until one of the guards sent a charge through his ankle bracelet to silence him.

Sean had predicted that Josh Carter would quit, just like he had expected Tyler to break. He seemed to have a sixth sense about his peers which gave him a valuable upper-hand. He often thought that his gift was only the ability to see his fellow human beings for what they really were. That no one was inherently good. That most people showed their true colours at the first hurdle, and that those colours rarely painted a pretty picture. It was this intuition which had led him to become so successful over the years. If he always expected someone to have a hidden sore spot, then all it ever took was for him to find that spot, and to press on it to get anyone to do his bidding.

Sean readjusted the collar of his shirt and his jacket, and checked his wristwatch. They had just under a minute before they were due to go live.

'Come on, let's keep moving, people!' he shouted, at no one in particular.

His words sent the entire backstage area springing into action again. Only a moment after the incident, it already looked like nothing out of the ordinary had taken place. Behind the panels, the audience hooted and cheered as the lights dimmed, signalling the imminent start of the show. Sean glanced over at Tyler who was leaning with his eyes closed against a wall, looking shaken. Sean watched as one of the production assistants tapped Tyler on the shoulder, causing him to jump in surprise. The member of staff pointed at the entrance to the stage and raised a hand up, fingers spread out wide, to signal he was due in five seconds. Tyler nodded and, with lightning speed, reached into his inside jacket pocket to pull out a little plastic bottle Sean knew only too well. Tyler gobbled a couple of pills and slid the container back inside his jacket. A moment later, he was walking onto the stage, under roaring applause from the crowd.

For the very first time since it had all started, Sean wondered if he had gone a step too far. He had done a lot of things people would shudder at throughout the years, but rarely had he questioned his own actions. As far as he was concerned, the means justified the end. That was the game of life. But for just an instant, he asked himself whether there could have been another way. One which would have seen Tyler live a long and healthy life past the show's final episode. He toyed with the idea for a moment, finding a sort of enjoyment in the novelty of it. Could he, Sean Cravanaugh, the great, the feared, the ultimate magnate, be suddenly developing a conscience? Now, *that* would be unexpected.

Sean felt a gentle squeeze on his upper arm. He turned around, and saw Camilla nod towards the stage. He readied his face and bent both arms, offering one each to his fellow judges. The women slid their arms in his, and together they marched confidently onstage.

The audience's delight might have overwhelmed less experienced individuals, but all three judges had had their share of such occasions in the past, and kept walking, smiling, all the way to their table. Fame, like most things, was a luxury one got accustomed to very quickly, provided one had the guts to endure what came with it. Not everyone did.

'Welcome, welcome, everyone!' Tyler said brightly, 'Tonight, six contestants will become three. But *who* will make it through to next week's big finale? Let's see what our lovely judges' predictions are...'

He walked to the judges' desk and his expression changed to one of great surprise.

'Dear me!' Tyler exclaimed, 'we seem to be down one judge today! Has anyone seen Josh Carter?' He called out to the crowd, and everyone looked around, as though the fourth judge was due to pop out of thin air at any moment.

Tyler brought a finger to his ear, like he was listening intently to instructions his earpiece. The audience fell silent, all eyes turned to their show host.

'I see…' Tyler said eventually, in a voice clouded with mystery.

He glanced up at the arena around him and added, in a deep voice:

'I have just been informed that Josh Carter will not be joining us either tonight, or for the competition's final challenge…'

The audience gasped, almost immediately breaking into a buzz of murmured conversations.

'I am told,' Tyler continued, silencing the crowd in an instant, 'that Mr Carter felt he could no longer bear the stress of the competition… That he felt our contestants were not being treated with enough *consideration*…'

He paused again here and made a face. The audience laughed.

'I mean…' Sean intervened, rolling his eyes comically, and turning to the audience, 'does anyone else think that we've been too harsh on people who, let's not forget, have committed such vicious crimes?'

'No!' The audience shouted.

'Does anyone here think that we should be kinder to the people who have brought our great nation to ruins?' Sean asked again.

'No!' The audience shouted again, louder this time.

'I don't know about you,' Sean added, standing up, and turning slowly on his heels, as though to address every single person in the crowd individually, 'but I don't think the victims of the crimes these people committed would say we're being too harsh!'

The audience got to their feet, cheering him on.

'Does anyone here think this is not justice?' Sean continued, raising his tone.

'No!' The audience screamed, hysterical.

'This *is* justice!' Sean boomed into his microphone, 'justice as it was intended to be. Fair and decisive. Giving the victims and their loved ones the solace that the crimes which broke them are being punished!'

'Time for justice! Time for justice!' The arena chanted.

The audience was primed for what was to come, and Sean knew they would need all the public support they could get before they triggered what they had scheduled for the night. He stole a glance towards Camilla, who met his eyes ever so briefly. They shared a look of understanding, before turning their attention back towards the stage.

'Tonight,' Tyler exclaimed, as the contestants' cage was rolled onstage, 'our contestants will need to demonstrate stamina and courage if they want to make it to next week's finals!'

As he spoke, a large structure was rolled onto the stage behind him, covered with a giant sheet of silky material which fluttered around as the structure was brought into position and secured tightly to the floor.

'Please give a round of applause for tonight's task...' Tyler said excitedly, 'the 'Fire Escape'!'

At the words the sheet of fabric dropped to the floor, revealing the structure concealed underneath it. It was a large piece of wall, at least twenty meters tall. It had been decorated to mimic the side of a building, complete with windows, drain pipes and red bricks. At the very top of the wall, attached towards the centre, was a golden star.

'Our contestants have to climb one of our six custom-made walls, reach the golden star at the top, before sliding down the back of the wall using our fireman-pole on the other side. The contestants will have twenty seconds to start climbing, before the wall is set on fire. The three contestants to complete the challenge in the shortest time will go through to the next round. Are you ready?' Tyler exclaimed, as the first contestant, a middle-aged man, was brought face to face with the wall.

A countdown started, and the crowd chanted the numbers down from ten, until the digital clock kicked off, indicating that the contestant needed to start climbing. He stepped on top of a close-by window sill sticking out of the wall, looking for the nearest gripping points. Slowly and tediously he climbed, resting his hands and feet on whatever he could. He had barely gone a couple of meters up when a loud buzzer resounded in the arena, signalling the fire had been ignited at the bottom of the wall. The contestant looked down, realising with terror that bright flames were now edging their way towards him. He looked up, searching frantically for his next step, resuming his ascent as fast as he could.

He must have been tired, Sean observed, because before long he was slowing down again, his hands slipping from their grip, struggling to pull himself upwards. Sweat was dribbling profusely from his forehead, down his face onto his shoulders, drenching his overalls. The flames were now mere centimetres behind him, and though he tried to go on, his body strength appeared to have left him. He hung on the spot for a few seconds, breathing hard, his face contorting with the effort. When he finally reached the golden star at the top of the wall, the audience cheered, and the man swayed over the edge of the wall, disappearing behind down the fireman pole. Two guards instantly ran to drag him to the other side of the stage, whilst a platoon of production staff ran to the stage with fire extinguishers, spraying the wall.

'Oh, my lord!' Tyler shouted over the frenzy of the audience, 'what an adrenaline rush that was!'

A second wall was installed, this time moulded into a replica of a white stone cliff, with rocks poking out at various angles. The second climber, a tall woman, was brought to the wall, and the same chain of events ensued. The contestant seemed prepared this time, having watched her predecessor endure the ordeal a few minutes before her. She wizzed to one end of the wall and hurried upwards, until the second countdown finished and the flames started low beneath her. As she reached the midway point she paused, hanging on for dear life, failing to make any more progress. The flames got closer and closer. The moment the leg of her overalls caught fire she forced herself back into motion, and she wriggled all the way to the top. By the time she reached the golden star, the bottom half of her overalls was on fire. She barely seemed to notice. She hoisted herself over the wall and, though the public could not see, the big thump they distinctly heard indicated her descent had been as arduous as her ascent.

'Our second contestant seemed to struggle a bit more than the first, didn't she?' Tyler commented. 'Let's see how the third one fares…'

CHAPTER 52

TERRENCE BLAKE

Watching the proceedings from his spot in the cage, Terrence felt sick to his stomach. He knew his turn would be coming up soon. At the centre of the stage, a new wall had been erected. This one was jungle themed. Thick liana plants intertwined with exotic foliage and colourful snakes. Bits of rocks and brown roots flowed in and out of the wall, giving it a mysterious, wild appearance.

Two guards came to pull Mad Spencer out of the cage and off to the centre of the stage to face the wall. The countdown began, descending from ten to zero. The buzzer rang, kicking off the task.

But instead of climbing right away, Mad Spencer stood watching the wall. He walked up and down the length of it, observing it and touching it in places. The second countdown started and, suddenly, Mad Spencer lurched at the wall, with surprising agility, landing almost two meters above the ground, taking hold of a large branch. Up he went, climbing with almost inhuman speed. He was like a grotesque spider, moving across the wall, not only upwards, but sideways too, as if the whole thing was nothing more than a game to him. He had gone almost halfway up when suddenly he lost his footing. Mad Spencer tumbled, catching himself just in time. He remained still for a moment or two, but quickly regained his countenance and started upwards again.

The second time it happened, Terrence saw it more clearly. A sort of wooden rod had poked out from the surface of the wall, hitting Mad Spencer in the thigh, causing him to lose his balance again. Because of the position of the wall, the audience would have been none the wiser, but from his vantage point Terrence stood at the perfect angle to catch every movement between Mad Spencer's body and the wall. Someone was trying to destabilise the climber. Once again, someone was rooting for him to fail.

It was not the realisation that the game was rigged which hit Terrence the hardest. That nothing was fair in this farce, he had known all along. No, it was something else. Something he could not quite put a finger on. Could it be pity? Could he feel sorry for an individual as monstrous as Mad Spencer? Amongst all of the hatred and fury the whole thing had awoken inside him, could he still be capable of compassion?

Mad Spencer made to keep going, the fire now centimetres from his feet. He gripped at two pieces of rock sticking out from the wall. Before he could move another muscle however, the two rocks underneath his fingers retracted suddenly and, with nothing more to hold onto, he fell back, dropping as though in slow motion through the flames, until he hit the ground with a loud thud. He lay there for several moments, gasping for air. The shock of the impact seemed to have knocked the wind out of him. His overalls had caught fire and flames were creeping their way from his calves slowly towards his torso. Yet he remained still, either unwilling or unable to move. Terrence guessed it was the latter.

From where he was positioned, he could see Mad Spencer's eyes darting around frantically, up to the wall, side to side, and up again, clearly unsure what had happened. He must have thought he had a good grip, thought he had found a sure way up. Then understanding dawned on his near paralysed face and his eyes widened with the knowledge that he had been tricked. Terrence could see it flush across his face. It seemed to spurt his body back into motion, making him roll to one side. He got to his feet, his overalls still ablaze. He took them off ever so slowly, deliberately, seemingly unaware of the blood-chilling melting texture of his skin underneath. The audience gasped, but he looked immune to pain, like the sensations that might immobilise so many of his fellow men had no effect on him. In fact, if anything, the pain appeared to fuel his determination. He glowered at them all, standing on the stage, ashen faced and bleeding all over, wearing nothing but filthy, greying underwear. Without any warning, he burst out laughing and lurched up at the wall once more, landing amongst the flames, zooming up through the fire. His skin was dissolving, as was the greasy hair on his head. None of it seemed to matter, he looked beyond reach, beyond agony, in a time and space where nothing truly was real, where humans could creep their way through burning flames and come out alive and well.

He reached the golden star faster than anyone could have imagined possible given his condition. Whoever had been working to impede on his progress before had either given up, or else had been so stunned they had forgotten their task. Mad Spencer sat atop the wall for a moment, laughing more madly still, brandishing the golden star like a trophy. He grabbed the star with both hands and tried to tear it apart, groaning angrily all the while. Mad Spencer's already damaged hands were now bleeding profusely. A couple of the star's spikes gave way, and Mad Spencer threw the pieces in front of him into the flames. He stayed perched where he was, on top of the wall like his getting there was an achievement he was not ready to let go of. Sitting there, burning in the flames, Mad Spencer was laughing. He laughed and he laughed and he laughed, and his insane laughter was the most wretched sound Terrence had ever heard. He laughed like he had known all along this was how it was meant to end, like he had been expecting this very moment, and rather than being scared of it, he was embracing the public's hatred with open arms. He was not just mad, Terrence thought, he was madness itself. He was the epitome of insanity. He carried the very essence of cruelty, in such concentrated levels that it obliterated whatever might once have made him human. He was beyond life and death, and beyond the everyday afflictions which others may suffer. He was such potent evil that nothing could ever touch him, and not even fire could bring him down.

Terrence could not take his eyes off the burning man, as much as he wished he could look away. The spectacle in front of him was like a morbid trick of hypnosis. The rancid smell of burning flesh spread through the air. From behind the wall, two men in thick overalls and helmets had climbed up a ladder and grabbed Mad Spencer by the arms, dragging him down. Mad Spencer was giggling a high pitched giggle which made Terrence's insides twist with fear.

Tyler Benson was standing a meter or so away, a look of utter disgust on his face. He stared at the distorted body, his eyes wide, his mouth slightly ajar, visibly unable to find the words to comment on the scene.

'Well…' He started, tentatively.

Tyler Benson fell silent again, and Terrence wondered what he could possibly say next. Silence stretched. The only sound that could be heard was Mad Spencer's incessant giggles. The audience was abnormally silent too. Could it be, Terrence thought, that a line had been crossed? That, despite the horrors they had witnessed, Mad Spencer's performance had been a step too far? Had this taken them all over that invisible line of right and wrong? Could this task be the one to finally awaken their collective conscience?

For a moment it felt like it might. For a short, fleeting, fragile instant. And then, as suddenly at it had emerged, the moment had gone, and it appeared the line had not been crossed after all. Tyler Benson found his countenance again, and with it his voice, and as he started commentating again, the audience came out of their trance. The moment had passed, and everything was back to the new cruel normality they had come to know. Terrence's heart sunk.

The production team brought over a new wall, this one moulded into the facade of a posh building, with flower-laden window sills, iron-cast water pipes and red bricks. Terrence's mouth fell open, because the wall featured several fire escape ladders, giving an almost clear way from the bottom till the golden star at the top. A familiar knot tightened in the pit of his stomach as two guards came to escort him to the wall. Terrence frowned. Knowing what he now knew, there had to be a trick somewhere. The ladder might collapse. Or the windowsills might not be strong enough to support his weight. Or, if they were, they might retract just as he stood upon them on his way up.

The countdown above the stage kicked off. Terrence stared at the wall, unsure what to do. His instincts, fuelled by week after week of twisted turns of events in this nightmare of a place, were screaming at him not to put his trust in anything which appeared too good to be true. He looked around, hopelessly aware that he was running out of thinking time. He took a step forward, resigned to the fact that whatever cruel joke was being played at his expense, he had no other choice but to face it.

He grabbed at an iron pipe and stepped onto one of the lowest window sills. He paused for a second, expecting the worst, but nothing happened. Tentatively, he reached for the next windowsill, using a nearby ladder for support. There again, nothing happened. He kept on climbing, tensing when the new countdown started, telling him the fire had ignited beneath him. He willed himself not to look down, but he could feel the heat from the flames down below. The crackling noise of fire unsettled him, but he kept on climbing. It felt like no time at all passed before he found himself sitting atop the wall, his hands clasped around the golden star. He glanced around, flabbergasted, almost waiting for the wall to collapse or a bucketful of gasoline to be poured over his head from a hidden trap door above him.

When after a few moments he was still unharmed, he flung his legs over the wall, and slid his way down the pole to the relative safety of the stage floor. The cries of excitement from the crowd were astounding. Terrence let himself be led away to join the others, his gait uncertain, still stunned that nothing abominable had happened.

Or, at the very least, a little voice at the back of his head whispered, not *yet*.

CHAPTER 53

SEAN CRAVANAUGH

Sean felt that the production team's support of Terrence Blake could have been better disguised. Looking at the wall the man had to climb, he thought they might just as well have handed him the golden star. Not that it mattered, really, because the audience had been so rattled by Spencer Martins' performance they seemed relieved at the simplicity and ease with which their favourite contestant had tackled his task. Sean had seen the look of utter disbelief on Terrence Blake's face as he saw what awaited him. He would have been surprised and, he had to admit, a little disappointed if Terrence Blake had embraced his good fortune without a second thought. He had come to expect more from him over time.

When the last two contestants had completed the task, Tyler announced an advert break. They needed the stage clean for what was to come next. Sean glanced sideways at Camilla who was looking resolutely ahead, a somewhat rigid smile set upon her face. He could imagine what she must be feeling. She seemed to feel his gaze upon her because she turned her face ever so slightly towards him, appraising him from the corner of her eyes.

It occurred to him, as it often did, how deceptive appearances could be. Before she had come to him many weeks previously, he would have struggled to guess what hid underneath the surface. He would not have taken her for a kindred spirit. And yet, there she was, beautiful and unattainable, and as fake as one could ever be. She reminded him of those stunning and deadly jungle flowers, which grew in the midst of bushes of greenery, but which contained such powerful poison they could swallow anything that came too close. Once the deed was done and they had devoured their prey, they would resume their position, find their deceptive stillness once more, as if nothing out of the ordinary had taken place, patiently awaiting their next victim. Sean admired her skills, which allowed her to remain so well concealed.

The advert break was drawing to a close, and Sean noticed Tyler looming awkwardly by the side of the stage, half concealed behind the passing-bys of the members of staff as they hurried to ready the stage before the broadcast resumed. Sean saw Tyler fiddle with something in his jacket pocket, then jerk his head back as he swallowed more pills before taking his place onstage. The broadcast resumed.

'What a show!' Tyler exclaimed in his typical jovial and candid manner. 'The three contestants who took the longest time to complete tonight's challenge are Contestant seventy-three, contestant twenty-one and contestant sixty-two!'

Red spotlights appeared over the three contestants. The audience boomed their approval. Sean felt them rise as one, screaming and yelling profanities.

Sean studied Spencer Martins, his insides lurching as he scrutinised the poor state of the contestant. The sight of him was revolting. Even by his own Machiavellian standards, Sean felt this was a little much. Even dressed in a fresh pair of overalls, it did nothing to conceal the irreparable damage to his head, neck and hands. The red light bathed his face in a deep scarlet colour, illuminating his melted off skin, making him look like a worn-out candle. Lumps of bodily matter had formed in odd places, giving him the eerily lumpy look of a badly made clay structure. His appearance was pitiable. His countenance however, told quite a different story. He stood tall and determinately impassive, the corners of his mouth twitching slightly from time to time.

A sudden noise, very much like the ringing of a fire alarm, erupted around them. Lights flashed around the Cradle, yellow and white and red, moving around in circles everywhere. From all around them the deep disembodied voice of the commentator rang out, unmistakably threatening. The collective inhale from the audience seemed to suck the air from the arena.

'Contestant number sixty-two…' The voice boomed around them as all lights zoned in on Spencer Martins once more, 'you have exhausted your lifelines. Tonight, on this stage, the nation will watch as your fate is finally sealed, and you are punished for the crimes you committed.'

The disembodied voice was so deep and powerful it seemed to come from the almighty himself. The ultimate judge, serving a long-awaited justice, honouring the law of nature which dictated that no deed of unimaginable cruelty and madness should go unpunished. But Spencer Martins was smiling. He was smiling his derisive and insane smile, clearly visible amongst the piles of damaged, reddened skin. His gaze burnt with his signature look of madness. Despite knowing his end was near, he kept smiling. He smiled because he seemed to know that none of it had ever meant to be fair. Not just the competition, but his entire existence. He looked as though he had always expected that his miserable life would lead to such a moment. And, rather than cower away from it, he embraced it with open arms. He had inflicted pain and death on so many occasions, the meaning of life probably had taken a whole different meaning to him. To Spencer Martins, it might simply be something which came and went. At times he inflicted the final blow, whilst in this very instance he would be at the receiving end of it. He probably did not even see it as justice at all, or repayment for his actions, Sean thought, he likely only saw this as the way things went.

Sean smiled too, because amidst the offended faces around him, he felt he understood the man in front of them. He could not endorse the madman's actions, of course, but he himself had treaded over the line in his life. Who was to say whose crimes were worse than others? Could he say with confidence that his own acts of revenge were any less or any different than Mad Spencer's? Or was the knowledge that he had never been caught simply giving him a rationale for the high horse he sat upon? Did any of it really matter? Spencer Martins was on the verge of death, whilst Sean was on the brink of pulling off his biggest, most daring coup yet. When it came down to it, did it really make a difference who had done what?

'Contestant sixty-two's punishment card is called...' Tyler announced, as large letters appeared on the large screens above them, 'Russian Roulette! One of our judges will be drawn at random to assist in this task. He or she will be given a fully loaded gun and stand on this spot here,' he pointed down at a red cross on the stage floor, 'and the contestant will be tied over here...' He walked a few meters away to where a tall wooden pole had been placed, securely fastened to the stage floor by heavy metal bolts. 'This gun, of course, contains no ordinary bullets...' Tyler paused and seemed to falter for just a second, looking momentarily unfocused.

Sean frowned, but before he had time to worry, Tyler had composed himself.

'Every bullet has been filled with a specially formulated substance which is designed to awaken every single nervous connector in the body, setting all of them on fire at once, generating pain such as no one has ever felt before.'

The audience was silent.

'The judge who has been chosen to assist with this task… is…' Tyler announced, dramatically, drawing an unmarked white envelope from the inner pocket of his jacket, and opening it slowly.

He drew a piece of paper from inside the envelope and stared at it for a moment. He glanced around to the backstage entrance, frowning. Slowly, he brought the microphone up to his lips and spoke the name in a doubtful voice.

'Camilla.'

The entire arena erupted in a thunder of low buzzing commentary. Of the three remaining judges, they had obviously expected the task to be assigned to one of the two senior members of the panel.

Sean smirked despite himself. People only ever saw what they wanted to see. If only they knew. He turned to look at Camilla and their eyes met. Her face was impassive, her fingers knotted on her lap. Sean placed a hand on top of hers and squeezed. As it had so many times before, a look of mutual understanding passed between them. She knew that of all people, he was the one to truly get what she was about to do.

Tyler walked towards the judges' desk and held a hand out to Camilla, who took it and followed him docilely onto the stage. She proceeded with such ease and grace she appeared to be floating rather than walking. Tyler led her to where the red cross had been drawn onto the floor. A velvet-covered pillow upon which the gun rested was placed on a high table by her side. Spencer Martins was tied securely to the pole. Sean watched Camilla turn slowly towards the side table and look at the gun set upon the pillow. Time seemed suspended.

After Sean had hung up from his first ever phone conversation with Camilla, after she had requested to see him, more than a week had gone by without Sean thinking about the meeting to come. He was reminded of his meeting with Camilla one morning, as he was rushing into his office.

'Camilla's waiting at the building reception,' his secretary had said, 'Should I let her in? I've slotted half an hour into your schedule.'

'Sure,' Sean had sighed, distracted. 'Give me two minutes.'

when Camilla had walked through the door, Sean had struggled to match the young woman standing in front of him with the image of the glittery diva he had seen so many times on television, or on the glossy cover of gossip magazines. She was wearing a simple black roll neck jumper, dark blue skinny jeans, and black leather boots.

'Mr Cravanaugh,' she greeted him politely, 'thank you for seeing me.'

'My pleasure,' he answered, more as a form of habit than out of genuine sentiment. 'Please take a seat.'

She had sat down facing him, her eyes slowly taking in the beautiful view the glass walls offered over the capital.

'So, Camilla, what can I do for you?' He did not have any time to waste.

'As I mentioned to you on the phone,' she turned back to look at him, her stare intense and determined. 'I'm interested in being a part of the recent proposal you released.'

'You're referring to 'No Pain, No Game', correct?'

'Yes.'

He had already known the answer, of course, as she had revealed that part on the phone, but he still could not understand why she would want to join him on his latest plan, or which role she thought she could play. He sat back into the sofa, his arms extending over to his sides, dominating her with his presence. Power, he thought, was just a game after all, and one at which he hated losing.

'When we last spoke you said you had more details to give me about your reasons for making this request?'

'I would like to be one of the judges on the show.'

'I had guessed as much,' he responded right away.

This was not entirely true but he had wanted to unsettle her. He wanted to get to the truth behind her intentions as quickly as possible, before he could make a call on whether she was worth his time.

'I'm more interested in *why*. This isn't quite your usual repertoire, as far as I can see'.

'You're right, this isn't something my brand would normally be associated with,' she answered. 'The truth is, Mr. Cravanaugh, I'm looking to diversify my portfolio, and I believe being a part of your new venture would be a great start to launching a new side to my career.'

She had given him her speech flawlessly, remaining professional and calm. Anyone other than him might have been fooled. But Sean had been in the game too long, and he could smell public relations spiel from miles away. He looked at her for some time, studying her face, trying to see whether she really thought she could play him so easily. If she did, he thought, she had grossly underestimated him, and he would make sure she paid for such a rookie mistake. She held his gaze with a force of determination which surprised him.

'Bullshit,' he called out finally, never taking his eyes off her.

She was quiet for a long moment, and he could almost see her mental gymnastics as she figured out her next move.

'You don't believe I would want to join the show for professional reasons?' She asked, testing the waters.

'Not for one second.' His tone was adamant.

Another minute had passed without either of them breaking the silence, waiting for the other one to fold first.

'Listen,' Sean leant forward, interlacing his fingers on his knees, 'you have two options here. You can either tell me why you're making such a request, when we both know you have absolutely nothing in common with my new scheme, or you can get the fuck out of my office and await the painful consequences of wasting…' He looked at his wristwatch theatrically, 'nine minutes of my precious time.'

She considered him for a few second, a smile playing at the corner of her lips. Eventually, she sighed.

'My name…' She started, her gaze far out of the window, 'isn't Camilla. My name is Santana Clarens. Camilla was my little sister's name, which I used as a pseudonym when I started off in the music industry.'

Sean remained quiet.

'Seven years ago, my sister was abducted,' She marked a pause. 'By a man called Spencer Martins,' she turned back to look at him. 'He raped her repeatedly, and then he murdered her, in the most brutal manner. It wasn't the first time he'd done it, and he was later convicted, and sentenced to life imprisonment. To this day this monster lives and breathes, whilst my sister died the most horrible death.'

Sean had suppressed an involuntary smile, because he could finally see where this was going.

'I want him dead. I want him worse than dead, in fact. I want him to suffer as much as he's made my family suffer. So, I will tell you exactly how this is going to go. I will join the panel of judges on the show and, let's face it, this can only do your audience levels some good. In return, you will ensure Spencer Martins is one of the contestants in the competition, and give me carte blanche on influencing his fate.'

Sean listened to her every word, which she had spoken in the most neutral of tones, almost matter-of-factly, as though she was used to the pain and anger they triggered in her. The woman sitting in front of him had nothing to do with the glamorous princess clad in brightly coloured outfits he had seen singing love ballads for teenage girls on television. She had transformed in a matter of seconds, her eyes glistening with fury. She was not a naïve little diva anymore, she was a woman with vengeance on her mind, running through her veins like poison. His opinion of her had changed instantly as he read the expression in her eyes.

'Fine,' he had agreed finally, causing her to raise an eyebrow in surprise.

'As I'm sure you understand, what we've just discussed should under no circumstances be made public.'

'Of course, that goes without saying. I'll have my people send over the paperwork,' he concluded, standing up.

She got to her feet, following his lead. He held out a hand which she shook, with much more strength than he had expected. As he held her hand in his for a moment longer, he looked straight at her, a wicked smile stretched out across his lips.

'Welcome to the show, Santana Clarens.'

CHAPTER 54

SANTANA CLARENS

Santana looked at the gun in front of her. It was an old-fashioned revolver, adorned with a smooth white layer of beautifully carved tusk over the grip. The gun was shiny and clean, as if it had just been polished moments before, which, she thought, probably had been the case. It had a spotless metal barrel and cylinder. Bringing her fingers to the cold metal, she caressed its smooth lines. She followed the outline of the trigger and the trigger guard. Picking up the gun, she felt its weight in her palm. She had been preparing for this, of course, so much that by now holding a gun seemed to make her arm whole. She slid the cylinder open and inspected it, angling the gun away from the cameras, so that no one could see all six compartments were full.

She turned around, ever so slowly, to face her opponent, and her eyes found the distorted face of Spencer Martins. The gun hung reassuringly by her side, her fingers safely around the handle. She felt oddly numb inside, devoid of any recognisable emotion. Spencer Martins' gaze was upon her. He was smiling broadly, though she was unsure whether the wide gaping hole his massacred mouth made could really qualify as a smile anymore. The lips were gone, buried under many layers of melted skin and excess tissue. She knew he was amused. She knew he was probably as entertained by the turn of events as the rest of them were. How could he stand here, about to die the most painful of deaths, and still find the situation even remotely pleasurable?

Santana closed her eyes, because the image of a younger Spencer Martins had popped uninvited into her head. The last time she had seen him was at the trial where he had been found guilty and convicted to a life sentence. Her sister had been his last victim. Santana remembered sitting in the courtroom between her mother and father, looking at the man who had broken their family beyond repair. Spencer Martins had sat in the accused box, his hands heavily chained, wearing his unceasing smile. He had not looked like he was about to lose his freedom forever. When the sentence was announced, he had simply laughed, a shrill, blood-freezing laugh which told them all he could not care less where they sent him. He had laughed, and laughed, and laughed, and the sound of his laughter had sent Santana's mother into a fit of hysteria.

They had left the courtroom not as a family who had seen justice done for their lost child, but as three individuals who seemed to have little more in common than a shared history. Everything had changed after that. Santana had watched her mother starve herself to death and her father drown himself in whatever substance allowed him to escape the new reality of their existence. The real Camilla, their youngest daughter, had vanished forever, and they refused to face a life without her in it. It did not seem to matter that their elder daughter was still around, and Santana learnt that no matter how much her parents might have loved her when Camilla was still alive, it had not been enough to make them want to keep on living now that their youngest was not with them anymore.

Whilst her parents edged ever closer to their own demise, Santana, then in her teens, had devoted all of her attention and energy to her passion for singing. She had made her own way to achieve her ambitions, knowing to rely on no one but herself. It was then that she had changed her name. Maybe in some way she felt that she was giving Camilla a chance at a life she would never experience. Santana stepped aside and Camilla came back to life.

As children, Santana and Camilla could not have been more different. Their personalities were such polar opposites it was hard to believe they were even related. Camilla had been everything Santana was not. Despite being the youngest, Camilla had been extroverted, bubbly and charming. She was as pretty and blonde as Santana was dark and brunette, one taking after the mother, the other after the father. Everything seemed to come so easily to Camilla, and she had been the apple of her parents' eyes. Santana, on the other hand, was a quiet child, preferring being on her own to playing with friends, speaking very little, reading extensively.

And so when she had started on the route to stardom, with her borrowed pseudonym, the name had become more than just a name. Camilla had become her persona. Where Santana had been too shy for public performances, becoming Camilla had allowed her to overcome her quiet disposition. By being Camilla, she had become a woman who could step onto a stage and astound everyone around her. One who could muster the courage to get what she wanted.

After her parents had died, the number of people who had known the full extent of what had happened had considerably reduced. Very few people knew the truth behind the facade, or the story behind her determination, and Santana had ensured her secret remained well-concealed. At times, she felt that she could barely make out the reality from the story she had built for herself. The thin lines between Santana and Camilla became blurry. There were times when she could not be quite sure who she was anymore.

She knew that deep down Santana was still there, lurking, biding her time, even as Camilla's appeal and strength had grown over the years. In the beginning, she had managed to convince herself she was doing this to honour her sister's memory, to give her the life she would never live, to avenge a death which had come too soon. When she had got wind of Sean Cravanaugh's master plan, she had seen her one and only chance to fully atone for her sister's unfortunate fate, though she had been unable to explain to herself why she felt somehow responsible for it.

Santana opened her eyes again, resolutely raising her arm so that the gun was pointing straight at Spencer Martins. She placed both hands on the handle, sliding a finger through the trigger guard, readying herself. Spencer Martins was now giggling softly. Santana looked him straight in the eyes, aimed, and pulled the trigger. She shot once, twice, three times. Three red dots formed on the man standing before her. One in the shoulder, one in the thigh, one through the arm. She had taken care not to aim for any fatal spot. The man had to suffer and die a slow death. She watched as the red circles widened, like little bloody halos around the spots where each bullet had landed. She lowered her arms, waiting for the promised chemical reaction to take place. It only took a couple of seconds, but the spectacle was worth the wait. Spencer Martins squirmed on the spot, like something was eating him up from inside. He twitched and convulsed, his restraints keeping him steadily upright. He clenched his jaw, apparently trying hard not to scream. Santana guessed he did not want to give them that satisfaction. She knew *she* would not have wanted to in his place. She raised her arms and shot again. Once and twice. The first bullet landed in his calf, and the second in his flank. He now appeared to be in so much pain he could no longer contain the cries of agony. He screamed at the top of his lungs, with such force that Santana realised she had not known anyone could feel such pain, even after what her sister had endured before she passed away, and after she had watched both her parents slowly perish from their broken hearts.

Santana watched, impassive, until Spencer Martins breathed his very last breath, taking in the final moment when life exited his despicable body, his head drooping lifelessly onto his chest. Suddenly, he was still. As unmovable as a statue.

Santana waited.

She waited for some time, though she was not too sure what she was waiting for. She had avenged her sister's death, what could it be that was still missing?

She felt nothing.

She was as numb as she had ever been, as cold and insensitive as though nothing of importance had just happened.

And then the shadows of understanding dawned upon her. She knew exactly what it was she had refused to acknowledge all this time. She had been desperately waiting to feel something. Anything. She had been waiting for relief. For a feeling of redemption. For mercy she thought would never come. Deep down, in the confines of her heart, she now knew one fact for certain. When everyone around her had felt lost and sad when Camilla had died, she, on the other hand, had felt nothing.

No, she corrected herself. That too was a lie.

Now was no longer the time to fool herself with these prettier versions of the truth. She had not felt *nothing*. In fact, she had felt... glad. *Glad*. Her sister had been brutally abducted, raped and killed by a lunatic and she, Santana, forever eclipsed by her sister's talents and charms, had felt *pleased*. She had been jealous of Camilla from the day she was born, jealous of how naturally beautiful and amazing she was without trying too hard. Jealous of how much her parents loved her and how little they tried to conceal their preference. She had loathed how Camilla always came first, despite being born second. For the entire time they had shared a home, it had all only ever been about Camilla. And the moment Santana heard she had died, she now recognised what she had felt in that exact moment. She had been *relieved*, because maybe then her parents would finally look at her, pay attention to her, *love* her just a small fraction of how much they had loved Camilla.

But they had not.

They had chosen to give up their own lives rather than turn to their eldest for comfort. And, on some level, Santana knew that her lack of grief had affected them too, and maybe distanced them even more from her than anything else. Naively, foolishly, Santana had felt she could atone for her lack of an appropriate emotional reaction by keeping Camilla alive in some way, and by tracking down and finishing off her murderer. Surely, she had thought, surely *then* she would feel something. Anything. Any sort of reaction which was somewhat in line with the situation. Maybe she would feel forgiven. She would feel Camilla's understanding wrap around her, she would feel free of the prison she had made for herself, of this life she had built which was not really her own. She had expected she would find redemption.

But nothing came.

Despite herself, standing there, facing the body of the man who she had so desperately wanted to kill for so long, Santana burst into a fit of laughter she could not control.

She laughed because she realised how pointless it had all been. She laughed because, whilst she had tried hard to come into her own after her sister's demise, her entire existence had ended up being exactly what it had always been when she was alive. Seven years after her sister had died, Santana's life was still very much all about Camilla. And she laughed because even after everything that had happened, after murdering in cold blood the man who had ruined everything, she felt nothing.

How meaningless it had all been. How little her efforts at making a career and a life for herself mattered in the end. How stupid she had been for trying so hard. There she was, so many years later, still living in Camilla's mighty shadow, her perfect sister, unable to let Santana step into the light. She did not even know who she was anymore.

Maybe if she had had the strength, if she had known how, she could have flourished as her true self. Maybe she could have embraced being quiet and introverted, and never having the same emotional responses everyone else did. Maybe she could have accepted that what made her always stick out so much was also what made her so special. But things had taken a different turn, and she found herself at a crossroad, with one path leading off the edge of a cliff and the other into a giant fire pit. She knew there was no way back. She was stuck, and the only person she had to blame for it all was herself.

Game over, Santana. You lost, and quite miserably so, too. You silly, silly girl. You did not even put up a fight. Look at how pathetic you are. No wonder your own parents did not want to live for you.

She laughed, and she kept on laughing at the waste of it all, at how ridiculous the situation was. She was still laughing as she lifted the gun up to her temple, and she was still laughing the moment she pulled the trigger, freeing the final bullet from its metal enclosure.

She was dead before her body even hit the ground, her eyes wide with mad ecstasy, her mouth stretched into a manic smile, the very last burst of genuine emotion she had felt, forever etched on her beautiful face.

CHAPTER 55

TYLER BENSON

All Tyler could remember was running. He had watched the bullet spurt out of the side of Camilla's head, as if in slow motion, splattering blood and fragments of brains everywhere. And, then, he had started running.

He ran away from it all, as fast as he could. He had not stopped until he reached the solitude of his changing room, where he bolted the door locked behind him, and slouched in one of the armchairs. What just happened, he kept repeating in his mind, what just happened? Had this been for real? Were the contents of Camilla's skull truly pouring out onto the stage at that very moment? What on earth was going on?

The more he thought, the faster his heart beat, and he was certain that it would eventually burst out of his chest and ricochet onto the carpeted floor. He tried to calm himself but there was no forcing it. He was out of breath and sweating profusely, and before long he was drenched in a pool of his own bodily fluids. The mad panting made the back of his throat ache and itch. He foraged into the inside pocket of his jacket for the little container. Just a pill or two and he would be fine. Water, he thought, I need water.

He popped the pill container onto his makeup table, catching a glimpse of his appalling reflection in the mirror in the process. He did not recognise the man who stared back at him. For a split second he wondered if someone else was standing behind him and, turning around wildly in his chair, scanned the room, only to realise that there was no one there. He got to his feet, swaying dangerously as he stood up, looking around frantically for the water bottles he was sure should be there somewhere. His hands were shaking so much that everything he touched ended up escaping his grasp and rolling around in all directions. His heart was pounding too hard and too fast now, and it occurred to him that this could not be right. He gasped for air, quickening his search for the hidden water bottles.

Everything was a blur, piles of things were layered everywhere, merging into patches of colour around him. He turned on his heels. He was no longer sure whether he was the one spinning or whether the world around him had started whirling. Everything seemed to be melting, nothing made sense anymore. He could feel his heart beat everywhere, from his torso, to his temples and into his toes. It was like it had expanded beyond his body, reverberating through the room, bouncing off the walls and the ceiling. A sharp pain shot through his chest and he fell to his knees, clutching at his shirt, desperately trying to rip it off his body.

It was then that he knew he was about to die.

He wondered if his whole life was about to flash past his eyes. But all he could see in front of him was a sea of little red pills which had spilt from the open container onto the carpet, just a short distance away. They seemed to shine like so many tiny fairy lights, calling out to him, mocking him almost. He extended a hand towards them, but they lay resolutely out of his reach. He knew it was too late. He was going to die. He was probably just seconds away from breathing his last breath, and whilst the room still zoomed around him in mad confusion, the one thing he knew with absolute certainty was that there was nothing he could do to save himself.

In a way, had he not always known this was to be his fate? Had he not always known he was to die someday? Or was it that he had expected it to come much later and in much smoother a manner than this? He wondered what might have ever given him the arrogance to think he would be blessed with a soft, pain-free ending. In truth, he supposed he had never thought of dying at all. He had been aware that it was bound to happen somehow, but it had seemed so far away and so inconsequential that for some time he had fooled himself into believing that it would never come to pass.

His very last thought as he felt blood trickle down his mouth and nose, was that he wished he had known better. Not just that he had been more aware of his own mortality, but that he had truly, fully *known* how fragile and how temporary life was.

In that moment, he thought he might have gone about his short existence differently, though as the very last exhale left his body, he realised with immense sadness that he would never find out.

CHAPTER 56

SEAN CRAVANAUGH

Whilst Spencer Martins' death had been part of the deal, Camilla's suicide was an act of improvisation Sean had not cared for. It was unfortunate, Sean thought, that she had chosen the course of action she did, though he could not say with honesty that he was entirely surprised.

He had felt it from their first interview, he had known she was like him. They were of the same species. The difference was she did not seem to be dealing with the way she was as smoothly as he did. She had gone for a complete reinvention of her whole character, in a desperate attempt to fool everyone around her into believing she was one of them. He had wondered if at times she had also fooled herself. Though they had never discussed it, Sean now knew that she probably was looking for something she thought she could not grant herself.

Pardon. Forgiveness for the way she had been from the day she was born.

Like him, she must have gone misunderstood for such a long time, she might have thought there was something wrong with her. He had come to accept his way of being early on, to use it to his advantage as a strength rather than a weakness, regardless of what everyone else said. She clearly had struggled. She had chosen to hide rather than face the truth. Maybe she had felt that avenging her sister's death, that giving herself a purpose would make her feel worthy of her own existence. But Sean knew too well that the sort of acceptance she had been desperate for could not have come from anything or anyone other than herself.

Sean's phone had been ringing incessantly ever since he had stood up from behind the judges' table and sprinted to the relative safety of his office, closely followed by his personal security team. He locked the door behind him, instructing the guards to let no one in. With one call to the head of the production team, he had ordered for the arena to be evacuated, the convicts to be escorted back safely into their cells, and the mess on the stage to be cleaned up.

He marched to his drink cabinet and poured himself a large scotch, which he downed in one gulp. He poured himself another which he swallowed with difficulty. With his third glass of scotch in hand, he went to sit down on one of the chesterfields. A glance at his phone showed he had seventy-two missed calls already. The screen lit up again as the Prime Minister attempted to reach him. Sean ignored the call.

The swirl of emotions he was experiencing felt new to him. Was it sadness? Or grief? Or sheer annoyance that his endeavour had been messed with when he was so close to his goal? A mix of all the above, he guessed.

He leaned back and closed his eyes, pondering what to do next. Ideas and strategies swam across his mind, intertwined with visions of Camilla's beautiful, blood-covered face. What a waste, he thought, what a bloody waste. Quite literally.

He breathed in deeply, and breathed out slowly, forcing his body and mind under his control. A familiar sense of numbness overtook him, a sensation of cool, calculating calm which had helped him in many a dire situation. He made himself think logically. He led himself through a clear, objective train of thought, down a path where he could get out of the situation unscathed. It would be no mean feat if he was able to extirpate himself from this mess with minimal damage.

In half an hour he had a plan. Whether it would work, he could not be entirely sure, but as always he had to follow his instincts. He drunk his scotch in one go and slammed the glass down on the coffee table, before walking off to his desk and picking up the receiver.

'Yes, Mr Cravanaugh?' His secretary's voice came through instantly.

'Get Benson in my office,' he growled. 'Now.'

'Yes, Mr Cravanaugh.'

Sean put the phone down and pulled his mobile from his pocket. The Prime Minister's panicked voice barked at him from the other end of the line.

'Cravanaugh! What happened? *What* is going on! Was *that* part of your masterplan, too?'

'Sir,' Cravanaugh said coolly, 'If you calm down, I can tell you how we can spin this into...'

'Spin this? *Spin* this?!' Derren Clarke shouted, his voice a hysterical shrill. 'The girl *shot* herself! On bloody live television! Surely even *you* can't get us out of this mess.'

Sean stayed quiet, waiting for the Prime Minister to vent out his frustration. He needed the man alert and composed. He wished they did not have to waste time in such frivolous human weakness, but a lifetime of living amongst his peers had taught him it was a pointless affair to expect people to be as detached in a crisis as he was.

'Cravanaugh? Are you listening?' The Prime Minister bellowed.

'I am, sir. I'm simply waiting for you to be quiet so we can talk about our plan of action.' Sean heard the man on the other line gasp, but he did not give him a chance to round up on him again. 'I know this is a challenging situation, but there *is* a way out. Are you ready to hear what I have to say or shall we postpone our conversation for when you are better disposed to listen?'

'Very well,' Derren Clarke conceded finally, his tone sarcastic, 'what genius idea have you concocted to get us out of this nightmare?'

The Prime Minister listened carefully to what Sean had to say. When Sean finished speaking, there was silence on the line.

'Are you sure this will work?' The Prime Minister eventually breathed, his voice just a whisper.

'Have my methods ever failed you?' Was Sean's immediate response.

'Well... I suppose not. I just...'

'If you do as I say, everything will work out as planned,' Sean assured him, his tone commanding.

'Fine, I leave it in your hands, Cravanaugh. I'll see you in a couple of hours.'

Sean slid his mobile phone into his pocket and looked around the room, suddenly remembering what else he had requested to be done. He pushed a button on the phone on his desk.

'Yes, Mr Crav...'

'Where is Benson?' He growled into the receiver. 'Get him into my office. Now!'

He slammed the phone down without waiting for an answer, and sat back behind his desk, massaging his temples. A minute later, he heard a knock on the door.

'Come in!' He shouted.

The door opened and the producer walked in, looking dishevelled and petrified.

'What?' Sean stood up, glaring at him, banging his fists on the desk in front of him, growing tired of everyone's lack of efficiency.

'Sir... Tyler Benson... He's... He's dead,' the producer started speaking very fast. 'We went to his dressing room. When he didn't open the door we tried taking it down by force. When we finally got in he was... He was...' He looked flustered, '...he was lying there. *Dead.*'

Sean kept staring at him, impassive. He almost wanted to laugh, partly because the producer looked so crestfallen it was almost comical, but mainly because the timing could not have been worse. But Sean was nothing if not resourceful.

'What was the cause of death?' Sean asked.

The producer seemed taken aback.

'We're not sure, sir. It looked like an overdose. He was surrounded by a lot of medication... We've called an ambulance but I'm not sure there's much they can do...'

'Very well,' Sean nodded, aware that his choice of words at that very moment was not the most sensible.

He sent the producer off to handle the situation with the emergency services. Back behind his desk, he made several phone calls, and sent a long note to the Prime Minister. There was a lot to be coordinated, and quickly, if he wanted to pull off his coup. He then sat back into his chair and closed his eyes, his mind fixed on the task at hand.

Over an hour later, his secretary informed him that the press conference he had called was ready to begin. Sean stood up slowly and made his way decisively across the arena, to a small room where Derren Clarke was waiting, his head bent over a few sheets of paper. He looked up when Sean entered, but he said nothing.

'Shall we?' Sean jerked his head to the door in the opposite corner of the room. Behind the wooden door, they could hear the buzzing of conversations, as dozens of press representatives impatiently awaited their appearance.

The Prime Minister simply nodded, and straightened up his tie. Sean opened the door and together they walked through. They were welcomed by a shower of shouts and flashes of lights. They stepped onto an elevated platform, up to a stand mounted with a microphone, facing the crowd. Derren Clarke stepped to one side, and Sean approached the microphone. The journalists were on their feet, leaning in towards him, their recorders extended at arms' length, shouting and fighting for his attention. A lesser man than him might have cowered before such an audience, but he was not one to be easily scared. He looked at them in silence, towering over them from his pedestal, his stare travelling across the crowd without as much as a flinch. He gave them a few more seconds to indulge in their emotions before raising a hand. They fell instantly silent, and he revelled in the sense of power he held. Several cameras' red lights indicated the scene was being aired live.

'Ladies and gentlemen,' he said gravely, 'thank you for joining us at such short notice... and on such a distressing occasion. Today, the penultimate episode of 'No Pain, No Game' bore witness to a tragedy. It saw its brightest star take her own life. Tonight, we mourn the loss of our beloved Camilla, and I would like to begin this emergency press conference by marking a minute of silence for her.'

He lowered his gaze, arms hanging in front of him, one hand placed on top of the other. The entire room imitated him. The seconds ticked by and silence stretched, breaking in an instant the frenzy which had reigned over the small audience just moments before.

'Many knew Camilla for the talented young woman she was,' Sean continued when the minute ended. 'For her generosity and her kindness. Over the short time I worked with her, I have got to know the woman behind the name, and she was every bit as kind and genuine as she seemed. But I also got to know how fragile she was, and she shared with me the shadow which tainted her entire life. A shadow which never left her. A shadow with a name: depression.'

The audience gasped.

'A few weeks into the show, Camilla revealed to me that she suffered from depression. And though I tried to help her, and encouraged her to leave the show, she refused. She wanted to prove to the world that she was stronger than her ailment, and she wanted her example to serve as an inspiration for us all. She wanted to show that anything is possible when you put your mind to it. I admired her for that,' Sean's voice broke a little, and he looked down.

Murmurs rose from the group in front of him.

'But, despite the help and care of all around her, today she must have felt she could not do it after all...' Sean paused again. 'It is my deepest regret that we... that *I* failed her. I wanted to believe she could do it, but somewhere along the way she drifted to where no one could reach her...' He let his eyes travel over the crowd. 'Though it is little consolation for the loss we have all suffered today, I would like to announce that a considerable donation has been made by the 'No Pain, No Game' production company to the country's leading charity supporting the victims of mental illnesses and funding major research in cutting edge treatment. Because no one should ever feel as desperate as Camilla felt tonight.'

Whispers of approval buzzed around the room, and a few bursts of applause erupted here and there.

'It pains me to say that Camilla's tragedy is not the only one we mourn today...' Sean looked around to take in the audience's sudden alertness as he delivered the breaking news. 'Shortly after the episode's sudden end tonight, Tyler Benson was found dead in his changing room, the heart-breaking victim of an overdose.'

The journalists were on their feet again. Sean raised a hand to silence them.

'Tyler Benson was more than just a colleague. He was a good man, and a dear friend. He was a loving husband and father. He was the friend everyone wished they had. The news of Tyler's addiction, and his dependence to a dangerous and lethal substance, came as a shock to all who knew him. He had a happy, fulfilling life, and no one can explain what might have led him on the horrific path of substance abuse,' Sean brought a hand to his chest, as though in a pledge, 'I wished I had been able to see what Tyler was going through, because then I might have been able to help him... My heart goes to Tyler's family, to his wife and his children. And whilst nothing will bring Tyler back, I would like to announce that 'No Pain, No Game' has also made a large donation to the nation's largest charity supporting victims of substance addiction and their families.'

This time the applause was widespread, as the audience stood, dignified and respectful.

'With the night's tragic events, we have decided to cancel the final episode of the competition,' Sean announced.

Moans of disappointment erupted in the assembly, and Sean almost wanted to smile, because at the end of the day, despite the turn of events, the people still craved entertainment.

'The contestant with the highest amount of points, contestant seventy-seven, has been declared the winner of 'No Pain, No Game'. He will be released tomorrow, with the winnings he has accrued on the show.'

Excitement spread through the room. The audience cheered and clapped, and the sounds of the country's delight could be heard from beyond the doors of the room they were in. Sean moved aside to let Derren Clarke take his spot. The Prime Minister cleared his throat.

'On this sad occasion, I would like to first send my heartfelt condolences to Camilla and Tyler Benson's friends and families. It breaks my heart that such talented young people have met with such a tragic demise. Tonight's events serve as a reminder that every single one of us has their own challenges and that it is our duty, as a nation, to look after each other. To take care of our own. To nurture our community. To ensure that no one should ever have to suffer alone like Camilla and Tyler did. It is our responsibility to ensure that they did not die in vain, to learn from their unfortunate circumstances to better ourselves.' The Prime Minister's words resonating around the quiet room. 'It is also our duty to look to the future. To rebuild our nation into the heaven it should be for its citizens. I'm glad to announce that our criminal rates have greatly improved. A few weeks ago, every single one of our two-hundred and eleven penitentiaries were overflowing. Today, only fifty-two of these prisons remain in active service, and are all operating at half capacity.'

The journalists exchanged looks of incredulity.

'These are unprecedented results, and they are the first milestone to getting our country back to growth and back to its former glory.'

Sean found himself drifting off. He knew the Prime Minister's speech by heart. He was the one who had written it, after all. He watched the audience's reactions and was pleased to see they were lapping it all up. He knew the toughest part was behind them.

On his way out of the Cradle, in the secluded comfort of his chauffeured car, he picked up his mobile phone and distributed a final set of instructions. By the time he reached the luxury hotel he had been booked into for the night, sneaking in through the back door like a thief to escape attention, every news channel and social media platform in the country and abroad was dissecting the night's events. The reaction to the unfortunate way the episode had ended had, at first, been shock and disgust. People had demanded explanations. After the press conference however, the country's outrage had slowly morphed into more elaborate debates on the topics Sean and the Prime Minister had introduced into the conversation: mental illness, addiction and the way ahead for the country.

Once more, human nature had proved every bit as predictable as Sean had expected. The nation had something else to grind their teeth on, quickly relegating Camilla and Tyler's fate to mere footnotes.

Nevertheless, Sean had decided not to linger. He would settle his affairs, cash his earnings and set off into the sunset without another glance back at the situation he left behind.

He walked across the presidential suite he was to occupy for the night, and climbed into the plush king size bed, pulling the soft duvet all the way to his chin.

'Ethics…' He found himself muttering once more, as he switched off the lights and closed his eyes, 'my arse.'

CHAPTER 57

TERRENCE BLAKE

Terrence had stood rooted to his spot in the metal cage, his eyes wide with horror, his mind replaying the scene over and over again, on a continuous loop. All he could see was the young woman lifting the gun to her head, pressing the trigger, and the bullet zooming in agonisingly slow motion through her cranium, exiting on the other side, splashing blood all over the stage. The devastating feeling of powerlessness was too strong for him to bear. Despite the weeks of pain he had witnessed and the abominable scenes he had been made to endure, the sight of Camilla's brain splattering through the air was one he would never be able to erase from his memory.

The moments after the young woman's body had hit the ground triggered utter chaos through the arena. The audience was on their feet, screams of panic and fear resonating all around them. In the midst of the confusion, the production team rushed the small group of convicts off the stage and down into their cells. Sitting in his solitary cemented cupboard of a prison, Terrence wondered what could possibly come next. Would they be made to go on with the competition? Could the show's marketing powers gloss over something as horrendous as what had just happened?

Terrence was not sure how long he was made to wait in his cell, curled up into a ball on the cold floor. It might have been hours as well as days.

He was too lost in the whirlwind of his own thoughts to keep track. Eventually a group of guards came to escort him to Sean Cravanaugh's office. They sat him in one of the sofas, removed his ankle bracelet and handed him a small plastic bag.

Terrence was so baffled that it took him a moment to realise the room looked different to the last time he had found himself on that same couch. The office appeared to have been stripped off all of its contents. Piles of cardboard boxes were numbered and lined up in a corner. The large desk remained, though all of the items which once adorned its surface had been removed. The two Chesterfields still held their original position, but every other piece of furniture had been taken away. Terrence frowned, wondering what twisted game he was being made to play this time.

The door opened and Sean Cravanaugh walked in, clutching his mobile phone in one hand.

'Mr Blake,' Sean Cravanaugh came to sit opposite him. 'I won't beat around the bush. As you are aware, the competition has taken a rather unexpected turn.'

Terrence snorted. Many words to qualify his recent experience had swirled around his mind as he laid prostrate in his cell after Camilla's death, but 'unexpected' had not been at the top of the list. Sean Cravanaugh ignored his reaction.

'As a result, there's been a change of plan. The competition has ended, and you have been declared the overall winner of 'No Pain, No Game'. Congratulations, Mr Blake, you're free to go.'

Terrence involuntarily clutched the bag on his lap and stared blankly at the head judge. Sean Cravanaugh slid a hand into his jacket pocked and fished out a thin unmarked white envelope.

'Here are your winnings,' he handed it to Terrence. 'The bag you've been given contains a change of clothes. When you leave this room, someone will escort you out of the arena.'

Terrence took the envelope, unable to say a single word. Sean Cravanaugh was watching him intently and he looked like he could guess his train of thoughts.

'This is not a trick, Mr Blake. You truly are free to go,' he gestured around the room, 'I'm just about to head off too. There is little else to be gained from sticking around, wouldn't you agree?'

'Gained?' Terrence repeated uncertainly.

'You and I probably have a different perspective on the matter, of course,' admitted Sean Cravanaugh.

'You could say that, yes.'

Sean Cravanaugh studied Terrence's face with interest.

'I should thank you, really,' he smirked.

'*Thank* me?' Terrence was puzzled.

'Absolutely. The show was always going to be a resounding success, but your story gave people something more to latch onto. Your contribution was priceless.'

Terrence said nothing. He pondered Sean Cravanaugh's words in silence, shaking his head with disbelief.

'This really was just a game to you, wasn't it?' His voice was coarse.

Cravanaugh burst out laughing.

'You say this like it's a revolting idea. Isn't *everything* a game? Isn't everyone's goal to get as much as they possibly can with the hand they've been dealt? All people ever want is material gain. Given the choice they will sooner pick their own survival over anyone else's wellbeing. It's the game of life. I just happen to know the rulebook inside out. Better even, I *make* the rules. I've achieved more in this lifetime than most people could ever dream of. I *won*.'

Sean Cravanaugh spoke animatedly, with alarming fervour.

'The competition was nothing more and nothing less than the game people have been perpetrating for ages. Someone made the rules, chose the players, and made everyone else abide by subjective laws. And people went with it, because they knew nothing else and were too absorbed in their own misery to think of alternative options. They don't know how to think for themselves. But I… *I* went counter current. I figured a way out. *I* decide who does what, who goes where, who lives or dies. I've rigged the game so that I can never, ever lose. I've made it. Don't you see? I understand how the world works. When I die, someone else will take my place at the head of the pack. This is how it'll always be. Surely, after what you've been through, even you can see that.'

Terrence was speechless. He shook his head again.

'You and I,' he whispered, 'have very differing ideas of what the purpose of life is. I'm sorry to say that you're wrong. So wrong. You're deluded beyond recovery.'

Sean Cravanaugh and Terrence stared at each other, each rooted in their own convictions, mutely agreeing to disagree. Eventually, Sean Cravanaugh smiled and stood up, signalling the conversation was over. Terrence imitated him and got to his feet. He eyed Cravanaugh's outstretched hand for a second before briefly shaking it.

'Goodbye, Mr Blake,' his voice was amused, 'someone is waiting for you outside to escort you out of the arena.'

Terrence walked out of the room, closing the door behind him, still unable to process what was going on. A member of the production team led him through the maze of staircases and corridors, and into a small room where he was instructed to change.

'Whenever you're ready, Mr Blake, you can just leave through that door over there,' the assistant told him with a smile. 'Just go all the way down the corridor, make a left and you'll see the exit. And congratulations again on winning the show!'

The young assistant left him without another word, leaving Terrence standing sheepishly on the spot, unsure what had just happened, clutching the bag and envelope against his chest. Shaking himself back to attention, he changed and walked through the door, down the empty corridor.

The moment he turned a corner, the sight that awaited him immobilised him. Delilah's ghost was standing by the door, fixing him determinedly. She walked slowly towards him, and as she got closer he noticed that her face was streaked with tears. When she stopped in front of him, it took him a few seconds to realise that she was not Delilah. She was the girl who had come to interview him.

'Hi,' she said with sorrow in her voice. 'They said I could come in and wait for you…'

They looked at each other in silence, and eventually she took something from her jacket pocket and handed it to him. He would have recognised the patchwork stuffed rabbit amongst millions. He had made it himself, roughly piecing fragments of old clothes together, once upon a time, when he could not afford ready-made toys.

He held Leon tightly between his fingers and looked up at the girl. At the look of sadness and affection in her eyes, he understood.

He fell to his knees, weeping, and thanking a God he was not sure he still believed in for returning his daughter back to him safely. She knelt down beside him, her hands on his, and they remained there, shivering and sobbing, until he completely lost track of time and space.

'Let's get out of here,' she said finally, handing him a hat and scarf. 'You should cover your face, it's pretty chaotic out there.'

Terrence did as she asked and, without another glance behind them, they stepped out into the street. The night air was charged with noise and excitement. A short distance away, Terrence could see a large crowd facing away from them.

'That's the main entrance,' Maddison explained, answering his unspoken question. 'People have been camping out here since last night, everyone's waiting for you or Sean Cravanaugh to come out.'

She grabbed his elbow, pulling him in the opposite direction, and together they half-walked, half-ran down the street. She led him into a car parked nearby where a young man was waiting behind the wheel. Terrence lay across the back seat and Maddison covered him with a large blanket.

They drove in silence for a long time, struggling to dodge the crowds milling around the Cradle. Terrence lay still, listening to the sound of animated conversations growing fainter and fainter as the distance between them and the arena increased.

Terrence carefully lifted the side of the blanket and peaked through. He watched Maddison, now Medina, from the corner of his eyes and occasionally she returned his gaze. They did not speak. They both knew that there was much they needed to discuss before they could indulge in any sort of small talk.

They reached a house in the suburbs, where a man and a woman, whom Maddison introduced as her adoptive parents, ushered them all into their home. They sat in the warmly lit living room whilst Miranda fussed over tea and biscuits, until Clive and Pedro forced her to leave Maddison and him alone.

They stared at each other in silence for ages, neither of them too sure where to start. There was so much to say, so much time to make up for, and yet the words did not come easily. Terrence felt he had forgotten how to speak altogether. Thankfully for him, Maddison spoke first. She had always been the stronger one, he thought.

'I spent my life not knowing who I was, or where I came from… When I came to live with Miranda and Clive, they were told that I may never remember the life I had. They said my brain had triggered a knee-jerk reaction to the trauma and repressed my memories.'

She explained, her voice trembling, how she had come to look through the folder Miranda and Clive brought to her. How the barrier suddenly lifted, and it had all come rushing back to her. There were still things which she was not sure about, she admitted, things which were confusing, but she told him of the pieces she did remember clearly. Events and occasions Terrence could still picture in his mind's eye.

She told him of her life after they had parted, and though he could tell there was a lot she was not saying, he understood that despite it all, she had been loved. She had been given the care he had failed to provide for her. For that, he was grateful.

Eventually, she asked the question he had hoped would never come, but one he knew he would have to answer sooner or later.

'What happened…' She murmured. 'What happened that night? The night you were arrested.'

Terrence did not know where to start, so he told her everything from the very beginning. From the day he met Delilah, to how they had fallen in love and built a life together. He told her, his eyes downcast, how he had failed to see that Delilah was not as pleased to find out she was pregnant as he had been. He said, his throat burning under the weight of the confession he had never been able to give, how, day after day, Delilah had drifted away from him, and he had done nothing to acknowledge the problem that was staring him in the face. He retold the story of Delilah's admission into the clinic, and of his own struggle to raise his newborn daughter as a single parent, with the help of a kind neighbour.

Terrence's tone lightened up at that point, as he recalled the happy times he and Maddison had enjoyed for those first few years. And Maddison smiled too, because she could remember fragments of it. Terrence needed to pause before he felt ready to say how everything had changed when Delilah had come home. How Delilah had still hated their child and refused to see how wonderful she was. He whispered that he had started to notice odd marks and bruises on Maddison's body, but he had tried to lie to himself for just a little longer. He had not left Delilah, and he knew that short borrowed time had been the catalyst for everything that had unravelled afterwards.

'I came home one night...' He paused, looking for the right words. 'And she... She was bent over you, threatening you. She had a knife in her hand. You looked so scared, I didn't think... I just... I just ran. I ran at her and I pushed her out of the way. But she fell and she hit her head on the kitchen counter. I think she died on the spot... So much blood... There was so much blood everywhere...'

Terrence paused again, unable to say another word. A heavy leaden silence had settled between him and Maddison as he struggled to find the words to continue his tale. He knew he had to carry on, he had to let the words out before he no longer had the strength to say a thing.

'I failed you…' he continued, his voice weary. 'I failed to protect you. The police came. Someone must have heard the noise and called them. And I just… I couldn't move. I couldn't help you. And you were so scared. You didn't understand what was going on. I should have been there for you… You needed me… I should have…'

He should have fought the trial, and he should have explained that everything had been an accident. He should have denied that he had been the one who was abusing their child, and told them what had truly happened. But there again, he had failed. He had been in such shock he had been unable to say anything for himself. He had felt so guilty about Delilah's death it had been impossible for him to try and wriggle out of a prison sentence.

He had felt he had to pay.

After all, whether or not it had been intentional, *he* had been the one to administer the fatal blow. Much before that night, *he* had been the one who had started it all. He felt responsible for Delilah's descent into madness, for not catching the signs earlier on, for forcing her into a state of motherhood she clearly did not want to endure. He was guilty of pushing his wife over the edge, and for allowing his daughter to be hurt at the hands of a woman who wanted her unwanted child to pay for taking away her happy life. If only he had seen it. If only he had done something about it all. But he had not. And for that he had needed to redeem himself.

Terrence was quiet for a long time after finishing his story, weeping silent tears. Maddison sat opposite him, looking at her shoes, hugging herself and gently rocking back and forth on her seat. And then, eventually, as the glowing pastel shimmers of dawn sifted through the windows, she stood up and came to sit next to him. Lifting her gaze towards him, she observed his face in silence, her face pink and glistening with tears. She gave him a smile of such sorrow he felt his heart break a little. Then she placed her hand on top of his and she said softly:

'It's over now, Daddy. Everything will be fine.'

He took her in his arms and they embraced, crying and sobbing with relief, only breaking apart when Miranda, Clive and Pedro walked back into the room, carrying trays laden with food for breakfast. As they sat at the dining-room table, talking of nothing of consequence, in the midst of the aromas of freshly brewed coffee, melting butter and warm bread, Terrence felt like a new man.

He looked over his coffee cup at Maddison. He took in her beautiful face and the way she smiled. He revelled in the sound of her laughter and the delicate tones of her voice. However arduous his journey, he had finally arrived. He had reached his destination, because all he had ever seen at the end of the road was her. He had paid a heavy price for his mistakes and he had been rewarded with a second shot at life. A mixture of relief and contentment filled his heart; the ordeal was finally over.

He closed his eyes and inhaled deeply, the strong flavours of steaming coffee filling his nostrils and awakening every cell of his body. The long-forgotten smell sent his mind cascading back many years, to a time when life was much simpler, when the incident, the competition, the pain and horror were still unknown and unimaginable. He travelled back to days when he would sip his morning coffee with one eye on the newspaper, and the other on making sure Maddison ate all of her breakfast before school. He could still picture her, sitting on her chair, spoon-feeding Leon some of her cereal. The clinking of cutlery against plates and cups gently guided him back to the present moment.

When he opened his eyes, he met Maddison's gaze and he knew that everything would be alright. The certainty he read in her face told him that though they had been stranded for a while, they *would* make their way forward. A new way. A better way. One in which they would care for and protect each other.

With a deep sigh, Terrence forced himself to close the door on all that had happened, on all of his failures and all of his remorse. And though he knew that it would take some time to overcome the memories of the hurdles he had faced, and to heal the scars carved on his body and inside his mind, for the first time in a very long time he was confident that peace was within reach.

He was ready to let go, and as he admired his daughter's serene smile, he felt it was divine confirmation that he was finally allowed to move on and live again.

EPILOGUE

The sun was shining bright in the clear blue sky, gently warming Terrence's skin. He shifted comfortably in his deck chair and readjusted the blankets around his legs and shoulders. A soft breeze caressed his cheeks and he shivered slightly. He closed his eyes, and not really knowing why, he started humming to himself.

He still could not believe he was free.

Five years had passed since the abrupt end of the competition. To this day, his nights were still haunted with nightmares of what he had experienced. Worst of all was the vivid image of that young judge taking her own life, sending her head exploding over the smooth stage on live television.

No one had quite been able to explain it, though speculation had continued for quite some time after that. Bits and pieces from her past had surfaced, dark tales of how her sister had been the unfortunate victim of Mad Spencer's crimes. As for Tyler Benson, the police concluded that he had had a heart attack, triggered by an overdose on a highly abrasive and addictive chemical, which use and sale was illegal in most of the developed world. The autopsy reports had leaked to the press, spreading the gory details of how the substance had eaten Tyler Benson from inside for weeks on end before eventually causing his death.

Far from deterring the public from their attachment to the show, its unexpected and bloody end had created even more of a sensation all over the country. People had rallied behind it, enthused by the incredible results it had yielded in lowering the nation's criminal rates. After years of fear and hardship, people finally felt a renewed sense of safety and hope, bonding communities together for the first time in decades. It was not long before the press referred to it as the best thing that could have happened to get the nation back on its feet. It served as an example to other countries, who rushed to Sean Cravanaugh's door to buy the rights to run the show in their homeland. 'No Pain, No Game' became the most popular franchise of all time, spreading like wildfire across the globe.

The mighty Sean Cravanaugh became the richest man on earth, and allegedly retired to a large and idillic private island off the coast of Costa Rica. He became a role model, an example to follow for all young people wishing to make something of themselves. Whatever horrors the man might have orchestrated, he had reached such high peaks of success in return that none of the atrocities he had engineered mattered much when it came to adding up the scores. The end justified the means, people said, without batting an eyelid at what the 'means' had been. To this day, the deaths of Camilla and Tyler Benson were still treated as collateral damage in the rebuilding of the nation, a small sacrifice to have paid for the benefit of the greater good.

Five years later, Terrence found himself occupying the top floor of the little country cottage Maddison and Pedro had bought together, a year before they got married. He had repeated that he refused to be a burden on them, but nothing he had said had made any difference. Maddison had insisted that she was not ready to let go of him after being apart for such a long time. They had settled into a comfortable life, a happy life, one which he never thought he deserved after what had happened.

Terrence shifted again in his deck chair, opening his eyes to glance at the pale blue sky above him. He felt warm and content. He felt that, though his debt may never be paid in full, he had earned these past five years of happiness. This was more time than he had ever hoped to have with his daughter, and he knew he could not be so greedy as to wish for much more. He had sensed age and fatigue creep up on him, slowly but surely and he had not tried to fend it off. After a lifetime in jail, dragging life on from day to day, and after what had felt like an eternity surviving as best he could on the 'No Pain, No Game' ordeal, he was well acquainted with the fragility of life. He had seen death from such a short distance that it had been impossible to ignore it was there, all the time, all around him, ready to strike when you least expected it to. He had always hoped to live just long enough to see Maddison again, and now that his wish had been granted, he knew his time was near.

For all of that absolute knowledge, he was not afraid. He had stopped being scared of death a long time ago. He comforted himself in the certainty that Maddison was happy and well, that she was loved, that she would be alright. That was all he had ever cared for, all he had ever wanted. He opened his eyes slowly, and in the distance he glimpsed Maddison coming down the stairs from the house into the garden.

She was coming towards him, one hand over her prominent belly, walking with difficulty under the weight of the baby which was due any day now. Her figure blurred as his vision started to shut down. He felt a twinge pulling through his heart, and a tingle run up and down his arm. He forced himself to keep his eyes open for as long as he could, revelling in the last look he would ever get of his beloved daughter. He thought she might have been speaking to him, but his hearing seemed to have switched off, too. He could vaguely hear her turn around to call out for Pedro. Whatever her words were they only reached him in muffled noises. She sounded distressed, and he wanted to tell her that it was all ok, that he would be fine.

That he was ready. That being around her again had been the best gift life had given him, and that it had made the horrors he had endured a price worth paying.

He wanted to say thank you, for her kindness, for her forgiveness, for her love and care over the few years they had together. A second form rushed from the house towards him, as Pedro joined them. Terrence felt Maddison's hand on his, and he smiled a weak contented smile.

The last breath he breathed had her name in it, forever hanging off the edge of his lips.

THE END

Acknowledgements

This book has been thirty years in the making and it could not have seen the light of day without the incredible help of those who have, often *literally,* held my hand along the way.

Thank you to Vicky Blunden, my editor, the first person to ever meet Sean Cravanaugh. Her guidance and support have been invaluable, she gave me the confidence I needed to persevere and take *No Pain, No Game* to print.

Thank you to all of you, friends and family, who patiently listened to me talking on and on (and on, and on) about writing and editing and editing again and getting rejected by agents and publishing houses. Your enthusiasm and words of encouragement kept me going!

Last but not least, thank you to my wonderful husband, my absolute rock, who never lost faith in me, and who believed in me more than I ever believed in myself. Who picked up the slack whilst I frantically went through round after round of writing and editing. Who lifted me up when I doubted - which was often. Who read and heard more about *No Pain, No Game* in the past three years than anyone should ever have to. From the bottom of my heart and soul: thank you.

Please leave a review!

Reviews greatly improve the chances of success of any book and are a great way for you to support Indie authors.

If you enjoyed reading *No Pain, No Game* please post a review on Amazon and Goodreads.com

ABOUT THE AUTHOR

Lucie Ataya grew up in Tours, France where her passion for writing and her love for the English language were born. She studied modern languages, took a random detour through Radford, Virginia in the U.S. and moved to England to complete a Masters' Degree in Sociology at the University of Bristol. She now lives in London with her husband, their Cocker Spaniel Veer and their Burmese cat Leela.

A yogi at heart, Lucie practices yoga as a qualified Vinyasa Flow Yoga Teacher. For her day job, she works as a Product Manager in an Ad tech company.

When she's not writing, working or practicing her Sun Salutations, she can be spotted walking with Veer, trialing independent coffee shops, or indulging in crafty projects.

Her first novel, *No Pain, No Game*, was published in 2020.

Find out more at https://www.lucieataya.com

  @lucieataya

Printed in Great Britain
by Amazon

55052804R00199